THE
KILLING
LUCK

THE
KILLING
LUCK

A PROJECT MOLKA NOVEL
FREDRICK L. STAFFORD

My Thanks

To Michelle Kirk for helping create the Molka character.

To my Mother and my Aunt Susan and her husband Chuck for being early and enthusiastic supporters of this series.

To my wonderful beta reader Cass.

To my wonderful beta reader Jae.

To my wonderful beta reader Jude.

To my wonderful beta reader Olivia.

PROJECT MOLKA

At the peak of her warrior skills, Molka resigned from an elite special forces unit and chose veterinary medicine as her post-military career. She opened a small clinic, built a small practice, and sought to live her life in humble obscurity.

And she did—until the Traitors Scandal intervened.

Her country's foreign intelligence service—known as the Counsel—suffered an unprecedented disaster when moles burrowed in deep for 10 years popped up and exposed the identity of almost every covert operative.

In a small state with many enemies sworn to annihilate it, the safeguarding role of covert operations is indispensable. The Counsel, gutted and demoralized, fell into panic mode.

In the short term, they used a few uncompromised retired operatives—along with some career bureaucrats who never qualified for field-work—to fill the gaping void. The results disappointed, to put it mildly.

In the long term, new operatives would be recruited and formally trained, but the process would take several years.

It was the time in between when the country faced the most danger.

The Counsel's solution was Operation Civic Duty—more often called the Projects Program. They recruited ordinary citizens who held what they deemed a useful skill or skills. Each citizen recruit, or project as they were dubbed, received some quick, very basic operative training before being sent straight out to complete what the Counsel called a task.

It sounded desperate and borderline suicidal, and it was. Even so, they found willing projects everywhere: university students, the factory workers, athletes, scientists, housewives.

But the Counsel's prize recruit was Molka.

Their best recruiter, Azzur, told her as much when he came to her office. He said she was the preferred age range—not yet thirty—maintained superb physical condition, retained a useful skill-set from her military service, and could claim an excellent cover. Who could be suspicious of a person who lives to help animals?

He told her that the Counsel required her help. She told him she was a patriot, but she had already done her duty. She wasn't interested. Please leave her alone.

He smiled and left.

He came back a week later with more information for her. Azzur can always find more information. He told her all about her worst special forces mission, how that mission led to the unavenged murder of her little sister, Janetta. He said the Counsel knew the identity of the one responsible and where this one hid. And if Molka completed 10 tasks for them, her 11th task could be personal. They would give her the identity and location of the one she would die to kill.

She agreed to the Counsel's offer.

She agreed to serve under Azzur.

She agreed to become his project.

Project Molka.

 **CHAPTER ONE**

On what could have been the first flawless sunny day of a hopeful new spring, an immaculate lakeside park bloomed with loving and laughing moms and dads, daughters and sons, grandmothers and grandfathers, and dogs, puppies, babies.

On a hill overlooking the park's serene perfection, an unremarkable man seated in an unremarkable van held a video camera before his face and pressed record.

"The first ones about to die will be the lucky ones. They'll never see it coming. But you will not be so fortunate. Witness your fates."

The man exited the van, attached the video camera to a tripod positioned next to it, and focused on the park. Satisfied, he stepped to the van's rear, removed a small tablet device from his jacket, and tapped the screen.

A high-pitched buzz echoed from within the van's cargo area.

A thousand angry insects?

The man opened the van's back doors, moved aside, and tapped the tablet again. A black swarm—not comprised of angry insects but, rather palm-sized four-rotor drones—floated out and climbed into the innocent blue sky.

The drone swarm flew in a tight, high formation to the park, hovered a moment, and split into three smaller swarms.

One swarm each moved over the park's three most populated areas: a lakeside walkway, benches near an ice cream stand, and a playground.

All below continued to enjoy their lives unaware.

The unremarkable man watching from the hill tapped his tablet again.

A single drone broke from its swarm, dove on a pretty young woman jogging lakeside, hovered before her face, and with a bright FLASH and loud BANG, exploded a projectile-like object into her forehead.

The drone remnant fell away.

The woman died and dropped.

The unremarkable man smiled and tapped his tablet yet again.

All three swarms dove simultaneously on individual human targets.

FLASH-BANG!

FLASH-BANG!

FLASH-BANG!

Blood and brain tissue.

Brain tissue and blood.

Buzzing drone death annihilated the people lakeside.

FLASH-BANG!

FLASH-BANG!

FLASH-BANG!

Skull fragments and falling.

Falling and skull fragments.

Buzzing drone death annihilated the people on the benches.

FLASH-BANG!

FLASH-BANG!

FLASH-BANG!

Screaming and running.

Running and screaming.

Buzzing drone death annihilated the people on the playground.

FLASH-BANG!

FLASH-BANG!

FLASH-BANG!

It finished.

The park was silent.

The unremarkable man removed his video camera from the tripod, placed the tripod in the unremarkable van, closed the doors, got behind the wheel, and drove away at a leisurely pace.

Back in the park, the lone remaining survivor—a small, terrified dog dragging its leash—ran through the motionless, blood-spattered bodies.

The screen faded to black.

The lights came on in the theater.

"The end?" Molka said. "Well…that was thoroughly nauseating. Glad I passed on the popcorn." She sat mid-theater as the lone audience member wearing a tight white hoodie and white joggers. "Where are you hiding anyway?"

Azzur stepped from behind a red curtain flanking the screen. Molka's Project Manager—with his clear, dark complexion and neat, gray-specked black hair—still appeared fit for his early fifties. He wore his usual fashionable brown leather jacket and carried his usual brown leather satchel.

Molka rose and stretched. "Next time you invite me to the movies, how about picking something a little less gory? Like maybe a nice sweet, light-hearted teen-slasher zombie-massacre war-atrocities film."

Azzur centered himself before the screen and ignored Molka's grin. "Time for us to talk again."

"More like past time. It's been four months. How's Tel Aviv? Still there?"

"The situation you just watched portrayed in the dramatic simulation is not a question of if it could happen; it is a question of when it will happen and to whom."

"Oooo…an ominous warning." Molka's eyes widened in mock dread. "You should have used that as the ending. Leave the audience with something profound to ponder instead of worrying about what's going to happen to the poor little dog whose owner lay dead."

He remained unamused. "What is your initial assessment of the simulation's actual content?"

3

"Alright. I get why you showed it here for the big screen effect. But the bad guy was forgettable. The playground scene was way too disturbing. And what was that horrible soundtrack, royalty-free stuff from the mid-2000s? All in all, pretty cheesy."

Azzur took out and lit a cigarette. "Have you any further sarcastic remarks? Or may we proceed to the briefing?"

"Let's proceed." Molka grinned again. "But I can't promise you anything remark-wise."

"A quantum leap forward in autonomous micro drone technology has arrived. They are operated by artificial intelligence and feature a processor that reacts many times faster than a human brain. Each is equipped with a wide field camera, tactical sensor, facial recognition, and—as graphically depicted in the simulation—they are weaponized with three grams of shaped explosive, which can penetrate and explode inside a human skull. Virtually anyone, even individuals with limited capabilities like the unremarkable man represented, can enter the target profiles they wish, deploy the drones as a swarm, and drive away worry free. Designed to work in teams, they can breach walls, fences, doors, windows, or find the smallest entry points, then evade people, bullets, and any other known countermeasures. And since these so-called *slaughterbots* take away the expense, danger, and risks of conventional warfare, all current weapons systems may eventually be rendered obsolete. A new era of ultra-efficient, unstoppable death is upon us."

Molka shook her head. "What kind of disturbed minds would think to create such a horrendous weapon?"

"One mind. An engineer named Mr. Aden Kayne Luck." Azzur headed up the aisle toward the exit. "And you are going to bring him to me."

CHAPTER TWO

Azzur didn't bother to inform Molka that he had returned to Florida until his message to meet him at the theater interrupted her morning workout. And in the theater lobby before leaving, he only provided her with his hotel information, told her the briefing would continue in his suite, and ordered her to be there in fifteen minutes.

No "how have you been?"

No "what's new?"

No "did you change your hairstyle?"

Social niceties never impeded Azzur's time. So his impoliteness could be ignored. But his failure to mention the promise he had made to her the last time they had talked could not.

Molka collected her bike parked beside the snack counter and pushed it toward the exit. The theater manager presented a proud smile as he held the door open for her. He had agreed to Azzur's before hours private screening because he served as an associate, "associate" being the unofficial name given to foreign sympathizers who provide discreet, invaluable assistance to the Counsel.

She rolled her bike onto the sidewalk and prepared to make the short ride to Azzur's oceanside accommodations. The drenching South Florida July humidity prompted her to strip off her hoodie and joggers. Underneath, short black workout shorts and a black crop top accentuated her tall, lean muscular form. She tucked the hoodie and joggers into her backpack, pulled her long, straight, dark hair into a high ponytail, and placed tactical sunglasses over her large, oval-shaped blue eyes.

When she straddled the bike, a passing car honked approval.

The door opened before Molka knocked. Azzur admired her scantiness as she and her bike entered.

The spacious luxury suite contained a chain-smoker's reek and haze, stinging her nose, and air-conditioning set on maximum sprouted goose bumps on her bare legs and arms.

Molka halted her bike in the entry foyer and moved her sunglasses atop her head. "Nice room. And you've personalized it with the classic Azzur freeze and gag ambience."

He closed the door behind her, crossed the living room area to a workstation desk, and sat. "Let us continue the briefing." He motioned to a chair positioned next to the desk. "Sit down."

Molka stiffened. "Before I do…well…first let me say I'm sorry for calling your movie cheesy. It did a great job showing the insane danger of these killer drone slaughterbot things this guy created."

"Thank you."

"And if you want me to bring him to you as one of my future tasks, fine. But what happened to your promise from four months ago?"

"I do not make promises."

"You did to me," she said.

He lit a cigarette from a pack on the desk. "My main recollection from our conversation of four months ago was your vehement protests that your last task was part of a training exercise."

"That's not what I'm talking about."

"What are you claiming I promised you?"

"You told me the one responsible for murdering my little sister was operational again and you needed me to help you locate them."

"And what was your reaction?"

"I said, give me this one's name and last known location, and I would take care of the rest."

"And my reply to your request?" Azzur said.

"You reminded me of our agreement."

"That is correct."

"However," Molka said, "you also told me circumstances were fluid. And you could very well see me receiving that information before I completed all 10 of my tasks for the Counsel."

"And after that, what were the last instructions I gave you?"

"You told me to remain here and keep working in my legend until you returned to give me further instructions."

"Precisely," Azzur said. "And in what part of our conversation did I make you a promise?"

She tugged on the base of her ponytail. "Ok. Then the promise was implied."

"I do not agree."

"Azzur, with great difficulty, I've accepted you withholding the identity and last known location of the one who murdered my little sister as being a sensible requirement of our agreement. But if you plan to dangle the promise of giving me that information sooner as a loyalty or motivational tool before each of my tasks, we're going to have a serious problem. I don't respond well to mind games. And it's not professional. And it's just plain cruel. And I won't take it."

"What makes you think the information you want is not actually part of your next task?"

"Because you just asked me to bring you this engineer Aden—"

"Mr. Aden Luck," Azzur said.

"You just asked me to bring you this engineer, Aden Luck, and you would never ask me to bring you someone you know I'm going to kill on sight."

"That is correct."

"So what does Aden Luck have to do with the one who murdered my little sister?"

"Sit down, Molka."

"Are you going to keep your promise or not?"

"Sit down, Molka. Talking loudly to someone across a large room is always ridiculous and sometimes dangerous."

Molka dropped her bike on its side, slammed her backpack on the floor, and rushed to Azzur's desk. "ARE YOU GOING TO KEEP YOUR PROMISE OR NOT?"

Azzur smiled, unintimidated. "Yes."

"Good. Why didn't you say so in the first place?"

"Now sit down and allow me to finish your briefing."

She complied.

Azzur held up a hardcover book. "Are you familiar?"

Molka read the book's title: *Going Back to Go Forward: Repairing Your Lost Childhood to Live Happy, by Dr. Thomas Moore.* "Never heard of it. Looks like a weird self-help book."

Azzur thumbed through it. "Doctor Thomas Moore was a pseudo-therapist who claimed the simple theories in this book would guarantee people permanent happiness. And millions of unhappy people paid him to find out."

"And let me guess," she said. "Millions of still unhappy people want their money back?"

Azzur continued, "When Doctor Moore passed away 11 years ago, he left two separate wills. One bequeathed his exceedingly valuable estate to his three adult children from previous marriages, and the other will bestowed everything to his fourth and final wife, Mrs. Darcy Hazlehurst-Moore. A contentious legal battle ensued, at the end of which the children were awarded all the money and the most valuable assets, while Mrs. Hazlehurst-Moore received the publishing rights to his bestselling books and a large parcel of vacant ranch land." Azzur removed a standard briefing tablet from his satchel and swiped to an attractive blond woman's headshot. "This is Mrs. Hazlehurst-Moore. Your impression?"

Molka rubbed her freezing arms and leaned forward. "She's very pretty. Looks friendly. On the other hand, I've never trusted someone with a hyphenated name. It's like their hedging their bets as to which side of the name will be more valuable."

"An astute observation." He flicked ash into a repurposed brass ice bucket. "Another interesting fact about her is—"

Molka raised a hand. "Hold on. You said Doctor Moore has been dead for 11 years, so he can't be the one who murdered my little sister. And I also assume his widow, Mrs. Darcy—"

"Mrs. Darcy Hazlehurst-Moore."

"I also assume Mrs. Hazlehurst-Moore is not the one either."

"A safe assumption," he said.

"Then how is your tedious little documentary on their lives relevant to my task?"

"Any piece of information I give you is relevant."

"You said the same thing before Cyprus. Look how that turned out."

"Allow me to finish telling you about Mrs. Hazlehurst-Moore and you will find—"

"What does this have to do with the one who murdered my little sister?"

"Allow me to finish telling you about Mrs. Hazlehurst-Moore and you will—"

Molka leaned toward Azzur. "Just give me the name and last known location of the one I need to kill!"

Azzur laughed. "Molka, you must learn to master impatience, as I have."

She shoved her chair back and stood. "It wasn't your little sister who was blown into pieces! You can afford to be patient! I can't!"

He shoved his chair back and stood. "Do you think you are the only one?" He strode to the drapes covering the balcony sliding glass doors and yanked them open to reveal a spectacular ocean view. "Maybe you have been here in this peaceful utopia too long, but do not forget where you come from. Everyone there has lost someone. Everyone on every side. What makes you think you are something special?"

Molka took three composing breaths and dropped back onto the chair. "You were saying about Mrs. Hazlehurst-Moore?"

Azzur returned to the desk, sat, stubbed out his cigarette, and lit another. "Our latest and best assessments indicate Mrs.

Hazlehurst-Moore is in direct contact with the one responsible for your little sister Janetta's death."

CHAPTER THREE

Adrenaline jolted Molka's heart. "Where is Mrs. Hazlehurst-Moore?"

Azzur smiled. "Oh, are you more interested in my tedious little documentary now?"

"Where is she?"

"First, understand this: Due to the connection between Mrs. Hazlehurst-Moore and the one responsible for your little sister's death, there was a serious debate within the Counsel."

"Where is she?"

"I strongly recommended the task be assigned to a project who did not have your emotional motivation, which may hinder logical judgement."

"Where is she?"

"Nevertheless, after taking my concerns under advisement, it was decided you are still the most uniquely qualified asset we possess to complete the task."

"Where is she?"

"Therefore, be advised, you will not only carry the burden of my expectations but also of those at the Counsel's highest levels."

"Where. Is. She?"

"In the hinterlands of British Columbia."

"Hiding?" Molka said.

"Hiding in plain sight, you might say." Azzur swiped the briefing tablet to a college-like campus promotional photo. "Mrs. Hazlehurst-Moore is the founder of Hazlehurst Institute."

"Looks fancy and expensive. What kind of school is it?"

"Hazlehurst Institute is a non-accredited and non-affiliated venture of Mrs. Hazlehurst-Moore. It is located on the ranch land awarded to her from Doctor Moore's estate settlement: 75,000 acres in an isolated region of British Columbia some 650 kilometers north of Vancouver. Doctor Moore acquired the property for a planned spiritual retreat center. After his death, Mrs. Hazlehurst-Moore made other plans. She applied timely political donations in Victoria and got approval for her private school." Azzur swiped to a satellite campus view. "The school opened four years ago and is totally self-contained and self-sufficient."

"I see it has its own airstrip too," she said.

"Small airport actually. The road connecting the school to the nearest highway is not suited to handle heavy trucks, so everything must be flown in. This is intentional, as it fits with the school's desire to be severely sequestered."

"Severely sequestered, meaning what?"

"There is no phone, cell, television, or internet service available in the greater area. The only connection to the outside world is by specially encrypted satellite phone. All other satellite and radio communications are jammed from within."

"Disconnected from the world," Molka said. "Why would a school need such extreme isolation?"

"Mrs. Hazlehurst-Moore based the school's curriculum upon her late husband's theories. Those being, the best way to true happiness is to leave all adult responsibilities behind and reconnect with your lost childhood. Concerns of the cruel, mature outside world are unnecessary and forbidden. All they need is the guidance of a caring, understanding, and loving educator. Mrs. Hazlehurst-Moore believes she is this educator. She even insists the students, faculty, and staff call her Principal Darcy."

"Principal Darcy?" Molka raised cynical eyebrows. "I smell the sweet jungle death-stench of a cult leader."

"The 379 *students* live in dormitory style-housing, attend classes, and engage in organized activities. Their days are strictly scheduled and monitored. Only a select number are allowed enrollment. The main qualifications are a minimum net worth of 200 million US dollars and payment of six-figure tuition fees. As of this date, no student has graduated."

She nodded. "And as long as they keep paying, no one ever will. That's also the real reason she keeps them so isolated: total control."

"Exactly. It is an ultra-lucrative swindle on the ultra-wealthy."

"And I'm going to this school, right?"

"You are," Azzur said.

"What's my new legend going to be? Depressed billionaire heiress or bored bratty princess?" She shook out her ponytail and put on her sunglasses. "I would love to play a bored, bratty princess."

"Neither. A staff of approximately 150 workers act in a support capacity at the school. They live in a separate compound from the students and handle such duties as operating the utilities, food service, laundry, maintenance, etc. A student resource building features an infirmary with a physician, registered nurses, EMTs, a dentist, an optometrist, and a veterinarian. You will be the new veterinarian."

Molka placed the sunglasses back atop her head. "Why does the school need a vet?"

"The students are permitted to keep pets to help connect to their lost childhoods—another Doctor Moore theory. Consequently, they have need for a full-time veterinarian. The regular veterinarian left suddenly, and the school seeks an immediate replacement."

She retied her ponytail. "How did they like my application you filled out?"

"It was eagerly accepted because you are available at once, speak fluent English, and had no objection to living and working in the isolated conditions."

"What happened to the other vet?"

"Dismissed," Azzur said. "Caught by security in possession of alcohol. Alcohol, tobacco, drugs, gambling, pornography, and prostitution are all forbidden at Hazlehurst Institute."

"Sooo…you're saying it's not a party school?" Molka snapped her fingers. "Darn. I looked forward to doing some serious keg stands this weekend."

He blew smoke. "I have missed your sarcasm, Molka."

She beamed. "Really?"

"No. Not really."

"Ha. You got me. By the way, how are things back home?"

"Still in perpetual crisis," he said. "You have not been following events?"

"I meant things back home as in my home, and my office."

"The rent on your apartment and the lease payments on your clinic, as well as their utilities, are being maintained. I also employed a cleaning service to come once a month to dust and air them out."

"Thank you," Molka said. "Ok. Back to Mrs. Hazlehurst-Moore. I assume she lives on campus to keep a close watch on the suckers…I mean…the students?"

"She keeps a modest apartment and office in the school's classroom-administration building. She promotes this as a great personal sacrifice in that she is forgoing her two California mansions to be close to her students. Although, she is often absent from campus for long periods using the school's private jet. The school's dean, Dean Besnik, actually oversees the day-to-day operations."

"Alright. I'll go there as the new vet, see a few pets while I gather intel on Mrs. Hazlehurst-Moore's routines, get her alone, obtain the information about the one I need to kill from her, and go kill them. Not a problem."

"One problem," Azzur said. "You are forgetting about the one *I* need, Mr. Aden Kayne Luck."

"Right. How is he tied in with Mrs. Hazlehurst-Moore?"

"He is her supreme contingency plan."

"How so?" she said.

"Even though her students are devoted to her and the money flows in unimpeded, all is not well in Mrs. Hazlehurst-Moore's fraudulent paradise. Many student's family members have grave concerns about their welfare, more specifically, about the welfare of their own dwindling inheritances."

Molka shrugged. "Well, you know what they say: 'Where there's a will, there's a greedy relative.'"

"And these greedy relatives have alerted the media and employed a cadre of lawyers and private investigators. There are also rumors mercenaries have been hired by some families to abduct and return their loved ones. All this caused Mrs. Hazlehurst-Moore's abnormal paranoia level to increase to the point of establishing a campus security team of her own mercenaries commanded by the retired Russian special forces legend Colonel Nikolai Vasilyevich Krasnov."

Her eyebrows raised. "Colonel Krasnov—the Red Wolf. A smart, tough, ruthless commander. In the Unit, we studied some of his operations in the North Caucasus conflict. If I was a reporter or a lawyer or a private investigator or even a mercenary, I wouldn't poke my nose anywhere near the Red Wolf's lair."

"Shrewd advice," Azzur said.

"But wasn't he involved in a controversy or something?"

"He is wanted for questioning by an international war crimes tribunal. However, Mrs. Hazlehurst-Moore has used her aforementioned political influence to so far shield him from extradition requests."

"Sounds like she has things well covered."

"For the moment, but the concerned student's families have pushed back in other ways too. They applied their own timely donations in Victoria, and a major investigation has been opened by the Canadian National Police into the questionable business practices of Mrs. Hazlehurst-Moore and alleged mistreatment of her students. Consequently, she realizes it is only a matter of time until they shut down the school and indict her. And there enters Mr. Luck as her contingency." Azzur swiped the briefing tablet to a handsome, brown-haired man's photo. "He bears a strong resemblance to someone you once knew, does he not?"

Molka lied. "No one I can think of." She stood. "I can't take this. It's too cold in here for me." She returned to her backpack, removed and put on her hoodie, and cuddled back into the chair with her knees up.

He flicked ash. "Mr. Luck, age 36, only child born to an Israeli mother and a wealthy industrialist Canadian father. Mr. Luck served in the Canadian Air Force as a fighter pilot, resigned, and went on to found AKL Technologies. His genius in industrial robotics and drones led to numerous patents, which made him wealthy in his own right, at which point he sold his company and went on a spiritual odyssey."

"Define spiritual odyssey," Molka said.

"He moved into an ashram in India to follow a widely discredited guru, joined a commune in Switzerland which prepped to be evacuated by extraterrestrial aliens, and enlisted in a religious sect in Oklahoma, which contained no less than three warring leaders claiming to be the new messiah. He has also, over the years, and without explanations, abandoned mansions housing fiancées in South Korea, Romania, and Costa Rica."

She reexamined his photo. "He looks normal but sounds unbalanced."

"A trait he shares with many geniuses. Over a year and a half ago, when the Traitors Scandal broke, Mr. Luck immigrated to our country and offered to develop his slaughterbot drone technology for us. His stated reason for doing so was that his late mother would have expected him to do his part to help defend her beloved home country during a time of perilous crisis. We accepted his proposal, and he was entrusted to our friends in the ISS, who provided him with a world-class research facility, a world-class seafront mansion, and a world-class fiancée."

Molka sighed, exasperated. "Yet I still can't get my friends in the Counsel to reimburse me for my range ammo. You know that's in our agreement, right?"

"Five months ago, on the verge of completing an operational drone prototype, and without warning, Mr. Luck destroyed the prototype in his world-class research facility, abandoned his world-class seafront mansion—along with his world-class fiancée housed there—slipped his ISS handlers, left the country, and enrolled at Hazlehurst Institute."

She grinned. "Oops on the ISS. A massive embarrassment for the prime minister's favorite service."

"I am told the prime minister wept in rage upon hearing about Mr. Luck's sudden loss."

16

"But if we can bring him back, it might make us the prime minister's new favorite." Molka smiled. "And when I say us, I mean you."

Azzur looked away and blew smoke from the side of his mouth.

"Anyway," she said. "I have no love for the ISS, and I didn't support the prime minister in the last election, but I wouldn't want to be on their bad sides either. This Aden Luck is gutsy to walk out on them."

"He likely has no clue as to the repercussions. Mr. Luck is an exceedingly brilliant engineer, but he displays an unusual disregard and naivety concerning his actions and his worth. Much like a child."

"And if he's bought into the 'recover your lost childhood' nonsense they teach at that bogus school, he might have totally lost it."

Azzur stubbed out his cigarette and lit another. "Mrs. Hazlehurst-Moore recognized the value of Mr. Luck's talents and built him a new state-of-the art research facility on campus." Azzur returned to the school's satellite view on the briefing tablet and pointed to a large gray building. "This is the new research facility known—for obvious reasons—as Building A. This smaller building across from it is the security headquarters." He zoomed out to a wider view. "The area containing Building A and the security headquarters is called the Security Zone and, as you can see, it is surrounded by a formidable fence and connected to the campus by a zigzag road with tree concealment to keep prying eyes from its activities."

"Which are?" Molka said.

"Mrs. Hazlehurst-Moore provided Mr. Luck with an ample budget and resources, and he finished the slaughterbot prototype and tested it successfully. The research facility was then adapted into a production facility and staffed with an illegally imported skilled workforce from Asia who assemble drone swarms under Mr. Luck's supervision."

"What does she want those awful things for?"

"Personal enrichment. Mrs. Hazlehurst-Moore opened the bidding on a swarm order of what is believed to be into the billions of dollars."

17

Molka sneered. "Which is why Aden Luck is her supreme contingency plan. She's using him to make her a new fortune to fall back on before the authorities end her school scam."

"That is correct. The initial 50,000-unit drone swarm produced is the most desirous, as it will achieve the maximum shock value when used. The nefarious potential buyers included several of our old enemies and the other usual bad actors. But the one responsible for your little sister's death submitted the winning bid. Hence, Mrs. Hazlehurst-Moore's direct contact with them. Of course, we cannot allow the sale to occur nor allow Mr. Luck's dangerous technological knowledge to remain out of our control."

Molka's jaw tightened. "Ok. Let's bottom line this. You want what Aden Luck has in his head. I need what his…patron, Mrs. Hazlehurst-Moore has in hers. How do we both get satisfaction?"

"Your task is as follows: Make contact with Mr. Luck, by any means necessary. Convince him to leave Hazlehurst Institute with you, by any means necessary. Destroy the research and production facilities and all drones, by any means necessary. And obtain the relevant information from Mrs. Hazlehurst-Moore, by any means necessary. A contractor team will then extract you and Mr. Luck by helicopter."

Molka frowned. "I'm relying on contractors again?"

"No choice. Normally, I would use our own people for a dangerous extraction like this. But the Traitors damage cut deep. Some of our country's finest pilots remain in hiding."

She nodded with respect. "Understood. Anyway, you said the school has no cell or internet, so I can't use an encrypted phone again, and all radio and satellite communications near the school are jammed from within, so how will I contact the extraction team?"

Azzur zoomed the school's satellite photo out even farther. "The school is enclosed within a tall masonry security wall. This wall, and an outer perimeter distance of two kilometers in every direction, is under constant surveillance by drones. Drones of Mr. Luck's design. However, on a foothill, 4.6 kilometers west of the school, the contractors have emplaced an advanced sensor panel, which is connected to a satellite uplink. You will send a signal to this sensor panel which will in turn signal the contractor helicopter extraction team waiting for you in the nearest town which is…" He zoomed out further yet. "Alex Creek, 210 kilometers away."

"Sounds iffy at best," she said. "And how do I send the signal?"

Azzur reached into his leather satchel and removed an 18count tampon box. "With one of these."

Molka smirked. "Very funny. What am I supposed to do, bounce a menstrual rage scream off the sensor panel?"

He opened the tampon box, removed a floral wrapped plastic applicator tube, and unwrapped it.

"Huh," Molka said. "I would have bet cash money you were a pad man."

Azzur disregarded her mischievous smile, pointed the tampon's insertion end at the far wall, and pulled the string hanging from the plunger end. An intense green laser-like beam emitted and dotted on the wall.

"Oh, that's classy," Molka said. "A perv friend of yours in the R&D department having a good laugh?"

"No. The contractors fabricated these signalers specifically for your task. They have an effective range of 10-kilometers and use a special filter, which makes them the only light source the sensor panel will recognize. They are also made from a composite material that will not alert any security scanners. And even under X-ray, it appears as a normal feminine device."

Molka giggled. "Feminine device?"

Azzur pulled the string again—shutting off the green beam—and placed the signaler on the desk. He reached back into his satchel and removed another tampon box sealed in factory-like shrink wrap. "This is the special package you will take with you. You will pack it next to an open box of identical looking regular feminine devices. In the past three weeks, two separate associates have flown from Miami airport to Vancouver airport with the opened and sealed boxes arrangement in their luggage without any security incident."

"Makes sense. Once you've seen one of those, you've seen enough."

"You can also expect your baggage to be searched upon arrival at Hazlehurst Institute, but this should not be an issue either."

"Let's hope not," she said.

"In the special package, three signalers are mixed in with regular ones. You can identify them by the blue and white flowers on the signalers wrapping as opposed to the red and white flowers on the regulars."

"Thanks for the warning. Could you imagine if I accidently..." Molka cringed. "Ouch."

Azzur returned to the briefing tablet and re-zoomed into a campus satellite view. "When you are ready to be extracted, you will send the signal from the school's landmark bell tower. At 160 feet, it is the highest point on campus." He placed a finger on the screen. "This opening in the belfry on the tower's west side is in a direct line of sight with the foothill containing the sensor panel. It is suggested you signal during darkness for optimal efficiency."

Molka super-focused on the screen. "Ok. I prefer a night extraction anyway." She pulled her hand from hoodie warmth, used her fingers to zoom the view out again, and traced a line from the tower to the foothill. "Where on this hill is the sensor?"

"The contractors say if you aim near the approximate center of the foothill, the sensor panel will pick it up. Basically, you can't miss."

"But how will I know for sure?" she said.

"When your signal is received, a small muted red acknowledgment light should appear just to the right of the foothill's center. You may need optics to see it though."

"And how long do I maintain the signal?"

"Activation from it should be instantaneous."

"You used the word *should* twice," Molka said. "*Should* I be concerned?"

"Once the contractors receive your signal, they require 20 minutes staging time. Then the flying time from Alex Creek to the Hazlehurst Institute is 48 minutes with a plus or minus of five minutes."

Molka tucked her re-chilled hand and arm back under the hoodie. "Two hundred and ten kilometers in 48 minutes is moving pretty fast."

"Their helicopter is modified with increased speed and an auxiliary fuel system. It also has new noise suppression technology I understand works quite well."

She lifted unbelieving eyebrows. "I'll believe it when I don't hear it. Where's the extraction point?"

"They will land here…." Azzur scrolled over. "The campus central courtyard. The contractors will approach the landing zone as low as possible from the opposite direction of the research and production facility, your destruction of which should be used as a diversion."

Molka assessed the research and production facility's position in relation to the central courtyard. "Yes. A diversion would be good. And the bigger and uglier I can make it the better."

"Agreed," he said. "The contractors will then fly you to a private airport in Vancouver, where you will personally hand over Mr. Luck to Counsel representatives for processing. Questions?"

Molka sat back. "What's my time frame on the task?"

"Ideally, I would have given you at least eight weeks to work there in your legend while ingratiating yourself with Mr. Luck and formulating a suitable plan to get him to extraction. However, there is an unbreakable deadline of September 1st."

"What happens on the deadline?" she said.

"A leased cargo aircraft is scheduled to arrive at the school from Vancouver at 11:00AM Sunday, September 1st to remove used electronics equipment. This equipment is actually the first slaughterbot swarm order."

Molka perked. "The final destination of that cargo aircraft could be very useful to me after I'm done."

"Agreed. Unfortunately, we have not been able to establish that yet."

"September 1st," she said. "That gives me…."

Azzur flicked ash. "Thirty-nine days from your arrival to complete the task."

"I'm not complaining, because faster is better with me, but if you preferred I had at least two months to complete the task, why are you just now assigning it to me?"

"Finalization of the first drone swarm is moving faster than we anticipated. And the asset we have within the school providing intel only confirmed the delivery date a few days ago."

"Who is the asset, and how reliable are they?"

"The reliability of the asset is beyond question, and they will present themselves to you when, and if, they deem it appropriate."

Molka smirked. "I just love all the silly gamesmanship this job comes with."

"Silly gamesmanship, in what sense?"

"Never mind," she said. "Weapons? I'll need some, but obviously I can't take any with me."

"Colonel Krasnov's campus security headquarters has a well-stocked armory. Procure from it whatever you need to accomplish the task."

"And what about my own military background? If Mrs. Hazlehurst-Moore—"

Azzur interrupted. "You should start referring to her as Principal Darcy, as she requires."

"Alright. If Principal Darcy is as paranoid as you say, and she digs up my time with the Unit, it might interest her in a bad way for me."

"Not an issue," Azzur said. "I cleansed your military record when you joined the program. It now records that you served in a mundane transportation company."

"Hey, don't hate on military transportation. They do vital work."

He rubbed jet lagged eyes. "Any other questions?"

"After I obtain the information I need from Principal Darcy, what's her fate?"

"Leave her to the Canadians to deal with. Now speak to me in English."

Molka cleared her throat. "Only a lunatic would wear a leather jacket in South Florida in July."

Azzur's bloodshot eyes opened, impressed. "A marked difference in your accent. As I hoped, being here alone and immersing yourself in the culture has paid dividends."

"I also took an acting class and played an American character in several community theatre plays."

"Your initiative is commendable, Molka."

"Well, I know I'm not one of the *legendary* operatives you worked with the *glory days*. I'm just a lowly project. But I'm doing my best."

"The Traitors have necessitated that we must all exceed our abilities to survive."

"When do I leave?" Molka said.

"Your flight to Vancouver departs at 6:10 AM tomorrow. There you will meet Dean Besnik from Hazlehurst Institute for orientation and be taken to the campus aboard their private jet. The rest of your instructions are in the file." He turned off the briefing tablet and handed it to Molka, along with the special tampons box. "I see on your face you have another concern."

"What if I can't persuade Aden Luck to leave with me...by any means necessary?"

"Prevent him from ever leaving there. By any means necessary."

"He's a troubled man," she said. "He needs real help. He doesn't just need to be—"

Azzur laid a fist on the desktop. "Before you make your usual ethical protestations, consider this: It is imperative we have Mr. Luck's technology before our enemies. And not necessarily for us to use on our enemies, rather for us to get a head start in developing counter measures for when our enemies eventually do acquire it. And if that does not persuade you, think of his creation unleashed on our people in a real park or shopping mall or grade school. We no longer have a say about the morality of this situation. And Mr. Aden Kayne Luck sacrificed his right to self-destiny when he chose to develop such a weapon. Do you understand?"

"In other words, if we can't have him, no one can."

"Just get our engineer back."

"Alright. I'll do my best." Molka stood.

"There is something else," Azzur said. "After you make contact with Mrs. Hazlehurst-Moore, your inner rogue may try to talk you into committing a selfish personal act. I cannot impress upon you strongly enough what a fatal error in judgment this would be."

"You mean my inner rogue may tell me to just get the information I need from her and abandon my task and the program?"

"That is correct."

"My inner rogue is crazy," Molka said. "But she's not stupid. And she appreciates the importance of the task. And she also appreciates the Counsel allowing us to still have it considering, as you say, emotion is where logic goes to die. No worries though. I'll stow those emotions and get Aden Luck for you before I go commit a selfish personal act. You have my word."

He nodded. "Good enough."

She recovered her backpack in the foyer, righted her bike, and moved toward the door.

"Molka," Azzur said. "A parting contemplation."

She stopped and turned.

He had spun his chair to face the balcony windows. "Twenty years ago, when I was your age, and before I went to do what you are about to go do now, a very important and wise man reminded me of one absolute fact: The affairs of the heart must always bow to the affairs of the state."

CHAPTER FOUR

Molka returned to her modest one-bedroom apartment in the exclusive beach community of Cinnamon Cove, showered, made a protein shake, and plopped on the couch. She rebooted the briefing tablet and—as always—a countdown clock appeared in the upper right-hand corner. When the clock reached zero, the hard drive would be wiped clean. But unlike her previous tasks, Azzur had expanded the time allotment for memorization from two hours to four.

She read through her departure instructions. Her cover story—or legend as Azzur referred to it—practicing as a guest doctor from the veterinarian exchange program at Kind Care Animal Hospital, required an exit tale. As planned, she would inform them she must return home to care for her "gravely ill sweet Aunt Zillah." A quick call handled it. The hospital manager didn't sound surprised or ask any questions. Molka always suspected her as another Counsel associate.

A little sadness seeped into her leaving. All her co-workers treated her with respect and friendliness. And she enjoyed each day working with them. She declined their invitations to meet afterward for drinks and dinner and weekend get togethers though, because it's unfair to be friends with people you lied to.

Molka moved on to an official Counsel bio on Aden Luck. It pretty much presented the same picture Azzur had given her: a troubled genius who had lost his way, destined to be exploited by whoever possessed him. No way to live. They attached several more photos to help her identify him, but she couldn't miss a face like his.

Next, she found a large supplemental file on Mrs. Darcy Hazlehurst-Moore, aka Principal Darcy. No doubt the reason Azzur gave her the extra viewing time, but odd considering Principal Darcy wasn't her target.

Listed age: 44.

Surprising. She appeared about 32.

Born and raised in a small town in Mississippi, she had also lived in Italy, Florida, California, and Canada. Prior to marrying Doctor Moore, married and divorced twice.

Well-traveled and well-used.

Worked as an exotic dancer, a grade-school teacher, a grade school Principal—which explained her Principal Darcy title—and an exotic dancer again.

A bizarre career path and life story, to say the least.

Then met Doctor Moore and became a very rich widow.

Ha. But sounds like a happy enough ending.

The Principal Darcy file also contained several news articles about her work and travels with Doctor Moore, the ensuing legal battle over his fortune after his death, and the opening of Hazlehurst Institute.

Conclusion? Principal Darcy operated as a clever opportunist who married and schemed her way into extreme wealth. She also carried a checkered, if not scandalous, past she tried to conceal with supposed good works.

The reason Azzur had included her sketchy background in the briefing went unstated. Maybe he expected her to be a problem and wanted Molka to better understand the personality type she would be dealing with.

But considering Principal Darcy manufactured slaughterbot drone swarms to sell to the highest bidder, her large supplemental file could have been edited down to a single word:

Dangerous.

It didn't matter though. Molka would go to Principal Darcy's fake school and first keep her promise and charm or con or force super engineer Aden Luck into leaving with her.

And she would destroy his disgusting killer drones.

And before they left, she would threaten or beat or torture the information she needed from Principal Darcy and go straight after the one who had murdered her little Janetta.

And the Counsel and Azzur didn't know it, but after she killed the one, it would be over.

No more Counsel.

No more Azzur.

No more tasks.

No more Project Molka.

Molka set aside the tablet, removed her glasses, and flipped on the TV. *Take a quick break. Watch the news channel and learn about the other badness in the world.*

The lower screen headline read:

What Happened to The Missing Mogul?

Crazy how they still talked about it.

The mogul in question—billionaire Mr. Gaszi Sago—had gone missing without a trace four months earlier in the infamous Bermuda Triangle on a flight from Miami to Budapest. And every day following on every news outlet, relentless "expert panels" debated hijacking, terrorism, mechanical failure, pilot error, pilot suicide, and wackier theories around the 24-hour news cycles. And each floating fragment spotted in the 500,000 square miles of the Atlantic considered the probable crash area caused the breaking news and anticipation and debates and disappointment to recycle once more.

But Molka knew the answer to the mystery the whole time.

Mr. Gaszi Sago had been the target of her second task. And when that near-death debacle had ended, she watched a Counsel employed contractor team in Bermuda spirit him from his aircraft and take him to a secret detention facility in her home country. And his beautiful Airbus 350 private jet—containing his insane security giant Maur's naked, bloody corpse—had been flown by hyper-competent US intelligence operatives Nadia and Warren to a non-existent island near the Azores. An island where the answers to many other unsolved mysteries, legends, and conspiracies would never be found.

And Molka's second task should have ended there. Time to move on to her third task. But it hadn't quite ended. Something remained unfulfilled. A craving. An overwhelming urge to…

She turned off the TV, put her glasses back on, and picked up the briefing tablet to finish reading her exit instructions.

Pack clothes for four weeks and leave the rest in the closet.

Her issued weapons—Beretta 96A1 and Baby Glock semi-automatic pistols—placed in the dresser.

The remainder of the 25 thousand US dollars given to her for task expenses to be left in the top desk drawer—although she had already donated it to two good causes.

Leave the apartment keys on the kitchen counter and lock the door behind her.

And final instruction: Park her leased Mazda in the Pelican Garage at Miami International Airport with the keys left inside.

But all those things could be done the next morning. A suppressed desire required satisfaction that afternoon.

Molka headed to the bedroom to change clothes and load her weapon.

 **CHAPTER FIVE**

The South Florida Regional Executive Airport still didn't live up to its big name. It offered the same small terminal, same small hangars, same small maintenance buildings, and same two long runways as the last time Molka had visited four months before.

But the last time, she visited, Mr. Gaszi Sago's huge private had jet dominated the scene.

And the last time, she had bordered on hysterical at the fear that Sago would escape in his jet.

And the last time, she had made a quick plan to stop him from escaping.

And the last time—before she could launch her plan—the airport manager, Joe Gomez, the airport security chief, Ed Reynolds, and his two young security flunkies, Bobby and Nick, had been tricked by Sago into believing that Molka was his violent mentally-ill wife. And for their safety, they should point their weapons at her, deploy a Taser into her back, and allow Sago's man-beast bodyguard Maur to inject her with a powerful, sedative, and carry her unconscious body aboard his aircraft, and leave her to his sick intentions.

And the last time she visited, she almost never visited anywhere ever again thanks to those four clowns.

Molka entered the terminal wearing a black tank top, black jeans, and black tactical boots. She accessorized with contact lenses, her old pilot's watch on her left wrist, and a high ponytail with bangs swept across her forehead right-to-left to keep her aiming eye clear. Her Beretta waited in a concealed behind-the-back holster.

She proceeded to the airport manager's office. A different woman than the last time sat at the secretary's desk.

"May I help you?" the woman said.

"I would like to see Mr. Gomez, please."

"He's out of the office for lunch."

"When do you expect him back?"

"Two hours or so."

"Mm, frustrating," Molka said. "Is the security office still down the hall on the left?"

"It's down the hall last door on the right. Would you care to leave a message with me for Mr. Gomez?"

Molka smiled. "No thank you. I'll leave my message for him with the boys in security."

She approached the last door on the right. Open blinds in a window next to it revealed a large office with an empty desk in the center, a couch against the left wall, and a table and chairs against the right wall. At the table—inhaling sandwiches—sat young Bobby and Nick's puffy bodies squeezed into tan uniforms.

Molka pulled her Beretta, opened the door, rushed in, shut the door behind her, and assumed an Israeli combat stance on the boys. "Quiet cooperation or quick death. Choose now."

"Quiet cooperation," Bobby and Nick said in startled unison.

She side stepped and used one hand to close the blinds. "Stand-up, put your hands on your heads, and interlace your fingers."

They complied.

Molka masked wrath with a grin. "Hello, Bobby. Hello Nick."

"Mrs. Sago?" Bobby said.

"No," she said. "I don't think anyone misses Sago. I see you're both still right-hand draws. Bobby, when I tell you, I want you to keep your right hand on your head and use just two fingers of your left hand to remove Nick's pistol, toss it on the couch, then put your left hand back on your head. Do you understand?"

"Yes," Bobby said.

"Do it now."

Bobby complied.

"Nick, you repeat exactly what Bobby did. Do you understand?"

"Yes," Nick said.

"Do it now."

Nick complied.

"Sit back down, boys."

The boys complied.

Molka scooped the pistols from the couch and placed them in a corner file cabinet's top drawer.

Nick's face gaped. "I...we...I mean the aircraft disappeared. Mysteriously. You were on it. They never found it. Did they find it?"

Molka kept the boys at gunpoint and took their radios from the table. "Where's Reynolds?"

Bobby said, "He's in the customs office."

"Where's that?"

"Other side of the terminal."

"How far of a walk from here?"

"Maybe a minute."

She tossed one radio on the couch and spoke into the other. "Reynolds, are you there? Over."

Reynold's voice: "Reynolds here. Who is this? Over."

Molka: "Code silver in the security office. Come fast. Over."

Reynold's voice: "Code silver in the security office? Who the hell is fooling around on the radio? Over."

Molka: "Code silver in the security office. Come fast. Urgent. Over."

Reynolds angry voice: "On my way."

Molka tossed the radio on the couch. "You can put your hands down, boys. Sit." The boys complied. "Go ahead and finish your lunches. I see you have a meatball sub, Bobby. What are you eating, Nick?"

"Cheesesteak," Nick said.

"Where did you get those?"

"South Beach Famous Subs."

"Nice," she said. "Their sweet onion teriyaki is my favorite."

Molka cracked the door and peeked out. A tall tan-uniformed, white-haired man fumed toward the office. Molka closed the door and pressed her back to the wall on the door's hinge side. "Alright. Take big boy bites. Bigger than that. Stuff your mouths full."

The boys complied.

The door swept opened.

Reynolds stomped in. "What in the hell—"

Molka greeted him with a side kick into his lower back.

Reynolds bounced from wall to floor.

Molka shut the door and removed the pistol and Taser from Reynolds' duty belt. She added his pistol to the boy's collection in the file cabinet and pointed her pistol and the Taser at him.

Bobby swallowed his bite. "It's Mrs. Sago, Uncle Eddie!"

Nick swallowed his bite. "And she's still crazy!"

"Shhh!" Molka said. "Quiet cooperation or quick death, remember?"

Reynolds got on hands and knees and grimaced at Molka.

"Stand up," she said. "I didn't hit you that hard. Yet."

Reynolds stood. "I'm glad you're alive, Mrs. Sago. I hadn't heard the good news."

"Thanks," Molka said. "I can tell how happy you are to see me again."

Reynolds held out his hands. "Please calm down, Mrs. Sago. We're here to help you. Please give me the weapon. Everything will be ok."

"That lame trick again? You patronized me the same way last time, right before you Tasered me in the back. Now I'm going to return the favor."

"Please take it easy, Mrs. Sago."

Molka kept the Taser on Reynolds and holstered her pistol. "Bobby, Nick, don't do anything foolish over there. I can pull my weapon and fire before you can unstick your big rear ends from your seats. Tell them, Reynolds."

"Sit tight you two," Reynolds said. "Mrs. Sago isn't going to do anything rash. She's going to give me the pistol and the Taser and let us help her. Aren't you?"

"I saw that." Molka's face perked up. "Yes. Good. Just what I wanted to see."

"See what?" Reynolds said.

"A look in your eyes saying you think you can take the Taser away from me before I can use it. And here's what's going to happen: I'm going to Taser you like you did me. Except, unlike you, I'm going to do it face to face. But first I'll give you something you didn't give me, a sporting chance. I'm going to set the Taser on the floor between us, step back, and count to three. First one to grab it gets to use it. Alright?"

Reynolds' body stiffened. "Alright."

She placed the Taser on the floor and took two steps back. "Ready?"

Reynolds locked on the Taser. "Ready."

"One, two—"

Reynolds dove for the Taser.

Molka leapt forward and dropped an axe kick on the back of his skull.

Reynolds flattened facedown, stunned.

Molka smiled. "I figured you would try that." She seized the Taser, rolled Reynolds onto his back, and deployed the Taser darts into his chest.

Reynolds screeched and arched in pain. His eyes closed over an anguished face.

She continued to click electric agony into his body. "Here's a one…two…three…count you gave me. One more for being incompetent at your job. And one more…just because." She released the trigger and tossed the Taser on Reynolds' stomach.

Reynolds writhed as he recovered his senses. A wet spot appeared on his crotch.

Molka frowned, disappointed. "Not as satisfying as I thought." She turned to Bobby and Nick. "You guys want to do something about it?"

Bobby and Nick did not.

"Bobby," she said. "Look at him lying there. Are you going to let me get away with that?"

No response.

"He peed his pants," Molka said. "Your Uncle Eddie, new name Uncle Wetty, peed his pants like a little baby. How humiliating."

No response.

She pulled out her phone, quick-videoed Reynolds' accident, and re-pocketed her phone. "Cop wannabe pees his pants. It's guaranteed viral hilarity. Your family will never live down the shame. Aren't you going to avenge him, Bobby?"

Bobby raged. "You're a crazy bitch."

Molka's face perked again. "Yes. Get mad. Come do something about it."

"You have a gun. I don't."

She removed a pistol from the file cabinet, detached the magazine, and placed them side by side on the floor. Next, she unholstered her pistol, detached the magazine, and placed them side by side on the floor next to the other pistol. "New game. I'll stand way over here." She moved to the far corner. "You stand up. That puts you a lot closer than me. When I say GO, whoever gets to their weapon first and loads it, controls the situation. Ready?"

Reynolds strained onto his side. "Get her ass, Bobby."

"Yes, Bobby," Molka said. "Listen to your Uncle Wetty. Get me. Ready?"

Bobby dove-stumbled, grabbed a pistol, grabbed a mag, inserted it, and started to stand.

Molka lunged and landed a front kick on Bobby's chin. Both he and the pistol clunked on the floor. "You didn't wait for me to say GO. Cheating must run in the family." She bent to collect both pistols. "But cheaters never prosper. They only get their faces kicked."

Nick overturned the table, bull rushed Molka, caught her, and attempted a rear chokehold.

She jerked her head back, mashing Nick's nose, spun, twisted her head from his grip, fired two knees to his groin, and thudded a hook kick to his temple.

Nick joined the floor party.

"Nice try, Nick," Molka said. "A surprise rear attack while your target is engaged is a good tactic. You're not as stupid as you smell." She placed hands on hips and surveyed her carnage.

"That's all you guys got? No more? Ok. It was ok for me. Not great. Not terrible."

Molka recovered her pistol, reinserted the magazine, and re-holstered it. She picked up Bobby's pistol and removed the other two from the file cabinet. "I'll drop your sidearms in the trash can outside the terminal. And tell Gomez if I ever get back here, he'll get the same as you. No. He'll get worse for inconveniencing me with another visit to this dump. It brings back bad memories. And you can also tell him and the real police that the ghost of Mrs. Sago did this to you." She smiled. "Cheer up guys; you'll have a great story for the news channels."

No one from the floor dared comments.

Molka's face contracted in vengeful fury. "But I came here to get some vengeance. And I got some vengeance. And you'll never forget the vengeance I got on this day. You'll always remember...." Her vengeful face released into a smile-giggle. "No. That's not true. I'm lying to you. I've been lying to people on a daily basis and it's becoming too easy. I really didn't come here for vengeance. And I really don't even hold a grudge against you. I'm sure you aren't the first group of morons Gaszi Sago deceived into doing his dirty work. But it's been a long time since I've...since I've took out some stress. It's also been a few months since I've experienced any live fire—so to speak. And I wanted a little sparring session. Things are about to get serious for me again. So thank you. This was just what I needed."

PROJECT MOLKA: TASK 3
THURSDAY, JULY 25TH
39 DAYS TO COMPLETE TASK

CHAPTER SIX

Twenty-six hours later, Molka deplaned at a real airport—
Vancouver International—in a travel-comfortable sleeveless blue
summer dress, white sneakers, braided ponytail, and black-
framed glasses.

A wide-smiling man wearing a forest-green blazer—
displaying a gold Hazlehurst Institute crest—greeted her by
name. With unabashed pride, he identified himself as a friend of
Principal Darcy, hand-picked to personally welcome Molka. He
went on to inform her that the staff orientation would be held in
the airport hotel's fifth-floor meeting room, and it would be his
great honor and privilege to load her luggage onto the school's
private jet.

In Molka's home country, a gregarious stranger approaching
you in an airport—let alone offering to handle your luggage—
would give you good cause to alert security. But Principal Darcy
had sent a hand-picked welcoming friend with a sincerity too
zealous not to be trusted.

A 12-seat conference table dominated the airport hotel meeting room. At the far end, two men occupied opposite seats.

On the left side, a pleasant-faced overweight, middle-aged black man wearing a red flannel shirt and khaki work pants two-hand texted. A pleasant smile matched his pleasant face.

On the right side, dozed a wiry, brown-bearded, pale man, sporting new camo hunting boots, pressed green tactical pants, a fresh camo hoodie, and a fresher camo hat with the brim covering his eyes. A Styrofoam cup rested between his legs.

Molka chose to sit next to the pleasant-faced black man who shared his pleasant smile with her.

"How was your flight?" he said.

"Long," she said.

"Mine too. I flew in all the way from Ottawa. But I'm really from Gloucester. That's a suburb of Ottawa—if you consider a smidge over 10 kilometers east a suburb. And where did you come from?"

"I flew in all the way from Miami. But I'm really from Haifa. That's a suburb of Miami—if you consider a smidge over 10,000 kilometers east a suburb."

His pleasant chuckle suited his pleasant face and pleasant smile.

The meeting room door opened and a half-century old toad in an expensive dark blue suit entered carrying a high-end titanium attaché case. He wasn't a real toad, of course, but his bulging eyes, flat broad nose, and pock-marked, gray-brown skin hinted that he might not have been a too distant relative from the Amphibia class.

He smiled with a trial lawyer's sincerity, laid his case on the table, and took the head seat. "Good afternoon. My name is Besnik. I am the dean of Hazlehurst Institute. Before we begin, let us take care of formally signing your contracts. I am hopeful you read over the standard six-month employment agreement and our non-disclosure."

He opened his case, removed three contracts sheathed in blue covers and three black ink pens, and passed them to the appropriate signers. Molka and the pleasant-faced black man took a moment to scan through them before signing. The camo guy signed his without seeming to wake from his doze. The pens and contracts were passed back.

"Thank you," Besnik said. "Now I must ask, as stated in your contract, if you have brought any electronic devices to please turn them over to me now."

The pleasant-faced black man handed over his phone. Molka removed hers from her purse and did likewise.

The camo guy tipped back his cap. His sinewy face carried too many wrinkles for about 35 years of use, and black circles saddened his hollow chestnut eyes.

Molka recognized a combat veteran when she saw one. And she saw one.

He raised the Styrofoam cup close to his mouth and spit out a chunky brown liquid with a pungent snuff whiff. He set the cup on the table, reached into his hoodie pocket, and took out and slid a camo covered phone across the table toward Besnik.

Besnik placed the phones in his case and locked it. "Thank you. Your devices will be left here in the hotel safe to be collectable upon your return." He rose, walked to a flat screen mounted on the wall, removed a controller from his jacket pocket, and started a PowerPoint presentation titled: *Welcome to the Hazlehurst Staff.* "For the benefit of the newcomers, I will cover the amenities you will enjoy as staff members."

Next screen: "The staff compound, where most staff members live and work, features a commissary where you may purchase a large variety of dry goods, snacks, soft drinks, toiletries, etc. Payment is made by simply scanning your staff ID card, and the amount will be deducted from your paycheck."

Next screen: "A self-serve laundry is available for your use."

Next screen: "You may also enjoy the campus library."

Next screen: "Campus workout center."

Next screen: "And last, but certainly not least, your included three meals per day served in our school cafeteria, in which you will not be disappointed."

"Now during the early days of Hazlehurst, some staff members had a difficult time adjusting to being disconnected from the world. However, we believe we have made great strides in resolving this issue by the introduction of Hazelnet."

Next screen: "Hazelnet is an intranet system operated by the school. An intranet is a private network, if you are not familiar. Hazelnet offers a large selection of information and entertainment choices accessible from touch screens in your rooms. You will also use Hazelnet to access your assigned school email account from which you will receive official school communiqués and use to contact other staff members."

Besnik ended the presentation, returned to his seat, and consulted a thin, luxurious gold watch. "In 32 minutes, you will be boarding the school's jet and be taken to Hazlehurst. So while we have a few moments, let us do introductions. We like to establish a communal atmosphere among the staff." He smile-nodded at the pleasant faced-black man. "Welcome back, Custodian Truman. I trust you are feeling better?"

"Much better, Dean Besnik. And I'm raring to resume my duties."

"Are you sure? If you need to take some more time, please do so."

"I get what you're getting at. But don't worry about any liability. My doctors have fully cleared me. I can have them send you a note stating that if you like."

"Yes, I would. Thank you."

The pleasant-faced black man turned to Molka. "Dean Besnik is also a very sharp attorney who looks out for Hazlehurst and Principal Darcy's interests like a fanatic."

Besnik's trial lawyer smile reappeared. "And Custodian Truman is a valued member of the Hazlehurst janitorial staff, which keeps our campus unspoiled." He smile-nodded at Molka. "Your name and job description please."

"I'm Molka. I'll be taking over as the school veterinarian."

"Welcome, Doctor Molka," Besnik said. "The students cherish their pets and will be happy you have arrived to provide them care." He smile-nodded at the camo guy. "Your name and job description, please."

The camo guy spit into his cup again. "My given name is Owen Longstreet Cooper. My friends call me Coop. For a couple of reasons, some ladies call me the 'Spitting Cobra,' and my men called me first sergeant in the 5th Special Forces Group. But you all will call me First Sergeant Cooper until I say otherwise."

Besnik raised a finger. "Principal Darcy insists on a first-name basis. Recall, this is in your contract?"

"Yeah, but I'll bet you everything you got in your rich lawyer wallet you don't refer to Colonel Krasnov as Security Chief Nikolai."

Besnik addressed Molka. "Colonel Krasnov is the chief of campus security and retains his former military title as a courtesy."

"And so will I," the camo guy said. "I've earned it too."

"I am sure you have." Besnik straightened his tie. "However, I would hate for Principal Darcy to terminate your contract before you even begin. Would First Sergeant Owen be an acceptable compromise?"

Owen cup spit yet again. "I reckon."

"Thank you. Your job description, please."

"I'm to be the colonel's second hat. He needs an experienced NCO to retrain, organize, and motivate his team. I've heard there's not much action though. Something about shooting the occasional stray bear and running off the occasional stray reporter. Or maybe it's the other way around on who gets run off and who gets shot. Either way, the pay is sweet."

Molka's wide-smiling personal greeter in the forest-green blazer appeared at the door and motioned to Besnik for a word.

Besnik excused himself from the table and stepped into the hall.

Owen looked to Molka. "I've also been told about all the beautiful scenery I'll see up there." His look became a leer. "Whoo-yeah...I surely look forward to seeing some beautiful scenery up there. Right up close."

Molka sneered at Owen's leer. "I imagine your duties won't leave you much time for sightseeing."

"I can always make time for beauty."

"And I never waste time on ugly."

"What did you call me?" Owen said.

Truman showed Owen his pleasant smile. "First Sergeant Owen, I believe Doctor Molka was being playfully sarcastic."

Owen aimed annoyance at Truman. "Mind your business, flabby. She knows what she was being." He aimed anger at

Molka. "Is that right, doc? You were being playful and sarcastic?"

She shrugged. "If that's how you want to take it, sergeant."

"It's first sergeant, and I was just being friendly with you. No need to get sassy with me."

"Sassy?" Molka leaned back and folded her arms. "If I ever get *sassy* with you, you'll know it…first sergeant."

CHAPTER SEVEN

After a smooth one-hour flight on the Hazlehurst Institute's
magnificent Gulfstream G650, the final approach into the school
airport revealed a sudden clearing in a pine-covered valley.
Distant snowcapped mountains provided a spectacular backdrop
for the stately scarlet-red brick campus buildings laid out on
virgin emerald-green grass and overlooking a pristine Tiffany-
blue river.

If nothing else, it ranked among the most impressive sights
Molka had ever witnessed.

But a broader view—revealing a lone single-lane road
leading away from the school and vanishing into a thick forest
and no other human made landmarks from horizon to horizon—
contextualized the beauty as isolated to a paranoid extreme.

The jet landed on a commercial-sized runway serviced by a
wide taxiway and apron. A large white aluminum hangar and
maintenance building on one side and a control tower and two-
truck fire department on the other completed a tidy modern
facility.

Something at the apron's far end caught Molka's interest
most though: a matte black Airbus H135M light helicopter
configured as a gunship. It menaced from atop a helipad with a

20-millimeter Gatling-style cannon mounted on its port pylon and a 40-millimeter grenade launcher mounted on its starboard pylon. A formidable, customized weapons platform—someone wasn't fooling around.

Of course, in normal circumstances, a school having such firepower on hand would be absurd. But considering the nefarious work their prized student Aden Luck carried out there, the fact they didn't have a lot more might have been even more absurd.

The jet taxied to a stop across from the hangar, the door opened, and Besnik led Molka and her two new co-workers down the airstairs. A 25-seat electric powered transporter cart driven by another forest-green-blazer-wearing guy arrived and stopped next to them. And a woman wearing yet another green blazer took Besnik aside for a private conversation.

Owen used the pause to pull a red dipping tobacco can from his back pocket. He shook it while finger tapping it with one hand, opened it, removed a thick pinch with his thumb and index finger, and packed it into his lower lip.

Molka turned away from his off-putting habit and faced Truman. "What's the story with all these green blazer wearers?"

"Those are Friends of Darcy—that's Friends with a capital F. They're not her real friends. It's just the title she gave them."

"They have special status here?"

"You could say so. All hardcore disciples of Doctor Moore and now her. They're super loyal volunteers and handle duties she doesn't trust to *old thinkers*—as they call people like us. They also act as instructors for the students."

"Friends of Darcy," Molka said. "FODs."

Truman chuckled pleasant. "Good use of acronym. But everyone on the staff calls them greenies. Never in front of Principal Darcy or Dean Besnik though."

Besnik finished his confab and addressed the trio. "Doctor Molka, First Sergeant Owen, please get on board the transporter. Your baggage will be taken to your accommodations. Custodian Truman, Head Custodian Randy has asked you report to the cafeteria at once for clean-up duties."

Molka and Owen got in the transporter, and Truman departed to obey his orders.

Molka sat in the back rear-facing seat and watched still more greenies unload their luggage from the aircraft and onto a cart and push it into the hangar, no doubt to be hand searched for contraband. The box of special "feminine devices" Azzur had issued her had passed through the Miami and Vancouver airports without incident, and she expected they would do the same there. But she made a mental note to rewash all her underwear.

Besnik sat next to the driver and turned to the passengers with assured pride. "We will now take a campus tour."

The transporter crossed the apron, passed through an automatic gate watched by security cams, and entered the campus grounds. As they drove along a tree lined gray brick path, Besnik identified the cafeteria, library, gymnasium, auditorium, student dorm, student resource center, central courtyard, and the five-story classroom-administration building with the attached bell tower Azzur had briefed her on.

Besnik pontificated on the neo-classical Jeffersonian style campus architecture, as illustrated by the red brick, white painted columns, and ample use of arches. Trees in perfect position and proportion, manicured lawns, vibrant flower beds, and wrought iron lamp posts accentuated the buildings. If Molka didn't know it was only four years old, she might have guessed the place had been there for over a century.

But at another glance, it resembled a movie set—a movie set with something phony going on behind all the fancy facades.

The transporter drove into a small stadium located next to the river. A grandstand rose on the nearside and faced a grass playing field surrounded by an all-weather running track. The transporter drove onto the track and stopped.

Across the river—in direct line with the grandstand and atop a small hill—towered a massive Principal Darcy statue. Her smiling dress wearing likeness stood with arms spread in a welcoming manner.

Besnik radiated at the monument. "Hazlehurst Institute commissioned the finest sculptor in Italy to honor our beloved founder. She stands a full 80 feet high atop a 20-foot-high pedestal. They say the granite used should last for 1000 years."

The transporter left the stadium and moved across campus. They passed a large two-story mansion-like house on a slight knoll, which sat separate from all the other structures. Also done in neo-classical Jeffersonian style, it featured another well-manicured lawn, and a newer model forest green Range Rover was parked in the driveway.

"Sweet crib," Owen said. "And a bitchin' Rover out front too. Who lives there?"

"That is the dean's residence," Besnik said.

"Damn, you're living pimp-rich, aren't you? I guess with all the billions gushing around here, it don't hurt to siphon off a little taste for yourself, right?"

Besnik straightened his tie. "There is no impropriety on my part. The house is provided to me by Hazlehurst Institute, and the vehicle is on loan from Principal Darcy."

"Sure." Owen spit dip juice on the campus grass. "Whatever you say, Deanie."

Besnik's beaming demeanor returned. "And now I have a special treat for you. Principal Darcy is on campus today and is about to conduct a convocation in the auditorium with all the students." His eyes glistened with ecstasy. "And she has graciously requested you to attend."

Male, Caucasian, pasty, and portly individuals over 65 years old dominated the student body filling the auditorium. But a sprinkling of women, other races, ethnicities, and physiques registered on closer view. No one could accuse Principal Darcy of discrimination; all with an acceptable net worth were equal in her eyes.

The students wore identical loose-fitting beige tops and bottoms similar to surgical scrubs—but made from a higher quality material—and thick soled brown sandals over white socks. The Hazlehurst school uniform combined comfortable conformity with ridiculous humility.

Besnik directed Molka and Owen to two empty seats in the last row. They sat, and he paced with eagerness next to them in the aisle.

A podium with a microphone waited on stage, and courteous applause greeted a tall, eagle-nosed older male greenie with dyed jet-black hair approaching it.

He smiled into the microphone. "Welcome, students."

The students answered in unison: "Welcome, Friend Greg."

"She's here!"

Excited applause.

"Are you excited?"

"Yes, Friend Greg!"

Anticipative applause.

"I said, are you excited?"

"Yes, Friend Greg!"

Desirous applause.

"ARE YOU EXCITED?"

"YES, FRIEND GREG!"

Untamed applause.

"Ok, without further ado, our wonderful Principal Darcy!"

The students erupted to their feet and unleashed exuberant, cheer-fueled clapping.

Greenie Greg stepped aside.

A gorgeous petite figurine in a white designer dress and heels emerged from stage right and glided toward the podium. Her blonde hair shined delicious. Her ivory smile gleamed epic. And her gray eyes radiated empathy.

Principal Darcy made it difficult to look at her and not like her.

And difficult not to want her to look at you and like you too.

The students increased their ovation in noise and enthusiasm when Principal Darcy centered herself behind the podium and dialed her smile to the upper charm level.

She slowly raised both hands with her palms facing the students.

The students went silent.

She smiled again and slowly lowered her hands.

This queued them into passionate group song:

I love me, this I know,
For Principal Darcy tells me so;
To myself I belong;
I was weak, but now I'm strong.

Yes, I love me!
Yes, I love me!
Yes, I love me!
For Principal Darcy tells me so!
The students sat in unison.

Principal Darcy adjusted the microphone to her height. "Good afternoon, students!"

The students in unison: "Good afternoon, Principal Darcy!"

"I'm so very happy to see you all."

She spoke with the soft southern drawl Molka had only heard in some old American movies. And she enunciated somewhat dramatic, but not to the point of irritation.

She continued. "Are you happy?"

"Yes, Principal Darcy!"

"Do you love your school?"

"Yes, Principal Darcy!"

"Do you love your studies?"

"Yes, Principal Darcy!"

"Do you love yourselves?"

"Yes, Principal Darcy!"

A balding obese student stood and yelled, "And we love you too, Principal Darcy!"

The students bounded to their feet again and broke out in fresh cheers and chanting.

"Principal Darcy!"

"Principal Darcy!"

"Principal Darcy!"

"Principal Darcy!"

Owen leaned to Molka's ear. "Ever see *Triumph of the Will?*"

Principal Darcy savored the adulation for a long beat before bringing the students back to their seats and silencing them with her hand movements again. "Let me gaze upon your beautiful faces." She scanned the audience side to side and paused on a middle row. "Student Gerard, has there been any improvement with your sciatica, and has the physical therapist I brought in from Los Angeles been helpful to you?"

Student Gerard stood and smiled, waiting for an attending greenie to bring a wireless microphone. "Yes, Principal Darcy, my condition has improved, and the therapist you provided has been very helpful. Thank you for asking and thank you for caring."

Principal Darcy presented a compassionate smile. "I'm so glad to hear you're feeling better my sweet man."

The students clapped supportive.

Principal Darcy scanned the audience again. "Student Martha? Where is Student Martha? Oh, there you are dear heart. I'm told the gourmet chocolate chip walnut cookies you baked for the faculty were positively scrumptious."

Student Martha stood and smiled, waiting for the microphone greenie. "Thank you, Principal Darcy. Wait until you taste my fall desserts preview at the student fair: apple caramel cheesecake bars and my ultra-moist pumpkin bread with brown butter maple icing."

Principal Darcy's smile broke playful. "Sweet Savannah! You're going to devastate our diets! But…if you have to go down, you may as well go down like a boss, right?"

The students laughed with agreeable nods.

Principal Darcy sighed. "I'm sorry I have been away from you for so long. I've missed you all desperately. My work keeps me ever busy. But I'm never really away from you." She laid her hand over her heart. "I hold you close every moment. And I value and love each and every one of you so very dearly."

Many students wept, unashamed.

Besnik's eyes filled too.

Principal Darcy went on, "Now I believe for today's convocation, we will have testimonials. Who would like to volunteer?"

Every student raised a hand.

Principal Darcy perused faces. "Yes, Student Warren."

A short, white-bearded man stood and waited for the microphone. "When I was an old thinker, I strived from prep school to conquer Wall Street. And I didn't disappoint myself. I became the most successful hedge fund manager they ever saw. Then after I bought and experienced everything I ever desired, I no longer had a purpose or a reason to live. But this school gave me a new purpose and a new reason. I love you, Principal Darcy."

Principal Darcy blew him a kiss. "And I love you too, Student Lawrence."

Impassioned applause.

Principal Darcy stilled the students. "Who's next? Yes, Student Rolf."

A slender, dignified man stood and took the microphone. "When I was an old thinker, I was quite a good footballer. That is a soccer player to my American classmates. I had dreams of a professional football career. When I was 10 years old, my father informed me he was dying from terminal cancer, and I was to be immediately groomed to take over the family business. My football dreams ended in that moment. By the time I was 30, I operated the biggest import-export business in Europe. By the time I was 40, I operated the biggest import-export business west of Hong Kong. By the time I was 50, I had been divorced three times and in and out of rehab six times. By the time I was 60, the thought of one more day of my wretched existence was unthinkable. But then a dear friend, who is also a student here, had Principal Darcy reach out to me. Everything changed for the fantastic after that. Next week I turn 70 and I cannot wait to see the joys 80 and 90 will bring me. Thank you, Principal Darcy. You saved my life."

Even more impassioned applause.

Principal Darcy stilled the students again. "Thank you, Student Rolf. Your journey is an inspiration to us all. Who's next?"

The affirmations continued for another 30 minutes, each one an emotional tale of extreme adult success achieved at the expense of lost youth, leading to desperate depression, before finding redemption at Hazlehurst and ending with all praise and credit to Principal Darcy.

She reveled in each syllable.

The convocation ended with a repeat rendition of their tribute song and Principal Darcy blowing too many kisses to the cheering students on a too slow stage exit walk.

No question, Principal Darcy's manipulation game played strong. And if her concern and affection for the students was all fake, her acting game played stronger. But even the strongest players have a weakness. *Better find it before the time comes to break her.*

Besnik summoned Molka and Owen to follow him backstage to a small room. Principal Darcy sat in a throne-like, high back chair, legs crossed with elegance. The tall greenie the students called Friend Greg and several other greenies surrounded her.

Principal Darcy smiled at the newcomers. "Who are your guests, Dean Besnik?"

"Principal Darcy," Besnik said. "These are our newest staff members. Doctor Molka and First Sergeant Owen."

Darcy smiled at Owen. "Welcome, First Sergeant Owen."

Owen tapped his cap brim, impressed. "Thank you, ma'am."

"You sound like a country boy. Where are you from?"

"West, by God, Virginia, ma'am."

"Oh, a mountain man. Well, our surroundings here should make you feel right at home." Her eyes strolled over him. "Dean Besnik tells me he has a very special assignment in mind for you. Do you believe you're up for it?"

"I'm up for anything you've got for me, ma'am."

"We shall see. And please call me, Principal Darcy."

"Yes, ma'am, uh, Principal Darcy."

"Colonel Krasnov requested you report to him at security headquarters. You are excused to do so now."

Owen started to salute her, caught himself, and departed.

Principal Darcy recharged her smile and moved to Molka. "And where did you come to us from, Doctor Molka?"

"South Florida."

"That's a full day of travel, isn't it?"

"About 13 hours with the layover."

"Whereabouts in South Florida?"

"Cinnamon Cove," Molka said.

"Is that a fact? Were you part of the exclusive Cinnamon Cove set?"

"No. I just took care of their pets."

Principal Darcy laughed and assessed Molka's body. "You're much younger and more attractive than I imagined a veterinarian could be. Of course, the only other veterinarians I've met in person were your predecessor—who set a very low bar— and an old drunken farm vet back home in Mississippi. He would come into the establishment I worked in, always reeking of apple pie moonshine and manure." Her smile and focus faded. "I pushed him away and called him a disgusting, repulsive pig. It only seemed to excite him more." She refocused on Molka and smiled again. "Your assistant, Vet Tech Rosina, has been doing a fine job filling in. You've had a long flight. What would you say to taking the rest of the day off and reporting to your office tomorrow at 10:00 AM?"

"I would say I really appreciate that. I also want to say I really admired your performance out there. There's definitely a lot I could learn from a knowledgeable educator like you. I hope I'll get a chance to pick your brain someday very soon."

Principal Darcy shined with appreciation. "Well, aren't you just a doll? Thank you so much for those sweet words. I have a feeling we're going to get along like sisters."

CHAPTER EIGHT

Short sleep and cross-continental travel sent Molka straight to bed after the Principal Darcy meeting. She woke the next morning and judged her staff dorm room to be a lot like her old college dorm room, except a lot newer and nicer and cleaner, and she didn't have to share it with a little drama queen from Netanya.

She reached for her phone on the nightstand. Not there. Where did she leave it?

Wake up, Molka! Your phone is locked in the airport hotel safe in Vancouver. You're disconnected from the world. Get used to it.

She rose and dug her old pilot's watch from her suitcase. 9:04AM Cinnamon Cove time made it 6:04 AM local. Still four hours until she needed to be in her office.

She showered in a tiny shower, hung hanging clothes in a tiny closet, and folded folding clothes into a tiny dresser. In the tiny bathroom, her toiletries filled the tiny countertop, and she stored Azzur's special tampon box in the same place she stored hers at home: under the bathroom sink.

The entire procedure didn't take as long as she had hoped.

Molka powered up the Hazelnet monitor mounted on the wall over a tiny desk. A welcome screen prompted her to create a username and password.

Next, she activated her assigned Hazelnet email—doctormolka@Hazelnet—and for fun and boredom's sake, she tried to email her real email account. A pop-up stated that Hazelnet provided no internet access, and her message went unsent. A second pop-up instructed her to please not attempt again. Obviously, she wasn't the first one to try it.

The Hazelnet main menu offered school news and events, student services, staff services, and entertainment.

She tapped on the student services, hoping to find a campus map to study for her task, but instead found the student's current daily academic schedule.

10:00 AM-12:00 PM: Classroom Study: The theories, teachings, and solutions for living a truly happy life from Doctor Thomas Moore and Principal Darcy.

Made sense. Keep them well indoctrinated to keep their tuition fees flowing.

12:00 PM-2:00 PM: Lunch

A nice leisurely two-hour lunch break.

2:00 PM-3:30 PM: Rest Time

That would be nap time.

3:30 PM-4:30 PM: Physical Wellness

That would be recess.

4:30 PM-6:00 PM: Organized Activities

The Organized Activities drop down menu included arts and crafts, cooking, drama club, book club, volunteerism, and mentoring.

Mentoring? Maybe the committed Principal Darcy disciples convincing doubters to stop doubting?

In any case, it read as a joke curriculum for a joke school.

Molka tapped on staff services and learned that the commissary opened at 6:00 AM for the staff's convenience.

Alright. Go do a little time-wasting shopping.

She logged off, outfitted in tight white running shorts, a tight white crop top, and white running shoes, grabbed her staff ID, trotted down the stairs from her second-floor room, and headed across the quiet staff compound.

The morning sky dawned clear, the pine fresh air stimulated, and the low humidity offered an invigorating change from South Florida.

Unlike the neo-classical Jeffersonian-style architecture and well-maintained landscaping on campus, the staff compound featured functional no-frills buildings laid out on grid pattern streets, giving it an industrial park atmosphere.

The commissary—like a modern drug store—stocked a little bit of everything. Molka purchased a bottled water 12 pack, protein bars, a cheap digital alarm clock, a notebook, a roll of duct tape, some tacks, and—to track the days in her new phone-free existence—a bizarre school calendar featuring a different Principal Darcy photo for each month.

Back in her room, she loaded the water bottles into her tiny refrigerator, setup the alarm clock on her nightstand, stashed the duct tape next to the special tampon box, used the tacks to tack the Darcy calendar over her bed, and ate a protein bar for breakfast.

Time check:

It's only 7:19 AM? Wow. Now what?

Ok. As she figured out after her arrival in Cinnamon Cove, it's best to keep your normal routines while adjusting to new surroundings and a new time zone. Her normal routine at such an hour would be heading to the gym or going for a run. She opted to use a run to reconnoiter the campus—a logical first step to completing her task.

Molka fast-stepped back downstairs and ran across the staff compound and through the open gate separating it from the school campus. First stop, the most important stop to her task: the extraction point.

The deserted central courtyard encompassed a half-soccer-field-sized greenspace crisscrossed by gray brick paths leading to the various campus buildings. A wider brick path encircled the entire courtyard, and large, healthy oak trees encircled that path.

On site, it appeared somewhat smaller than it had on the satellite view photo from her briefing. That photo had been taken the previous fall, and since then, the trees had reached their full summer growth. A pilot making a night landing and takeoff would have to keep careful watch on their rotor diameter.

Other central courtyard features included green benches, wrought iron lampposts, squirrel movements, bird calls, and—at the far end—a small white building.

She approached it. Cartoon kids holding ice cream cones formed the exterior décor. An ice cream stand? Yes.

Why not. Adults playing children would demand sweet treats. Maybe she would find a playground next.

Molka headed for the other important location required for her task: the bell tower she would signal the contractor team from.

The square-shaped red brick tower abutted the classroom-administration building's left wing. A mansard roof at the top covered the belfry, which featured a white arched opening on each side. No external entrance visible though. Access must be from inside its adjoining building.

Molka did a 360-degree location check. Still no one around. Good time to go up there and inspect the layout.

She entered the classroom-administration building. No occupancy sights or sounds registered in there either. She turned left and walked the hallway. Sure enough, it ended at a door marked *bell tower*. The door waited unlocked, and she stepped inside and jog-climbed the 16 flights.

Whew. Good cardio.

The stairs ended at a metal hatch. She pushed it. Unlocked too. Lax security. Then again, how many Hazlehurst-aged students would make the climb?

Molka crawled through the hatch and into the belfry but found no bell. Instead, on the metal floor where a bell should have been mounted, a pencil-drawn circle with jotted dimensions still waited for its arrival and installation. Maybe Principal Darcy had diverted those resources to somewhere else on campus.

Like into manufacturing slaughterbot drones.

The four large arched belfry openings—protected by metal safety rails—offered a comprehensive view of the entire school grounds and hundreds of square kilometers beyond. She moved to the west-facing opening and identified the pine-sheltered foothill 4.6 kilometers away containing the contractor's sensor panel. It sat in perfect unobstructed alignment. Hitting it with

Azzur's "feminine device" signaler beam would not be a problem.

Back downstairs and outside, Molka resumed her run. She cut around the classroom-administration building's corner and almost collided into Custodian Truman pushing a janitorial cart from the opposite direction.

"Whoa," Truman said. "Close call."

"Sorry," Molka said.

"No problem. And good morning, Doctor Molka."

"Good morning, Custodian Truman."

"Out for a run, I see?"

"Yes."

Truman admired the cloudless sky. "It's a very beautiful day for it."

"Very beautiful and very quiet."

"Well, the students don't start classes until 10 AM because, you know, it takes many of them a little longer to get ready, get breakfast, and such."

"Understood," she said. "Guess we have the campus all to ourselves right now."

"Not quite. I watched First Sergeant Owen head into the stadium a few minutes ago. And listen to this," Truman lowered his voice, "he was carrying a machine gun."

"Was he?"

"He was. Seems like excessive firepower for campus security."

Molka shrugged. "I wouldn't know."

"He's an interesting man, don't you think?"

"If by interesting you mean obnoxious, crude, and delusional."

Truman chuckled his pleasant chuckle. "No comment." He pushed his cart on. "Have a good day, Doctor Molka."

Although she played it unconcerned, Truman's observation rang ominous. Owen stalking the campus with an automatic weapon posed a possible future threat to her task. It warranted another recon mission.

Molka jogged to and entered the stadium. A matte black electric golf cart with Owen seated inside waited near the running track start-finish line. He had exchanged his camo apparel for dark gray fatigues, a matching fatigue cap, and black combat boots. An MP5 submachine gun rested on the seat beside him. He watched something on the track—a man in a white tee shirt and blue shorts running laps. Hard.

Molka watched too.

The man they watched was Aden Kayne Luck.

And as Azzur had suggested, Aden did resemble a man she once knew. A beautiful man she called her American captain. A man she once knew intimately. Until she found out she didn't know him at all. He told her his lies were well intentioned and for her own good.

That only made them even more hurtful.

Want to keep your heart? Take the malicious truth every time.

OK! That's enough! Secure the sob story, soldier! Get back to your task! You can feel sorry for yourself when you're dead!

CHAPTER NINE

On a second lap closer view, the resemblance diverged between Aden and the one love of Molka's life.

If you took away Aden's close-cropped full beard, facially they could pass for brothers. Both modeled strong jawlines, broad foreheads, and short brown hair with a sexy gray hint at the temples. But physically her American captain showed off a lift heavy, supersets, never-skip-leg day, body type, whereas Aden sported a leaner, more defined, cardio-heavy physique.

Maybe her long intimate male company dry spell had biased her judgment, but if forced to pick which one attracted her more, she would have to go with Aden.

Hmm.

Mmm.

Well...

Anyway, the first step in talking Aden into leaving with her was to find a reason to talk to him. She waited for him to come around the track again. When he had traveled about 20 meters past her, she fell in behind him at the run and maintained the 20-meter interval.

Aden didn't look back at her. He just ran on.

And on.

And on.

Two kilometers in…

He sets a good pace.

Four kilometers in...

He sets a really good pace.

Six kilometers in...

I run. He's a runner.

Eight kilometers in...

We're about at my limit for the day.

After kilometer nine, Aden stopped next to Owen's cart and removed a bottled water.

Molka arrived, stopped next to him, put hands to knees, and recovered her wind. Owen spit dip and spanked her with a stare. She ignored his new lechery and addressed Aden. "Either you're in great shape, or I'm out of shape."

Aden wiped his face on his shirt and appraised her with gentle brown eyes. "You're not out of shape." He tossed the empty water bottle back into the cart and ran toward the stadium exit.

Molka followed him.

Owen followed them both in the cart.

Aden traversed the empty campus to the zigzag road—with tree lines concealing what lay beyond the next zig or zag—which led to the Security Zone.

Aden increased his pace, and Molka lost him. Owen accelerated around her to catch Aden, and she lost him too.

After about a half kilometer of zigging and zagging, Molka turned the last zag. The road ended at a prison-high chain-link fence topped with razor wire and bisected by an automated gate covered by security cameras.

Molka reached the gate. A white sign with black letters warned:

SECURITY ZONE
AUTHORIZED PERSONNEL ONLY

Aden had already passed through the gate and was running toward a large three-story gray warehouse-like structure.

Recall from her briefing photos confirmed it as the drone research and production facility—aka Building A—and the smaller two-story building 40 meters adjacent to it as the security headquarters.

Aden reached the building, climbed an external staircase to the third floor, and entered.

A black blur flashed in Molka's left peripheral vision.

She spun to it.

Owen's cart emerged from concealment in the tree line outside the fence and sped toward the gate.

Molka stepped back to let him pass, but he cut it sudden and clipped her leg. She stumbled back, smacked the pavement— skinning elbow and knee—and sat on her backside facing a grinning, parked Owen.

"The Security Zone is off limits to students and staff," Owen said. "And so is he." He motioned toward Building A.

"Why did you hit me?"

"Just doing my job."

"It's your job to plow into a new staff member out for a run who loses her way?"

"I don't think that's quite what you were doing."

Molka examined her elbow abrasion. "What do you think I was doing?"

"Trying to flirt with my man."

"And if I was," she said, "how is it your business?"

"It's my business because the boss assigned me to watch him when he's out and about and discourage anyone from bothering him while he is."

"You don't say?"

"Yes, I do say. So no hard feelings, right?"

Molka smiled, rose, and approached the cart with her hand extended for shaking.

Owen extended his hand in return. "That's a way."

She took his hand, yanked him from the cart, kneed his abdomen, slung him to the pavement, and snatched his MP5 submachine gun from the seat.

He roll-recovered into a combat stance and gripped his holstered sidearm. "Damn it! Cheap shot!" He eyed the submachine gun muzzle pointed his way, eased his hand from his pistol, and grinned. "Course, I love a well-timed cheap shot. What are you trying to do, get on my good side, girl?"

"Doctor or doc will be fine," Molka said. "And I'm not trying to get on any side of you."

Owen examined an abrasion on his elbow. "Where did you learn that move?"

"Where did you learn not to see that move coming?"

"Ok, you caught me off guard. Just lucky though. Bet you learned it at one of those cute little women's self-defense classes."

She crinkled her nose. "Something like that." She inspected his submachine gun. "New issue. Not German Army surplus trash."

"Hey, be careful there," Owen said. "It's ready to rock, and it would be a helluva note if I got killed with my own weapon."

Molka viewed his sidearm. "And you're carrying a new model Gen5 Glock too."

"You know a little about weapons, do you?"

"What other fun new toys do you security guys have around here?"

Owen puzzled a moment and said, "I won't—but I should—report you for this incident."

"And you won't—but you should—report yourself for *this* incident." Molka tapped the submachine gun.

He spit dip. "Well, you got me there. I'll give you that. But I won't forget this either, doc."

"Neither will I…first sergeant."

Molka tossed the submachine gun on the cart seat and jogged back toward campus.

CHAPTER 10

"**D**on't let all the fresh air and beautiful scenery and open space and peace and quiet fool you. It gets depressing around here fast. I've got three months left in my contract, and then I'm going straight back to my dirty, smelly, crowded, noisy, wonderful little Bronx."

This was the second thing, after good morning, that Vet Tech Rosina said when Molka arrived in the veterinarian's office at 9:45 AM.

A late 20s, slim, five-foot, firecracker of Puerto Rican descent, Rosina talked loud and proud and left no doubt that she could back up every decibel and declaration.

Molka liked her on the spot.

Rosina next offered Molka an office tour. Located next to—but separate from—the campus infirmary, the veterinary facility was well designed, well-equipped, and spotless. The tour ended back in the oversize waiting room, which doubled as a pet supplies store.

"Most appointments are walk-ins," Rosina said. "But the students can also book through Hazelnet."

"What's our clientele like?"

"Eighty-seven dogs, 34 cats, three hamsters, two gerbils, not sure how many birds right now, and a royal python I hope we never have to see."

"Alright," Molka said. "I'll need you to go over your lab and pharmacy procedures, record-keeping, inventory and ordering of supplies, and the bad news about my paperwork requirements."

"No problem," Rosina said. "I can familiarize you with everything." She turned away and moved from shelf to shelf straightening and re-straightening items. "I want to talk to you about something first, Doctor Molka."

"Sure. And just call me Molka."

"Ok, so the doctor you replaced, Doctor Brantley, didn't spend much time in the office. He chain-smoked and liked to drink. So, he spent most of his time in his room smoking and drinking."

"I thought alcohol and tobacco are prohibited here."

"They are, but the greenies run a nice side business selling cigs and booze and other contraband. They say Dean Besnik knows all about it and takes a cut of the profits."

"Really?" Molka said. "Dean Besnik struck me as a by-the-book, loyal Hazlehurst man."

"Oh, don't get me wrong. He's a true believer in Principal Darcy. Just like all the students. And he would never allow the greenies to sell to them. But he figures we old thinkers on the staff have lost our souls anyway, so what difference does it make if he takes our money? I mean, it's no big secret. That's why everyone was a little surprised when security investigated Doctor Brantley and got him fired for it."

"Interesting information," Molka said.

"But what I wanted to talk to you about, with Doctor Brantley never around, I basically—ok, more than basically—I ran this office myself. If I needed him for something, which I rarely did, I sent for him. I'm damn good at what I do and know as much or more than some vets I've worked with. I'm not being boastful, I'm being truthful."

"I don't doubt it," Molka said. "I recognize a good vet tech when I see one. And I see one."

"Thanks. But this is the closest I'll ever get to having my own practice. And no matter what I say about this place, it's been one of the most fulfilling times in my life. So, I hoped you and I could have a similar arrangement?"

"You mean where you run the office, and if you need something from me, you'll send for me?"

Rosina frowned, determined. "Right."

"Rosina, believe it or not, I couldn't ask for a better arrangement."

Rosina smiled, relieved. "Exactly what I wanted to hear. Well, I have some business to take care of before classes start." She opened the front door and let in seven waiting students with leashed dogs.

"Are those all appointments?" Molka said.

"No. We have none scheduled today. They're here to buy grooming stuff to get ready for the dog show at the student fair tomorrow."

"How cute."

"It's a pretty big deal they tell me."

Molka admired the wandering, sniffing, panting dogs. "Some real contenders here now."

"The fair is open to staff," Rosina said. "Think you might want to go?"

"May as well. Doesn't look like I'll have anything to do around here tomorrow."

That's exactly what Rosina wanted to hear too.

 **CHAPTER 11**

Welcome to the Hazlehurst Institute 4th Annual Student Fair!

The massive white banner with green letters hanging above the hangar's open doors confirmed that the student fair—as reported on Hazelnet—would be held at the airport. But it didn't explain why they had chosen such an impersonal, shade-less area over more comfortable or scenic campus venues like the auditorium, stadium, or central courtyard.

Molka arrived in her preferred off-duty veterinarian guise—tennis shoes, khakis, white polo shirt, ponytail, and black-framed glasses—and joined the noon time student and staff throng awash on the apron.

Her fellow fairgoers meandered among booths displaying various arts, crafts, and cooking exhibitions crewed by other students. A greenie trio manned a booth offering Doctor Thomas Moore's works in hardcover, paperback, CD, and DVD—old formats for those old enough to love old formats.

A roving clown passed out balloons, and a concession stand served cotton candy, candy apples, soft drinks, and ice cream.

Not the worst fair she ever attended, or maybe it appeared better because it provided a distraction from the school's isolation shock.

But the real reason for her presence fell into the "make contact with Aden by any means necessary" category. He hadn't shown at the track that morning. So if she couldn't run with him, maybe she could run into him.

She made three slow passes up and down the fair's block-long midway.

No Aden sighting.

Keep searching.

During pass four, Molka's eyes paused on the helicopter gunship still parked on its helipad at the apron's far end. Such a hot little ship. After pass number five and another gunship glance, her inner pilot couldn't resist any longer. She headed toward it.

The helipad, and an area next to it, had been roped off. Joining the gunship inside the rope barrier was a matte black 6x6 weapons carrier truck with—bad memory for her—twin 23-millimeter cannons mounted on its open flat bed, a giant matte black four-wheel-drive SUV equipped with menacing push bumpers, and two matte black ATVs, each mounting a light machine gun.

The Hazlehurst Institute security force was showing off to the students the tools it used to keep them safe and secured.

Aside the gunship, a diminutive security officer in his early 30s with brown curly hair stood watch, sporting a dark-gray uniform and a shoulder holster. He switched on a standard flirtatious smile as Molka approached.

"Hello, *belle*," he said. His French accent sounded legit.

"Hello," Molka said. "Are you the pilot?"

"I am. And you are the new school veterinarian with the feisty attitude?"

"I'm the new school veterinarian. But the feistiness of my attitude depends on the company."

The pilot laughed. "I understand. And we share the same opinion. You like the look of my powerful gunship, *belle*?"

"It's impressive."

"Yes, it is impressive. And so is my helicopter."

Molka smirked. "How charming. Mind if I get a closer look at it? At the helicopter, I mean."

"It is not permitted. But for you *belle*—with me—anything is possible."

The pilot lifted the rope, and Molka ducked under. She opened the pilot-side door, poked her head inside, and found state-of-the-art electronics and ergonomics. Nice. The pilot's helmet rested on the seat. It carried a newer model helmet-mounted display for digitally enhanced optics, such as night vision or infrared and weapons targeting. Very nice. The fire controls for the six-barreled 20-millimeter cannon and 40-millimeter grenade launcher were located on the cyclic grip.

Molka pulled her head out. "What's her range?"

"Six hundred and fifty kilometers," the pilot said.

"Cruise speed of about 140 knots?"

"Yes."

"Ceiling of about 6,000?" she said.

"Yes."

"I can understand why you went with the Gatling over a 12.7-millimeter gun pod, but why the retro grenade launcher over 70-millimeter rockets?"

The pilot's face perplexed. "Because 40-millimeter grenade ammo is more readily available on the aftermarket…how do you know so much about attack helicopters and helicopters in general?"

"My uncle flew them in the wars. He took me for a ride on my 16th birthday, and I've been fascinated by them ever since."

The pilot grinned creepy. "Maybe I can take you for a ride sometime and you can become fascinated by me."

"I don't think you'll—"

"HERE SHE COMES!"

YEWAAAHHH!

Molka turned toward the source of the shouting and roaring cheers.

The students geriatric fast-walked en masse toward the apron's edge and another rope line separating it from the runway. They jockeyed for prime positions to watch Hazlehurst's private jet approach the airport and broke into a chant:

"Principal Darcy!"

"Principal Darcy!"

"Principal Darcy!"

While the glossy white and forest-green Gulfstream G650 had impressed Molka from the inside on the way from Vancouver, the exterior inflight view raised her appreciation to a higher degree. Its sleek form presented fierce, unapologetic beauty—like its mistress.

The student body pressed the rope line to watch the jet descend for an apparent landing. Molka moved behind them to watch too. But she identified two problems: the jet was coming in way too fast, and the landing gear wasn't down.

The students continued their chant:

"Principal Darcy!"

"Principal Darcy!"

"Principal Darcy!"

The jet reached the airport's edge, leveled off, and made a low, ear-filling, air-shaking, high-speed pass down the runway's entire length.

The waving, screaming students thrilled to the sight.

Molka did too.

When the jet pulled up, circled back around, dropped the gear, and landed, the reason why they had chosen the airport as the fair venue became apparent: staging.

Before leaving Florida, Molka had done a little research on cult leaders. A common trait was their desperate need to be the center of attention. And Principal Darcy using such a grandiose arrival demanded full attention.

But she also used it for symbolism. The high-speed spectacle in her beautiful jet showed the students that she retained the means and power to go anywhere in the world. However, she chose to turn around and come back to them. What a generous gesture from their loving leader. And how fortunate and appreciative they must have felt.

Clever.

The jet taxied to the rope line. Greenies moved the students back.

"Principal Darcy!"

"Principal Darcy!"

"Principal Darcy!"

The aircraft door opened, and Besnik stepped out. He smiled his toad smile and waved to the students. Their underwhelming response came from disappointment. They wanted their adored one. And she made them wait.

"Principal Darcy!"

"Principal Darcy!"

"Principal Darcy!"

A frenzying five minutes later, she emerged in the doorway.

The students detonated into cheers and applause.

Principal Darcy descended the airstairs in a tailored off-white pantsuit, smiling and waving like a queen. Greenie Greg led a six-greenie cordon to escort her majesty across the apron toward the hangar.

The students fell in behind her.

Molka assessed the situation. Still no Aden sighting. Might as well find out how the performance would end. She joined the students.

Inside the spotless hanger, a podiumed and microphoned stage awaited along with several hundred stage facing chairs. A pedestaled sign on the high-shine white floor reserved the seats for the students. Molka joined other staff members standing to the side.

The hangar reverberated with renewed cheers when Principal Darcy and Besnik mounted the stage.

Principal Darcy savored the exaltation before stepping to the microphone and silencing the crowd with her hand gesture. "Greetings students!"

The delirious students shouted in unison: Greetings, Principal Darcy!"

"I want to congratulate you on another successful student fair. Each and every one of you should be very proud of yourself for the efforts you have put in because I am very proud of each and every one of you."

Honored cheering.

"Which is why I broke away from my important work just to be here with you all on this special day."

Beholden cheering.

"The highlight of last year's fair was the student dog show, and I'm sure this year's will be equally exciting. Dean Besnik and I look forward to judging another spirited contest. Now let the show begin."

Anticipative cheering.

Forty student contestants entered the hangar with their leashed dogs and paraded them before the stage. Molka found each one more adorable than the last. But she found all dogs adorable.

Principal Darcy and Besnik watched and consulted together. They narrowed the 40 to 20, the 20 to 10, and the 10 to 5.

Each time they passed a smooth-coated white Chihuahua to the next round, the students cheered, extra satisfied. But when a black and tan Cocker Spaniel also passed through, boos sprinkled the subdued cheers.

The final five became the final two—the Chihuahua and the Cocker Spaniel. The Chihuahua's wild cheers got wilder, and the Cocker Spaniel's mild cheers became more peppered with boos.

The student body reaction—and comments Molka overheard from them—revealed the contest devolving into a referendum on the dog's owners. And "Principal Darcy's favorite donor" leading the Cocker Spaniel was far less popular than the "impeccable lady" leading the Chihuahua.

Principal Darcy and Besnik consulted again, and she stepped back to the microphone. "I'm afraid we've come to an impasse."

A discontented murmur passed through the students.

Principal Darcy went on, "I have picked the Cocker Spaniel as our winner."

Mild cheers and increasing boos.

"While Dean Besnik favors the Chihuahua."

Enthusiastic cheers.

Principal Darcy raised and lowered her hands to silence the mob. "Therefore, I believe it appropriate we ask a knowledgeable mediator to break the tie. And I can think of none more qualified than our new school veterinarian, Doctor Molka." Principal Darcy rotated and locked in on Molka. "Doctor Molka, would you please come join us?"

When the queen calls, you must answer. Molka came forward, climbed the stage steps, and joined the judges. Principal Darcy and Besnik flanked her, and Principal Darcy asked that the

Cocker Spaniel and Chihuahua be paraded again for Doctor Molka's evaluation.

As the students reacted with even more defined passion for the Chihuahua and even more disdain against the Cocker Spaniel, Besnik leaned his head close to Molka's, and through smile-clinched teeth said, "Principal Darcy wants you to pick the Cocker."

Ha. They're fixing the contest.

Principal Darcy picked the Cocker Spaniel for obvious selfish monetary reasons—her favorite donor was its owner. But since the other students loathed him, Besnik picked the more popular owner's Chihuahua to placate the student masses. And to solve the dilemma, they recruited a clueless newcomer—Molka—to make the final unpopular decision.

Principal Darcy gets her way without taking the blame. So clever.

But another thing Molka had learned about cult leaders is that they cannot abide having their authority challenged. She would have to break Principal Darcy's will to get the information she needed about her little sister Janetta's murderer. So why not lay the foundation for the process by defying her—in a passive-aggressive way—before her ardent followers?

Principal Darcy motioned Molka to join her at the microphone. "Doctor Molka, please give us your decision."

Silence filled the hangar.

"It's so hard to pick," Molka said. "Both dogs are amazing. But it's obvious there is only one clear and fair choice to be made." She looked at the Cocker Spaniel and then smiled at Principal Darcy.

Principal Darcy smiled back.

Molka continued, "So…I declare…BOTH dogs are winners!"

The students roared approval.

Besnik smiled, mortified.

Principal Darcy smiled, enraged.

Molka smiled, satisfied.

The students rose to a standing ovation.

Principal Darcy curled her arm around Molka and released a devastating new smile to charm them back to her. But the eyes and admiration remained on Molka.

See how easily I can undermine you, Mrs. cult leader? Better tell me what I need to know before I really do some damage to your power.

Molka added defiant insult to Principal Darcy's authoritative injury by mimicking her kiss-blowing acknowledgements to the students until Owen and another man watching from outside the hangar door caught her attention.

Owen's submachine gun hung across his chest on a tactical sling. No more leaving it lying around to be snatched by veterinarians with feisty attitudes. He didn't applaud though. He spit into a plastic cup in his right hand.

But the man standing next to him—Aden—applauded with vigor and looked at her with a look she knew well, the look of desire.

He waved to Molka.

Molka waved back.

The look, the wave...does he want to talk to me too?

She stepped from the stage and headed toward him. A student congratulatory flock surrounded her with smiles and kind words and handshakes and back pats. She ease-pushed through them all the way to the hangar door.

But when she got there, Aden and Owen had gone.

 **CHAPTER 12**

"**G**et your fucking hands off me, you fucking pedophiles! I swear I'm going to castrate you both and ram your little pedophile balls down your fucking pedophile throats."

Azzur chuckled at the girl's profane symphony in the hallway outside his Tel Aviv office. From his desk, he pressed a button, which unlocked the door. A uniformed military police corporal and private led a tall, slim, attractive girl into the room.

Her green eyes and long blond ponytail matched the photos in Azzur's file, but the neck tattoo must have been a recent addition. She wore a baggy brown short-sleeved utility shirt, matching pants, white tennis shoes, and handcuffs.

"Here she is," the corporal said. "And you're welcome to her. She fought us all the way here."

The girl twisted away from him. "You haven't seen me fight yet, motherfucker."

"Please remove the handcuffs, corporal," Azzur said. "And you men wait outside the door."

The corporal complied, and the two MPs stepped out.

The girl's face animalized. "You should have heard the things they were saying on the way here! What they wanted to do to me!" She jumped to the door, kicked it, and yelled into it. "Pedophiles! Too bad I'm 19, you sick fucks!"

Azzur took out and lit a cigarette and motioned to a chair in front of the desk. "Sit down, Laili."

The girl locked desirous eyes onto the cigarette. "Can I have one?"

"I am not sure smoking is right for you."

"What are you, my fucking daddy?"

Azzur lifted a tablet from his desktop and read aloud: "Gross insubordination, dereliction of duties, absent without leave, assaulting a fellow soldier, assaulting an officer, and theft. Sentence: two years."

"Yeah," the girl said. "They went over all that at my court-martial."

"Sit down, Laili."

"Why are you calling me by my first name?"

"Because I am not with the Army."

"If you're another shrink, you're wasting your time. They already made me take two psychiatric exams and they said I was crazy, but not crazy enough to get out of conscription." Laili sneered. "Guess I proved them wrong though, didn't I?"

"Sit down, Laili."

Her face became annoyed. "What's your name?"

"Azzur."

"That's a stupidly idiotic name."

"Sit down, Laili."

"Is this going to take long?" Laili approached and examined a world map on the wall. "The sooner I start serving my sentence, the sooner I can get the hell out of this country once and for all."

Azzur read on, "At age 13, you ran away from home with a man to Europe. At age 15, you ran away with another man to the United States. At age 17, you ran away with yet another man to New Zealand. You speak very good English, excellent French and Spanish, decent German, and passable Russian."

"Well, I was only in Russia for two weeks before the bitch found me and had me dragged back again. Are we done now?"

He set the tablet aside. "If you want to go spend the next two years in Prison Five, it is of no concern to me. But let me tell you, they have a certain type of woman there, a type of woman which makes those two policemen seem like perfect gentlemen. A type of woman who would love to get a hold of a sweet little piece of ass like you."

"You think I'm afraid of those fat lesbian bitches?"

"Perhaps not," Azzur said. "But they would soon make you afraid of them. And you would become their property. And then what would young Eitan think of you?"

Laili charged Azzur's desk. "Don't you ever say that name to me! Ever!"

"What is wrong with saying your little brother's name?"

Laili bared her teeth and brandished her nails—a young green-eyed tigress. She leaned over the desk and raked Azzur's cheek, raising three scratches.

He stood and backhanded her face, buckling her knees.

Laili recovered, snarled, and lunged at him.

He sent a moderate straight right to her chin, knocking her back.

She recovered again, snarled again, hoisted the chair, and charged.

Azzur side stepped her attack, grabbed her ponytail, and slung her toward the wall.

Laili impacted hard, dropped the chair, and crumpled to the floor, stunned.

Azzur sat and resumed smoking. "Are you done now?"

Laili winced, groaned, and sat with her back against the wall. "Can I have a cigarette?"

"I said, are you done now?"

"Yeah."

"Answer me with proper respect."

She pulled a long, loose hair clump from her ponytail. "Yes. I'm done."

"Good. You have always lived your life by your own rules. Done things your own way. But now you must learn my ways, Laili. First lesson: controlled violence—very useful. Uncontrolled violence—very dangerous."

"Can I have a cigarette?"

"Pick up the chair, sit down, and you may have a cigarette."

Laili scowled but obeyed.

Azzur gave her a cigarette and lit it for her.

Laili closed her eyes and relished the inhale, leaned her head back, and blew smoke at the ceiling. "Now what?"

"Now I will tell you about the Projects Program."

PROJECT MOLKA: TASK 3
FRIDAY, AUGUST 2ND
31 DAYS TO COMPLETE TASK

CHAPTER 13

Now what?

Molka reached behind her head and tugged on the base of her ponytail while leaving the stadium.

Six straight mornings she had come to the running track hoping to catch Aden, and six straight mornings he had never showed. Making contact with him by any means necessary required a little participation on his part too.

Puzzling. Men who looked at her the way he had at the dog show usually didn't leave her alone.

Molka returned to her room, showered, changed, and reported to the veterinarian's office.

"Good morning, Molka," Rosina said from behind the reception counter. "How was your night and day yesterday?"

"The same as the last five nights and days after you kicked me out of here at lunch time."

Rosina laughed. "Sorry. What do you do?"

"Well, after lunch, I've been wandering around school grounds until dinner. But I did break the boredom yesterday by visiting the campus library for some reading material. Have you ever been to the campus library?"

Rosina nodded. "I know what you're going to say. Besides Doctor Moore's books, there are no books in the campus library. They've all been checked out, and there's at least a month's waiting list to get one. That's because there are about 500 other bored-out-of-their minds people here. Reading material is like gold."

"So I found out," Molka said. "Then after dinner, I go back to my room and watch the Hazelnet entertainment channel's nightly lineup: old cartoons, followed by old Doctor Thomas Moore speeches, followed by newer Principal Darcy speeches followed by a self-produced two-hour documentary on Principal Darcy's work to save humanity."

Rosina sighed. "I have it memorized."

"And then I lie in bed missing real TV and my phone and the internet and civilization while waiting to fall into merciful sleep and wake up and do it all over again."

"Told you this place quickly gets depressing."

Habit led Molka to don a white lab coat over her light-blue Oxford shirt and jeans. "Do we have any appointments today?"

"One. A rash coming in any minute."

"Oooo…a rash. Excitement. Can I stay and help?"

Rosina laughed. "You're so funny. Ok, please stay."

The rash dog came and got treated.

Rosina opened the door for the departing student and his poodle and paused to view something. "Uh-oh. There goes another unhappy camper."

Molka spotted what Rosina viewed: a student slumped in a wheelchair, wearing a yellow safety vest over his school uniform, being pushed by a nurse toward the infirmary.

"Guess they stay pretty busy over there," Molka said. "Considering the age and health level of the students."

"They do. But I think his problem is he just came back from a field trip. You can tell when they're wearing the vest."

"Field trip to where? There's nowhere to go within 200 kilometers."

"I'm not sure," Rosina said. "I heard it's like a nature hike or something. They all come back totally exhausted like him though." She checked her watch. "Ok, I got this, Molka. It's almost 11:30, so you might as well—"

"I know, I know, I might as well go to lunch then take the rest of the day off. And if you need me for anything, you'll send for me."

Molka crossed the central courtyard and headed toward the cafeteria. Midway, a big black buzzing wasp swooped past her face. The wasp swooped past her face again. And again. On the fourth swoop, it stopped in midair, reversed, did a wide sweeping circle around her, and stopped to hover before her.

That's no wasp. That's a drone.

The drone swooped away and didn't return.

The Hazlehurst Institute cafeteria always smelled like a five-star restaurant to Molka—well, at least what she imagined a five-star restaurant would smell like. And it wasn't an olfactory fluke. The cafeteria boss—as profiled on Hazelnet—had served as a top executive chef at an exclusive LA restaurant until Principal Darcy coaxed her away.

Three times a day, giddy students formed a patient line and waited for food service workers to ladle their meals onto compartmented trays. But unlike the usual school cafeteria menu choices—cold cereal, hot dogs, chicken nuggets, etc.—they feasted on fare like eggs Florentine, sesame-seared Ahi tuna salad, and prime bone-in rib-eye.

They might be mega millionaires pretending to be children, but they still maintained their mature mega millionaire's standards.

The staff enjoyed the five-star dining perk too, which the school hyped as a hiring incentive. But they segregated the seating with the student section upfront and the staff in the rear.

Molka waited in a long line and opted again for the excellent seafood salad and a bottled water. She sat as usual alone at the backmost table.

A few bites in, two greenies arrived and moved the students from the frontmost table. Some grumbling occurred, but they complied. A minute later, Owen entered escorting Aden.

Aden sported a blue cardigan over a white tee shirt, blue jeans, and black-framed glasses. Owen came dressed for duty submachine gun included. The greenies cut them to the food line's front—where they got prompt service—and seated them in the cleared spot at the first table.

Two utility workers across from Molka watched too. One said to the other, "Never seen the genius eat here before. I thought he had his meals catered in."

The other worker shrugged, "Slumming with us peasants, I guess."

Fifteen minutes passed, Owen stood, took his tray to the tray return, and headed back toward Molka. As he passed her, he flipped a small folded white paper note next to her water bottle. He continued on and assumed a sentry-like position beside the door.

Molka opened the note and read:

Will you join me for lunch, doctor?
Aden Luck

Molka looked to Aden.

He looked back at her.

Same look as at the dog show.

He motioned for her to sit in Owen's vacated seat.

She gathered her tray and approached him. He had chosen the seafood salad too. She liked him in his glasses. Handsome. Her American captain had refused to wear his. Too vain.

"Hello, Doctor Molka. I'm Aden Luck."

Molka sat next to him. "You know my name?"

"If a stranger runs behind me for nine kilometers, I make inquiries."

"Very sensible. But maybe you heard my name announced at the dog show. I saw you there with First Sergeant Owen."

Aden went back to his salad. "First Sergeant Owen says you're a first-class bitch."

Molka went back to her salad. "And from what I've seen of First Sergeant Owen, he's a third-class First Sergeant."

"I spent some time in Israel," Aden said. "You've Americanized your English, but I can still hear your accent. It's sexy."

"Sexy?"

"Oh yes. It brings back memories."

"Good or bad?" she said.

"Some of each." He pushed his tray away. "You mentioned the dog show—quite a performance."

"Yes. They were all so cute."

"I meant your performance. Going against Principal Darcy's wishes is something not done here."

Molka shrugged. "She'll get over it. Or not."

"Athletic, beautiful, and charming, I'll bet the boys never had a chance against you, did they?"

"The men haven't done all that well either."

Aden beamed at Molka, showing dimples that would melt most women's hearts. She forced her eyes back to her salad. "You're younger than all the other students I've seen here—by about 30 years."

"I'm not part of the old big-money club. Principal Darcy allowed me enrollment because of the work I'm doing."

"And what are you doing in Building A? No one on the staff seems to know."

"All I can say is it's very important to the future success of Hazlehurst Institute." Aden's face flipped from judicious to juvenile. "Hey, would you like to ride ATVs with me?"

"You mean all-terrain vehicles?"

"Yeppers. Principal Darcy gave me one. It's the same machine the security officers have, except it doesn't have a mount for a machine gun."

Molka pushed her tray away. "I've never ridden an ATV before."

"It's easy. Uses the same basic controls as a motorcycle. I can teach you."

"Oh. I've ridden a motorcycle before."

Aden's face popped excited. "Then you can handle an ATV no problem. I'll ask the colonel if we can borrow another one from security, and we'll go riding."

"Alright. When?"

"Tomorrow morning. Right after our run."

"We're running together again?"

"Yes, now that I know you're not a crazy stalker."

Molka smiled. "How sweet." She motioned her eyes toward Owen. "But will your personal protector be ok with us hanging out?"

"Owen will be ok with what I tell him to be ok with." Aden winked. "You might not know it, but I'm kind of special around here."

CHAPTER 14

"**A** fine brunch ruined." Principal Darcy tossed a fine linen napkin aside a fine China plate presenting a fine herb rice stuffed Cornish Game Hen served with a fine tomato ginger salsa.

Greenie Greg waited beside her umbrella table seat located next to a rooftop penthouse's infinity pool. "Was there a problem with Dean Besnik's message, Darcy?"

Principal Darcy handed him a satellite phone. "He always interrupts something good with something bad."

"I'm sorry, Darcy."

"Turn on the screen. I'll be there directly."

"Yes, Darcy." He ran to obey.

Principal Darcy popped two white bars from a prescription bottle and chased them with an oversized mimosa. She sighed and stood, wearing a black bikini under a white wrap, and walked inside with annoyance.

A white Italian marble hallway brought her to an ultra-high-tech media room. Greenie Greg handed her a remote, and she dropped into a sumptuous front-and-center leather recliner. The lights dimmed, and a 200-inch theater screen—split into 20 individual screens—came into focus. Each smaller screen showed a different security drone or surveillance camera view of Hazlehurst.

Principal Darcy used the remote to expand the view from a drone observing high over the central courtyard to full screen. It showed the student body filling the space and watching Aden tear laps around the outer walkway on an ATV.

She sighed again. "He begged me to let him have that ridiculous thing. I said no. It's too dangerous, and he's too valuable to me. But he kept begging and pouting like a little boy. So, I gave in." She slammed her fist into the chair arm. "Damn it!"

Greenie Greg jumped. "Are you ok, Darcy?"

"Why isn't he wearing the helmet I gave him? If he dies, I'll kill him. Do you understand me?"

"Yes, Darcy."

"This kind of carelessness isn't like him. Why is he suddenly acting like a little fool who—"

Aden flew around the walkway again and grinned over his shoulder at Molka riding an ATV a half lap behind.

"Oh, that's why." Principal Darcy smirked. "Well, well..."

Molka crouched and accelerated.

Aden crouched and accelerated.

"She's trying to catch him. He's trying not to get caught."

Another lap completed; Molka gained on Aden.

"Looks like a race to me."

The student spectators chanted something at the racers.

"I knew this feature would come in handy someday." Principal Darcy used the remote again to activate a microphone installed on a tree-concealed courtyard security cam.

Her surround sound speakers blasted the student's chant:

"Go, Doctor Molka, go!"

"Go, Doctor Molka, go!"

"Go, Doctor Molka, go!"

Another lap completed; Molka neared Aden's tail.

"Go, Doctor Molka, go!"

"Go, Doctor Molka, go!"

"Go, Doctor Molka, go!"

Another lap completed; Molka on Aden's tail.

"Go, Doctor Molka, go!"

"Go, Doctor Molka, go!"

"Go, Doctor Molka, go!"

Another lap completed; Molka passed Aden just before the ice cream stand.

Aden slowed, pulled over into the grass, and stopped.

"Race over." Principal Darcy frowned. "She won."

Molka raised a fist, drove to the courtyard's center, and spun victory doughnuts in the grass.

The students encircled her and celebrated with another chant:

"Doctor Molka!"

"Doctor Molka!"

"Doctor Molka!"

Principal Darcy slammed her fist into the chair arm again. "It was the damn dog show! The students loved the way she handled it so *fairly* and *generously*. It gave her instant folk hero status. But don't they realize how deeply that embarrassed their loving Principal Darcy? Don't they even care how low it made her feel?"

"I care, Darcy," Greenie Greg said.

Principal Darcy turned off the screen. "Leave me."

"Yes, Darcy." Greenie Greg left the media room and closed the door to darkness behind him.

Principal Darcy lowered her face into her hands and sobbed.

Molka left her victory party and parked her ATV next to Aden's beside the ice cream stand.

Aden smiled. "I owe you one double scoop waffle cone of your choice, right?"

"Right." Molka smiled. "The sweet taste of victory."

She received her trophy cone—vanilla and strawberry—and Aden chose a frozen yogurt as his consolation. They sat on a nearby tree-shaded green bench.

"You're deceiving me," Aden said.

"Am I?" Molka said.

"Yes. You're a much better rider than you let on. You're better than me."

"I'm not so sure. It seemed like you slowed down a little at the end. I'd be very disappointed if you let me win."

"You really love to win, don't you?"

"No," she said. "I just really hate to lose."

"I had fun today."

"So did I."

"Thanks for doing this with me," Aden said.

"Thanks for asking."

Aden smiled at Molka with those dimples again. "Maybe we can do something else fun sometime?"

Molka demurred. "Maybe."

"So."

"So."

He glanced toward Building A. "So I better get to work."

"Me too. I mean, I guess I'll go check-in at the office. Should I return the ATV?"

"You can leave it here. I'll get Owen to put it away."

"Alright," Molka said. "He looked pretty upset when we ditched him outside the Security Zone though."

"He'll get over it."

She shrugged. "Or not."

He laughed. "See you at the track in the morning?"

Molka stood. "I'll be there."

"Ok…um…goodbye."

"Goodbye."

Molka headed toward the veterinarian's office. She wouldn't realize it until some years later, but that was the moment it happened. That was the moment a tiny crack opened in the armor she had forged around her heart.

CHAPTER 15

"**L**ook at my busy little bees go." Principal Darcy said.

"They're superb workers," Besnik said.

The pair watched from an office window looking out on Building A's first-floor drone production line.

Besnik preened in a silver tailored silk suit. Principal Darcy dazzled in a tight charcoal-colored dress.

She smiled. "And they're so happy to get what little I'm paying them too."

"What you are paying them is many times what they earn in their home country."

"What would the world be like without cheap commie slave labor?"

"Unaffordable."

Aden ambled by in a white tee shirt, jeans, untied sneakers, and post-run shower-wet hair.

"Well, good morning, smartacus," Principal Darcy said.

"Good morning." Aden sat in an ergonomic chair behind an ergonomic desk and booted up a laptop. "Surprised you stopped by. The last three times you've been on campus, you didn't bother."

"Oh, don't be that way. My schedule didn't permit it. But let's not talk about my schedule. Let's talk about yours. Are you on schedule to make delivery?"

"Right on time." Aden started playing on the laptop.

"Dean Besnik informs me the buyer isn't one for patience, understanding, or excuses. Period. Are you sure things are right on time?"

Aden nodded. "Yeppers, right on time."

Principal Darcy crossed the room, came to Aden's desk, and slapped his laptop closed. Aden flinched and froze.

"In my teaching days," she said, "when I told a student to be right on time for class, I meant for them to be at their desk with their book open at least five minutes early. Do you understand me?"

Aden folded his hands on the desktop. "I'll see what I can do."

"What you can do is spend more time here watching their asses," she pointed out the window at the workers, "and less time running around campus watching Doctor Molka's. Yes, I know all about the great race yesterday."

"I was only trying to be friendly with her."

"I know what you were trying with her. But when I allowed you to come here, I made it understood that your priorities are first, last, and always the greater good of this school. Did I not?"

"Yes, Principal Darcy."

"So, get your priorities straight."

"I will, Principal Darcy."

"Good boy." Principal Darcy reopened his laptop and moved toward the door.

"Principal Darcy?" Aden said.

She paused and turned. "Question, Aden?"

"A weapons expert explained to me what the shaped charge these drones carry does to the human skull and brain. It's devastating."

"Well, that's the whole purpose of a weapon, isn't it?"

"Yes, but don't you ever think what you've asked me to do is possibly…on some level, immoral?"

"Immoral?" Her arms lowered to her sides with fists clenched, and she smiled. "Oh yes, I forgot. You told me you're a pacifist at heart. But do you even know what pacifism really is? It's an excuse for letting other people solve the world's problems. Pacifism has never solved anything. Anything worth anything was solved by bold, decisive action. You said yourself the people you previously worked for would eventually figure out and finish what you started. Is that correct?"

"Yes, in a few years' time."

"And then they would share the technology with their likeminded friends. Is that correct?"

"Yes, that was my understanding."

Principal Darcy pointed at the production line again. "So the people I sell those little monsters to will act as a counterbalance. Meaning, if both sides have them, neither side will dare use them. It's the greatest deterrent doctrine ever, called…what's it called again, Dean Besnik?"

Besnik came to attention. "Mutually Assured Destruction. Some historians suggest the Mutually Assured Destruction doctrine, also known as MAD, was primarily responsible for preventing a nuclear holocaust during the—"

Principal Darcy silenced Besnik with a hand. "It prevented a nuclear holocaust. You say what I'm asking you to do is immoral? I say what I'm doing is bold and decisive and, yes, even noble. Because what I'm doing is saving the world from the hideous appalling insane weapon YOU, have created. Do you understand me?"

"Yes, I understand." Aden's chin dropped to chest and his lips pouted. "I understand I have created a hideous, appalling, insane weapon. I'm sorry."

"If you're sorry, why do you want to disappoint me?"

Aden's eyes rose and pleaded with her. "I don't want to disappoint you."

She turned her back to him and moved to the viewing window. "I'm not so sure."

"It's true, Principal Darcy. I don't want to disappoint you."

She came to Aden, knelt beside him, and placed her hand on his shoulder. "Do you still believe in the work I'm doing to end suffering in the world?"

"Yes, Principal Darcy.

"Do you still believe in me?"

"Of course, Principal Darcy."

"And what were you before I let you come here?"

"Before I came here, I was lost."

She used both arms to hug him tight. "That's right. You were a lost little boy. And don't you ever forget that."

Aden laid his head on her breast. "I won't, Principal Darcy."

Principal Darcy rode with Besnik back to the school airport in her custom-built electric transporter cart. It featured a much more powerful motor than the other school transporters for faster travel. And an enclosed passenger cabin with air conditioned or heated comfort provided her privacy from her driver Friend of the day.

"Do you think Aden believed your MAD theory?" Besnik said.

"I'm not sure," she said. "But Doctor Moore used to say the bigger the lie, the better chance people will believe it."

"An adage which has led to tragic consequences throughout history."

She slapped Besnik with a raised eyebrow. "I hope guilt isn't creeping into your loyalty too?"

"You know me, Darcy. I am with you all the way on this deal."

"But I sense a *but* coming."

"But I would not be truthful if I said Aden's concerns had not crossed my mind as well. You see, my better judgment was formed years ago by—"

"Yes, I know. You got into the law for all the right reasons. To comfort the afflicted and afflict the comfortable and all that bullshit. Graduated at the top of your law school class. Got hired by the most prestigious firm in LA. Made partner. Got rich while still doing a lot of pro bono work. But when you botched that suit against big pharmaceuticals and lost your stellar reputation, who urged Doctor Moore to hire you off the scrap heap?"

"You did, Darcy."

"Who talked sense into you after you divorced sweet Janice and wanted to marry a young gold-digging blond whore?"

"You did, Darcy."

"Who pushed you protesting and screaming to take Friend Clarence's class action suit that restored your stellar reputation?"

"You did, Darcy."

"Yes, I did it all. Because my better judgment is better than yours."

"Yes, Darcy."

"And here's the way I judge our current situation: Ever since the first caveman grabbed a rock and bashed in his fellow caveman's head to steal his cavewoman, humans have devised a never-ending parade of deadlier and deadlier ways to exterminate each other. Yet, the world population continues to grow. So what difference has it really made? Yes, I might give them a new and better way to kill for a while, but in a few years, they'll find an even better new way to kill. Any guilt I might have now will be made obsolete soon enough. Do you understand?"

"Yes, Darcy. I never considered the deal with such a perspective."

"Take away Aden's ATV. Tell him I said it's too dangerous."

"Yes, Darcy."

"He's behaving like he's backed up, isn't he?"

"You mean he is backed up as in his work?"

"I mean he's backed up as in he's horny," she said. "He needs a little carnal relief. Once he batter dips his corn dog, he'll get refocused."

"It seems he is pursuing that type of relief with Doctor Molka."

"She's not right for him though."

"Why not?" Besnik said.

"Because she's a fellow idealist. And when idealists get together, they start to get ideas. I don't need idealists in my life. I need mindless disciples, right?"

"Of course, Darcy."

"Oh, get the sourpuss off your face." She pinched his cheek. "I didn't mean you, Bezie. However, I believe it's best we separate those two."

"Would you like me to dismiss Doctor Molka?"

"Normally, yes. But she's already become popular with the students. Getting rid of her might cause unrest at a time when we need stability."

"Yes, Darcy. Would you like me to have a word with her about not associating with Aden?"

"No. I'll deal with her myself tomorrow."

"As you wish, Darcy."

The transporter parked beside the jet's waiting airstairs, and Principal Darcy stepped out. "Go ahead and grant Aden's old visitation request, but don't tell him. Let's make his visitor's arrival a nice surprise for him. And maybe we can kill two problems with one favor."

CHAPTER 16

Molka answered her door to a submachine gun muzzle. The weapon hung on Owen's chest from a tactical sling.

"Morning, doc," Owen said. "Up early and all dressed for your run, I see."

Molka nodded at his hand resting in the weapon's grip. "Some people might take that personally. And I'm one of those people…first sergeant."

"Nothing personal. I'm working and that's how I carry my tools."

"If you say so…first sergeant."

Owen side-cocked his head. "Every time first sergeant comes out of your mouth towards me, it sounds more insult than respect."

"It does?"

"Yeah, it does. You know, when I was a punk PFC, everyone called my first sergeant, Top Sergeant. In our unit, the title of Top Sergeant meant the highest respect." Owen leaned back on the balcony railing and squinted at the distant mountains. "And after I earned my three up and three down, I always hoped my men would call me Top Sergeant too. But they never did."

Molka side-cocked her head. "I wonder why?"

Owen pushed off the railing. "Your smart-ass mouth wakes up early too, doesn't it?"

"If you're working, why are you skulking around outside my door? Is Aden waiting for me at the track?"

"Nope."

"Is he ok?"

Owen grinned. "He's fine. But you won't be running with your boyfriend this morning."

"He's not my boyfriend."

"Some may beg to differ. I came to tell you Principal Darcy wants to see you in her office right away. Follow me."

Molka folded her arms. "I know where the classroom-administration building is. I'm sure I can find her office without an escort."

"That office is just ceremonial. I hear the only thing in it is a shitload of her dead husband's books. Her real office is in her place in Vancouver. She sent her jet, and it's burning fuel waiting on you. You can come just the way you are. Let's get moving."

"Why did I rate you as a special messenger? Why didn't she send one of her Friends?"

"I don't know. She just said to make sure you get on the jet and don't take no for an answer." Owen grinned again. "Hope you're not in any trouble."

A lumbering male greenie in a chauffeur's cap met Molka upon arrival at the Vancouver airport and led her to Principal Darcy's limo—a regal Mercedes-Maybach S650 Pullman finished in pearl white.

He secured Molka in the lavish onyx-black leather passenger cabin and departed the airport. En route, from behind a glass partition, he informed her via intercom that their destination was the West End neighborhood in downtown Vancouver, ETA 35 minutes under current traffic conditions.

On the drive north, Molka took mental notes on the street names and prominent landmarks. After she got Aden out, she might have to retrace the path.

The trip ended curbside beneath the tallest, most modern glass tower on a boulevard of tall, modern glass towers. A waiting dark-browed greenie opened Molka's door and identified himself as Darcy's Friend Omar. He bid her to follow him through an opulent revolving entrance into an opulent hotel's opulent lobby and into the opulent private penthouse elevator.

On the 60 floor ride to the top, Friend Omar boasted that Principal Darcy's two-level penthouse provided 15,000 square feet and featured six private bedroom suites, entertainment-sized living and dining areas, eight terraces, an outdoor lounge with an infinity pool, three gas fireplaces, a full bar, a wine room, a billiard room, a state-of-the art media room, a CEO-quality private office, and an unrivaled view of the entire city, Coastal Mountain Range, and the Pacific Ocean.

His sales-like pitch suggested he might have been a big-ticket properties broker before he was Friended by Principal Darcy.

The elevator opened onto a great white room further whitened with a white vaulted ceiling, white carpet, white furniture, and a white grand piano. Molka didn't know much—if anything—about high-end designer décor, but if she guessed, that was what it should look like. Floor-to-ceiling windows, surrounding the space in every direction, validated Friend Omar's claims about an unrivaled view.

Wow.

Friend Omar led Molka across the room to a smaller elevator. One flight up, the door opened onto a long white hall with more extraordinary floor-to-ceiling window views. The hallway ended at a black mahogany door.

Friend Omar courtesy knocked, opened the door for Molka, and departed. She stepped into an enormous, windowless, gray-carpeted office highlighted by well-filled carved black mahogany bookcases, black leather furniture, and a massive floor stand globe with dark-gray continents and light-gray oceans. At the room's opposite end sat a huge black mahogany desk. And behind the desk, in a commanding gray business suit, waited a smiling Principal Darcy.

"Thank you for coming, Doctor Molka," she said. "Please come sit."

Molka sat in a vintage chair facing the desk. Her head swiveled across the extravagant surroundings until it was halted by an oddity. On the wall behind the desk hung a larger-than-life-size painting of Principal Darcy. It resembled a school yearbook photo, and a brass plaque on the lower frame named her the Lee School District Educator of the Year, 17 years before.

Principal Darcy caught Molka's perplexed stare. "All the art snobs were horrified when I commissioned that. But what it stands for, means more to me than the combined value of all the priceless crap in all their snobby galleries."

Molka played it gracious. "It's a perfect likeness."

"Maybe seventeen years ago. But now...I am what I am."

"You don't look like you've aged a day."

"That's a polite lie," Principal Darcy said. "However, a polite lie is as good as a compliment to women of a certain age." She smiled. "So I thank you."

Molka smoothed her white track pants. "I'm sorry for my appearance. I wasn't given time to change."

"I don't believe you'll ever need to apologize for your appearance, doll."

"Thank you, Principal Darcy."

"We're not in school right now. Why don't we dispense with the formalities? Call me Darcy. And I think I'll just keep on calling you doll. If you don't mind?"

Molka smiled. "Alright. But I hope I'm not in any trouble. Getting summoned to the principal's office—wherever it's located—is usually not good."

Darcy laughed. "No, you're fine. I just like to get to know the staff on a more personal level. You've been at Hazlehurst going on two weeks; how do you like it?"

"I've enjoyed my time there."

"You've already become quite popular with the students. From what I hear, they're raving about you in the classrooms. It seems they're becoming fonder of you then they are of me."

Molka feigned humility. "That's not possible."

"You've also been spending time with Aden."

"Yes. A bit."

"It's nice to have a close friend in a lonely place, isn't it?"

"I suppose," Molka said.

"Do you have many close friends back home?"

"Not really."

"Brothers and sisters?" Darcy said.

"One younger sister."

"I had three brothers—half-brothers, I should say. They were never around much. But I always desperately wanted a sister to laugh with, to cry with, to commiserate with. It must be wonderful."

Molka's eyes dropped to her running shoes. "It was."

"Then maybe you and I can become as close as sisters?" Darcy brightened. "Yes. I've decided we will become as close as sisters." She stood. "And what better way to start becoming as close as sisters than a sister's night out preceded by a sister's day out?"

The most exclusive women's boutique in the greater Vancouver area locked its doors to all other customers when Darcy walked in with her new sister.

Molka stepped from the dressing room modeling a minuscule white dress Darcy had chosen for her. "Isn't this a little too tight and too short?"

"Not for where we're going tonight," Darcy said. She turned to the salesclerk. "I'll take the same thing in black. And bring us some shoe choices. Sexy is good. Slutty is better."

The most exclusive spa in the greater Vancouver area rescheduled all their appointments for the afternoon when Darcy walked in with her new sister.

After their Swedish massages, saunas, and facials, Molka and Darcy—wrapped in thick white robes—reclined side by side in pedicure chairs. Darcy drank from her third glass of wine. Molka still sipped from her first. Two Asian women attended to their nails and pretended to ignore their conversation.

Darcy smiled at Molka. "I know what you're thinking right this moment, doll."

"You do?"

"You're thinking I'm a charlatan, a con artist, a cheat, a fake, a fraud, an imposter, a phony, a pretender, a quack who is not what she seems, aren't you?"

Molka viewed her toes. "I was actually thinking I should have gone with the midnight-blue polish instead of the turquoise."

"No you weren't, but it's ok." Darcy took another wine swig. "My official Hazlehurst bio talks about my time as an educator, award-winning elementary school Principal, and my work with my late husband. But I lived a whole other lifetime before that. I'm from the little town of Deatsville Mississippi. It's just south of Tupelo and just north of hell. It's known for two things: a paper mill and a giant locust plague in 1935 which caused locusts to flow from the faucets and overflow from the toilets. Have you ever smelled a working paper mill?"

"No," Molka said. "What does it smell like?"

"It smells like you'd rather have the toilet locusts."

"Wow, that bad?"

Darcy went on, "My momma was a drunk and my daddy was killed when I was eight. They told me he worked on the railroad and died in a train accident. Later, I found out he was a boxcar hobo who passed out drunk on the train tracks one night. Then my momma got remarried to what they call a functional alcoholic. Which is defined as a person who maintains jobs and relationships while exhibiting alcoholism. But to me, it meant a big fat sweaty drunk coming home and sneaking into my room to paw me under the covers."

Molka's face cringed in revulsion. "That's revolting."

"When I turned 17, I figured if I'm going to get groped every night, I may as well get paid for it. So, I went up to Tupelo and applied for a dancer job at a strip club called The Eager Beaver. It was a real dive which catered to the paper mill workers. I lied about my age, not that they cared anyway, and got hired. And I didn't have a car, and I didn't dare ask anyone I knew for a ride to work, so every evening I walked the lonely backroads six and a half miles to The Eager Beaver. And every early morning when I got off, I walked the six and a half miles back home. And I'll tell you something, that solitary 13 mile walk round trip gives you plenty of time to think and get your mind right."

"I can imagine," Molka said.

"One morning after my shift, my step daddy caught me sneaking back into my room. He told me his friends saw me stripping and he wasn't going to have a dirty little slut shaming his *good* name. Yes, preposterous, I know. He told me to go fetch a shovel from the shed, so he could dig my grave out in the backyard after he killed me—it was his sick way of terrorizing me and making me beg. He'd done it many times before. But that time I didn't beg. I said fine, he would be doing me a favor. I went to the shed and fetched the shovel and gave it to him. I gave it to him right upside his big fat, sweaty, drunk head. Then I dragged him out to the backyard and started digging his grave. But he wasn't dead yet, and I didn't believe he was worth anymore of my time. I left and never came back."

"Who could blame you?" Molka said.

"Then I met a boy I thought I was in love with. I got pregnant. As soon as I told him, he married another girl and moved away. I decided to keep the baby. I told myself I could handle it, work two jobs, go to college, make a good life for my child and me. But a state counselor talked me into giving him up for adoption. A nice couple from Meridian wanted him. I only got to see him for two minutes before the nurses took him away from me."

Darcy hit the wine again. "A few years ago, I hired a private investigator to find my baby. He did. My boy's 27 now. Lives in Oklahoma. Works as a land surveyor for the county. Good, honest work. He's married with a two-year-old boy of his own. My grandson. Yes, my little boy turned out just fine. Just fine. I expect giving him up was the mistake of my life." Closed-eyed tears stained Darcy's makeup. "Sometimes I want to die. Sometimes I want to die."

No doubt Principal Darcy's early life carried a heartbreaking tale with a sad ending. But why share such intimate tragedies with a relative stranger?

Darcy wiped her eyes and composed her face. "When a student comes to Hazlehurst Institute, they're out of answers. They have obscene wealth and everything they thought they ever wanted in life, but they're still completely miserable. They don't understand why and try to fill their big empty happiness hole with possessions, alcohol, drugs, sex, and every type of *legitimate* therapy. And still nothing has worked. So they believe they have nothing left to live for. What I do is give them hope and purpose and joy in their golden years. And I truly take pride in that. And I truly love and care about them. And yes, it also puts a little coin in my pocketbook at the same time. But is that so wrong?"

Molka laughed. "What you call a little coin other people might call *obscene wealth*."

Darcy's face blazed defiant. "I was married twice before I met Doctor Moore. And both swept me off my feet, took me away, teased me with a taste of the luxury life, and promised to take care of me forever. And both dropped me on my ass, and I ended up right back in Deatsville. And teaching doesn't pay much—at least not enough to live the luxury lifestyle I tasted and desired—so I also went back to The Eager Beaver and stripped on the side for those smelly paper mill workers. And I'll be damned if I ever let it happen to me again."

"Don't misunderstand me," Molka said. "I'm not judging you. I respect talent. From what I've seen, you're incredible at what you do. You may be the best who ever lived at what you do. Even if what you do is a total scam."

Darcy smiled and took Molka's hand. "That's why I like you. There's a stubborn honesty just below the surface."

"Thank you."

"But there's a sadness hiding within you too. Did you have a good childhood?"

Molka nodded. "Yes."

"Tell me about your parents."

"They were both college professors. My father wrote several books. He received some literary awards. My mother was a lifelong athlete. She competed in triathlons right until the end."

"Your mother passed prematurely?"

"Yes," Molka said. "Both my parents did."

"What happened to them?"

Molka took another wine sip.

Darcy squeezed Molka's hand. "It's ok, doll. You don't have to tell me if it's too painful to talk about."

Stupid! She had blundered right into Darcy's trap. That's why she had shared something deeply personal: to get Molka to share something deeply personal too. She wanted to form an emotional bond. Her first step in gaining control.

So clever.

Alright. Tell what happened to your parents. But stay strong. If Darcy sensed a weakness, it could cause her to hold out when the time came for her to give up the needed information. Tough subject though. But if she can do it, you can do it.

Molka took her biggest ever wine sip. "On their 20th anniversary, my parents went to a neighborhood pizza place where they had their first date. They sat at the same table and ordered the same pizza. A 16-year-old girl walked in and detonated a suicide vest. Fifteen people were killed besides my parents. They hadn't even gotten their pizza yet."

Darcy laid her hand on Molka's shoulder. "I'm so sorry. How old were you and your sister when it happened?"

"I was 16. My little sister was six."

"What's your little sister's name?"

"Janetta," Molka said.

"Such a pretty name."

"For such a pretty girl."

"What happened to you girls after your unspeakable loss?"

"We went to live with my grandfather on a kibbutz for about a year until he became too ill to look after us. Then we went into foster homes. When I turned 18, I left for my military service."

"And where's your little sister Janetta now?" Darcy said.

Molka started to sip her wine again but set the glass aside. "I don't want to talk about my family anymore."

"I understand. Come on, doll; let's go get drunk."

The doorman at the trendiest club in the greater Vancouver area allowed Darcy and her new sister—in their hot new dresses—to skip the long line out front and enter as VIPs.

At the bar, Molka switched from wine to bottled water. Darcy switched from wine to vodka Martinis, to whiskey shots, to agreeing to dance with a college-aged kid wearing a too-tight shirt, a gold chain, and gel-spiked blond hair.

He left behind his bigger, similar clad—but shaved bald—partner who asked Molka to dance each time the song changed.

"And again," he said. "Would you like to dance?"

"And again," Molka said. "No."

"Then I guess a blowjob is totally out of the question?"

Molka folded her arms and leaned back against the bar. "Totally. But a compound fracture is not."

"Oh yeah, baby; now you're talking my…wait, what?"

"Nothing. Go away, little boy." Molka side stepped so she could watch Darcy on the dance floor.

"Come on baby, I was just messing with you. My bro is being a good wingman dancing with your MILF friend so I can get with you. Is there a problem?"

"Yes. And I'm going to take care of it right now."

Molka left the bald bro at the bar, pulled Darcy away from the blond bro on the dance floor, spoke in her ear, and led her outside the club.

"Hey!" Darcy said. "This isn't the ladies' room; this is the parking lot."

"It's time to get you home," Molka said.

"I need a shot." Darcy moved back toward the door.

Molka caught her arm and turned her around. "You've already had six shots."

"How many?"

"Six. Which is about five more than you needed."

"Then I want some food," Darcy said. "Because I'm starving, and all I want are some fresh, hot doughnuts." She pulled away from Molka and approached the massive doorman. "Hey killer, where's the nearest Jim Thorntons doughnut store? I know it's close because there's one on every corner up here."

"Yes, ma'am." The doorman pointed. "Straight down Georgia Street. About two kilometers on the right."

"Thanks, killer." Darcy hooked Molka's arm and led her away. "Two kilometers on the right. What's that in real distance? Kilometers, meters, centimeters, Canadians are an annoyingly understanding and polite people, but they insist on holding onto their archaic traditions like the metric system."

"Actually," Molka said, "most of the world uses the metric system."

"Well, as my old Uncle Thad used to say, if they don't do it in Mississippi, it don't mean shit!"

Darcy texted and called the limo driver and received no answers. "The big lumber-head is a local Friend. Not one of my regulars. He probably fell asleep on me. What time is it?"

"Almost 11," Molka said.

"It's still early! Let's go back inside!"

"I see the limo over on the far side of the lot. We'll walk it."

Molka hooked Darcy's arm and led her to the limo. Sure enough, the driver sat head back, zonked out.

Darcy pounded on the window. "Wake up, you big lumber-head!"

The driver startled awake, stumbled out, and opened the passenger door for the ladies.

Molka got in.

Darcy started to follow...

"Wait for me, baby!" The blond bro ran toward Darcy.

Darcy twirled and smiled. "Hey, studley!"

"Gotcha!" The blond bro snatched Darcy by the waist, flung her small body over his shoulder, and ran in the opposite direction.

"Woo-hoo!" Darcy yelled. "My prince charming has come!"

Molka scrambled out and chased.

Ugh! Running in high heels!

The blond bro reached a wannabe drift car, opened the driver-side door, pitched Darcy into the passenger seat, and got in.

Molka caught up to them and skidded to a stop. "Let her go!"

The blond bro lowered the driver-side window and smiled past Molka. "Better check your girl, bro."

The bigger bald bro came from behind Molka and moved between her and the car. "Hey baby. Change your mind about the blowjob?"

Molka ignored him and glared at the blond bro. "Let her go! Now!"

"We're not about hurting anybody," the blond bro said. "We're basically nice guys and just wanted to invite you babes to our place to party."

"Yeah, baby," the bald bro said. "We just want you babes to come to our place and party."

"Woo-hoo!" Darcy yelled. "Let's party!"

"See," the bald bro said. "Your girl is down."

Molka gave serious evaluation to the bald bro for the first time: enhanced bodybuilder. He could hurt her if he went hands on. Careful.

"Please let her go," Molka said. "We don't want any trouble."

"Forget her, bro," the blond bro said. "This one says she'll do us both."

The bald bro pointed at Molka. "This one wants it too. I can tell by the primal look in her eyes."

"Whatever," the blond bro said. "See you back at the beast cave." He lit the tires, sped past the limo, and exited the parking lot to the right.

The bald bro crowded Molka. "You're riding with me, baby. We can do this the fun way or the mean way. Which way?"

"Fun way," Molka said.

"Cool. My ride is right over there."

"How do you like my new shoes?"

The bald bro grinned. "Hot baby."

"Take them off for me."

"Take them off?"

Molka smiled. "Yes."

"Oh, ok. I'm down with the whole feet thing. I'm down."

"Sure, you're down?"

The bald bro knelt and lusted at Molka's shoes. "Yeah, I'm down."

"Not quite." Molka fired a knee into his jaw and an elbow into the back of his head. "But you are now."

Molka removed her shoes, side stepped the bald bro's nap, and barefoot sprinted back to the limo. The driver still gaped clueless.

"You saw that guy take Darcy!" Molka said. "Come on!"

"You mean chase them?"

"Yes!"

"Shouldn't we just call the police? I could lose my 4C license."

"Some Friend of Darcy you are!" Molka pushed the driver aside, jumped into the driver's seat, pressed the start button, shifted it into gear, and floored it from the parking lot onto the same four-lane boulevard the blond bro had left on.

The Mercedes-Maybach presented itself as a big heavy slow brute, but its twin-turbo V-12 shattered the impression. Within a kilometer, Molka caught the blond bro's unsuspecting bumper at a stoplight.

Now what? Use a pit maneuver? No. She had never attempted one before. And if you did it wrong, people could get hurt. Best to follow them to his place and take Darcy away from him there.

Ok. Back off a little. Don't let him notice you followed. No traffic to lose them in anyway.

Molka allowed a 10-car gap to open between them. The blond bro cruised the speed limit unaware.

What a ridiculous situation. Darcy hadn't even fought her semi-abduction. Instead, she had enjoyed the attention and gone along with it—like an irresponsible drunken sorority girl. Darcy's head rested on the passenger windowsill, and her blond hair flapped in the slipstream. If Molka hadn't needed the information waiting in that head, she would have left Darcy to the bros. Believe it.

But something unexpected disagreed with her—a real concern for Darcy as a tragic and vulnerable person.

And besides, sisters are supposed to look out for each other, aren't they?

The blond bro turned into a not-so-exclusive apartment complex and parked. Molka parked crossways behind so he couldn't leave, exited, and jogged to the driver-side door.

The blond bro stepped out. "Hey baby, where's my bro?"

"Same place you're going."

"Where's that?"

Molka stepped back and landed a perfect front kick to his chin.

Naptime for the blond bro too.

Another wannabe drift car screech-stopped behind the limo and the bald bro powered out. "Yo bitch! What's up with hitting me? And what's up with my bro?"

Molka approached him. "Your perseverance is starting to win me over."

He smiled. "Really?"

"No. Not really."

Molka dropped him unconscious again with a no-nonsense roundhouse.

"Hey, why did you do that?" Darcy crawled over the center console and out the driver-side door. "They were cute." She gawked at both sleeping bros. "Sweet Savannah! Look what you did! Where did you learn how to do that? You're a real hellcat. Woo-hoo!"

Darcy corkscrewed onto her rear end and leaned against the back bumper. "Ok, I'm drunk. So what?" She curled a finger at Molka. "Come down here with me, doll."

Molka joined Darcy on the pavement.

Darcy laid her head on Molka's shoulder. "Did you know, unlike males, the ability for a female to achieve orgasm serves no biological purpose in the reproduction process?"

"I've never really thought about it."

"So why were we created with that ability?"

"I'm not sure," Molka said.

"To enjoy our bodies, of course. And we could've had a lot of enjoyment with those boys tonight. What do you have against enjoying your body?"

"I have nothing against enjoying my body. I'm just choosey about who I enjoy it with."

Darcy raised her head. "You mean like Aden? No, no, no, no. Aden's not for you. He's too confused and needy. A lost little boy, really. Best to stay away from that smartacus."

"I wasn't necessarily referring to him," Molka said.

"You're a lonely girl a long way from home desiring some warm company. Trust me, I can appreciate the feeling. But a woman like you needs a real manly man. Why don't you bump uglies with one of the security officers? They're all manly men and all really good in…I mean…I would imagine they're all really good in bed. Being virile, vigorous, potent soldiers and all."

Molka stood and yanked Darcy to her drunken feet. "Come on. Let's get you home."

Darcy draped herself around Molka's neck. "This was fun. This was a fun day, and this was a fun night. I want you to come visit me again. Will you come visit me again?"

"Darcy, you can count on it."

"We bonded tonight, like real sisters. Didn't we? So we can have another sister-to-sister talk."

"Definitely."

Molka walk-carried Darcy to the limo.

"Do you really want to be my sister?" Darcy said.

Molka opened the limo's passenger door. "In you go."

"Do you really want to be my sister?"

"What?"

Darcy jerked away from Molka. "I asked if you really wanted to be my sister."

"Yes, Darcy. I really want to be your sister. Now get in."

Darcy beamed. "You mean it?"

"Yes. Get in."

Darcy hugged Molka's neck again. "And you know what?"

"What?"

"I love you like an older sister loves her younger sister."

CHAPTER 17

"**W**ho's the little old fart?" Laili sneered at a short, older—but ripped—man in sweatpants and a tee shirt standing on the mats in a closed south Tel Aviv gymnasium.

"He is Yossi," Azzur said. "He will instruct you in Krav Maga. His methods are unorthodox, but his results are unquestionable."

"Krav Maga? I don't need that crazy shit. You said I was starting my weapons training today."

"You are. Your first and most reliable weapon is yourself."

"Which stupid martial arts movie did you steal that from?"

Azzur walked toward Yossi. Laili yawned, looked around, and slowly followed.

"Yossi," Azzur said. "Here is the girl I spoke of."

"Welcome." Yossi held out a weathered hand for shaking.

Laili dissed his greeting. "Let's make this waste of time quick, grandpa. I'd like to get to the shooting range sometime this month."

Yossi smiled. "You like to play with guns, do you?"

Her green eyes flared confident. "When I have a gun, I don't play."

Yossi addressed Azzur. "Give me your weapon."

Azzur removed a Sig P226 pistol from a behind-the-back holster and passed it to Yossi.

Yossi chambered a round and handed it to Laili. "Show me how you don't play."

She pointed the pistol at Yossi's head, slid behind him, and placed the barrel to his temple. "Never underestimate me."

"I would not do that if I were you," Azzur said.

Laili pointed the pistol over Yossi's shoulder at Azzur's face. "That's because you're not me."

"Go ahead and shoot him," Yossi said. "Believe me, the world will not mourn."

Azzur laughed.

"Don't fuck with me, grandpa. I'm a bad-ass little bitch." She scowled at Azzur. "Give me your car keys. I've decided to leave your stupid little program right now."

Azzur removed the keys from his coat pocket and complied.

Laili put the barrel back against Yossi's temple. "Ok; grandpa, you're going to shield me outside to my new ride. Be good, and I might only shoot you once."

In an almost un-seeable flash, Yossi's right hand came up, grabbed the barrel, and turned it away from his temple. Simultaneously, his left hand came up and grabbed the back of the pistol. He punched both arms forward—ripping the pistol from Laili's hand—spun around and pointed the barrel into her chest.

She froze in confused terror.

Azzur laughed again.

Yossi smiled. "The last one you brought me was impetuous too. But more respectful." He tossed the pistol to Azzur, kneed Laili in the stomach, doubling her over, and struck an elbow into the back of her head dropping her hard to the mat.

Azzur laughed again, harder.

Yossi stared down at Laili. "This is the first of several beatings you will take from me. They will never be this gentle again. You will first learn how to take a beating. Then you will learn how to prevent a beating. Then you will learn how to give a beating. And then you will truly become what you call, a bad-ass little bitch."

PROJECT MOLKA: TASK 3
TUESDAY, AUGUST 6TH
27 DAYS TO COMPLETE TASK

CHAPTER 18

Less than three hours of sleep after Darcy's jet brought Molka back to Hazlehurst, she learned that the school featured a robust loudspeaker system.

At 4:19 AM, a recorded looped message blasted her awake:

This is a security drill.

All students, faculty, and staff, remain in your rooms, and lock your doors.

This is a security drill.

All students, faculty, and staff, remain in your rooms, and lock your doors.

This is a security drill.

All students, faculty, and staff remain in your rooms and lock your doors…

Molka didn't consider herself any of the stated, so she added sweatpants to her sleeping panties and tee and eased out onto the balcony. There she learned that Hazlehurst also featured a robust flood light system, which lit security activity on campus outside the student dorm building.

Investigation warranted.

She ducked back into her room, changed into a tight black mock turtleneck, tight black jeans, and tac boots, and pulled her hair into a high ponytail on the way downstairs.

Molka jogged through the staff compound, entered the school campus, and headed toward the student dorm. She paused behind a tree 40 meters away to observe. A security cart and the 6x6 weapons carrier truck with the bed mounted twin 23-millimeter cannons sat outside the three-story building.

She crouch-ran to a tree 20 meters away and identified Owen leaning against a lamppost. He talked up to another security officer on the truck bed manning the cannons.

The auto-message coming over the speakers cut.

Perfect. Try to eavesdrop the discussion. Get closer.

She crouch-ran to a tree 10 meters away, pressed her back to it, and captured Owen's conversation in mid-sentence.

"…they aren't worth a damn at night though. We need more boots and eyes on the ground."

The gunner with a Spanish accent said, "But wasn't it the drones, that detected the breach?"

"Even so, we're still dangerously undermanned. And you can bet your ass the word's out on us. So, shit like this will keep happening."

"Dean Besnik's working on getting us some more guys, right?"

"Supposedly," Owen said. "But anyone who's any good headed south to that civil war fracas."

"I wish I was down there too. Good money and plenty to shoot at from either side."

"And now old boy Deanie is talking about bringing some of the greenies onto the security team."

"What?" the gunner said.

"Yeah. I guess the greenies handled security here before they brought us in. The colonel is highly pissed about it too. Said the most qualified one of them was only a former mall cop."

"Mall cop? I hate working with amateurs."

"Working with an amateur is like—" Owen put a finger to the earpiece on his headset and talked into the microphone. "This is Spitting Cobra…Yes, sir. Roger that." He turned back to the gunner. "That was the colonel. He reviewed the surveillance vid, and he's on the way here with new orders."

Besnik emerged from the shadows and approached Owen at a fast walk. He wore a red silk robe over white silk pajamas and silk slippers. His gray hair was bedhead mussed. "What is the trouble, First Sergeant Owen?"

"No trouble," Owen said. "I've got everything under control now."

"Good. But what was the trouble?"

"Go back to bed, Deanie. You look damn ridiculous running around like that out here."

"You are aware it is Principal Darcy's expressed order I am to be briefed on all security related issues."

Owen sighed. "One of the students activated his medical emergency button. The EMT responded and found he was missing from his room and notified us. Security cams showed him being led from his room by a man wearing black tactical gear and hood. Obviously, part of a merc team sent by his family to bring him home."

"And what is a merc team?" Besnik said.

"Mercenaries."

"Unacceptable. And who is the student?"

"Name of Howard."

"Unacceptable. He is one of our most…what are you doing to stop them?"

"They breached the northwest perimeter wall," Owen said. "Found a blind spot behind the sewage treatment plant. Thirteen kilometers beyond the woods outside the breach, our gunship located a helicopter in a small field. The helicopter pilot fired several small arms rounds at our gunship."

"Why would he fire on our gunship?" Besnik said.

Owen shrugged. "Maybe to try and scare him off or maybe he panicked. Our gunship engaged and eliminated the threat and is now on station over the woods. The situation is contained."

"What does all that mean?"

"It means the merc team who took Student Howie is hiding with him in the trees out there, and they ain't going anywhere because their ride home is a smoking flaming wreck."

Another security cart arrived. Owen came off the lamppost to semi-attention. The driver boasted a no-nonsense neck, staunch torso, and heavy, uncompromising hands. He wore the same dark-gray uniform as the other security officers except for three gold stars forming a triangle on each shoulder board, denoting a Russian Army colonel.

Colonel Krasnov—the Red Wolf.

When he exited the cart, the lamp illuminated his face. Molka scrutinized a rock-like jaw line softened a bit—but just a bit—by late middle age, an oversized nose to smell an enemy's fear, and thin, serious lips that gave away few secrets.

The colonel addressed Owen in heavily Russian accented English. "First Sergeant, sitrep."

Owen motioned to the weapon's carrier truck. "As per orders, I've secured the student dorm. I've issued night vision and the team is assembled and ready to go after the intruders. I would be honored if you led the assault, sir. The mercs might have the numbers, but we have you and a gunship. What do you estimate their strength? About ten?"

"No more than two," the colonel said. "Including the one now dead in the helicopter."

"Sir?"

"The one who took the student is still on campus waiting to be extracted. The only feasible place for this is the airport. Search the airport area and buildings surrounding it. There you will likely find the missing student and the intruder."

Owen smiled, excited. "Yes, sir. I'll go neutralize the threat."

"First sergeant, I prefer the intruder be captured alive."

"I beg your pardon, sir, but as I understood campus security doctrine, Principal Darcy considers any trespassers to pose a clear and present danger to student safety. Lethal force is authorized. Warning signs saying so are posted on the perimeter walls. Right, Deanie?"

Besnik nodded. "Yes."

"Besides that," Owen said, "they're disrespecting us. We need to send a message we ain't to be messed with up here."

"Nevertheless," the colonel said. "I prefer the intruder be captured alive."

Owen frowned. "Yes, sir. If it's possible."

"Colonel Krasnov," Besnik said. "I would like to speak to you in your office right away."

Molka crouch-ran back to the previous tree she had hidden behind, paused, moved to the tree before that, and paused again.

From her recollection of Colonel Krasnov's operations discussed during her time with the Unit, he rated as a brilliant tactician. But armor and mechanized infantry experience dominated his background. He wouldn't have an aviator's eye. He had missed one other feasible—and much less conspicuous—place on campus for the mercs to land their extraction helicopter. The same place her extraction helicopter would land: the central courtyard. She would bet cash money the merc was hiding with the student somewhere near there waiting for a ride that was never coming.

Should she suggest her conclusion to the colonel?

No. Go back to bed. Molka headed for her room. *Best not to get involved with security matters.* She stopped.

On the other hand...

Her father favored a simple positive axiom: View every problem as an opportunity.

The security team's problem—being "dangerously undermanned," as Owen had said, and Besnik's difficulty finding qualified people to join them—might be her opportunity. Because both the easiest way to get close to Aden and the safest way to destroy Building A was to get into the Security Zone. And the easiest and safest way to get into the Security Zone was to be on the security team.

So, in their moment of chaos, crisis, and desperation, she could offer Besnik and the colonel her services. Crazy? Maybe not. She held a solid résumé with her military background. Of course, she couldn't disclose her time with an elite special forces unit, but what she could give them still surpassed the former mall cop they were considering.

Every résumé can always use an enhancer though. And bringing the colonel the missing student and the intruder could be a great deal closer.

Molka cut across campus to the dimly lit central courtyard and scanned over the large grass expanse and crisscrossing walkways—all quiet, except for the crickets.

117

She moved to each tree, green bench, lamppost, and trash can.

No one concealed.

Hmm…

Wait.

Yes.

Obviousness struck.

At the far side, the ice cream stand shuttered for the night—a perfect helicopter ride waiting room.

She looped around and approached the ice cream stand from the rear. The backdoor sat cracked open. She edged to it and peered through the crack. A gray-haired, 60-something male lay on the floor in his jammies with his hands flex cuffed to the ice cream dispenser machine. Black tape sealed his mouth. He waited alone.

Molka slipped inside and knelt next to him. His eyes panicked. She peeled back the tape.

"Don't let him take me, Doctor Molka!"

She winced. "Quiet. Where is he?"

"His radio wouldn't work. He's upset. He thought it would. He was cursing. He's very anxious."

"Where is he?"

"He told me he wouldn't hurt me. He told me to be calm. He told me he was here to help me."

"Ok," Molka said. "But where is he?"

"He said was going to the top of the bell tower to see if his radio will work up there."

"Alright. I'm leaving you here and go get help."

"Please, Doctor Molka. Don't let him take me back. Don't let him take me away from Principal Darcy."

Molka replaced the tape over his mouth, stepped outside, and viewed the student dorm. Deserted. The weapons carrier truck and carts moved to the airport search, no doubt.

She jogged across the courtyard and entered the darkened classroom-administration building. She jogged the hall to the bell tower entrance, opened the door, and startled at Truman's pleasant face staring up the staircase.

"Custodian Truman," Molka said.

"Doctor Molka."

"Cleaning at this hour?"

"Cleaning at any hour. Hazlehurst must be kept unspoiled."

"Yes. It must."

Truman smiled his pleasant smile. "And what brings you here at this hour?"

Molka motioned for Truman to step out and close the door. "Seems to be a disturbance on campus."

"You mean the alert a while ago? I believe that was only a drill."

"No drill," she said. "Security is searching for an intruder."

"Oh my."

"I think he might be in the bell tower."

"You do?"

"I do. And you do too, don't you?"

Truman nodded. "I saw a big, tall man in all black run in there."

"We should report him."

"Yes, we should."

"Do me a favor?" Molka said.

"Sure, if I can."

"He's a mercenary. He grabbed a student and is trying to take him out of here."

"Oh my."

"Security is searching over at the airport for him. Go tell them the missing student is safe and cuffed in the ice cream stand, their man is in the bell tower, and I'm negotiating with him."

Truman's pleasant face fell serious. "What do you mean negotiating with him?"

"Maybe I can talk him into surrendering."

"Not sure if that's a good idea. He's likely to be armed. Let's both go get security to be safe."

Molka shook her head. "He might get away before they can get here. If he won't surrender, at least I can try to delay him until they arrive."

"I don't know, Doctor Molka. I would hate it if you got hurt. Why don't you go get security, and I'll stay here and watch him?"

She shook her head again. "He's probably nearing panic mode. But he'll see a woman as less of a threat. Now go."

"Doctor Molka, I really don't—"

Molka pushed past Truman and opened the door. "And make sure to tell First Sergeant Owen I'm up there with the intruder and not to open fire."

Truman sighed. "Ok, I will. Please be careful."

Truman departed, and Molka fast-soft-stepped the sixteen stories.

The belfry access hatch waited open. Molka paused for a breath catcher and peered inside. A giant-like black-clad and black-hooded man loomed near the west-side opening arch with his back to her. He adjusted a radio with a long antenna. An AR-15 carbine leaned against the railing on the east-side opening, probably from where he first tried to get his radio to work. It waited equidistant between them.

She eased in, lowered the hatch, and stood on it. "Your radio is useless now."

The merc twirled around. "Not this one. It defeats your jammer. It already worked once tonight."

"I meant there's no one to answer you. Your teammate is dead."

"Bullshit."

"Helicopter in a small field 13 kilometers on the other side of the northwest forest. The pilot took a shot at our gunship. Our gunship shot back."

"Shit. The idiot. No. I'm the idiot for agreeing to work with an amateur. I tried to tell them combat experienced pilots are worth the extra…guess I'm next to go down?"

"Yes," Molka said. "They're going to kill you on sight."

The merc pocketed the radio. "I kinda figured."

"But there's another way."

"Which is?"

"I'll take you in."

"Take me in?" The merc's eyes laughed in the hood's vision slit. "Are you promising me mercy from the Red Wolf?"

"No. I can't promise you Colonel Krasnov will show you any mercy. But I can promise you his second hat won't."

"Who's his second?"

"He goes by First Sergeant Owen."

"That would be Owen Cooper," the merc said.

"You've heard of him too?"

"Ours is a small community. We had a little disagreement once. He definitely won't be happy to see me."

"So come in with me. It's your only chance."

The merc viewed the clear, quiet, star-filled helicopter-free night behind him, the ground below the tower, his waiting weapon, and then he returned his eyes to Molka. "You're not armed."

"I'm not with security."

"Then who are you?"

"The school's veterinarian."

"Veterinarian? We knew they were shorthanded here, but..." The merc's eyes flashed fight or flight at Molka. "I'll get into the woods and evade for a few days until a rescue chopper arrives. I need a head start though. So I'll have to neutralize you first. Sorry, but you shouldn't have come up here."

"It doesn't have to go this way," Molka said. "Please, come with me."

The merc glanced behind him again and then to Molka's boots atop the access hatch, and then to his waiting weapon again. "This is beyond embarrassing. Like I said, ours is a small community. Once the word is spread, I'll never get another job in this business."

"Get into a new business."

The merc chuckled. "Way too late for that."

"Come in with me. Please."

"I know I should. And a part of me wants to." The merc pulled off his hood to reveal a hard-veteran campaigner with a graying beard. "But I just can't. You know?"

Molka nodded. "I know."

"Nothing personal. And I'm truly sorry."

He lunged for his weapon.

Molka met him with a serious side kick that spun him around face-first toward the north-side belfry opening. Due to his extreme height, he slammed into the safety rail at mid-thigh.

Forward momentum and gravity pulled him over the rail.

He disappeared without a scream.

Molka charged down the stairs and ran from the building to the base of the bell tower.

The merc lay splayed in the grass. His neck's grotesque contortion made checking for a pulse unnecessary.

Molka sighed. "Nothing personal. And I'm truly sorry too."

Owen arrived in his security cart, jumped out, and aimed his flashlight on the merc's face. "Well, look who it is. Hello, Too Tall Tommie. Been awhile." He focused on Molka. "I saw him take a header out of the tower. You know anything about how it happened?"

"Yes."

Owen talked into his microphone. "Red Wolf, this is Spitting Cobra. Over…Colonel, the intruder is dead…Affirmative…And you ain't gonna believe this, but I didn't kill him."

CHAPTER 19

"**J**ust luck," Colonel Krasnov said.

Molka's explanation didn't sound any more believable when the colonel repeated it back to her. She stood before him in his office, which contained a functional desk enclosed by bare walls—a spartan room for a spartan man. Next to him sat a haggard and anxious Besnik still in his silk robe and pajamas. And behind her in the corner, Owen straddled a backwards-facing chair spitting dip juice into a cup on the floor.

Time: 5:11 AM.

"We shall go over your story again," the colonel said. He removed his cap, exposing adamant blue eyes and a military haircut almost entirely transitioned from red to gray. "You say it was just luck you happened to be out for an early morning walk when the security breach occurred. And it was just luck you happened to walk by the ice cream stand and find the missing student who told you the intruder's location. And when you confronted the intruder in the tower to delay him for capture, and he attacked you, the fact that he—an imposing professional soldier—fell to his death, and not you, was also…just luck."

"Yes, sir," Molka said.

Her story wasn't all lies though. Luck did favor her in the outcome—luck in violence often did. On missions with the Unit, the assault team who rode on her helicopter almost always found and destroyed the target.

They said she possessed the killing luck.

The colonel rubbed thick fingers on thick chin stubble. "I have heard it said a half-truth is a whole lie."

Shrewd. The colonel used an old proverb—from her people no less—to call her a liar without calling her a liar. But she would have to give him a whole new set of half-truths anyway.

"Colonel, I have a confession," Molka said. "I'm not exactly what I seem to be."

"People seldom are."

"And I didn't come here just to be the school's veterinarian."

Besnik's haggard eyes widened in alarm. "Why did you come here?"

"I read Doctor Moore's book in college," Molka said. "It helped me tremendously. And I've admired the work Principal Darcy carries on in his name. Obviously, I'll never have the means to be allowed admittance to this school. So, I thought working here would be the next best thing. And after meeting and spending some time with Principal Darcy, I'm more convinced than ever what she's doing here is important. I believe she's trying to change the world."

The colonel's face hardened, incredulous.

Besnik's face softened, empathetic. "You really want to help Principal Darcy?"

"Yes. Very much. I want to help her in any way I can. And I can help her by helping you, colonel."

"In what way can you help me?" the colonel said.

"I served in the IDF," Molka said. "I have basic weapons training. Some martial arts. I also have experience with sentry duties and operating radios. Rumor is you're shorthanded. Maybe I can assist your security team?"

The colonel suppressed amusement. "I have no further questions. You may leave now."

"One moment, colonel," Besnik said. "Principal Darcy informed me how Doctor Molka capably handled two overzealous admirers during their meeting yesterday. And the results of the incident tonight validate her prowess further. Combined with her military training, perhaps she can be of assistance to you."

The colonel again suppressed amusement. "I do not think so."

"Doctor Molka," Besnik said, "could you please step out for a moment?"

She nodded and left the room, closing the door behind her.

"Colonel," Besnik said, "if I may be so bold, you need all the help you can get. You are authorized for a force of 15, yet still operate with only five men."

"Five men complemented by state-of-the-art drone surveillance technology. This is more than adequate."

"In theory. But tonight was the third security breach this year."

The colonel raised irritated fingers. "The other two were reporters posing as Friends of Darcy."

"Breaches, nonetheless," Besnik said. "Security is paramount above all with Principal Darcy. Most particularly at this time. And of the last 20 men I offered a security position to, all but First Sergeant Owen have declined. Desperate times, desperate measures."

Owen spit into his cup. "Sounds like you're in full CYA mode, Deanie."

The colonel ignored his insolence. "Bring her back in."

Besnik stood and summoned Molka back to her chair.

The colonel re-scrutinized her. "I have much respect for the IDF. In which branch did you serve? Armor? The Merkava is a fine tank."

"No, sir."

"Paratroopers?"

"No, sir."

The colonel brightened. "Ah, the famed Golani Brigade?"

"No, sir," Molka said. "Transportation."

"Transportation?" Owen spit again and laughed. "Hell, she was just a damn truck driver."

The colonel's eyes hit Owen like a tank round. "And where would your great American army be without trucks and those

125

who drive them? Amateurs talk strategy, professionals talk logistics." He looked back to Molka. "What rank did you carry?"

"Lieutenant, sir."

The colonel leaned back, exhaled heavy, and frowned at Molka. "Lieutenant who drives truck. I am still not convinced you can be of any use to me."

"Why not use her in a support capacity," Besnik said. "Perhaps assign her some of the more mundane, but necessary, security jobs. Which could free one of your regular men to help prevent another incident like we had tonight."

"This is your order?" the colonel said.

"This is my recommendation. And I believe Principal Darcy will concur. Of course, the final decision is yours, Colonel Krasnov.

"And what of her responsibilities as veterinarian?"

"May I answer?" Molka said. "My vet tech Rosina handles the office flawlessly. I'm rarely needed there." She came to attention. "Sir, I understand my résumé to serve on your security team is not overly impressive. But with respect, it's better than a former mall cop."

"First sergeant," the colonel said. "What do you know of the man she dispatched from the tower tonight?"

"Too Tall Tommie MacDonald?" Owen said. "I know he served in Canadian Special Ops. And he stole a good job and a bad woman from me in Indonesia. Other than that, I heard he knew his business."

"Well, colonel?" Besnik said.

The colonel squared his shoulders. "I will consider it and give you my decision tomorrow."

"One second, colonel," Owen said. "Before you do decide, remember everyone else on the team had to pass my PAT to keep their job. It's going to be holy hell on morale if you exempt her."

The colonel addressed Molka. "Report to the gymnasium at 1200 hours. The first sergeant will give you his physical aptitude test. If you pass, I will give you my decision immediately afterwards. You are dismissed, lieutenant who drives truck."

CHAPTER 20

At a quarter to noon, Molka jogged toward the gymnasium wearing a black tank top, black training pants, and black cross trainers with her hair in a high ponytail.

While all the running in humid South Florida the previous months had made her extra lean, she wasn't quite in peak shape by her own standards. Her arms and chest could have used a little more strength work. Still, she had passed some brutal military physical assessments in lesser condition. So experience said passing Owen's physical aptitude test wouldn't be an issue.

Molka entered the gym, exchanged greeting smiles with Truman mopping near the entrance, and crossed a scuff-free hardwood floor. A large blue wrestling mat—with a five-meter white circle outlined on the surface—covered center court.

Four men in gray sweatpants and white tee shirts performed stretching exercises around the circle. The colonel and Owen, both in uniform, observed from the side. A whistle and stopwatch hung from Owen's neck.

Molka came to attention before the colonel. "Reporting as ordered, sir."

The colonel moved toward the men on the mat, and they lined up abreast. "You already know the first sergeant. I now will introduce you to the rest of my team." He moved to the first man in line: Hispanic, medium height, well-muscled, mid-30s. "Security Officer Gervaso. Specialty: weapons. Former member of Columbia's Anti-Terrorism Special Forces Group. Sold out his unit to a drug cartel, then sold out the cartel back to his unit. Both have open contracts on his life."

He moved to the next man in line: the flirty Frenchman she had met at the airport. "Security Officer Narcisse. Specialty: he is our gunship pilot. Formerly served in France's Special Forces Helicopter Brigade. Dismissed after numerous affairs with the wives of the unit's officer corps."

He moved to the next man: East Indian descent, tall, hulking, early 30s. "Security Officer Hamu. Specialty: surveillance. Former member of the Indian Army's Special Parachute Regiment. Court martialed for running a covert side operation selling bootleg pornography. Escaped a military stockade by disabling their security system."

He moved to the last man: Asian, short, thickset, intense dark eyes, late-30s. "Security Officer Yeong. Specialty: reconnaissance. Former member of North Korea's People's Army Special Operation Force, where he killed his commanding officer and fled to China. Joined The People's Liberation Army Special Operations Forces, where he killed his commanding officer and fled to Canada. So far he has not killed me."

The colonel vacated the mat. "Carry on, first sergeant."

Owen addressed Molka. "I was going to give you my basic PAT: two minutes of push-ups, two minutes of sit-ups, and a timed two-mile run, but based on our previous skirmishes, I decided to bring back a more challenging classic test from the past especially for you."

"How considerate," Molka said. "What do you need me to do?"

"It's called the Circle of Pain. You'll face all four members of my team, individually, in hand-to-hand combat for 30 seconds inside the circle. If you're knocked out of the circle or knocked unconscious or tap out to any opponent, you fail."

"Any other rules?" Molka said.

"I used to say no striking the head or face, but I won't say that today. Step in the circle and prepare to defend yourself. Gervaso, you're up first!"

Gervaso stepped into the circle across from Molka and assumed a fighting stance with his hands in front held low Jiu Jitsu style, which meant he was grappler. He would try to get her on the ground. But the ground is death.

Owen blew the whistle.

Gervaso juked left, juked right, came at Molka, and grabbed her shirt front.

Molka swung a hammer fist into Gervaso's right temple.

Gervaso released his grip and side-stumbled.

Another hammer fist to his chest.

Gervaso retreated.

Molka advanced.

Another hammer fist to his chest.

Gervaso collapsed to his knees.

Molka dropped a hammer fist to his head.

Gervaso covered his head.

Another hammer fist to his head.

Another.

Gervaso tapped out.

Owen blew the whistle. "Match! Narcisse, you're up!"

Molka resumed a fighting stance and waited for Gervaso to stagger from the mat and Narcisse to enter the circle.

Owen leaned to the colonel's ear. "She's trained in Krav Maga. Surprised the shit out of him. Could've killed him."

The colonel flashed a discreet smile. "She is cunning and sudden, like the she-wolf."

Molka and Narcisse squared off.

Owen blew the whistle.

Narcisse smiled. "Just choose to go down and tap out, *belle*. I do not wish to hurt you."

Molka's answer: a flawless front kick to Narcisse's groin and a side kick to his jaw.

Narcisse just chose to go down and tap out.

Owen blew the whistle. "Match! Hamu, you're up!"

Hamu lumbered into the circle with a creep's grin.

Owen blew the whistle.

Hamu didn't wait for more Molka kicks; he surprised her with a nimble body roll and cut her legs out.

But before Hamu could exploit the takedown, Molka wrapped her thighs around his neck—trapping his left arm against his carotid artery—locked her ankles and rolled onto her side.

Her triangle chokehold restricted blood flow to his brain.

Hamu flailed twice, ceased resisting, and blacked out.

Owen blew the whistle. "Match!"

Molka released her hold and stood.

Hamu slept.

Owen charged the mat, bent, and slapped Hamu. "Wake up!"

Hamu snorted awake.

"Move your loser ass!"

Hamu coughed and crawled from the mat.

Owen looked to Yeong who had remained seated during the frays. "It's on you, Yeong. You got anything for her?"

Yeong rose slow with a wince, pulled up his right pant leg, and tightened a big black brace on his knee.

Owen addressed Molka. "A KPA border guard gave him a 7.62 caliber souvenir on his way out of the country. That knee is bone-on-bone now. But don't you dare hold back on him. The man has his pride."

Yeong limped to the mat with his head drooped.

Molka resumed her fighting stance. Did Owen save the crippled guy for last because he didn't think she would make it that far? *Surprise… first Sergeant. Give Yeong a break though. Stay away from him and run out the clock.*

Yeong took pained steps into the circle toward Molka, head still dropping.

Owen blew the whistle.

Molka relaxed her stance and stepped back.

Yeong's head snapped up and he snapped off a frightening-fast jump kick toward Molka's chin.

It didn't land solid, but it knocked Molka sideways.

Yeong closed on Molka and spun a roundhouse kick at her face.

Molka ducked under the kick but caught a follow-up breath-shortening side kick to her ribs.

Yeong pressed the attack with a front leg double kick.

Molka stumbled back.

Yeong's inverted roundhouse kick confused and connected.

Molka fell near the circle's edge.

Yeong could have pushed Molka out to elimination, but instead he dropped an axe kick finisher.

Molka rolled right. Kick missed.

Yeong dropped another axe kick.

Molka rolled left. Kick missed.

Owen blew the whistle. "Time."

Molka writhed back to her feet and guzzled air. Close call. *Only a fool underestimates an opponent—you fool.*

"First sergeant," the colonel said. "I say the trainee has passed your physical aptitude test. Do you agree?"

"No, sir, I don't agree."

"Your reason?"

"She hasn't lasted 30 seconds in the circle with me yet." He glared at Molka. "You havin' any of it, doc?"

Molka wiped brow sweat on her forearm. "You only said I would face your four men."

"Yes or no?"

"Don't like the results, you change the rules?"

"Yes or no?"

Molka nodded and re-entered the circle.

Owen tossed his cap, pitched the whistle and stopwatch to Gervaso, unbuttoned and removed his shirt, and stepped into the circle in front of Molka.

Molka resumed her fighting stance.

"I still owe you one for the cart incident," Owen said. "So, you're about to get an old-fashioned Fort Benning beatdown. Oh, and I should mention I did a little semi-pro MMA fighting. Blow the whistle."

Gervaso blew the whistle.

Owen came at Molka with boxer hands and threw a mediocre jab, cross, hook combination.

Molka slipped and blocked.

Too easy. A feint?

Owen dropped his shoulders, attacked, and drove Molka into the mat with a violent double leg takedown.

Molka twisted on her side and covered her head to protect it from real punches, but Owen flipped her onto her stomach and dropped both knees into her lower back.

Molka wheezed and lost her wind.

Owen straddled Molka and pulled her left arm behind her back into a merciless arm-lock.

Molka screamed.

"Hurts, don't it?" Owen said.

Molka swung her free arm back at Owen. It missed.

Owen leaned forward and laid his face cheek to cheek with Molka's. "That unbearable pain burning in your elbow is your bursa sac about to rupture. I saw it happen to a guy once. Of all the bad things I've seen, that was one of the worst."

Molka screamed again.

"That's it. Don't tap. Take it, baby. It's almost there."

Molka tipped her head back and to the side and chomped into Owen's left ear.

Owen screamed.

Gervaso yelled: "Time!"

Molka locked her jaw and yanked cartilage.

Owen screamed again and released Molka's arm.

Molka released Owen's ear.

Gervaso yelled again: "Time!"

Owen jumped to his feet and into a fighting stance.

Molka jumped to her feet and into a fighting stance.

Owen grabbed his left ear and took away blood covered fingers. His pale face raged red. "I'll fucking kill you for that!"

Molka spit his own blood toward him. "Or die trying."

Both coiled for another clash.

The colonel yelled:

"NYET!"

"NO MORE!"

"ENOUGH!"

"SEPARATE THEM!"

Yeong and Gervaso ran in and got between Molka and Owen.

The colonel turned to Owen. "First sergeant, do you now pass the trainee on your test?"

Owen touched dangling flesh on his ear lobe. "Damn! She like to bite my ear off!"

"First sergeant, do you now pass the trainee on your test?"

"Yes! God-damn it!" Owen checked his tone. "Yes, sir. She passed."

The colonel addressed Molka. "Lieutenant who drives truck."

Molka came to attention.

The colonel continued, "You may serve on my team with the brevet rank of lieutenant subordinate to the first sergeant. Do you accept?"

"I accept, sir."

"Very well. When the first sergeant returns from the infirmary, report to him at security headquarters for orientation and orders."

"Yes, sir."

Molka rubbed her pain pulsating elbow as she left the gymnasium. A smiling, pleasant Truman still mopped near the entrance door.

"That was amazing, Doctor Molka," Truman said.

"Thank you."

"First Sergeant Owen had them all here two hours before you arrived sparring." Truman chuckled his pleasant chuckle. "But they still weren't ready for you. Were you a professional martial arts fighter?"

"No. Just lucky."

"I think you're being modest," he said. "Word from the janitor's closet is Dean Besnik is having a hard time hiring qualified security people. Is that why the colonel offered you a job?"

Molka shrugged. "Maybe I can help out a little."

"Guess those mercenaries getting in and taking a student have them desperate. No offense. You looked capable, but an amateur on the colonel's team still seems unlikely."

"Do you know what they did with the mercenaries' bodies?"

"The infirmary has a small morgue," Truman said. "The local constable is going to have them flown out."

"And the local constable will also do an investigation?"

"If you call accepting Principal Darcy's explanation for what happened an investigation."

"And what explanation would that be?" Molka said.

"They broke into the school, abducted a student, and violently attacked the staff with the intent to kill. It was justified self-defense. Case closed."

"You hear that word from the janitor's closet too?"

"No, I happened to be cleaning the dean's residence this morning when he met with the constable. They talked loud."

Molka pushed through the door and headed for her room. Truman tagged along.

"You would think the authorities would still do an actual investigation," she said. "To confirm Principal Darcy's explanation, if nothing else."

Truman peeped over his shoulder. "I agree. But I guess the local constable goes along with Principal Darcy to get along with Principal Darcy. Like everyone else around here."

"Convenient for her."

He lowered his voice. "What happened with you and the mercenary in the tower. Was it really justified self-defense?"

"I'll just say a decision was made I didn't agree with, but I had to respect."

"Your answer opens a whole new line of questioning."

"See you around campus, Custodian Truman."

He smiled his pleasant smile. "I hope so, Doctor Molka."

She jogged away.

Truman was friendly. And chatty. And nosey. And gossipy. Did that make him annoying and avoidable? Under normal circumstances, yes. But he could be a useful information source to help complete her task. *Always seek to recruit useful assets.*

Ha. Sounds like Azzur talking. Scary.

Molka jogged straight to the cafeteria. Aden might be eating lunch there again and waiting for her. But he wasn't.

CHAPTER 21

"**H**ow's the elbow, doc?" Owen said from his cart parked outside the Security Zone gate.

"Still attached." Molka viewed a large bandage on his ear. "How is your ear?"

Owen hand cupped the bandage. "Huh? What did you say? Can't hear you?" He grinned. "Mount up. The colonel wants you to get the full tour."

The gate auto-opened. The entrance road ran between Building A and the security HQ building. Owen stopped halfway down it.

"The Security Zone is a perimeter within a perimeter," Owen said. "The outer perimeter here is called the Green Zone. If you catch anyone unauthorized in here, detain them and call me." He pointed toward Building A. "You'll notice that area is surrounded by its own fence and a cam-monitored gate. "That's the inner perimeter called the Red Zone. You catch anyone unauthorized in there, shoot them and call me."

"Who's considered authorized personnel?" Molka said.

"Besides security, Aden, Principal Darcy, Dean Besnik, and the techs."

"Who are the techs?"

"They work in Building A, but you won't be dealing with them."

They drove on past Building A, turned left into a paved lot behind the security HQ building, and stopped again. A vehicle inventory waited there in neat rows: six big matte black SUVs, six ATVs with machine gun mounts, and five electric carts identical to the one they had rode in. The truck with the twin 23-millimeter cannons occupied the lot's back corner.

"You said you served in transportation," he said. "So, you know what a motor pool is, right?"

"Yes," Molka said. "And I know that's a range over there." She pointed past the motor pool to a covered shooting position and targets downrange fronting an earthen berm. "And the bunker way back there is probably an armory." She pointed to a large steel door recessed into a manufactured hillside 150 meters away.

"Well damn. You just about know it all, don't you?"

Owen drove the cart to the security HQ's rear entrance and dismounted. Molka followed him inside to a long, white-walled, green-tiled hallway.

"First floor is operations," Owen said. "Second floor is the barracks, but the colonel said, for obvious reasons, you'll stay in your own quarters." He walked the hall pointing to doors left and right. "Those are the detention cells. That's a storage closet. That's a latrine. That's the squad room…we'll be going in there in a second. You saw the colonel's office last night. His quarters are attached to it. And this is the nerve center of campus security." He entered an open door across from the colonel's office. "The surveillance room."

Hamu filled a heavy-duty rolling chair before a massive control console and 20 plus monitor screens.

Owen back slapped Hamu. "How's it hanging big 'un?"

"Another quiet, boring day," Hamu said.

"Better than a sharp stick in the eye though, isn't it?"

Hamu shot Molka a dirty glance. "Maybe."

Owen turned to Molka. "The boys gave him holy hell about you choking him out. And I don't think he approves of you joining the team."

She shrugged with indifference.

Owen swept a hand over the console. "All the cams, the drones, and the gates are controlled from in here. Got it? Good. Let's go."

On the way back down the hall Molka said, "Is Hamu the only one assigned to surveillance?"

"Yeah. He pretty much works, eats, and sleeps in there 24/7."

"And it smelled like it."

Owen stopped and spun on Molka. "Your brevet rank don't mean shit around here. You're still bottom rung. So best watch your mouth."

You're in! Don't smart comment your way out!

"You're right," she said. "Sorry. I understand my place."

The squad room mimicked an office breakroom, with a long table and chairs, a coffee maker, a sink, a microwave, and a small refrigerator. It also mimicked a recreation room, with a foosball table and five Hazelnet screens with personal headphones—an off-duty Gervaso smiled at old cartoons on one. It also mimicked a squad room, with a duty assignment board, a key cabinet containing keys for the various vehicles, and security related posters and signs.

Owen opened a big carboard box on the table. "Ok, let's get you outfitted."

He first issued Molka two new uniforms. Since Narcisse measured the same height and about 10 pounds heavier than Molka, they carried a size to fit her. She requested permission to wear her own tac boots. Request approved.

Next, he issued her a radio, and a radio headset, and he gave her the security team's radio call signs:

The colonel: Red Wolf

Owen: Spitting Cobra

Gervaso: Bogotá

Narcisse: Frenchy

Hamu: Hindu

Yeong: Kia

Molka's call-sign, of course, would be: Doc.

Owen gave her high-end military grade Steiner binoculars and explained that the extreme distances they monitored required such powerful optics. She didn't mention they would also be useful for her task.

Her black nylon duty belt came rigged with a holster, a double magazine pouch, and a radio pouch. When he handed her a sporty fleece uniform jacket, she hoped for sporty fleece uniform jacket weather.

In conclusion, he issued her a factory fresh Gen5 Glock 19 semi-automatic pistol—the same model he carried—along with two spare magazines, two boxes of ammo, and a cleaning kit.

He answered her inquiry about also being issued her own MP5 submachine gun with dismissive laughter.

"Any more questions on your orientation so far?" Owen said.

"No. First sergeant."

"Gear up and meet me at the school's front gate in 30 minutes."

Twenty-five minutes later, Molka waited by Hazlehurst Institute's classical-style stone entrance arch. A modern metal gate secured it, and multiple security cams watched it.

She thought she looked sharp. It had been a while since she had worn a uniform. She even liked the dark gray. After wearing the same olive-green for years in the service, it offered a neat change. She styled her hair into a duty-hat-friendly bun, bloused her pants over her tac boots, and wore her old pilot's watch on her left wrist.

Five minutes later, Owen arrived in a security SUV and motioned Molka into the passenger seat.

He inspected her over his sunglasses. "Looks a helluva lot better on you than Narcisse. But what's on your wrist?"

"It's my uncle's old pilot's watch."

"It looks more like an old hunk of crap. Why is it all charred?"

"It's been through two crash and burns," Molka held up her wrist, "but it's still going strong. And if you have a problem with me wearing it, it's going to be a problem."

"Damn, doc. I was curious is all. Wear it till it rots and falls off for all I care."

"I plan to," she said. "What's next?"

He threw a thumb over his shoulder. "That's Student Woodrow. Woody. He's earned himself a field trip, and we're going to escort him."

Molka turned to the backseat. A chubby man in his late 60s with bright pink skin lay pouting. He wore a yellow safety vest over his school uniform.

"Where do we take him for a field trip?" she said.

"You'll find out when we get there." Owen leaned his arm and head out the window, grinned, and flipped the bird at a cam above the gate.

Hamu remote-opened it anyway.

Owen mashed the accelerator.

The one-lane paved road leading away from the school ran for about a kilometer and became a gravel road cutting through a dense forest. Towering pines shaded the afternoon sun, and their scent overpowered until the nose became deaf to it. A rising white dust tail obscured all behind them.

About five kilometers on, they passed a small one-lane gravel road veering to the right and disappearing into more trees.

"Where does that lead?" Molka said.

"That's what they call the Principal Darcy Memorial Causeway," Owen said. "It leads to the Principal Darcy Memorial Bridge that crosses the river to the Principal Darcy Memorial Turnpike which leads back to Principal Darcy Memorial Park. Home of the Principal Darcy Memorial Statue."

"You're joking with those names, but why did they put the access roads and bridge this far down-river from the campus?"

"How should I know?" Owen said. "I look like a genius engineer to you?"

Molka kept her eyes forward. "Not in the least."

Owen un-pocketed his dip can and used his wrists to steer while he opened it, took out a big pinch, and packed his lower lip. He tossed the can on the dash, reached under the seat for an empty plastic cup, and held it between his knees. Every few minutes, he lifted the cup to his lips for a disgusting brown spitting.

Molka checked the back seat again. Student Woodrow still lay gloomy. "Is he ok?"

"Don't pay attention to his act," Owen said. "He's just worried about his damn dog."

"What's wrong with your dog, Student Woodrow?" she said.

Student Woodrow said, "I'm worried if Duffy will be ok until I get back late tonight or tomorrow morning."

"Where's Duffy now?" Molka said.

"Student Blaine is looking after him. He lives in the room across from mine."

"Little bastard dog of his is mean," Owen said. "He tried to bite me when I picked Woody up."

"Because you scared him," Student Woodrow said. "He's very sensitive. I've never been away from him for more than a few hours. I'm so concerned about him."

Molka said, "When I get back, I'll ask Vet Tech Rosina to check on Duffy for you."

"Thank you, Doctor Molka. Duffy is the only real friend I have."

Owen talked into the rearview mirror. "Wouldn't you like to have me as your friend too, Woody?"

"I would prefer not to answer, First Sergeant Owen."

Owen laughed and unleashed an extra horrible spit stream into his cup. Molka sighed in disgust.

Owen grinned at Molka. "Maybe you'd prefer a dog to my company too?"

"Or a cat," Molka said. "Or a baboon or a jackass or even a six-eyed sand spider crawling up my leg."

Owen shuddered. "Eck. I ain't got no use for spiders. I saw some ugly ones in South America—big as your head. I had a dog once myself though. A stray pup I found when I was six."

Out of painful boredom, Molka offered a reply. "What kind of dog?"

"Little brown and white mutt of some sort. I named him Sarge. And that's before I ever thought about joining the army and becoming a sergeant myself. That dog followed me everywhere and slept beside the bed every night. When I started school, he followed me to the bus stop every morning and was always waiting for me at the bus stop every afternoon when I came home. One day, he chased a coon into a hollow log. He stuck his head in after the coon, and the coon plucked one of Sarge's eyes out clean."

"Oh no," Molka said. "Did he survive?"

"Hell yeah! They sewed his eyehole shut, and Sarge carried on. He was a tough little soldier. But a couple months later, he was waiting for me at the bus stop as usual. The bus backed up for some reason. Sarge didn't see it coming because it was on the side of his missing eye. The bus backed over him. We all felt the bump of it. When I got off the bus, I saw he was dead. I wrapped him in my shirt and carried him home crying. My old man told me to take him out in the woods and bury him. I did and came back crying harder. My old man told me to stop crying and be a man. It was just a damn dog. But I couldn't stop crying, so my old man beat me until I did stop crying. My old man wouldn't tolerate a sissy." Owen spit. "He was a good little dog though. And a good little friend."

She considered patting shoulder, but instead said, "I believe you."

An uncomfortable moment passed, and Owen said, "You know, it's funny. I still dream about little Sarge sometimes."

Molka couldn't be sure, but behind his sunglasses, she might have heard a tear or two.

Owen slowed, made a U-turn, and stopped. "We're here."

"We're where?" she said. "All I see is a massive forest and no end in sight to this road."

Owen pointed to the odometer. "We're exactly 20 kilometers from the front gate." He grinned into the rearview mirror. "Ok, Woody. You know what to do."

Student Woodrow sulked out and shut the door.

Owen reached into the center console, removed a canteen and flashlight, and tossed them out the window to Student Woodrow. "We'll see you when we see you, Woody. And remember what I told you: If you got to take a dump, best do it beside the road. Because bears really do shit in the woods."

Owen laughed, dropped it into gear, and floored it back toward the school.

"What are you doing?" Molka twisted in her seat and watched Student Woodrow vanish into a fresh dust cloud. "You're going to leave him out here?"

"That's what a field trip is, doc. He violated school policy. The nice long walk-back gives them time to think and get their minds right."

"Walk-back? He's not one of your 18-year-old recruits to abuse at Fort Benning. He's an out of shape senior citizen."

"He'll be ok," Owen said. "We strapped a tracker to his ankle so Hamu can monitor him, and he'll send a drone out to check on him too."

"Is this Colonel Krasnov's idea of acceptable discipline?"

"No. The colonel hates punitive discipline. He says punitive discipline is for weak minded commanders. This comes straight from Hazlehurst's boss."

"Dean Besnik?" Molka said.

"He's definitely weak minded, but I said from the boss."

"I can't believe Principal Darcy would approve of this."

"That's because you're a true believer in her bullshit," Owen said. "Yeah, I said it—her bullshit. I may work at Hazlehurst, but nothing in my contract says I have to believe in what's going on there. And I know you'll disagree with this too, but I think your little queen is pretty damn dangerous."

Molka couldn't disagree.

Owen parked the SUV in the security HQ motor pool and turned to Molka. "I'm assigning you the worst duty we have."

"I'm new to the team," Molka said. "I expected it."

"You'll be pulling the guard duty we call 'Death Watch.'"

"Why is it called death watch?"

"Because it will bore you to death watching."

"Which means what?"

Owen grinned with spite. "You'll see. Open the glove compartment."

She did and found a keycard on a black lanyard.

"That's all-access," Owen said. "Opens everything in this asylum. Take good care of it."

"No worries." Molka looped the lanyard around her neck. "I'll treat it as the very valuable asset it is."

CHAPTER 22

The terrorists never stood a chance.

Laili engaged the first five targets with a Tavor assault rifle on a tactical sling—three quick shots apiece dead center mass. For the last three targets, she unholstered a Sig P320 pistol and used a perfect point shooting technique to drop them clean.

Her instructor at the private training school outside Jerusalem smiled. "Outstanding, Laili. Make your weapons safe and pick up your brass."

Laili smiled back. "Ok!"

While she complied, the instructor and other shooters focused their desire on the lithe teen beauty, her tight jeans and crop top somehow made even sexier by her ear and eye protection accessories.

Azzur left a sandbagged viewing area and approached the instructor. "Like what you see so far?"

The instructor kept eyes on Laili. "Very much."

"I meant your assessment of her progress."

"She has the instincts of a natural predator."

"Perfect," Azzur said.

"But…"

"But what?"

"But maybe she enjoys it too much."

In the car leaving, Laili flashed Azzur an excited smile. "Today's training was sickly ill."

"I thought you enjoyed the tactical exercise?" Azzur said.

"I did. That's what I just said. As hot as it is, my hands weren't even sweating. And I actually like the smell of gunpowder."

"Good."

"Will you buy me my own Sig?" Laili said.

"You liked the compact Sig model? It felt comfortable in your hand?"

"Always. The rifle too. Like I've fired them my whole life."

"Laili, we may have found your natural gift."

"Thank you, daddy."

"I asked you to stop calling me that. It is disrespectful to your real father."

"My real father?" She erupted with scornful laughter and propped her sneakers on the dash. "Don't worry about that. I never had a real father."

"Then it is disrespectful to the man who fathered you."

"The only thing I was told about the man who *fathered* me is he beat the shit out of my mom while she was carrying me, and he finished in second place in a deadly two-man knife fight before I was born."

"Where is your mother now?" Azzur said.

"She OD'd on pills."

"So you are all alone in the world?"

Laili turned her face to the window. "Yeah. I'm all alone in this ugly world." Her head wrenched back toward Azzur. "But you already knew that. You know everything about me."

"Yes."

"Then why did you make me tell you?"

"To remind you," Azzur said.

"Remind me of what?"

"To remind you I am your family now, Laili."

PROJECT MOLKA: TASK 3
MONDAY, AUGUST 12TH
21 DAYS TO COMPLETE TASK

CHAPTER 23

"**D**eath Watch" earned its grim moniker.

Here's how it tried to kill Molka's spirit:

At 7:30 AM, she reported to Owen at the security HQ, signed in on the squad room duty board, exited the HQ, passed through the gate into the Red Zone, verified that the area around Building A was threat-free, and waited.

At 7:40 AM, a private passenger jet from Vancouver landed at the school airport. It brought the 120 skilled Asian workers— the techs—Darcy illegally employed to assemble the slaughterbot swarms. They boarded transporters driven by greenies and guarded by Security Officer Yeong and were brought to Building A. On arrival, Yeong issued each a pre-prepared bag lunch from the cafeteria, followed them into the first-floor production line, and locked the door behind them. Their shift started at 8:00 AM.

Molka spent the next 10 hours—minus a 30-minute lunch break in the squad room—foot patrolling the Red Zone to guard against the remote possibility that intruders may attempt to breach it or Building A.

At 6:00 PM, Yeong unlocked the door, and the techs re-boarded the transporters for the airport and the return flight to Vancouver.

At 6:15 PM, Molka left the Red Zone, returned to the security HQ, filled out a cursory report form, signed out, and went back to her room.

Repeat.

Repeat.

Repeat.

Repeat.

Same tedious day for five straight tedious days.

Death. Watch.

On the encouraging side, the ponderous routine gave Molka ample time to analyze the structure she would have to destroy. Building A's construction didn't match the campus red brick or the stout masonry in the staff compound. It presented a prefabricated, modular appearance. Maybe a rush job built for Aden's work. Good news, it wouldn't take much high explosive to implode it. And more good news—her newfound access to the Security Zone and its armory would provide her with the materials she required.

On the troubling side, her task would turn messy unless she got the chance to talk to Aden again. She needed to continue cultivating their friendship to make him receptive to leaving with her when she asked. And she considered them off to a promising—if not great—start. It should have been easy to reconnect because he lived and worked in Building A. But she didn't glimpse him during those five straight days.

Finding another opportunity to talk to Aden preoccupied her mind. She didn't find one. But just as the messy alternatives to this failure began to overpower her thinking, on the morning of her sixth "Death Watch," an opportunity found her.

Molka had completed yet another patrol lap around Building A when the "big black wasp" that had buzzed her in the central courtyard buzzed her again. No. It was a much smaller model.

The micro drone circled her three times, stopped, and hovered a meter from her face.

Hamu must be as bored as I am today.

Molka swatted at the drone.

It darted away and came right back.

She swatted again.

It darted again and came right back again.

A third swat.

Same result.

It reacted way too fast for her quickest reaction time.

The drone moved to her left half a meter and hovered. Moved another half meter left and hovered again. Moved another half meter left, hovered, and made a waggling motion.

Does it want me to follow?

She took a few steps toward it. It waggled again.

It does want me to follow. Ok, Hamu. I'll play along.

Molka moved toward it.

It buzzed away and around Building A.

Molka pursued at a trot.

On the building's opposite side, an always locked door waited open, and the drone flew inside. Molka reached the door and investigated. It led to a staircase. The drone already hovered at the top outside a second-floor door. Molka high-kneed the stairs to catch it. Before she could, the door auto-opened, and the drone flew inside.

Molka followed and entered an expansive workshop-like room. Shelves loaded with electronic gadgets lined its perimeter, and long tables overflowing with more electronic equipment ran its length. And at a workbench—tucked into a clearing in the creative clutter—lounged a cheerful Aden.

Molka approached him. He wore slim-fit jeans, white tennis shoes, a snug navy-blue V-neck sweater with the sleeves pushed up, and his black-framed glasses—preppy-adorable.

"Good morning, Doctor Molka," Aden said. "Or should I now say Security Officer Molka?"

"Just Molka is fine. Do you have a security emergency?"

Aden smiled. "Why? Have you come to save me?"

"Do you need to be saved?"

"Do I look like I need saving?"

"Not at the moment," she said.

"Then why did you come here?"

Molka folded her arms and leaned against a table behind her. "I don't know. You droned me."

"I'm told you threw a very big, very capable man from our 16-story bell tower to his death."

"I didn't throw him," she said. "He fell."

"But you helped him fall."

"Well, he tried to help me fall first, so..."

"I'm also told you beat up the entire security team and tried to bite Owen's ear off."

"That's an exaggeration."

"Is it?" Aden said. "Owen says you're probably the best man he's got, and you're only a woman."

Molka crinkled her nose. "Yes. I'm only a woman."

"Trust me, he's impressed. Me too. He said you served in the IDF?"

"Yes."

"I knew the IDF was tough, but I didn't know they fielded a lethal veterinarian corps."

"They don't. I became a veterinarian after I left the service."

Aden perched his glasses atop his head. "And how did a dangerous desert girl like you end up in a peaceful green place like this?"

Molka chuckled. "You're funny. But the long story short is I originally joined the veterinarian exchange program to get out and see the world."

"And what do you think of the world so far?"

Molka shrugged. "I've seen better."

Aden laughed. "You're funny too."

Molka smiled. "You think so?"

Focus not flirt!

She came off the table and scanned over its contents. "I haven't seen you out running or riding lately."

"After the mercenary incident, Owen suggested I confine myself in here for a few days until they get things squared away. Whatever that means." Aden sighed. "And Principal Darcy took my ATV away from me. She's afraid I might get hurt on it."

Molka looked back to Aden. On the workbench before him rested identical micro drones in the dozens—the same type she had followed there. "Are those your new little toys?"

152

"No. Those are PSDs."

"What's a PSD?"

"You're naturally inquisitive, aren't you?"

Molka smiled. "I've worked with a lot of cats. Maybe it rubbed off. Sorry."

Aden smiled. "No. I like it. It's endearing. But PSD stands for Personal Security Drone. I didn't come up with that name, by the way. This was a total Principal Darcy brainchild."

"What's their function?"

"After the intruder debacle the other night, Principal Darcy ordered a Personal Security Drone made for each of the students and vital staff members. She wants to use them to more quickly locate you in case of another emergency."

"How nice," she said. "If not terrifying. But I'm considered a vital staff member?"

"All security officers are. I just activated yours this morning."

"Oh, then it wasn't Hamu controlling it."

"No," Aden said. "And it wasn't me controlling it either. It found you on its own. I only entered a mission goal to bring you here."

"And here I am. How do they work?"

He picked up a drone from the group and glanced at its underside. "This is your unique PSD."

"How can you tell for sure? Does it have my name on it?"

"Each one has a serial number, and they can be assigned to any individual."

"And you memorized my number?" Molka smiled. "How sweet."

"I memorized all the numbers."

"How savant."

Aden stood, placed the drone in his palm, and held it for demonstration. "It uses facial recognition from your staff ID photo. It also has a profile uploaded containing your work schedule and personal habits, so it knows where to find you. Autonomous AI. Simple stuff, really."

"What's simple to you would amaze the world."

He set the drone back on the table. "Maybe."

"When I tried to swat it, it knew to move."

"Yes. That stochastic motion is a defensive feature."

"To make them impossible for a human to knock down?"

"Yes."

"Or shoot down?" Molka said.

"I suppose."

"So basically, it can find you on its own and can't be stopped once it does, right?"

Aden's face lit up. "Hey, I was about to go upstairs to my place and make a roasted strawberry and Greek yogurt smoothie. Want one?"

"Sounds delicious. But I should get back to my duties."

"You mean your boring duties."

"My duties aren't boring," she said.

"Making a lap around the building every 15 minutes for 10 hours isn't boring?"

"It's great steady state cardio."

"What about all your scanning of the vast terrain with your fancy binoculars?"

"Not boring either. I spotted a moose relieving himself yesterday."

Aden's eyes widened in mock amazement. "Exhilarating."

"And it sounds like you've been watching me."

"I get bored too. How about that smoothie?"

"I better not," Molka said. "First Sergeant Owen wouldn't approve."

"Well, Owen doesn't have to know about *everything* we do together." Aden melted Molka with his heart-melting dimples. "Does he?"

She followed him to a spiral staircase in the corner, which led to third-floor open loft-style apartment.

Aden walked to an all-stainless-steel kitchen, opened the refrigerator, removed some containers, and started tossing strawberries into a blender.

Molka checked the loft's layout. A king-sized bed occupied one end. The center area contained a leather sectional and a huge flat screen connected to several video game consoles. Expensive workout equipment filled the other end.

"Nice home gym," she said. "I see where you got those sleeve hugger arms."

"I haven't been hitting it lately though," Aden said. "Principal Darcy has me spending more time supervising the techs. But the techs don't need supervising. Supervising slows them down. I'm required to check their work before they leave each day and I never find a single flaw. They're outstanding."

Molka viewed a scale model of a Canadian Air Force fighter jet displayed on the counter. "You also into building model aircraft?"

He turned on the blender. "No. That's a memento from my old squadron."

"Wow. You were a fighter pilot?"

"For a brief time."

"Why brief? Didn't like it?"

"I loved it. I loved the training and the perfecting of deadly skills. And I got a real rush from the power over life or death those deadly skills theoretically gave me during the training exercises. But then they reminded me I might have to use those deadly skills to actually kill real people. I could never do that. So I resigned." Aden shut off the blender. "I guess a tough woman like you would see that as weakness."

"Not at all," Molka said. "My father was dedicated to non-violence, and he was the strongest man I ever knew."

Aden removed the container from the blender base and poured the pink smoothie into twin tall glasses. "I must warn you; these are addictive."

"Bold claim. Hope you can back it up."

"I've always let my work speak for itself."

"Noted," she said.

Aden moved to hand Molka her glass but hesitated. "Please take off your hat first."

"Why?"

"My house, my rules. Or call it indoor cover etiquette, soldier."

Molka saluted playful. "Yes, sir." She removed her duty cap and laid it on the counter.

"Now lose the bun."

She didn't want to, but for some reason she wanted to. She removed two hair pins and unwound the bun.

"Now the ponytail," Aden said.

Molka removed a hair tie and shook out her ponytail.

He smiled. "Much better. That's the way I like to see you."

Molka smiled. "You do?"

"Oh yes." Aden handed her the glass. "Now drink."

Molka took a sip. "Ok. I have to admit, this is really good." Another sip. "Really, really good."

"Thank you. Mine aren't bad, but there's a café in Tel Aviv that made these incredible smoothies called—"

"Café Jarrod."

Aden grinned delighted. "Yes! You've been there?"

"I have; it's the best."

"You miss your country?"

She swallowed another sip. "More than I thought."

"I miss it too. Like I said, I worked there for a while, but I first fell in love with it when I was a kid. Every summer my mother took me to visit a moshav where she was born and raised in the Jezreel Valley."

Molka nodded. "I know the area well."

"Caring for the livestock, all the hard work, I actually enjoyed. But when the work was done, there was also horseback riding, big campfires, group singing, games. It was a wonderfully pure and simple lifestyle. My mother said we could move there permanently. Just her and I. And my father wouldn't have minded. Their marriage was convenient like that. I was so excited. But then she got sick. Breast cancer took her. I was 16 when she died. She never even got to see any of my accomplishments."

"I'm sure she would have been very proud."

Aden's eyes glistened. "You really think so?"

Molka placed her hand on his forearm. "Of course."

"I just wish she and I would've had the chance to move to that little moshav. I felt more at home there than anywhere I've ever lived."

"Would you ever consider going back to my country—your mother's home country—again? Not necessarily to the moshav, but to live and work?"

Aden smiled. "Is that an invitation?"

Molka smiled. "Maybe."

"I would love to. But last time I was there…some things happened. I might have left behind some hard feelings."

"Well, we're a very forgiving people. I'm sure they would welcome you back."

Aden stared into his smoothie. "Yes, they probably would. And lately, I've been missing it more and more." He set his glass on the counter and stepped close to Molka. "And I've missed you too." He pulled her to him, grabbed her head, and staggered her with a deep kiss.

Molka pushed him away. "And I've missed you." She pulled him back, grabbed his head, and staggered him with a deep kiss.

Aden pushed her away. "You didn't come up here for a smoothie."

"No."

"Why did you come up here?"

"I don't know," Molka said.

"You're lying."

"Am I?"

Aden seized Molka's hand and pulled her across the loft to his bed. "Is this why you came up here?"

She jerked her hand away. "No! Maybe. I mean…I'm not ready for that right now."

Aden backed away. "I'm sorry." He turned, rushed into the living room area, and sank onto the couch.

Molka followed.

He sat with his chin dropped to his chest and his lips pouted. "I shouldn't have brought you here. It won't happen again. I'm sorry."

Molka came to him and touched his shoulder. "It's fine."

Aden raised his head. "You're not mad at me?"

"No. I'm a little flattered, to be honest."

He stood, put his arm around her waist, and pulled her tight. "You should go." He kissed her.

"Yes. I should go." She kissed him.

"Yes, you should go," Aden said.

They kissed each other.

"Better go now," he said.

"Alright." She ran to the counter and grabbed her cap. "Will we see each other again soon?"

Aden gave her the devastating dimples again. "Do we even have a choice now?"

Molka smiled and floated back to her boring duties.

 **CHAPTER 24**

Molka + Aden.

Aden + Molka.

Molka loves Aden.

Aden loves Molka.

Mrs. Molka Luck.

Mr. and Mrs. Luck.

I'm such a LUCKY girl!

Molka tossed her pen across the room, dropped her notebook on the floor, and face-flopped on her bed.

UGH!

It was just some innocent kissing. It didn't mean anything.

Yes, he's brilliant and funny and in great shape and handsome. And those dimples. Oh my, those dimples!

Whew!

See, this is what happens when a girl puts herself on an extended dry spell. She loses her composure and she starts thinking with her...

Now you sound as bad as the guys in the Unit.

Steady girl.

But I do like Aden though. And he likes me too. He likes me a lot. So when I ask him to leave with me, he will. I won't have to kill him.

He's waaaay too sexy to kill.

UGH!

I can hear the major now: "Get yourself refocused and do your job, soldier!"

He's right. And there's only one thing to do in a situation like this to get a girl's mind back on the business at hand.

Right after my watch ends tomorrow, go shopping!

CHAPTER 25

C-4 demolition block charges.

A remote detonator.

Thermite grenades.

And yes, worse case prepared for, a .22 semi-automatic pistol with suppressor.

Molka made her mental wish list during "Death Watch" laps around Building A while more than half hoping Aden would summon her again.

He didn't.

The minute her watch ended, she signed out, crossed the motor pool to the armory, and used her security keycard to open its heavy steel door.

Darkness widened her eyes and air permeated by dust and weapon lubrication oil clogged her nose. She flipped a switch next to the door, and fluorescents illuminated a space much larger than it appeared from the exterior.

Heavy-duty shelves—arranged in four neat aisles—held racked weapons and military-style crates, boxes, and cases.

A slaughter superstore.

No store directory though, so she browsed.

The first aisle stocked rifles and machine guns in varied vintages, makes, and models.

Aisle two carried a wide pistol variety. Her preferred Beretta model was not available, but she did find an old Czechoslovakian-made .22. with a suppressor, which could do a job she hoped she would never have to do. She concealed the pistol inside her pants front.

The third aisle packed ammo. She pocketed a 50 round .22LR box.

She figured that the final aisle would hold the high explosives or grenades she needed. It didn't. And although disappointing, it made sense because campus security's mission was to defend a position, not take one.

However, the aisle's first offerings showed great potential in several six-foot-long olive-green aluminum cases. Markings indicated that they contained Stinger portable shoulder-fired missile launchers. An excellent weapon system designed to shoot down aircraft, but not ideal for destroying a building. She moved on. Next to the Stingers, old Russian RPG-7s. Useless junk. And in a case next to those, a Javelin fire-and-forget anti-tank missile launcher. Definitely not junk, and definitely useful, but she had never fired one, and—after a peek inside—manual not included.

But stacked right next to it…

Hello old friends!

…three MATADOR rocket launchers.

A weapon Molka had fired before, several times during an anti-tank training course. And even more exciting, she had witnessed assault teams in the Unit use them to demolish good sized structures. Two would be enough to eliminate Building A. All three would be better.

The MATADOR. Toro, toro. Ole.

"Good evening, Doctor Molka." Truman popped into view at the aisle's end dressed in his usual red plaid shirt and khaki work pants.

"Good evening, Custodian Truman."

"A little cool for this time of year."

"Yes," Molka said. "Might need a sweater later."

"Just might."

"You certainly get around this school."

162

"I go where the dirt is." Truman chuckled his pleasant chuckle. "I'm actually supposed to be cleaning the security headquarters—they let me in there once a week—but I noticed the armory door open and couldn't resist investigating. I've been dying to see what's in here. Impressive cache of weapons, isn't it?"

"Yes. I was just leaving." Molka headed down the aisle toward the exit.

Truman trailed. "I hear right after Colonel Krasnov arrived, a big, unmarked cargo plane landed at the airport and dropped all this stuff off. Rumor is, it came from a black market arms dealer friend of his."

"Where did you get that information?"

"Oh, it's just word from the janitor's closet."

"That's a very well-informed closet," she said. "The only thing my closet ever says to me is, 'great, you bought more shoes you'll never wear.'"

Truman chuckled his pleasant chuckle again and was still chuckling when he and Molka turned the corner.

Both startle-stopped.

Owen blocked the door, outfitted civilian style in a truck logo tee shirt, jeans, and camo hat. He grinned at their anxiousness. "What's so funny, and why wasn't I invited to the party?" His grin morphed into a scowl at Truman. "But flabby, I let you in my Security Zone to clean my HQ. Not to be back here cutting up and snooping around my armory. What the hell?"

"It's my fault," Molka said. "I asked him what could be done about cleaning the dust from some of this equipment."

"He don't need to worry about the dust in here; he needs to worry about cleaning our shitter in the barracks. And make sure it's sparkling. I have to drop a big deuce. Go get on it."

Truman's pleasant smile stiffened. "Yes, sir."

"I'm not a sir. I work for a living, flabby. Call me First Sergeant Owen."

"I work for a living too, First Sergeant Owen. Call me Custodian Truman."

Owen glared him out the door. "Smart-ass fat-ass. Reminds me of a captain at Bagram who used to break my balls." He turned back to Molka. "Now what are you doing in here, doc?"

"Looking for range ammo," Molka said. "It's been a while since I fired a weapon. I want to get some practice time in."

"You figure you'll have to shoot somebody soon?"

"You never know, do you?"

"You surely don't."

"What are you all dressed down for?" she said.

Owen viewed his shirt and jeans. "What do you mean dressed down? Everything I have on is brand new."

"Oh. You look…nice."

His face hardened. "Be advised, I'll be off campus on official security business tonight. So, I may or may not be here in the morning when you report."

"Alright. I'll try to carry on without you."

Owen cocked his head to the side. "Always with the smartass remarks." He walked to aisle three, grabbed two range ammo boxes, and tossed them to Molka. "Knock yourself out."

"You're not going to charge me for these, are you?"

"What?"

Molka smiled. "Nothing." She moved toward the door.

Owen followed. "You have some strange ways, doc."

"Like what?"

"Like there's a little more to you than you're letting on."

"You think so?"

"Yeah. I can't place it yet, but I'll figure you out. Then what are you going to do?"

Molka paused and faced him. "I haven't decided." She smiled again and tapped the ammo boxes. "Maybe I'll have to shoot you."

CHAPTER 26

Darcy lazed nude. Her taut 44-year-old body—a rival to most 24-year-olds—spread atop white silk sheets on a huge white bed in a massive white room adorned in sheer white curtains and thick white carpet. The morning sun pouring through floor-to-ceiling windows made the massage oil on her skin glow lustrous.

She didn't lie alone in her extravagant penthouse's master bedroom.

A nude man slept facedown next to her.

And Besnik—dressed for expensive litigation—waited bedside with averted eyes.

Darcy held a tablet and watched surveillance cam video from Molka's gymnasium triumph over the security team. "I told you she's a hellcat! Whipped all their asses and took a chunk out of the hillbilly's ear!" She laughed on and on and on until she caught her breath. "Oh me. Oh my. Ok, whew. But good idea putting her on the security team. She'll flat out shame them into doing a better job."

"Yes, Darcy," Besnik said. "And thank you."

"And it has the added benefit of keeping her too busy for Aden to play with."

"This was also my thought. Although, the colonel assigned her to guard the Red Zone."

"He put her in Aden's front yard?" she said. "Why would he do that?"

"He seems to think highly of her."

Darcy nodded. "Yes, well we might need to get her reassigned. Anyway, you like to give me a good giggle before you drop bad news on me." She handed the tablet to Besnik. "So, go ahead and drop it on me."

Besnik kept his eyes averted. "Our constable Friend—"

She sighed, annoyed. "You've been my personal lawyer for 12 years and have known me for 18. You've seen me in much worse states than bare-ass naked."

Besnik's toad face flushed. "You know my feelings toward you, Darcy. And with him here." He viewed the naked, sleeping man. "It makes me—"

"Look like a jealous schoolboy. You sound like my other little fool. Now what did our constable Friend tell you?"

"When he made his report about the mercenary incident, they did not question it."

Darcy fingertip clapped. "That's a good thing. Right?"

"No. That is a bad thing. He believes their silence confirms the much larger ongoing investigation we feared."

"How long does he think we have?"

"Maybe eight weeks," he said. "Maybe less."

Darcy fluffed her pillows and scooched into a sitting position. "Collect next month's tuition fees early."

"Yes, Darcy."

"And solicit some more endowments."

"Yes, Darcy."

"And increase the techs to 12-hour shifts."

"Yes, Darcy."

"And I'll keep breaking my ruler across Aden's ass."

"Yes, Darcy."

Darcy gazed out the tall windows. "Summer's flying by. Fall is coming soon. The evenings are already getting cooler. Issue the students their fall uniforms, sweaters, and jackets."

"Yes, Darcy."

"And have maintenance make sure all the heating units are working in the student dorm. They can't focus on getting better if they're uncomfortable."

"Yes, Darcy. You are absolutely right. The students are so fortunate to have your constant concern."

She stretched and yawned. "Yes, summer's flying by and fall is a comin' soon. Better fatten your secret Dakar accounts in case we have a long, hard winter too."

Besnik's face mortified.

Darcy smiled. "Yes, I know all about them. I sent my creative accountant to talk to your creative accountant over drinks and hookers. Your creative accountant talks too much when drinking over hookers."

Besnik straightened his tie. "Darcy, I assure you those are personal investments, and there has been no malfeasance on my behalf toward you or—"

"It's ok, Bezie. I was relieved to find out how little you've stole—relatively speaking. Because if your crooked lawyer isn't stealing a little from you, he's stealing a lot from you. It's the cost of doing shady business. Now give me back that tablet."

He complied.

Darcy grinned. "I want to watch the hellcat doll do her thing again. She reminds me of a skinny little black girl I worked with in Tupelo who—there it is again." Molka's conversation with Truman before she exited the gymnasium was also caught on camera. She paused the video and turned the screen for Besnik to view. "What's this look like to you?"

Besnik shrugged. "A friendly chat?"

"They're commiserating. And that was before they were caught commiserating in the armory yesterday. And after they were commiserating right before she killed the intruder. That's a lot of commiserating for two people who have no reason to be commiserating a lot. What kind of background checks did you give those two?"

"The standard."

"How clean are they?" Darcy said.

"Squeaky."

"Nobody's squeaky. Go deep on them. Put your guy in Quebec on it."

167

"He was contracted to help us expose suspected traitors among the students. His fee is quite substantial. Do you really think Custodian Truman and Doctor Molka require such scrutiny?"

Darcy re-fluffed her pillows. "One of the few sensible things my late husband used to say was this: Assume everyone is out to screw you. And if they don't, you can be pleasantly surprised."

"I heard Doctor Moore use that colloquialism."

"And here's a colloquialism you can hear from me: Success breeds jealousy, and jealousy breeds traitors. We're too close to the end and can't afford to be frugal. From now on, I want *everyone* considered a traitor until proven otherwise. You understand me?"

"Yes, Darcy."

"Get those deep background checks done immediately. And while he's at it, have him check out our special visitor on the way from Rome."

"Milan."

"What?" she said.

"She is on the way here from Milan, Italy, by way of her villa in Tuscany."

"Well, hoo-ray for her. But I don't care if she's on the way here from Sow Tits, Mississippi by way of an outhouse in Tuscaloosa; get her and those other two checked out."

"Yes, Darcy."

Darcy used the tablet to reach over and slap the sleeping man's bare butt. "Wake up, soldier boy."

The man jerked awake and groaned.

Darcy went on, "Dean Besnik's here to fly you back. And I also believe he has something very rewarding to discuss with you. Get moving. Recess is over."

Owen opened his eyes and raised his head and sighed. "What happened last night?"

"I took you into my bed and made you a king, but now I'm putting you out in the morning as a lowly foot soldier again." Darcy smiled. "And such is the power of a queen."

CHAPTER 27

Aden rode circles around Molka on a two-wheeled electric
scooter as she exited the security HQ after her watch.

"How do you like it?" Aden said. "I built it myself."

"It's cool," she said. "Did you really build it?"

"Sure." Aden perched his glasses atop his head. "I already
had the motors, batteries, and controls from a robot design I've
been tinkering with. I fabricated the body from some stainless-
steel plates laying around my shop. The tires and the steering
handle I pirated from lawnmowers in the maintenance building.
Then I just put it all together. It was easy."

"How long did it take you?"

He did another circle around her. "I thought of it this
morning. And finished it by lunchtime."

"You're an engineering genius."

"So they tell me. I made one for you too."

"You did?" Molka said.

"Yes. Get changed and meet me outside your housing unit in
30 minutes. I want to show you something."

"Alright. How should I dress?"

Aden flashed the irresistible dimples. "For adventure."

Molka cantered down from her room in a green sleeveless tee shirt, blue jeans, and cute hiking boots she had hoped to have an excuse to wear. Normally, she would ponytail her hair for adventure, but she wore it down instead.

Because Aden said he liked it down.

Aden—attired outdoorsy in a blue flannel shirt, jeans, and boots—waited for her with two homemade scooters and a backpack. He gave Molka a quick tutorial on how to operate the scooter and said, "Any questions?"

"One glaring," she said. "Where's your bodyguard buddy?"

"Owen won't be joining us this evening. We made a little deal. He won't tell Principal Darcy everything I do at night, and I won't tell Colonel Krasnov everything he does at night."

"Good deal."

"Let's roll."

Molka followed Aden as he weaved across the staff compound. The scooter moved fast and a little scary at first. But Aden had built it with great balance and sturdiness, and she enjoyed it.

They reached the staff compound's far side where the single chimney powerplant operated. Aden explained its clean coal fueled, largely automated process. And like his earlier explanations of the Personal Security Drones and homemade scooters, he shared his vast technical knowledge in a non-condescending accessible way. His style reminded her of a great professor she had once known—her father.

They rode around the powerplant to the school's tall masonry perimeter wall. A gravel cart path ran along the wall's interior, and they followed it.

After about a quarter kilometer, Aden stopped and dismounted. "We'll leave our rides here outside the door."

"What door?" Molka said.

He pointed at a large concrete drainage channel running under the wall. A knee-high gap separated the wall bottom and the channel.

"That's a potential security breach," she said.

"No. That's a blatant security breach."

"Yes. It should have a secure metal grate covering it."

"It did," Aden said.

"Someone removed it?"

"Yes."

"Then I should report this."

"You better not." He smiled. "I'm the someone who removed it."

Aden unslung his backpack and pushed it through the gap. Then he sat in the drainage channel, slid his feet under the wall, lay back, and inch-wormed through to the other side. "Your turn."

Molka mimicked his technique and stood to find them atop a grassy hill overlooking the Tiffany-blue flowing river.

Aden grabbed Molka's shoulders. "We've escaped! Sweet freedom!"

"Not for long," she said. "Hamu's patrol drones will spot us shortly."

"No, they won't." He re-slung his backpack. "I did a little maintenance on the drone for this sector. It's now replaying yesterday's feed."

"Another blatant security breach." Molka smiled. "I like your style."

Molka followed Aden downhill and along the riverbank. As they hiked, a giddy Aden paused from time to time to skip stones on the river.

Twenty minutes into the journey, they trekked back up a less steep hill to a grassy plateau embraced by pines.

Aden dropped his backpack and swept his hand over the scene. "Can I pick a view or what?"

Below them, the immaculate river passed over bright white rocks with a soothing gurgle. Smaller white rocks made up the riverbanks, which gave way to tall pine tiers forming a rolling and rising green that ended at distant mountain peaks.

Molka didn't exaggerate. "I love it."

"Just wait; it gets way better."

"How did you find this place?"

"I located it when I stole a hi-res satellite photo of the school grounds from the surveyor crew laying out Building A."

She grinned. "Aren't you the clever little thief too."

"Well, it was more about boredom than banditry. I did some satellite image interpretation in the Air Force and the possibilities of this spot excited me."

"And now this is your hideaway?"

"It's more a getaway," Aden said. "I was thinking about building a mini-log cabin here and stocking it with snacks and a portable gaming system."

"You mean kind of like a little playhouse?"

"Maaaaybe. But it's nice to be outside the wall, don't you agree?"

"Definitely." Molka rubbed her bare arms. "You should have told me to bring a light jacket though."

"You're cold? It's like 12°C."

"I'm from the Middle East by way of South Florida. To me this is a little cool."

"Not a problem," he said. "I came prepared. I'll build us a campfire."

"You know how to build a campfire too?"

"I'm from Western Canada by way of Northwest Canada. We come out of the womb with basic camping skills."

Molka smiled. "Cute."

Aden opened his backpack, took out a large blanket, and spread it on the ground. Then he removed a two-person sleeping bag, unrolled it, and spread it atop the blanket.

Molka removed her boots, sat on the blanket, and covered herself with the sleeping bag. "Much better. I'm fine now."

"You sure?" he said.

"Yes." She snuggled more under the sleeping bag.

Aden scanned Molka with a skeptical grin. "You don't believe I can build a fire, do you?"

"Let's just say, I don't want you to burn down British Columbia on my account."

"You'll apologize for that remark shortly."

Aden reached into his backpack again and removed a folding spade and a small hatchet. He speared both into the ground and headed back down toward the riverbank. Five-minutes later, he returned cradling a dozen or more grapefruit-sized rocks. He dropped the rocks on the grass, used the spade to dig a shallow pit, and surrounded the pit with the rocks. Satisfied, he grabbed the hatchet and waded through scrub and into the tree line. Ten minutes later, he returned with an armload of dry wood, stacked it with purpose in the fire pit he had built, lit it with a wooden match from a box in his backpack, and watched.

Soon a comfy fire crackled.

Molka bowed her head to Aden. "I apologize; humbly."

Aden bowed his head to Molka. "Accepted; humbly."

Molka smacked a mosquito, then another. "Must be their feeding hour. Do you have any repellent in your magic bag?"

"No way. That stuff can be deadly toxic."

"Well, not if you use it in moderation."

"I meant deadly toxic to the poor little mosquitoes," he said. "Here, this is much better." He removed a large yellow Citronella candle, lit it, and placed it beside the blanket.

"If you pull a porta potty out next, I'll really be impressed."

"You mean…oh no…you have to—"

Molka giggled. "No. I'm fine. But you know what I am craving that would make this outing perfect?"

"I do." Aden went back into his backpack, produced a large stainless-steel tumbler, and handed it to Molka.

"You didn't?" She took a sip. "You did! Roasted strawberry and Greek yogurt! Perfect outing! You're perfect too!"

Aden joined her on the blanket. They shared the smoothie, staring in mesmerized in silence at the fire and taking in its smoky bouquet.

Sunset approached, and Molka was considering laying her head on his shoulder when—

Aden leapt to his feet. "It's about to happen!" He grabbed Molka's arm, pulled her to her feet, and pointed to the western horizon. "Look! Look! Look!"

The sun descended between two mountain peaks. As it lowered, the mountains themselves and the vast forest valley below became silhouetted in cool, dark purple, while the sky above exploded into vivid red and orange.

The contrasting color palette halted their breath.

Aden took Molka into his arms as they both continued to devour nature's unrivaled show.

"What do you think?" he said.

"I think that might be the most beautiful thing I've ever seen."

"I think you're the most beautiful thing I've ever seen."

Aden kissed Molka.

Molka kissed him back.

They kissed each other.

The kiss went unbroken as they lowered back onto the blanket.

Aden untucked Molka's shirt, pulling it over her head and off. He removed her bra and eased her on her back. He unbuckled the belt on her jeans. He undid her fly. His hand moved inside her jeans.

Molka sat up and grabbed his hand.

"Do you want me to stop?" he said.

Molka captured Aden's eyes. "It's been a long time since I've…you know…with a man."

"I understand." He kissed her neck. "I'll be gentle."

"No, it's not that. It's…please don't ever lie to me. I know it's not fair for me to ask. But promise you won't lie to me."

"Of course," Aden said. "I haven't lied to you yet."

Molka squeezed his hand hard. "Promise me."

"I won't lie to you."

Molka squeezed his hand harder. "Promise me."

Aden kissed her forehead. "I promise."

Molka released Aden's hand and lay back.

Aden exhaled. "Incredible. You ok?"

Molka exhaled. "To put it mildly."

"I think I pulled both my groin muscles."

Molka glowed. "You're welcome."

"I'm dehydrated too. My water bottle's in my backpack. Go grab it for me?"

"No way. I'm too comfortable. Grab it yourself."

He rose and walked nude through the fire lit darkness to his backpack. He retrieved his water bottle and sat and chugged it on the blanket next to Molka. "If you were my wife, you would've fetched this for me."

"Wrong," Molka said. "This girl doesn't fetch for anyone."

"No, I suppose you wouldn't." Aden toasted Molka and chugged more.

She rolled onto her side and propped her head on her hand. "Have you ever been married?"

"No."

"Why not?"

"There have been a lot of women. But never the right one. Have you ever been married?"

Molka took the water bottle from Aden and sipped. "No."

"Why not?"

"There was only one man. But he wasn't the right one."

Aden slipped back into the sleeping bag and took Molka into his arms. "So if we got married, we would live in Tel Aviv."

"We would live in Haifa."

"We'll live in Tel Aviv but have a vacation home in Haifa."

"Beachfront?" Molka said.

"Naturally."

Molka nodded. "I can work with that."

"And we'll have a Persian cat named Avro."

"No. We'll have a Boston Terrier named Shakespeare."

"And our first born will be a beautiful son named Zeke."

"No. Our first born will be a strong daughter named Dava."

"How about this?" Aden said. "Our first born will be strong beautiful fraternal twins, Zeke and Dava."

"That would be so adorable."

"And every Sunday morning, we'll sleep late, then head over to—"

"Café Jarrod for smoothies," Molka said.

"Yes! You see? Our marriage would be perfect!"

"Yes. It would be perfect."

They kissed with perfect passion.

"You really like my secret place?" Aden said.

"I do."

"Then we need a code word for it."

"You mean a secret code word only you and I will know?"

"Yeppers. Something we can use freely on campus. And I just thought of the perfect one: Café Jarrod West."

"That's three words," she said.

"Code phrase then."

"Café Jarrod West. Sounds good to me."

"Cool," Aden squirmed, boy-like. "Wait, I thought of something even better. All you have to do is say, 'I miss the smoothies at Café Jarrod West' to me, and that will mean you want to meet me here at high noon the next day. Got it?"

Molka smiled. "You're so silly."

"No. I'm being serious. Repeat and define the code phrase."

"Ok. Code phrase: I miss the smoothies at Café Jarrod West. It means I want you to meet me here at high noon the next day."

"Good." He smiled. "You can say it to me right now for real if you want."

Molka turned away from his silly face and pondered into the fire. "I'm leaving Hazlehurst."

"You're leaving?"

"Yes."

"When?" Aden said.

"Very soon."

"I don't want you to leave. When is very soon?"

"Before the end of the month," she said.

"Why are you leaving?"

"Because I don't belong here." Molka locked her eyes onto Aden's and took his hands into hers. "And neither do you. I want you to come with me."

"Where are you going?"

"Home."

"Home?"

"Yes," she said. "It's time to go home."

"You mean your home?"

"It can be your home too. Just like you wanted as a boy."

Aden rose again, walked to the hill's edge, picked up a stone, and tried to skip it on the river. The night hid the result. "Like I told you, I left behind some hard feelings there."

"Did you commit some kind of heinous crime?"

"No, I didn't commit a heinous crime. I...no one got hurt by what I did."

"Ok," Molka said. "And like I told you, we're a very forgiving people."

"I know this."

"They've probably already forgiven you and are desperate for you to come back. Let's go home."

"Well, I'd like to leave here." He returned to the blanket and stood over Molka. "I feel I'm ready to leave. I haven't felt lost in a while."

"Then come with me."

"What about my work?"

"Finish it when we get back home," she said.

"Principal Darcy expects me to finish it here. She's going to be deeply disappointed if I tell her I'm leaving. Plus, I signed an agreement. She'll hold me to it."

Molka kicked from the sleeping bag and stood nude before Aden. "Easy fix. Don't tell her you're leaving."

He gave a bark of sarcastic laughter. "No one comes or goes without her knowledge."

"There's a way around that too."

"I don't see one."

"I have friends with a helicopter," Molka said. "I can contact them. They'll come at night, pick us up, and fly us to Vancouver."

Aden's smile was dubious. "You have friends with a helicopter who will just fly in and sneak us out of here?"

Her face hardened.

"You're serious?" he said.

"I arranged it when I took this job. In case the extreme isolation freaked me out and I needed to get out of here fast with no questions asked."

Aden shook his head. "It sounds outrageous." He deliberated Molka's solemnness. "On the other hand, you've shown you're capable of the outrageous."

"Believe me. I can make it happen."

"When could you make it happen?"

"Anytime you're ready," she said. "Sooner is better though."

"Principal Darcy is coming to see me tomorrow. She worries about me. She counts on me. She needs me. She's had a hard life, you know."

Molka embraced Aden. "I know Darcy has her demons. Bad ones. And I feel sorry for her too. But she has to face them on her own."

"I feel I should be here for her."

"You don't owe her endless loyalty."

"I actually owe her a lot," he said.

"She's using you."

"How do you mean?"

"I mean…she's using your serious research to give her phony school legitimacy."

"You don't understand. Before I met Principal Darcy, I was… You see, after my mother died, everything…" Aden turned away. "It's hard to explain."

"No explanations necessary." Molka put her arms around Aden from behind and rested her head on his shoulder. "I only want you to leave with me."

"Can I think about it? Just for a little while, Molka baby?"

Molka kissed the back of Aden's head. "Yes, darling. But just for a little while."

CHAPTER 28

On the drive through campus in Darcy's forest green Range Rover, Besnik struggled to keep his eyes on the road. Passenger Darcy lured his side glances in a white pure silk Armani pantsuit and Clive Christian No 1.

Darcy's question interrupted his distraction. "Do you remember the reason I insisted the pedestal of my statue contain a vault with a secure door?"

"Yes," Besnik said. "It would eventually serve as a Hazlehurst Institute time capsule to be opened 100 years after your death. I thought that was very forward-thinking of you."

"Turns out it was even more forward-thinking than I planned, wasn't it?"

"Yes, Darcy."

"I asked Aden to do this job right after the mercenary incident, but he didn't want to. So, he procrastinated and made excuses. But I finally got his mind right."

"What did you offer as an incentive?"

Darcy smiled sly. "I sent him a message saying if he didn't finish it by week's end, I would turn his workshop-playroom into a Doctor Thomas Moore Memorial Lounge for the Friends."

"Brilliant, Darcy."

"And what did the colonel say when you informed him of this little endeavor?"

"He did not say anything."

"I wish he had," she said. "Unlike most men, he's more dangerous when he doesn't open his mouth."

"I wonder if it was a good idea to tell him at all."

"It was. Because he'll believe we showed him respect by keeping him in the loop—which makes him less likely to ask questions. Even though he's a wanted war criminal, he still sees himself as an honorable soldier who deserves respect."

Besnik smiled his toad smile. "You always uncover the exploitable weakness, Darcy."

"When you explain to Aden what the Doomsday Scenario is, and the other modification it requires him to make, tell him it's just a loyalty test."

"Do you think he will be receptive to that?"

Darcy admired the Hazlehurst crest over the school's front gate. "I'll make sure he's receptive."

Besnik drove through the gate, proceeded to the river crossing bridge, and backtracked to the Darcy statue. The hill mounting the statue and the immediate area around it had been landscaped with manicured grass and hedges. Twin green benches flanked the memorial, but rather than face the obvious scenic campus view across the river, they were angled for the sitters to look up at Darcy's towering face.

Besnik parked in a small, paved lot behind the pedestal next to a security SUV. Owen reclined in the SUV's driver seat with his cap covering his eyes.

Besnik and Darcy exited the Range Rover. Darcy waited and watched Besnik remove a black metal briefcase from the backseat.

"I'll be right in," Darcy said.

The pedestal's steel door—with a keypad mounted beside it—sat open. Besnik headed inside.

Darcy moved to the SUV and knuckle tapped Owen's shoulder. "Keeping yourself vigorous, virile, and potent, soldier boy?"

Owen lifted his cap brim and grinned. "You know it, queenie."

180

"I never did ask how you and Aden are getting along."

"Great. He treats me like a first-class watch dog. And we're becoming real close too. He even told me all about his life."

"What did he tell you?" Darcy said.

"He told me he grew up a rich boy spoiled by his mommy and how he lived in rich boy mansions and went to rich boy schools and how he laid hot women who only laid for rich boys."

"What did you say to all that?"

"I told him about how seven of us lived in a three-room shit-shack. That being my old man and me and my five brothers. My momma was there too, until she had enough and ran off with a trucker. And I told him we were on the hand-me-down plan for clothes. And by the time they got handed down to me, since I was the youngest, the clothes were six years old. And how the kids in school all laughed about that and called me poor white trash. And I told him I never had my own bed or three meals a day until I joined the Army."

"And what did he say to all that?" Darcy said.

"He just said, 'Guess it pays to be rich.'"

"Well, maybe you'll get your rich reward someday soon?"

Owen grinned. "I'm already spending it as we speak."

Darcy entered the fluorescent lit twenty-by-twenty-by-ten-foot pedestal vault. A tool belt wearing Aden—with safety goggles over his glasses—worked on a control panel mounted on the right-hand wall. Besnik waited with the black briefcase next to the space's central dominant feature: a gray refrigerator-sized safe.

"This is it?" Darcy said. "As much as I paid, and it doesn't even have a dial or a handle."

"Those were my specifications to the manufacturer," Aden said.

"Ok, smartacus, explain to us how it all works. And use simple language this poor dumb little old girl from Mississippi can understand."

Aden perched the safety goggles and his regular glasses atop his head and moved to the safe. "All of the students' and vital staff members' Personal Security Drones are secured inside the safe. To deploy them, you must first enter a PIN on the keypad outside to gain entry to the pedestal. Then enter the same PIN on

181

this keypad." He stepped to the digital keypad mounted on the wall. "This will unlock and open the safe and lock open the pedestal door."

Besnik raised a hand. "Why would the pedestal door need a lock-open feature?"

"To guard against an accidental or intentional closure, which would prevent the drones from exiting."

"And what if someone blocked the door opening in some way?"

"I embedded a small explosive charge in the wall next to the door. A separate code will blow open a one-meter in diameter opening, which will be sufficient to gain entry and for the drones to exit by."

"He thought of everything." Darcy smiled. "I approve."

Aden smiled. "Thank you. I hoped you would."

"Please continue," Besnik said.

Aden continued, "Once you're inside and have opened the safe and secured open the door, each PSD can be activated and deployed to locate the person it's assigned to by simply entering the individual's unique code number on the keypad. And as you instructed, the PSDs can also be deployed all at once as a swarm using a master code. But you still haven't told me why you wanted that particular feature."

"Where are the PIN and deployment code numbers?" Besnik said. "And how were they determined?"

"Randomly generated by computer." Aden reached into the main pouch on his tool belt and removed a white laminated card. "This is the only copy."

"I'll take that," Darcy said.

Aden handed her the card. "Principal Darcy, I wanted to tell you…I mean, I wanted to ask you. I've been thinking about my future."

"What future?"

"My future after Hazlehurst. And getting back to a normal life."

"What normal life?" she said. "You told me you were miserable in normal life."

"Yes, I was. However, I feel I'm ready to give it another try."

Darcy sighed. "There's a deadline coming in less than three weeks that's not going to wait for you, me, or the big bad bear in the tree. I don't have time to discuss nonsense right now. And neither do you. You've got too much work to do for me." She turned to Besnik. "Give him the list."

Besnik reached into his jacket pocket and removed and handed Aden a printed list of names.

"What's this?" Aden said.

Besnik opened the black metal briefcase. Inside, black padding surrounded 20 individual compartments. "Principal Darcy would like the Personal Security Drones of the individuals on that list placed in this case. She would also like them to be made reprogrammable and activated and deployed using a separate portable device."

"For what purpose?" Aden said.

"Are these modifications possible?" Besnik said.

"I asked for what purpose?" Aden said.

Darcy's arms lowered to her sides with fists clenched, and she smiled. "For my purpose, Aden."

"I don't see the need to—"

Darcy stamped her high heel. "I instruct! You listen!"

Besnik and Aden recoiled.

The outburst echoed within the vault.

Darcy recomposed herself. "I consider all the people on that list essential to the operation of this school." She pointed at the black briefcase. "That's the Black Night Case. A Black Night is a major emergency like we had recently. This case will always be in my possession. So, if there's ever another threat from outsiders, I can deploy these drones more quickly to locate my key people and hopefully avoid a total disaster. My PSD will be used by Dean Besnik if something happens to me."

"Once again," Besnik said. "Brilliant, Darcy."

Aden reexamined the list.

"You should be honored," Darcy said. "Your name is third from the top, right after me and Dean Besnik."

Aden kept his eyes on the list.

"Are you honored I consider you third most important?"

"Of course, Principal Darcy."

"I wonder if you really do, though? Because sometimes it seems you don't appreciate everything I've done for you."

Aden's eyes popped from the list. "But I do, Principal Darcy. I really do."

"Well, I'm still not convinced. Can you make these modifications, or do I need to find another more appreciative student who can?"

Aden's eyes begged. "No, Principal Darcy. I can do it, Principal Darcy."

"Good boy." Darcy patted Aden's shoulder. "And good boys get rewarded. And your reward is coming very soon." She moved to the door. "Now Dean Besnik wants to talk to you about another serious scenario and one more modification these drones will require. Keep being a good boy and listen and do exactly what he says."

 **CHAPTER 29**

Five full days.

No.

Five full days and half a sixth day since Aden had talked to her.

Molka walked "Death Watch" laps around Building A retracing steps and thoughts.

After their night together outside the walls, they had bonded on more than a carnal level.

Hadn't they?

And they had planned to meet the next day for a run on the track and lunch in the cafeteria, but he hadn't shown for either.

She had observed Aden leave his loft that morning—and the previous five mornings—get into an SUV driven by Owen and exit the Security Zone. She had waved at him a few times. But he had paid her no attention.

What was that about?

She never would've figured him as a "hit it and forget it" type guy. He gave off a sensitive and a little needy vibe.

Ok. He didn't owe her anything after what they had done together. It was what it was. It was great. But it was what it was. She was a big girl. She knew what she had allowed to happen.

And it wasn't like another betrayal either. The deep betrayable feelings hadn't taken root yet. She had only known him a little over three weeks.

Over three weeks gone already!

The Darcy calendar flew by fast.

Time to complete her task.

Time to hyper-focus.

Time to make a final plan.

Molka stopped, took out her binoculars, and viewed the Security Zone main gate.

Final plan step one: Wait for Aden to return, corner him, and press him for a decision on whether he would leave with her.

Willingly.

Owen and Aden returned to the Security Zone 40 minutes before the techs shift ended. Owen dropped Aden at the Red Zone gate. Molka waited for him beside the external staircase to his loft.

Aden approached; his dimples flattened by anxiety.

"What's wrong?" Molka said.

"Tell me how you're going to do it?" Aden said.

"Do what?"

"Get us out of here."

"Ok. First I'll—"

"No. Let's go upstairs. I need a smoothie."

Molka embraced Aden in his kitchen. "I'm so happy you decided to leave with me, darling."

Aden pulled her arms off him. "I haven't decided yet. I want to hear your plan first."

He started preparing the smoothies.

Molka sat on a stool and viewed a black metal briefcase sitting on the counter's end. "Hmm. I figured you as more of a vintage weathered messenger bag man."

"What's your plan?"

"It starts with you spending every night from now on with me in my room."

"A great start."

"It's not all fun and games," she said. "It's about getting Owen used to the idea of you being away from the Security Zone at night and safe and sound with me. My room is also where we'll be leaving from."

"Makes sense. And he won't have a problem with it. When could we leave?"

"What's today? I lose track of the days here."

"Everyone does," he said. "It's Monday."

"We could go early Thursday morning."

"How early?"

"I've noticed from late-night prowling that the last lights go out in the student and staff dorms by around 1:30AM. The fewer nosy eyes awake the better. So I'll contact my friends with the helicopter at 2:00 AM and—"

"Wait, how are you going to contact them?"

"They prefer to keep those details confidential," Molka said. "Is that ok with you?"

"Not really. But go on."

She spoke up over the blender whine. "I'll contact them at 2:00 AM. They need 20 minutes to get ready and then it's a 48-minute flight here. My friends are very punctual, but let's give them five minutes leeway either way and assume they'll land in the central courtyard between 3:03 AM and 3:13 AM."

"And then what happens?"

"And then they fly us to Vancouver, and we go home."

"It's just that easy?" Aden said.

"Yes."

He shut off the blender, poured two smoothies, and passed one to Molka.

Molka took a big drink. "Mmm…excellent once again. I could drink one every day."

Aden started to drink his smoothie but set the glass back on the counter. "What am I thinking? I can't leave here."

"I told you, you don't owe Darcy anything. She's not your—"

187

"It's not just her," he said. "It's…I've done something horrible. I've made a huge mistake. I've created something very dangerous here. It's more than dangerous, it's…it's evil. No. It's beyond evil. It's…I'm sorry, I can't leave with you."

"Yes, you can. And you must."

Aden closed his eyes. "No. No, I won't. It's totally out of the question. I can't leave what I've done behind for others to exploit."

"I know you can't," Molka said. "And we won't."

Aden's eyes shot open. "You know something…what…what do you know?"

Molka knew her task had boxed itself into an unexpected and unplanned tipping point. And she knew what she was about to tell Aden would decide which way it would tip. And she knew if it tipped the wrong way, not only would he not leave with her, he couldn't leave the room. And she knew she didn't have time to go get the more humane .22 pistol she had chosen to do the unthinkable. And she knew what the nine-millimeter hollow point rounds in her service pistol did to a human skull at close range. And she knew she wished she didn't know so much.

Aden's eyes reflected dread. "Molka…what do you know?"

She stood, positioned herself between Aden and the loft's staircase, and let her right shooting hand hang free. "I know about the weaponized drones you designed. And I know a swarm of them are being built here. And I know Darcy plans to sell that swarm to a very bad individual. But I'm going to destroy all those drones before we leave. I'm going to destroy this whole building before we leave."

"How…you…" Aden's face bloomed with panic. "Oh no." He backed into the built-in stainless-steel oven door and froze. "Oh no. Who sent you?"

"I'm here to bring you home."

"Who sent you?"

"They just want you to come home."

Aden's face fell from fear to self-disgust. "For someone so smart…I sure do miss the obvious sometimes. But I only thought there was a remote chance they would send someone after me. And I didn't worry about it because I figured I would never see it coming anyway." He fixated on Molka's sidearm. "You came in plain sight though."

"I didn't come as an assassin, Aden."

"But if I don't agree to leave with you right now, you'll have to become one."

"Just promise you'll come home with me."

Aden viewed the kitchen clock. "I'm due on the production line in 20 minutes to inspect the techs' work. And if I don't show, Yeong will come here to get me. And if he found me assassinated, you would never make it out of here either. The colonel would see to that."

"Probably," Molka said.

"You're ready to sacrifice your life over this?"

"That's part of my job."

"And what happened between us the other night, was that part of your job too?"

"Yes," she said. "I mean, no. I mean, yes and no. It was part of my job to get you to leave with me by any means necessary. But no, what happened the other night wasn't part of my job. That was all me."

Aden unstuck his back from the oven door and slumped onto a counter stool. "I'm sorry this fell to you, Molka baby."

"I'm sorry too, darling." Molka moved behind Aden and laid her head on his shoulder. "But we don't have to worry about it anymore. Please come home with me."

"What happens when we get to Vancouver?"

"Someone will meet us and take us home."

"You know what's going to happen when they get me back, don't you?"

"All I know is what they told me," she said. "Our country won't be the first to use your technology as a weapon. But they need you to give it to us first so counter measures can be developed before our enemies eventually produce their own...slaughterbots."

"Same story they told me. Do you believe it?"

Molka spun Aden on the stool to face her. "I believe if you don't come home with me, terrible things will happen—one way or the other."

Aden's eyes drifted from Molka. "Once again, trapped in my own self-created hell. I just wish I could go back to the days when…" He exhaled, resigned, and refocused on Molka. "At least you and I can be together. Tell me the rest of your plan. How are you going to destroy this place?"

"After I signal for the helicopter, I'll disable the school surveillance."

"How?" he said.

"I'll figure it out at the time. Then I'll go to the armory and grab my favorite rocket launchers."

"You know how to use a rocket launcher?"

"Yes," Molka said. "I learned in the military. At 2:50 AM I'll put this building out of its misery and come meet you in the central courtyard."

"Two-fifty? You said your friends will arrive between 3:03 AM and 3:13 AM, right?"

"Right."

"You might not make it. It's at least a 15-minute fast jog from the Security Zone to the central courtyard."

"But it's only a 10 minute fast run for me. I timed it."

"Still cutting it close," Aden said.

"I wish I could cut it closer. When Building A goes down, it's going to be a long, tough 10 minutes."

"What do you mean?"

"I mean what's security's response going to be? I'm sure the colonel has a prepared response for an explosion and fire on campus. His orders will depend on what he believes is happening inside Building A. Does he know what's actually happening here?"

Aden shook his head. "I have no idea what he knows or doesn't know."

"Alright. Well, if he doesn't know, it will be a great distraction for us by getting the security team to look the other way. They'll probably just wake up the school fire department, inform Darcy, and wait to see what's recoverable in a few days when the debris pile stops smoldering."

"And if he does know what's going on here?"

"That could be a problem." Molka moved onto a stool across from Aden. "The colonel might think they're under attack and look to counter. And he's renowned for the rapid ferocity of his counter attacks."

"Yes. Owen told me about the legend of the Red Wolf. Ok, best case scenario, you destroy Building A, the security team is distracted, we meet in the central courtyard and just hope no one notices or hears a helicopter landing dead center of campus."

"My friends will approach very low from the opposite direction of Building A. If we get lucky, we'll be out while security's backs are still turned. My friends will also be using a special helicopter with noise suppression."

"Noise suppression." Aden allowed an approving nod. "Nice touch by your friends."

"My friends' helicopter is not the helicopter I'm worried about though. It's the possibility of Narcisse's beastly gunship chasing down our tail that really scares me."

Aden frowned. "I forgot about that gunship. What are you going to do about it?"

"There's nothing I can do," Molka said. "The airport is on the opposite side of the campus from Building A. I won't have time to get over there, take it out, and get back."

"Could you disable it the night before?"

"No. Narcisse plays cards at the airport with the aircraft maintenance guys every night until at least midnight. Sometimes later. Can't risk it."

Aden perched his glasses atop his head. "How about at the same time you're taking care of Building A, I sneak into the airport and disable the gunship's avionics. I can do it quickly and quietly and then run back to meet you in time to—"

"No way," Molka said. "Too dangerous. I can get caught. I'm expendable, but you're not. Which brings me to this: If for some reason I don't make it to the courtyard when my friends arrive because something happened to me or I got held up or I'm holding someone up or whatever, promise me you'll get on that helicopter."

"I'll get on it and tell them to wait."

"They're not going to wait."

Aden stood and paced the loft's length twice, returned to the counter, and surrendered his eyes to Molka. "This is a lot to unpack. It's unreal and confusing and frightening."

Molka stood and put her arms around Aden. He laid his head on her breast. She stroked his head. "Just leave it to me. Everything will work out, darling."

CHAPTER 30

"You say this was the first time she's ever rode in a helicopter?" the young flight instructor said.

"That is correct," Azzur said.

Both stood on the private flight school's tarmac watching Laili. She sat in the pilot's seat of a Robinson R22 training helicopter and tinkered with the controls and instruments.

The instructor shook his head. "Her questions and understanding were well beyond a beginner."

"She has studied the flight training manual," Azzur said.

"For how long?"

"I gave it to her last night after dinner. She gave it back to me at breakfast and said, it's easily simple."

"Amazing," the instructor said. "Is she an avid gamer? Flight simulation games, I mean?"

"Not to my knowledge."

"Amazing."

Azzur lit a cigarette. "If I give you access to her for unlimited hours for the next week, can you teach her to fly solo?"

"That would be a substantial additional charge."

"Understood," Azzur said. "But can it be done?"

"With unlimited access to her time, it shouldn't be a problem. I believe you have a genius on your hands."

"When can she begin?"

"Now," the instructor said. "But I have one more question. She's gorgeous. And flirtatious. Is she single?"

Azzur pointed his cigarette's lit end at the instructor's face. "That part of her you do not have access to."

PROJECT MOLKA: TASK 3
WEDNESDAY, AUGUST 21ST
12 DAYS TO COMPLETE TASK

CHAPTER 31

"**Y**ou're going to make me late for work again." Aden pointed to 7:09 AM on Molka's nightstand alarm clock. "Second time this week."

Molka rolled off Aden and smiled. "Last time this week."

Aden smiled back. "Right. By this time tomorrow, we'll be wide awake and unemployed in Vancouver."

"We're not there yet. We have to get through today and tonight first. So once again, do and say and act as you normally would."

"Yes, mommy."

Molka punched his arm. "Get serious."

Aden sat with his back against the headboard. "It's been fun playing house these last few days, hasn't it? We get along great and make each other laugh, don't we?" He lifted the sheet exposing their nude bodies. "We would make a hot-looking couple too, wouldn't we? And you're in your prime childbearing years, aren't you? So, if we were to get married and start a family, now would be the optimal time, right? I mean, what did I say wrong?"

"I haven't disagreed with anything you said."

Because she couldn't.

Molka left the bed, put on a long tee shirt, entered her bathroom, washed her face, and brushed her teeth.

Aden called to her, "I can't decide what I want to do first when we get back to civilization, check all my social media or binge watch my favorite show, *Conflict of Kingdoms*. What about you? What's the first thing you want to do?"

"I'd love to see some of the new summer movies I've missed."

Molka's mirror reflection looked at a liar.

The first thing she wanted to do in Vancouver is make an unannounced return visit to Darcy's penthouse. And easy way or hard way, Darcy would give her the information she needed. And right after, she would go straight for the one she needed to kill.

And Aden would understand, wouldn't he? *Where have I been, darling? I went to kill the one who murdered my little sister, Janetta. But everything is ok now. And who's Azzur? I used to work for him. Well, I still do, but I'm quitting. No, he told me I couldn't quit yet. But I'll deal with him. What? Yes, I really killed the one who killed my little Janetta. No, nothing is bothering me anymore. Yes, I'm ok now. Why wouldn't I be ok?*

Knock.

Knock.

Knock.

Knock.

Someone at the front door.

"Expecting company?" Aden said.

Molka stepped from the bathroom. "No."

"Hope it's not your crazy ex."

"Me too," she said.

"Was your ex crazy?"

"Yes. In a sane sort of way."

Knock.

Knock.

Knock.

Knock.

"It's probably Owen," Aden said and bounced from the bed. "Tell him I'm in the shower and I'll meet him downstairs in 15 minutes, Molka baby."

"Ok, darling."

Aden went into the bathroom and shut its door.

Knock.

Knock.

Knock.

Knock.

Molka pulled on sweatpants and moved close to the front door. "First sergeant?"

An Italian accented female voice answered. "No. Valentina."

"Who?"

"Valentina."

"I don't know a Valentina," Molka said.

"You do know Valentina."

"Maybe you have the wrong room. I don't know a Valentina."

"Everyone knows Valentina."

"I'm sorry, I don't know a Valentina." Molka unlocked and opened the door to a tall stunning woman. She carried a shoulder bag with a little white-faced Maltese peeking from the end. "Oh. Wow. You're *that* Valentina."

The woman forced a sarcastic smile. "Yes, *that* Valentina."

Molka's face fell star struck. "I loved your TV show."

"Everyone did."

"Oh. Wow. Are you a student here?"

"No," Valentina said. "I am here for Aden."

"Aden?"

"Yes. Tell him I am here."

"Aden?"

"Yes. Go tell him. I can hear him in the shower."

"Do you know Aden?" Molka said.

Valentina's smile turned smug. "I should. I am his fiancée."

CHAPTER 32

Valentina looked just like she did on TV.

Just like on TV, she rocked her signature ensemble: a tight pink leather jacket, even tighter pink leather bell bottom pants, and pink velvet high heels. And just like on TV, she carried a white leather designer shoulder bag holding her adorable Maltese named Principe.

Yes. With her statuesque, impossibly perfect body, long, shiny brown hair, big brown eyes, and smooth olive skin, she looked just like the former Miss Italy, former Miss Universe, former world's top model, and former star of *It's Valentina's World: Deal With It!*, that Molka had seen on TV.

No. That wasn't quite true.

In person she looked even more spectacular.

Azzur said that when Aden had abandoned their country, he also abandoned his world-class fiancée. And it appeared his world-class fiancée had come half-way around the world to reclaim him.

Valentina used Molka's astonishment paralysis to brush past her, enter the bathroom, and shut the door behind her. Before Molka could object, a submachine gun with Owen strapped to it stepped into the room and moved between Molka and the bathroom door.

Owen relished Molka's perplexity. "Stay at ease, doc. We'll be gone shortly."

The bathroom door opened, Valentina stepped out, gathered Aden's clothes from the chair next to the bed, and took them back into the bathroom.

Owen grinned at Molka. "Whoo-damn. Stings, don't it?"

Molka's eyes dropped to the floor.

"What?" Owen said. "No smart-ass remarks for me this morning? Well, guess it's kinda hard to talk shit when you get blindsided right in the teeth."

Good point. But her silence came from confusion. Had she failed her task by losing her man or lost her man by failing her task?

The bathroom door opened again.

Valentina led Aden out by the hand.

Aden didn't make eye contact with Molka.

They exited Molka's room.

Owen followed.

The colonel appeared in the doorway a second later. "Good morning, lieutenant who drives truck."

"Good morning, sir," Molka said.

"Security personnel are now forbidden to fraternize with students."

"Yes, sir."

"You are also being reassigned from the Red Zone to general campus security. Report to the first sergeant at 1900 hours to receive instructions on your new duties."

"Yes, sir."

"There is one other thing." The colonel's adamant blue eyes yielded a tick. "I do not wish you to consider these new orders as a personal reprimand from me."

"I understand, sir. Thank you, sir."

The colonel turned and left.

Molka moved to close her door.

Darcy's face peeped around the door frame. "I heard you got caught with a boy in your dorm room. Oh, you naughty, naughty girl." Her face twinkled. "I'm one to talk though. In my college days, the boys would bump into each other sneaking in and out of my room."

Darcy invited herself in wearing a playful—but tasteful— knee-length black leather skirt and a gray sleeveless cashmere top. She sat on the bed and patted for Molka to sit beside her.

Molka sat.

Darcy curled her arm around Molka. "How are you doing, doll?"

"Great," Molka said. "I only wish I read the personal privacy section of my contract closer. Who's coming in my room next, the entire student body one by one in alphabetical order?"

"I apologize for the dramatics, but the shock, pain, and embarrassment of this moment will make you never want to see Aden again."

"No problem. Like you said before, I'm just a lonely girl a long way from home desiring some warm company. I was about finished with him anyway."

Darcy smiled. "You can't con a conner. But I also told you he wasn't for you. A week after he got here, he started begging me to let her come join him. It was Valentina this and Valentina that. I refused because I wanted him to focus on his recovery and on his work. Then you arrived, and he stopped talking to me about Valentina. He started talking about leaving and a life after this school. He's not ready to leave though. He's still a very troubled boy. So, I did what's best for him and for the good of Hazlehurst."

"And when you say for the good of Hazlehurst, you mean you." Molka stood, crossed the room, and took a position beside the still open door. "I didn't know you viewed me as such a threat."

"It's not so much you're a threat; it's just that pink piece of Italian trash isn't in your league as a woman. She'll take care of his manly needs without making him think so much."

Molka folded her arms and leaned against the door frame. "You brought her all the way here to see to his manly needs? They have a name for those kinds of women."

Darcy shrugged. "I don't judge a girl on how she makes her living. But she'll earn her keep here in other ways too. She's recently expanded into a singing career. I've made her head of the Department of Music, and she's agreed to put on a concert for the entire school."

"Should be great."

Darcy laughed. "You haven't heard her sing yet. But my entertainment-starved students won't mind."

Darcy rose, approached Molka with empathy, and took both her hands. "I truly hope this doesn't end our sistership, doll. It means more to me than you know."

"Don't think of it." Molka squeezed Darcy's tiny, soft hands. "I've already stowed this situation in the irrelevant bin."

"That's my brave girl. I'm moving into the dean's residence for the foreseeable future to spend more time on campus. So, promise me we'll get together and have another sister-to-sister talk."

Molka smiled. "Yes. Another sister-to-sister talk is definitely what we need to have. And we'll have it very soon. I promise."

CHAPTER 33

When a conspiracy is exposed, a co-conspirator is often hated even more than the original conspirator. A conspirator must be given at least some grudging respect for having the brains and/or the guts to take a bold action. The co-conspirator, on the other hand, is loathed and resented as a shifty opportunist seeking full rewards for half efforts. Therefore, the co-conspirator can receive a much harsher and more vicious punishment.

That theory—as explained to her by a notorious co-conspirator one night in Cyprus—made Molka fairly certain Aden hadn't told anyone about her true identity, her purpose for being there, or her plan to sneak him out.

Or maybe he just cared about her.

Still, she waited in her room all day expecting to be taken on a one-way permanent field trip.

At 1900 hours, Molka reported to Owen at security HQ. Her new assignment to general campus security meant she would take over night watch. Owen gave one standing order for her new duties: "Anyone trying to get in, shoot 'em and call me. Anyone trying to get out, call me and I'll come shoot 'em."

Owen's improbable scenarios aside, night watch involved driving security cart laps on the gravel path running inside the school's perimeter wall from 8 PM to 8 AM.

Molka started her new duty, and the previous boredom level sank to a brutal new low. After two full school circuits, she needed a monotony pause. She parked outside the classroom-administration building and climbed into the bell tower. The nights had grown cooler, and a fall preview wind swished through the campus trees and prompted her to zip her fleece uniform jacket to the neck.

She stepped to the north-facing belfry opening. No lights shone in Aden's third-floor loft. The happy reunited, couple had bedded down for the night.

Aden hadn't lied to her. Besides the one question about ever being married, they had never gotten around to talking about their past relationships—or still pending fiancées. But how could he walk away from her without saying a word? Yes, his bio said he walked away from many women all over the world. Even so, she wasn't just another woman to him, was she?

It hurt less than when she had found out her American captain was married. But for some inexplicable reason, not a lot less.

No time to ponder personal angst though.

The Darcy calendar above her bed indicated only 12 days left to complete her task.

Only 12 days!

Which meant she had worked on it for 26 days and was no closer to completing it than the day she had arrived. If anything—after the Valentina setback—she was farther away.

Only 12 days?

She might not be able to do it if she had 112!

Ha. But she could imagine Azzur's response to her complaints:

Our country famously won a major war in just six days. You have 12 days to escort one mild-mannered man a few hundred meters across a quiet, scenic campus and put him on a helicopter, destroy one undefended soft-target building, and obtain a single name and location from a petite former elementary school Principal. Twelve days are more than ample time to complete your task, and your excuses are less than unacceptable.

And he would have been right.

So within the next 12 days, she would obliterate Building A and end the slaughterbot threat. And Aden would get on the extraction helicopter, one way or the other. And if his famous fiancée tried to intervene, Molka would make her sorry she had. And the prissy prima donna shouldn't take her beating personally; it would be strictly task related. Personal jealousy would have nothing to do with it. Alright. Maybe personal jealousy would sneak in an extra elbow or knee.

And then she would go see Darcy.

But those would be the easy parts. As she had discussed with Aden, success or failure hinged on the security team's response to Building A's destruction. Good probability the initial shock and confusion would keep their backs turned long enough for the extraction helicopter to get in undetected. Getting out presented a much more difficult dilemma though.

Would the colonel's situational awareness switch from a probable industrial accident to a possible attack and cause him to turn around and spot an apparent hostile helicopter? And if so, would their sudden death by gunship be his fast response?

To plan a counter move, she needed more intel on the colonel's knowledge and mindset about Building A.

Molka's eyes fell from Aden's loft to the security HQ. The light in the colonel's office window confirmed another solitary drinking night. A latrine break would be her excuse to speak with him. You had to walk right by his always open office door to reach it.

She didn't really have to go, but with only 12 days left, she really had to get going.

CHAPTER 34

"More and more I find the rough edges this smooths at night only return even more jagged in the morning," the colonel said and downed a shot. He braced back, bleary-eyed, but not drunk, into his office chair. His right hand curled around an engraved shot glass; his left hand curled around a half-empty, blue-labeled vodka bottle.

Molka sat at attention across from his desk. He waved her in—as she had hoped he would—when she passed his office door on the way out from her staged latrine visit.

"Lieutenant who drives truck, I asked you in here to give me a current status report on campus security. But first, will you join me in a drink?"

"No thank you, sir," Molka said.

"You do not indulge?"

"Occasionally, but in my army, taking a shot of alcohol while on duty was cause for dismissal."

"As it was in my army," the colonel said. "Nevertheless, this rule was often selectively enforced." He poured and downed another shot. "Thankfully."

"Yes, sir."

"By the way you conspicuously passed my door, you wish to speak with me too. And with you now sitting before me, I can see you are troubled on this beautiful, gloomy night. However, if your discontent stems from a broken heart, I cannot be of any assistance."

"No, sir," she said. "I actually have a question about you. If I may ask?"

"Ask your question."

"That morning in the gymnasium when you introduced me to your team members, you made it a point to tell me each one's— less than stellar—background."

"And you wish to know why?" the colonel said.

"I think I know why."

"Why?"

"I told you I served in the IDF," Molka said. "An organization you are familiar with and respect. And from that respect, you wanted me to know you don't approve of the men Dean Besnik has brought in to serve under you."

"I will not say I agree with you. I will also not say I disagree. Now what is your real question?"

Molka sat even straighter for effect. "If you don't approve of them, why tolerate them? And if I may, sir, why did you even take this posting? Security chief of a fake school? I'm familiar with some of your operations. I learned you are both a brilliant tactical and strategic thinker. But above all, a soldier who always upholds the highest standards of professionalism and personal honor."

The colonel's adamant blue eyes softened, and his thin lips yielded a slight smile. "I thank you for your compliment." He poured and downed another shot. "During your service with the transportation unit, did you ever see any combat?"

"Yes, sir."

"Good. You are familiar with my operations; have you also heard of the alleged, *Schoolboys Massacre* for which the international war crimes tribunal seeks to find me?"

"No, sir."

Another shot poured and downed. "My experience in the North Caucasus conflict was that of a war of mutual degradation. The lines of acceptable military conduct were at first strictly adhered to. Then occasionally crossed. Then frequently blurred. Then completely erased. Many good men became bad men, and many bad men became monsters."

"During a difficult operation outside a small village, my unit sustained two dead and eight severely wounded. Remoteness of the location and foul weather prevented the immediate evacuation of the wounded. However, I was ordered to continue with the mission. We had friendly relations with the people in this village, so we left the wounded in the care of a local woman trained as a nurse. We…I trusted her."

"When we returned to the village two days later, it was abandoned. We found the bodies of our wounded stacked in the village market. All beheaded. Their severed heads were arranged next to their bodies to form the shape of an inverted triangle—to resemble our unit's shoulder patch. They were also castrated."

"We caught a boy hiding and watching us. This boy admitted his friends were responsible for the murder of our wounded, and he was to report back to them of our return so they might ambush us."

"Instead, he led us to his friends concealed in a school in the neighboring village. We surprised them and took them prisoner. But we did not find more boys. We found fanatical young men committed to ideological terrorism. And in the school, we did not find textbooks or blackboards or desks. We found automatic weapons and RPG's and mortars. And on a table, we found a trophy they kept—a jar containing the severed testicles of my men."

"I conducted a Field Court Martial to find the correct perpetrators. These *schoolboys* all proudly confessed to their war crimes. I accepted their confessions, pronounced sentence, and executed them in a much more dignified and humane manner than they afforded my men."

"Soon after, a corrupt press hears of this incident from corrupt mouths. They showed the world old pictures of these *schoolboys*—taken when they were schoolboys—to give the impression they were still schoolboys when I executed them. You can predict the reaction."

"This international war crimes tribunal says they only wish to question me. But they have already passed judgment and the cell in which I shall spend the rest of my life has been emptied."

"However, if righteous vengeance is what they consider a war crime, then I reject the legitimacy of this organization."

"You asked why I tolerate serving with such men as on my current team and why I would even accept a ludicrous position such as this. Because it is a term of my sanctuary here. Sanctuary I require until responsible men of honor will give me a fair accounting of my justifiable war-time actions."

The colonel poured another shot. "What do you say to my answer?"

Molka responded honestly. "I wasn't there, so I can't say I would have done the same thing as you under those circumstances. But I also don't consider honest vengeance a crime."

The colonel raised his glass to Molka. "Then we understand one another—warrior to warrior." He downed the shot with deference.

The mutual respect moment, while appreciated, opened the door to probe for needed intel. Molka pointed to Building A's dark form framed in the window behind the colonel. "Do you know what's going on in the research facility?"

"One would assume research."

"I heard a rumor before I came here—a rumor from highly credible sources—that weaponized advanced autonomous micro drones, with no known counter measures, are being manufactured there and will be sold in swarms of 50,000 to the highest bidders."

"A very troubling rumor if true," the colonel said.

"And what would you think if it was?"

"I would think weaponized advanced autonomous micro drone swarms, with no known counter measures, are not good for any country or any individual to possess."

Anxiety hid behind his understatement—an opening to push further. Molka pushed. "There have been times when my country thought it was of vital national interest to eliminate dangerous technological threats in foreign countries."

"You are, of course, talking about sabotage."

"Do you also have an opinion on that?"

The colonel capped the vodka bottle and placed it in the bottom desk drawer. "Yes, lieutenant who drives truck. I have a most definite opinion on sabotage. First I wish to hear what you would say to volunteering for a mission for me?"

"I would say it's been my experience when a commander asks you to volunteer for a mission—not only is it as good as an order—they've also already prepared a report for their commander on why it was your fault the mission failed."

The colonel's laughter boomed. "I am sitting with no fool tonight! But does this mean you are not interested?"

"What's the mission?"

The colonel removed a Hazlehurst ID badge from his top desk drawer and handed it to Molka. She viewed a younger Asian male wearing glasses.

"His name is Jun," the colonel said. "He was a tech working here and he shares your concerns about the activities in Building A. He expressed these concerns to the other techs. This came to Dean Besnik's attention, and he had the man brought to this office yesterday. He sat in the chair in which you sit. Dean Besnik informed him he was no longer needed here and—using me as an implied threat—told him it was in his best personal interests to never discuss Building A again."

"What happened to him?" Molka said.

"Dean Besnik told him he would be returned to the representatives from his employer in Asia. Jun said he does not wish this. He wishes instead to defect to this country. But these representatives of his employer—who are no more than paid guards—will not allow him to defect because he is in this country illegally and they fear he would incriminate his employer, who has smuggled in many such workers. Jun went on to say the techs were being held by these representatives during off-work hours at a motel in Vancouver. He named the motel for legitimacy. And when the representatives learned he was no longer employed here, he would be smuggled by them onto a private cargo aircraft owned by his employer and returned home to a sad fate."

Molka nodded. "If they don't just toss him out over the Pacific on the way there."

"A distinct possibility," he said. "For his part, Dean Besnik feigned ignorance and skepticism to Jun's claims and did indeed turn him over to these representatives yesterday evening."

"And I understand why," Molka said. "The last thing Dean Besnik wants is him defecting and telling the Canadian authorities about what's going on in Building A."

The colonel rubbed thick fingers on thick chin stubble. "That is a political matter, and I am only a simple soldier and do not wish to intervene in political matters. However, as one who has lived under—and seen—much repression, I think this man should be allowed to defect to this country."

"And my mission would be to help him?"

"Yes. I have obtained information his employer's private cargo aircraft is scheduled for departure from the Vancouver airport tomorrow at 1400 hours. Undoubtedly, Jun will be placed on it. Before this can occur, you will remove him from the motel he is being held in and take him to the local office of the Canadian National Police, where he may ask for his asylum."

"Does Jun speak any English?" she said.

"Principal Darcy insisted all the techs, like all the students and staff, speak English for her monitoring purposes."

Molka grimaced, embarrassed. "I should have figured. Sorry. And what do you know about these representatives holding him?"

"Nothing, except the penalties for human trafficking in this country are quite severe."

"A diplomatic way of saying they might kill anyone who tries to expose them."

"A judicious assumption," the colonel said.

"Ok. How will I get there?"

"You accept the mission?"

"Yes, sir," Molka said.

"Take an SUV. I will inform Security Officer Hamu I am sending you on a long-range patrol and he will open the gate for you. After you travel eight kilometers from the school, you will clear the internal jamming system and the SUV's GPS will function." The colonel wrote on a pad on his desk. "Here is the motel name Jun gave." He tore the paper from the pad and handed it to Molka.

It read, *The Pleasant Dragon Inn*

The colonel continued, "You will have to locate it and the room number Jun is being held in on your own." He pulled a thick envelope from another drawer and passed it to Molka. "Approximately 4,000 in Canadian currency—I insist on being paid with cash. Use it for any expenses and take his ID badge with you to identify him by."

"Yes, sir."

The colonel viewed his watch. "If you change clothes and leave now, you should be there in good time to plan and execute your mission."

Molka viewed her watch: 10:34 PM. "Yes, sir."

"Be advised, if you are captured or killed, I will disavow any knowledge of your actions."

"I understand, sir."

"This man Jun deserves a chance to be free. He has the gleam of honor in his eyes. Therefore, I consider you volunteering for the mission a great personal favor to me."

Molka stood. "I'll do my best, sir."

The colonel nodded. "Good hunting, lieutenant who drives truck."

She hesitated.

"Question?" the colonel said.

"Yes, sir. You didn't give me your opinion on sabotage?"

The colonel swiveled his chair around and viewed Building A again. "Sabotage is most often a political act. As I told you, I am only a simple soldier and do not wish to intervene in political matters."

Molka changed into a black mock turtleneck and black jeans. She restyled her hair from a bun into a high ponytail, with bangs swept across her forehead right to left to clear her aiming eye. She put her tac-boots back on, put her contacts in, and left her old pilot's watch on her left wrist.

Next, she removed a black tactical duffle bag from her luggage containing black leather tactical gloves. She unzipped it and added latex gloves taken from the veterinary office, her issued Steiner binoculars, and the .22 semi-automatic pistol with a suppressor she had lifted from the armory. She had chosen the .22 over her service Glock because a 20-year-old weapon from a country no longer in existence should be harder to trace if used. She hoped.

Molka returned to security HQ, chose the newest SUV in the inventory, topped off the fuel tank at the motor pool fuel pump, and raced for Hazlehurst's front gate.

Before reaching it, Azzur made her slam on the brakes.

What are you doing, Molka?

I'm going on a mission for the colonel, Azzur.

You have agreed to do a task within your task?

Yes.

You just complained about having only 12 days left to complete your task.

I know. But—

You should be making your final preparations.

I know. But the colonel asked me to volunteer, and when your commander asks you to volunteer for a mission—

I am aware of the implication. However, he is not your commander. I am.

I know. But the man he sent me to free is someone who spoke out about the slaughterbots. And the colonel also knows what's going on in Building A and disagrees with it and all but gave me his blessing to destroy it. I think the goodwill I'll earn for doing this favor for the colonel also assures he won't have an aggressive response to our extraction. So, this task within my task could be considered part of my final preparations. Don't you agree?

Just get our engineer back.

213

CHAPTER 35

Molka arrived in a cool, gray, misty, rain-coated Vancouver at 7:39 AM local time and rolled straight to a stop in rush hour traffic. No need to suffer it though. Jun's final flight didn't leave until 2 PM. So she could wait it out while getting something to eat and making her plan.

She exited, refueled, and pulled into a Jim Thorntons restaurant because she remembered Darcy pining to go there after their sisters' night out. The doughnut pics on the drive-thru menu looked yummy, but she opted for a more appropriate pre-mission breakfast: mixed berry oatmeal, orange juice, black coffee, and a bottled water.

Molka parked and inhaled her food with surprising ravenousness. Was she that hungry? Was it the best oatmeal she ever tasted? Or was it just good to be away from Hazlehurst and her task's crazy complications and have a straightforward mission with a clear and defined objective.

The GPS indicated that Jun's motel was located 14 kilometers south from the Canadian National Police's downtown headquarters. A right turn from the motel's parking lot, drive to the end of the block, a right onto Granville Street, and a straight shot due north would be the escape route.

A simple snatch-and-go operation.
She had participated in several with the Unit.
Should be no problem.

Across the Fraser River from the Vancouver International Airport, The Pleasant Dragon Inn deteriorated in a neighborhood slipping from working-class into ghetto. An off-brand car rental flanked one side and a homestyle eatery named Auntie Bernice's Diner flanked the other side.

At 9:17AM, Molka parked across the street in a shuttered strip mall and focused her binoculars on the two-level motel painted an uninteresting tan. She counted 20 room doors on each level and assumed the same layout on the opposite side, making 80 rooms total. The parking lot contained a few scattered cars and nine red passenger vans grouped together.

Two Asian women in white housekeeper uniforms stocked cleaning carts and chatted near the motel office.

How to find Jun's room? She couldn't call the motel and have them ring his room, could she? No. He might be a prisoner without phone privileges.

The housekeepers ended their conversation and pushed their carts in opposite directions. Housekeepers at small motels must know who and what's going on in every room, right? Maybe she could show them Jun's ID photo and some Canadian cash and…

Wait, who are they?

Three younger Asian males exited Auntie Bernice's Diner next door to the motel and headed toward it—two in black leather jackets flanked one in glasses, beige pants, and a blue windbreaker.

Is that him?

Molka compared Jun's ID badge photo to the middle man in the blue windbreaker.

Match.

Returning him to his room after breakfast? The condemned man's last meal? Go grab him? No. Too far away and too much traffic to cross. Never make it. Keep watching and get the room number.

Now what's she doing?

A blond woman chasing after the three men came into binocular view. She wore a red server apron with a white lettered *Aunt Bernice's Diner* logo on the front. The men stopped and turned. The woman handed one of the leather jacket guys a phone and returned to the diner.

He must have left his phone behind on the table and she returned it.

Nice gesture by her.

And telling about him.

Because a man who forgets his phone is a distracted man or a careless man.

The three men continued toward the motel in no hurry. Why didn't Jun try to run? He was out in the open. He might not get another chance. Afraid of getting shot in the back? Maybe. But better than what they had planned for him.

Well, hang on, Jun. I'll have your room number in a second and come get you.

The three men reached the motel and veered right.

Oh no!

The three men walked around to the motel's back side.

Darn it!

Impossible to see which room they went in.

Now what? Go door to door?

No. She would have to get more creative.

Think, Molka.

Molka drove to *Auntie Bernice's Diner,* entered, and made sure her server would be the same blond woman who returned the phone to Jun's captor.

Her nametag said *Randi.*

Molka's lie to Randi about how cute her non-existent Aunt Bernice would look in a red Auntie Bernice's Diner apron—and a

$100 tip—secured Randi's agreement to meet Molka behind the diner and give her an apron to take home.

Molka then drove around the area until she found a drugstore. She purchased cheap reading glasses which somewhat resembled the glasses Jun wore in his ID badge photo and drove back to the diner.

In the parking lot, she put on the Auntie Bernice's Diner apron, grabbed the reading glasses and Jun's ID, and walked to the motel. She located and approached one of the housekeepers beside her cart outside a ground-floor room. Time: 10:31 AM.

Molka falsified a smile. "Hello there."

"Hello," the housekeeper said.

Molka pointed at her apron. "I work next door. Jun left his glasses and ID on my table." She held them up for confirmation. "I wanted to personally make sure he got them back." She falsified another smile. "He's a great tipper. He's still in room 22, right?"

"I don't know who you talk about."

Molka showed her the ID again. "Jun. He's still in room 22?"

The housekeeper squinted at the photo. "Oh him. No. Room 57."

"Fifty-seven? Are you sure that's his room or his friend's room?"

"No. He always in 57. His friends just move into 58."

"Jun is in room 57," Molka said, "and his friends are in room 58. You're positive?"

"Yes, positive."

"And since they're friends, they're connecting rooms, right?"

The housekeeper sighed. "Yes, they are connecting rooms."

Molka legitimized her smile. "Thank you so much."

The housekeeper shook her head exasperated and went into the room.

Molka laid a small stack of 20s on her cart and headed back to the SUV.

217

Molka drove around again until she found a superstore, where she purchased a short sleeve white shirt, white slacks, and three white bath towels. She changed into the white shirt and slacks in the store bathroom and returned to the motel.

She located Jun's room 57 and his "friends'" room 58 on the second level and backed in next to the external staircase. She folded and stacked the three towels, removed and put on the black leather tactical gloves from her duffle bag, and pulled the latex gloves over those. Next, she slipped the .22 automatic behind her back, grabbed the towel stack, and exited the SUV with it still running.

She climbed the stairs, moved to room 58, and knocked. "Housekeeping. I have your clean towels."

A male voice inside answered. "We don't need towels. We're checking out today."

"Oh. Yes. You're checking out. I'm sorry. I meant to say, um, I have a gift. I mean, I'm dropping off your gift. Your parting gift, that is."

Pause.

"What's a parting gift?" the voice said.

"It's a nice little thank you present from the boss. For a job well done."

Pause.

The locked clicked, and the door opened to Jun's phone-forgetting escort. "Gift from the boss, you say?"

Molka pie faced him with the towel stack and shoulder-ploughed him back into the room and onto the bed. He cleared the towels from his face to find the door closed behind Molka and her .22 aimed at his head.

"Quiet cooperation or quick death," Molka said. "Choose now."

"Quiet cooperation," the man said.

"Hands on head. Interlace your fingers."

He complied.

"Stand up. Kiss the wall next to the dresser."

He complied.

She jammed the barrel into his back. "Where's your weapon?"

"Right jacket pocket."

Molka removed a Ruger nine-millimeter and tucked it in her waistband. "Where's your partner?"

"In the office, checking out."

"Where's Jun?"

He pointed at the connecting door into room 57.

"Move to the door."

He complied.

Molka opened the door. The connecting door on the other side sat open. She used the man as a human shield and pushed him into the room.

Jun jolted on the near-side twin bed and froze.

"You're Jun, right?" she said.

Jun nodded hesitant-affirmative.

"Ok. Stand up and step away from the bed."

Jun complied.

Molka addressed the man. "Have a seat on the bed. Keep your hands on your head."

He complied.

"You get to live if you close your eyes and count backwards from 50. Do it now."

The man closed his eyes. "Fifty, forty-nin—"

Molka's front kick to the head laid him sideways, asleep.

Jun scrambled into the corner. His eyes terrorized on the pistol and then Molka's face. "I know you. You're one of the Hazlehurst security officers. The colonel sent you to kill me!"

"Shhh!" Molka said. "No. The colonel sent me to free you so you can defect."

"Why would he do that?"

"Because he agrees with you about Building A, and so do I." Molka tucked her pistol behind her back and hid the man's pistol under the second bed. "Now let's go before his partner gets back and I really do have to kill someone."

She opened the room door and checked both ways. Clear. "Follow me."

She jogged with Jun jogging behind her downstairs and into the SUV.

"Where were you supposed to take me?" Jun said.

Molka verified Jun's face with his ID photo and typed into the GPS. "Downtown to the Canadian National Police headquarters. You're only…17 short minutes to freedom."

She exited the motel parking lot right, drove to the end of the block, and turned north onto busy six-lane Granville Street.

"This won't work," Jun said.

"What do you mean? Everything's worked great so far." Molka grinned and pulled the latex gloves off her tactical gloves. "If I do say so myself. How were they going to smuggle you into the airport and onto the aircraft?"

"In a van already fraudulently cleared through airport security and customs. My employer has friends working there too. But I shouldn't have come with you. Please drop me off on the side of the street. I don't want you to get hurt."

He sounded traumatized. Molka had witnessed a fatalistic attitude before with rescued hostages. Best to calm them and ease them back into normalcy.

"My name is Molka. Relax and put your seat belt on. It stopped raining. The sun's out. It's going to be a beautiful day. Are you thirsty? Hungry? We can stop and get—" She checked the rearview mirror—a red passenger van tailgated. "Pass me if you want, pushy red van. No need to ride my bumper." Molka looked back to a dejected Jun. "Want to stop at a Jim Thorntons?"

"Please let me out."

"I could use an energy drink. I don't drink them often, but I've been awake since…" Molka checked her rearview again. The red van still followed bumper close. "This guy is acting like a real…What color van were they going to transport you in?"

"Red."

"Like the red van right behind us?"

Jun turned. "Yes. It's them."

Molka smashed the accelerator, weaved, and put a few cars between her and the van. "I read there are about 2.5 million people in the greater Vancouver area. No way they could have found us so fast."

"Surprised it took them this long." Jun raised his right forearm and pointed to a tiny scar on the inside just below the wrist. "Microchip implant."

"For tracking?" she said.

"Yes."

"Now I get why you didn't run coming out of the diner."

"They prepared for runners," Jun said. "We all have an implant. Told you this wouldn't work."

"Your employer is a real modern-day slave trader, isn't he?"

"It wasn't his idea. It came from *HER*."

Molka observed the van back on her bumper. "How are they monitoring you?"

"Through a hand-held GPS-style device."

"Any ideas how to defeat it?"

"None," Jun said. "Do you have any?"

"We could cut off your arm and toss it out the window."

Jun stone faced her jest.

"I have another idea," Molka said. "But I might have to hurt your employer's guys a little."

"Those guys aren't just any guys. They're members of the local triumvirate."

"The local triumvirate being?"

"An organized crime syndicate."

Molka arched a doubtful eyebrow.

"It's true," Jun said. "My employer always uses them. They take us techs to the airport in the morning, pick us up in the evening, and watch us all night. They move us to a different motel every week to keep the immigration officials guessing. And one thing you should know about triumvirate members is—"

"Hold on." Molka jerked the wheel to the right, shot across two lanes of honking, dodging cars, and turned onto a narrow residential street made even narrower by cars parked along the curb on both sides.

Jun glanced back. "They're still following."

"Good, "Molka said.

"Where are we going?"

"To find a nice quiet place for the wreck."

"What wreck?" he said.

"It's been my experience during fast movement through a confined urban environment, people tend to be distracted by what's rapidly passing by on their periphery rather than focus on what's ahead of them."

"What's that got to do with anything?"

"You'll see."

Molka punched it and pulled away from the pursuer.

The van punched it in response.

She accelerated to 80 kph.

Less than an arm's reach separated the SUV from the parked cars it flew past on each side. Jun fixated on those dual periphery threats making him stiffen and grip the dash. "Ok, I see what you mean!"

Molka accelerated to 100 kph.

A 10-car gap opened between the SUV and the van.

Jun closed his eyes. "This is insane! Hope you know what you're doing!"

"Don't worry," she said. "I got this. I think."

Molka came off the accelerator.

The van didn't.

Molka buried the brakes.

The van didn't.

The SUV stopped in a screeching burnt rubber cloud.

The van buried its brakes too. Too late.

EEEEEEEECH-CRUMP!

The impact rocked Molka and Jun forward and back in their belts.

Molka unbuckled, pulled her pistol, and jumped out.

The van's totaled frontend steamed and hissed on the SUV's heavy-duty rear bumper.

She ran to the driver's door.

Airbags deployed.

Both men conscious but stunned.

Molka opened the door. A hand-held GPS unit with their current location displayed lay by the driver's feet. She snatched it, trotted back to the SUV, and got in.

Jun gaped out the rear window.

Molka tossed the GPS unit into the back seat and smiled. "Told you. Let's go get you defected."

"Uh, Molka."

Molka beamed. "Honestly, I'm shocked that actually worked. I just made it up and did it."

"Uh, Molka."

"A few months ago, I was being chased in a parking garage, and the guy chasing me wrecked too. But then——"

POP!

POP!

POP!

POP!

POP!

POP!

Small-arms fire shattered the SUV's rear window.

"Get on the floor!" Molka said.

Jun unbuckled and scrunched onto the floorboard.

Molka crouched. In the side-view mirror, she spotted a younger Asian male with a mini Uzi next to the van and a black car parked behind it. "I thought you only had two keepers!"

"That's what I was trying to tell you," Jun said. "Anytime there's a problem, triumvirates immediately call for back-up."

Molka punched it again, but before the SUV reached the end of the block, a white car stopped in the cross street and barred their path. The passenger window dropped, the driver pointed a pistol, and a shot ricochet off the SUV's massive front brush guard and push-bumper.

She fast stopped and fast reversed but couldn't go far because the van wreck blocked her way.

The mini Uzi shooter beside it smiled.

He recognized the same trap Molka did: front and rear blocking positions with a kill zone in between.

"Why don't they finish us?" Molka said.

"Because this is the part they love," Jun said. "They want to enjoy our terror."

Molka took out the .22, lowered her window, and fired two fast shots into the van and two fast shots into the white car to force the shooters into cover. It worked.

She assessed the street for escape possibilities.

Older two-story houses—most with detached backyard garages and separated by chain-link fences—formed a continuous barrier on both sides.

Molka grimaced. "I couldn't have handed them a better ambush if I planned it."

Jun peered at her. "Let's wait for the police. Someone will call them."

"For reasons I don't wish to explain, I can't have contact with law enforcement. I hope—" Molka fired another suppression shot each into the van and the white car and viewed the houses again. "I hope homeowner insurance is required here."

Jun's face mystified. "Why?"

Molka shifted the SUV into gear, turned left up the nearest house's driveway, turned hard left at the garage, drove over a lawn sprinkler in the backyard, smashed through the fence into the next backyard, ran over lawn chairs, smashed through the fence into the next backyard, ran over a tricycle and bicycle, smashed through the fence into the next backyard, ran over more lawn furniture, smashed through the fence into the next backyard, burst through an above ground swimming pool, smashed through the fence into the next backyard, turned hard left at the garage, drove down the driveway, turned right back onto the street—a half block behind the van wreck, black car, and perplexed unseeing Uzi guy—drove to the end of the block, and turned north back onto Granville Street toward Jun's freedom.

Fourteen minutes later, Molka parked curbside at the Canadian National Police downtown headquarters.

"Good luck," Molka said. "And here." She handed Jun the remaining cash the colonel had given her. "A little something to start your new life with besides the clothes on your back."

"Thank you," Jun said. "And I still can't believe you got me away from those triumvirates."

"And I hope word doesn't get back to Dean Besnik a woman who looked a lot like me helped you get away from them."

"Don't worry, he'll never hear about it. Because the triumvirates know if my employer finds out I got away, he would have them killed by day's end. So if anyone asks them, they'll make up a false story about getting rid of me and hope for the best."

Molka smiled. "Perfect."

"But what an amazing true story I'll have to tell."

"Well, when you tell the authorities about your escape from bondage, you might want to leave out the part about all the private property damage I caused. I've heard Canadians are an annoyingly understanding and polite people, but why push them?"

Jun smiled for the first time that day and laughed for what sounded like the first time in a long time. "Understood. No problem."

"Also, please don't mention I freed you at gunpoint. Or the car chase or the car wreck or the gun fire in a residential neighborhood. And please don't mention me either."

"Ok. But what should I tell them?"

"Tell them you slipped away, and a kind citizen gave you a ride."

"A VERY kind citizen gave me the ride of my life."

"Take care."

"Thank you again, Molka. Thank you for everything."

"Better get going."

Jun's face fell depressed again. "The first drone swarm is almost finished."

"I know."

"It's a horrible thing."

"I know," Molka said. "Time to go."

"When it's used it will be an unspeakable disaster."

Molka reached across Jun and opened his door. "Nothing is decided until it's decided."

Molka parked the battle-scarred SUV back in the motor pool at 11:38 PM and willed herself into the security HQ. The light shone on in the colonel's office. She entered and dropped into the chair across from him.

The colonel removed two fresh shot glasses from a drawer—both engraved with the inverted triangle symbol of the colonel's old unit patch.

He poured two vodka shots and passed one to Molka.

They raised the glasses to each other and drank.

Molka set the glass on the desk, stood, and walked out.

Nothing need be said.

It was understood.

Warrior to warrior.

CHAPTER 36

"**P**uppies!" Laili ran to the Haifa veterinary hospital's kennels and poked her fingers through the fence at the wagging, panting dogs. "Can we take one home, daddy?"

"Those animals are not for sale or adoption," Azzur said. "They are sick or injured and are being treated here."

"Aww…poor little things. Am I going to help them get better?"

"Yes. You are to be trained as a veterinary technician."

Laili smiled. "Ok."

"I want you to approach this training with the same intensity you did for your pilot training."

"Speaking of that," Laili said, "I want some serious flight time in a chopper bigger and more powerful than the R22 trainer."

"I have already arranged it."

PROJECT MOLKA: TASK 3
TUESDAY, AUGUST 27TH
6 DAYS TO COMPLETE TASK

CHAPTER 37

Darcy commandeered Besnik's desk in the dean's residence study clad in a black-over-black, double-breasted slim-cut business suit. She read from a tablet containing the summarized results from Molka, Truman, and Valentina's deep background checks.

Besnik watched with worry.

Darcy placed the tablet on the desk, arose thoughtful, strolled across the room to a fire in a carved Italian marble fireplace, and nodded into the flames. Then she turned and said, "A school can survive its fools, and even the ambitious. But it cannot survive treason from within. An enemy at the gates is less formidable, for she is known and carries her banner openly. But the traitor moves amongst those within the gate freely, her sly whispers rustling through all the campus, heard in the halls and the classrooms themselves. For the traitor appears not a traitor; she speaks in accents familiar to her victim, and she wears his face and his arguments; she appeals to the baseness that lies deep in the hearts of all men. She rots the soul of a school, she works secretly and unknown in the night to undermine the pillars of the school, she infects the student body so that it can no longer resist! A murderer is less to fear! THE TRAITOR IS THE PLAGUE!"

Darcy stormed back to the desk, snatched the tablet, and flung it into the fire.

Besnik recoiled.

"Six days!" Darcy said. "Six days until we make delivery, and you drop tragedy on me!"

"I am so sorry, Darcy."

She sank onto a red leather couch and laid her forearm across her eyes. "Truth be told, I'm a little sad too. I hoped I might become sister-close with that girl. You know how I've always wanted a sister."

"Yes, Darcy."

"One saving grace is we caught her in time. If she had taken Aden away before I was done with him, I would have committed a permanent solution for my temporary problem."

"I understand, Darcy."

"Bezie, the investigation against us, what is our legal exposure?"

"Substantial, I am afraid."

"What kind of deal could you cut for us?"

"To avoid the maximum, we would likely have to agree to prohibitive asset forfeiture and massive fines. They would also want the dissolution of Hazlehurst-Moore Incorporated and all the subsidiaries."

"What about prison time?" Darcy said.

"I think we could get them to agree to 24 months. Perhaps a little less."

Darcy turned her face to Besnik. "So, when I got out, I would be pushing 50. And be broke and homeless. And with nowhere to go but back to Mississippi and strip at The Eager Beaver. If they would even have me. Well, I'll promise you this; I'm not going down that way."

Besnik knelt beside Darcy. "We could leave now. Together."

"You mean to your Dakar stash haven?"

"Yes, Darcy."

"You don't have enough for us to stay gone forever though, do you?"

"No, Darcy."

"But if we can survive these next few days, and deliver the swarm, we'll have the means to truly disappear. Our last and only chance. Do you agree?"

"Yes, Darcy."

"Did you bring my medicine?"

"Yes, Darcy." Besnik opened his attaché case and handed Darcy a prescription bottle. "The doctor told me you should take no more than two a day."

Darcy's eyes daggered Besnik. "A doctor also told my mother after her fifth abortion she wouldn't be able to have kids anymore. But here I am." She poured more than four white bars into her palm and dry swallowed them. "What time is it? What time does the concert start?"

"It is just before eight. The concert begins at nine. Do you still feel up to attending?"

"Yes." Darcy ascended from the couch and straightened her suit. "Let no one see our distress. Let the show go on. And let the guilty rest easy." She smiled defiant. "For the moment."

CHAPTER 38

The stage loomed glittery and imposing. The laser lights strobed brilliant and mesmerizing. The production design boasted quality and expense. The band jammed tight and professional. And the backup singers serenaded sweet and soulful. The concert in the Hazlehurst stadium lacked but one thing: any appreciable musical talent from the star.

Undaunted by self-awareness, Valentina strutted the stage in a pink short-skirted schoolgirl-style uniform and butchered her way through pop songs.

The entertainment deprived audience devoured every painful note.

Molka—on night watch duty—sat in her security cart outside the stadium fence and binocular scanned. The student body filled the grandstand. Staff members danced on the field before the stage. And a VIP box erected on a raised platform stage right hosted Darcy, Besnik, and Aden.

Darcy and Besnik smiled politely at the travesty.

Aden watched, sublime.

Molka moved her observation away from his apparent happiness and spotted Gervaso, Narcisse, Yeong, and Hamu standing at the foot of the stage manning a security barrier. They didn't monitor the crowd though. They leered up at Valentina, who straddled a stool to abuse a ballad. Hamu compounded their sleaze factor by using a small camera to take upskirt shots.

Not a good look for campus security. But since Owen always hit his bunk early and the colonel would be hitting his bottle, they enjoyed unsupervised lecherousness.

Valentina finished the ballad—mercifully—and stood. "This next song is very special to me because it always reminds me of a very special man. Aden, my love, please come join me."

Aden joined Valentina on stage to sickening sappy aww's and applause. The couple held hands as she sung into his smiling eyes and heart-rending dimples.

Molka lowered the binoculars.

Stay positive.

Six days left and successful task completion moved from doubtful to possible. Right?

Focus.

Move forward.

Make final preparations.

Use the opportunity presented.

The Security Zone sat unguarded.

She headed for the armory.

Molka loaded the three MATADOR rocket launchers to destroy Building A into her security cart's backseat. She re-locked the armory door and turned to find Truman smiling his pleasant smile.

"You snuck them out of there," Truman said. "But now where are you going to hide them?"

"Fancy meeting you out here, Custodian Truman," Molka said. "Again."

"I clean the security headquarters every week, Doctor Molka."

"Yes. You told me that, didn't you?"

"I saw the door open and the light on out here again and got curious again."

"But you're missing the big concert."

"No, I'm not."

Molka smiled. "Cute." She viewed Truman reviewing her lethal cargo and said, "I'm just taking these to my room to…study them later. I'm trying to familiarize myself with all the weapons in our inventory. Doing a little homework on my own time. I'm embarrassed how ignorant I am compared to everyone else on the security team."

"I see."

"This is also against protocol, so I would appreciate you not mentioning this to any of my colleagues."

Truman raised big soft palms. "Don't sweat it. I don't speak to anyone else on the security team if I can help it. They're not the friendly types, you know?"

"I know."

"Word from the janitor's closet is you did a good deed recently."

"Did I?" Molka said.

Truman eyed the rocket launchers again. "Why don't you let me keep those for you until you're ready to…study them. The greenies sometimes randomly search staff members rooms while they're at work."

"Interesting information," Molka said.

"Principal Darcy's paranoia runs deep. But I have a real janitor's closet. No one else ever goes in there. I'll tuck those inside, and when you're ready for them, let me know, and I'll bring them straight to you. Sound good?"

"I couldn't ask you to do that."

"You didn't," Truman said. "I'm offering. I owe you one for covering for me when First Sergeant Owen caught me in here last time. I'm happy to do it, if you'll accept, Doctor Molka."

"Alright," Molka said. "I accept, if you'll start calling me Molka."

"Only if you'll start calling me Truman."

Molka offered a hand for shaking. "Deal."

Truman took it. "Deal."

Azzur had told her to always look to recruit useful assets. He hadn't told her that useful assets sometimes recruit themselves.

CHAPTER 39

Molka checked herself and stopped pacing her room and tugging on the base of her ponytail.

Why did she wake so frustrated?

The previous night, she had obtained the weapons she needed and secured them in a safe place.

And before she had fallen asleep, it had occurred to her she'd received a huge bonus with Darcy's decision to move into the dean's residence. It would give her quick and easy access to Darcy for a surprise sister-to-sister talk right before she left Hazlehurst with Aden.

And, of course, Aden still wanted to leave Hazlehurst with her. Because despite Valentina's arrival—and the nauseating, teenage crush-like attention she gave him on stage—the look in his eyes when had they talked about home hadn't been short-term faking. It had been long-term longing.

And because the look in his eyes toward her had been the same.

A brief private conversation with him to confirm his wishes and coordinate a new day and time to meet her in the central courtyard for extraction would be enough.

They could even go that night!

Don't be frustrated. Be happy.

Five days left and successful task completion moved from possible to probable. Right?

Molka opened her tiny closet and browsed her tiny wardrobe.

But what if Aden didn't want to leave with her?

What if he wanted to stay with Valentina?

Molka paced her room and tugged on the base of her ponytail.

Molka timed her arrival at Building A with the techs' departure for the day. She wore her hair down and styled the lone sexy outfit had she brought with her: a skintight burgundy mid-thigh sweater dress with over-the-knee black suede boots. She bought the ensemble in an over-priced SoBe boutique. It had cost almost her entire paycheck from the Kind Kare Animal Hospital, but she thought she looked hot in it. And she believed Aden would think so too.

Molka climbed the external stairs to Aden's loft. Pop music wafted from its open windows. She knocked and Principe's alarmed high bark sounded from inside.

Valentina opened the door in alluring nudity under a long sheer pink robe.

"Yes?" Valentina said.

"Is Aden here?" Molka said.

"Who is asking?"

"I am."

"And who are you?"

"You know who I am."

Valentina looked Molka up and down and smirked. "Sweater dresses went out of style two seasons ago."

"Well, it's all I have. I forgot to pack my pink stripper-whore school-girl outfit."

Valentina placed hands to hips. "How dare you."

"I didn't come here to argue with you. Can you please tell Aden I would like to speak with him?"

"No."

"I know what you think of me," Molka said. "But it's not what you think."

"What do I think?"

"I'm trying to take your man away from you."

"You?" Valentina giggled. "Take a man away from me?"

"May I speak to Aden please?"

"You are wrong. I do not think of you at all. But I know what you think of me. You think I am just a clueless diva high on my own fame."

"I don't care what you are," Molka said. "Please tell Aden I want to see him."

"Wait here."

Valentina closed the door.

Molka leaned on the railing and revaluated her outfit versus Valentina's. Conclusion: A sorority girl cannot compete with a goddess.

Owen entered the Red Zone gate in a security cart, raced to Building A, stopped at the foot of the loft stairs, and vaulted out with his submachine gun at the ready position.

The door opened again, and Valentina stood holding a quivering Principe.

Owen looked up to Valentina. "What's your emergency, Miss Valentina?"

"Does this woman have any reason to be inside the Red Zone, let alone at my door?"

"What are you doing here, doc?" Owen said. "Shouldn't you be getting ready to go on duty?"

Molka looked down on Owen. "I'll report on schedule…first sergeant."

Valentina sighed, annoyed. "I asked if she had any reason to be in the Red Zone?"

"Uh…no." Owen covered his mouth and spit dip to the side. "Guess not. Not anymore, Miss Valentina."

"Then I suggest you remove her and restrict her access to it immediately."

"Yes, Miss Valentina." Owen laid his hand on the grip of the submachine gun. "Ok, doc; let's go."

Molka descended the stairs, stepped close to Owen, and looked with disrespect at his hand resting on the weapon's grip. "I told you I would take that personally."

Owen spit dip again—mouth uncovered—near Molka's new boot. "Take it any way you want. But take it outside my Red Zone."

Valentina's laugh slammed into Molka's back before her door slammed shut.

 **CHAPTER 40**

Right on time, Molka reported for duty at 8:00 PM.

And right on Valentina's cue, Owen confiscated Molka's security keycard and issued her a new one with blocked access to the Red Zone.

An unnecessary complication—and obvious major setback—forced on her by a jealous, petty, catty, little interloper.

Alright. Must set aside personal emotions and figure a way around the new problem. Fast.

In the next five hours, Molka's livid patrol cart laps alongside the campus perimeter wall didn't produce any solutions, but they did produce five years wear on her cart's tires, steering, and motor and drained her batteries five miles premature. She headed back to security HQ to get the keys to a charged cart.

Inside, the colonel had succumbed to head-on-desk vodka-fueled unconsciousness, and quiet dominated the first floor. But upstairs roared in full party mode. Loud thumping music thumped loud, and trash talking drunks talked trash.

The revelry wasn't unexpected. When Molka had come on duty, she had overheard Hamu and Gervaso whispering in the surveillance room about a "free pass" after Owen announced he would spend the night at the dean's residence due to an unspecified security threat.

Molka didn't give their gossip a second thought at the time or while heading toward the squad room key cabinet until two teen girls in bras and panties—with a beer in each hand—giggled ran down the hall and up the staircase to the barracks room. A smiling, growling Yeong in tee shirt and boxers ran close behind them.

Ok. That's so wrong on multiple levels.

Molka backtracked, climbed the stairs, and "cop-knocked" on the barracks door. It took three cop knock sets before the music cut, the door cracked open, and Gervaso's nose peeked through. He stepped out fast and closed the door behind him with an inebriated smile.

"Who are those girls?" Molka said.

"They work here," Gervaso said.

"Where?"

"In the student laundry."

"How old are they?"

Gervaso smiled and shrugged. "Twenty-one-ish?"

"I would say more like 17-ish."

"Well, we didn't ask them how old they are."

"Then I will." Molka reached for the doorknob.

Gervaso moved to block her. "No women allowed in the men's barracks afterhours."

"No women allowed, but underage girls are fine?"

Gervaso smiled and shrugged again. "We are all soldiers a long way from home, bored and lonely."

"Does the colonel approve of your rest and recreation activities?"

Gervaso smile-shrugged yet again. "What happens in the barracks stays in the barracks."

Molka took two steps back. "Fine. I was going to ask you to move out of my way very nicely. But…"

"But what?"

Molka's hook kick landed on Gervaso's temple and escorted him to the floor. "But I'm not in a very nicely mood tonight."

Molka entered the blacked-out barracks room. She found the light switch and lit up the girls sitting on a bunk with Yeong between them. Narcisse lay on the next bunk in boxer shorts caressing a wine bottle. Hamu sat clothed on a chair in the corner with his hand down his pants.

"*Belle!*" Narcisse said. "Welcome to the party!"

Molka focused on the girls. "How old are you two? And if I think you're lying, I'll go ask your supervisor in the laundry."

One girl said: "I'll be 18 in October."

The other girl said: "I'll be 18 next month."

"Get dressed and get out of here," Molka said. "And never come back."

"Hey!" Yeong staggered to his feet and got in Molka's face. "No! They stay! You fuck off!"

Molka's neck clinch with blistering knee strikes dropped him. He stayed dropped.

The girls snatched clothes and shoes and fled.

Narcisse took a swig and sat up. "I prefer my women older anyway." He grinned. "Like maybe one half-hour before their 18th birthday."

Molka spun and fired a straight right punch into Narcisse's nose. Blood followed.

Hamu remained seated and laughed at Narcisse's pain.

Molka approached him.

Hamu slurred. "I just paid to watch. I wasn't going to do anything to those girls."

"Maybe not," Molka said. "But if you were a real man, you would've done something for them."

"I could kill you; you know." Hamu unsheathed his hand from his pants and started to stand.

Molka's front kick to his chest reseated him and her side kick to his head humbled his homicidal threat.

"Your rage excites me, *belle!*" Narcisse's voice was muted through the bed sheet blood blotter he held to his nose. "When will you come for a ride in my powerful gunship?"

Gervaso woozed back in the room holding, his head and collapsed on a bunk.

Molka addressed the assaulted. "Anyone want to wake the colonel and report me?"

In unison: "No."

Gervaso rolled into a sitting position. "Are you going to wake the colonel and report us?"

"No," Molka said. "What just happened in this barracks can stay in this barracks."

Molka moved to the door and flipped off the light. "One more thing though. Normally, taking out my frustrations by beating on four drunks is nothing I would be proud of. But you guys made the exception pleasurable. Thank you; this was just what I needed tonight."

CHAPTER 41

"What's the problem?" Molka undid the bun from her hair and put on a fresh lab coat. When she had returned to her room after night watch, she had found Rosina's Hazelnet message to come to the veterinary office ASAP and she hadn't taken time to change.

"Come look," Rosina said.

Molka joined Rosina behind the reception counter and viewed the appointment page on their monitor. A message read: *Male Maltese, age three years, must see a real veterinarian, not just an office assistant.*

Molka smiled to lift Rosina's deflated feelings. "Don't take it personally. These people are very rich and consider themselves entitled. So, they expect—"

"OH MY GOD!" Rosina face froze in shock at the front door.

Valentina entered wearing a pink-over-white designer pantsuit and pink heels. She carried Principe in his white leather carrier purse.

Rosina bolted around the counter toward Valentina. "I'm such a huge fan! I loved your TV show! I love your clothes! I love everything about you! Your concert the other night was amazing! I can't believe you're right here in our clinic! Why can't I have my phone to take a pic? Oh my god, no one will ever believe I met you! Of all the times not to have my phone! I hate this place! But I love you!"

"Thank you," Valentina said and addressed Molka. "After what happened between us yesterday, I know we are probably not welcome here, but Principe needs help."

"All animals are welcome here," Molka said. "What's wrong with Principe?"

"I am not sure. Since we arrived, his behavior has radically changed. He never barked much, but now he is barking all the time, even at the slightest noises. He is also licking himself excessively. And he is having accidents all over the apartment. Something he has not done since he was a puppy. I do not know. He was professionally trained and has always been such a good boy. I am very worried about him."

"Alright," Molka said. "We'll examine him."

Valentina removed Principe from the carrier and placed him on the floor. He tail-wagged straight to Molka. Molka picked him up and stroked his head.

"Remarkable," Valentina said. "He has never allowed anyone besides me to hold him."

"Please wait out here for us," Molka said.

Molka and Rosina gave Principe a comprehensive examination. Forty-five minutes later, they returned to the waiting area with Molka carrying the pant-happy Maltese.

Valentina was amazed. "My good boy. He looks so much better. What did you find wrong with him?"

"Nothing physically," Molka said. "He's in good health. But I think he's experiencing a lot of anxiety about his new environment."

"That makes two of us."

"I'm prescribing some low dose tranquilizer tablets you can add to his food for a few days. Rosina will go over the dosage and side effects with you."

Rosina gave Valentina a fan-girl smile. "It will be my honor. I'll get that scrip for you right now." She jogged back to the lab-pharmacy room.

"Anything else I should do?" Valentina said.

Molka passed Principe to Valentina. "Give him lots of loving reassurance to show him he's in a safe place. If he continues to have problems, let us know."

"You are very professional. Thank you."

"Don't think of it."

Valentina started to speak, paused, and spoke. "Aden has been lonely here without me. Having a friend from his adopted home country to talk to has meant a lot to him. For this, I also thank you."

"And I still would like to talk to my friend again."

"I cannot permit it."

"You cannot permit it?" Molka said. "He's a grown man."

Valentina laughed. "No. He is a scared, lost little boy who trusts me to protect him from those who have devious intentions." She pulled her shoulders back and raised her chin. "But do not take that as a compliment. Because I am not afraid of you stealing Aden from me. Because this is not possible."

"You're not afraid of me?" Molka held up the new security keycard hanging from the lanyard around her neck. "Yet, you had First Sergeant Owen block my access to the Red Zone."

"Why is it so important you talk to Aden again?"

"He needs help. I can help him."

Valentina flipped a dismissive hand. "You have known him for a few weeks, I spent every day with him for nearly two years. What do you know about what he needs?"

Molka stroked Principe's ears. "Valentina, you're Aden's fiancée, and I respect that. So I respectfully ask if I may please be permitted to speak to him, only as a friend."

"My answer is no, and I will be leaving now."

Molka stroked Principe's ears again. "Goodbye handsome. Don't worry. You'll be ok."

Valentina's shoulders fell, and she sighed. "Your kindness to Principe has touched my heart. So…so, I will pass along a message to Aden from you."

"Thank you. Give me a minute to write it."

"I will give him a short verbal message is all."

"Ok. Um. Tell him that, tell him I—"

"What?" Valentina said.

"Just tell him I miss the smoothies at Café Jarrod West."

CHAPTER 42

Another day off the Darcy calendar.

Another night in the security cart.

Four-days left to complete her task.

During Molka's time with the Unit, the major had formulated a policy about collateral damage during a mission: Avoid collateral damage if you can. If you can't avoid it, stop worrying about it, and accomplish the mission.

No one could ever say Molka hadn't tried to complete her task clean. She had asked Valentina face to face woman to woman for a chance to talk to Aden. And still no doubt, Aden would have agreed to leave with her, and only Valentina's love life and Darcy's financial well-being would take a hit.

But Valentina's jealousy had opened the possibility for real collateral damage.

Molka would have to force her way into the Red Zone to get to Aden—which meant first disabling Hamu in surveillance and whoever might be hanging around the squad room or whoever might happen to wake up. And after their drunken barracks beatings by her, getting close enough to incapacitate them non-lethally might be unrealistic. They might force her to incapacitate them lethally. And although they all probably deserved to be incapacitated lethally, she would hate to have to do it.

And how would the colonel react? Looking the other way when she destroyed Building A was one thing. Taking out his team members—no matter what he might have thought of them—was another. Pride is unpredictable. He might force her to incapacitate him lethally too, and she would hate to have to do that even more.

The major had formulated his policy about collateral damage to absolve people from normal human guilt so they could finish the mission. But his policy said nothing about living with that guilt afterwards.

Those ugly thoughts occupied Molka as she drove her cart along the perimeter wall behind the sewage treatment plant—the school's loneliest and most remote section. The stench always called for maximum acceleration, but arriving aerial company paused her foot.

A large four-propeller drone with a toolbox-sized container attached to the bottom circled her twice, landed two meters away, and shut off.

Molka stopped, got out, and shined her flashlight on it. It didn't appear to be a surveillance drone—more like a cargo carrier. She popped the latches on the underside attachment and opened it. Secured inside was Aden's stainless-steel insulated tumbler. She removed the tumbler and opened the lid. A roasted strawberry and Greek yogurt smoothie greeted her. Yum.

Valentina had given Aden her message and allowed him to reply. Decent of her.

Aden's answer was sweet, but she hoped against hope he remembered their silly Café Jarod West code phrase and took the hint that she seriously wanted to meet him there. And she would show up at Café Jarod West the next day at high noon in case he did. But she didn't expect it.

Molka took a sip. Something solid bumped her lips. She removed the lid, reached inside, and pulled out a zip-locked bag with a note inside. She opened the bag and read the note:

I miss the smoothies at Café Jarod West too. Hope to see you there soon.

CHAPTER 43

"**Y**ou can take the girl out of the ghetto, but you cannot take the ghetto out of the girl."

"A charming old cliché," Azzur said. "But can you do it?"

The elegant, stylish woman Azzur addressed was attractive for her 50s. She circled, Laili who was seated in the private salon make-up chair again. "I am not sure it is possible."

"You said yourself she has the chiseled bone structure of a top model."

"It is not her external attributes which concern me. True seduction grows from the inside out. This is where the unlikelihood lies."

"I am disappointed," Azzur said. "I was told the legendary Lady Elka, even on her worst day, could make a well-worn Bangkok hooker look, walk, talk, spit, and shit as gracefully as the Princess of Monaco."

Lady Elka viewed Azzur with contemptable intrigue. "Tell me again what you expect."

PROJECT MOLKA: TASK 3
FRIDAY, AUGUST 30TH
3 DAYS TO COMPLETE TASK

 **CHAPTER 44**

The white smoke wisp and wood burning scent ahead transformed Molka's joyful jog along the riverbank into an ecstatic run.

I was so happy when I got your message!
And I have wonderful news, darling!
We're leaving tonight!
Everything is set!
We're going home!

Molka ascended the hill, onto the plateau, and into Café Jarrod West at high noon.

Aden's backpack was there again.

Aden's blanket was there again.

Aden's sleeping bag was there again.

Aden's fire was there again.

But Aden wasn't.

"I'm here!" Molka said. "Where are you, darling?"

"Right here, darling." Owen—with submachine gun—swam through the brush line laughing and zipping up his fly.

"Where's Aden?" she said.

Owen crouched next to the fire. "Looks like we're having a campfire cookout." He grinned. "I brought the extra-long weanie if you brought the buns."

"How did you know about this place?"

He spit into the flames. "I broke an agreement and tracked Aden here."

"How did you know I would be coming here too?"

"Principal Darcy made Aden tell me."

"Where's Aden."

"Wouldn't you like to know."

"Are you going to tell me or not?" Molka said.

"You could beg me to tell you."

"Or I could just beat it out of you."

Owen eased to his feet. "What did you say?"

"You heard me. You still have one good ear left."

Owen touched his ear bandage. "Whoo-yeah...you love to turn up the heat, don't you, doc?"

"Can you handle some more of it?"

"I can handle all you got. And I would love nothing more than to oblige you. But I have my orders. Let's go." Owen pointed his submachine gun at Molka.

Molka recognized bluffing when she saw it.

She didn't see it.

 **CHAPTER 45**

Rumors that Darcy's ceremonial office on the classroom-administration building's fifth floor functioned as nothing more than a storage closet for her late husband's books proved false.

Owen ushered Molka into a large room decorated with dark mahogany paneling, gray carpet, black drapes, and a beautiful antique Queen Anne desk.

Next to the desk—also submachine gun armed—brooded an ill-tempered Yeong.

And seated before the desk, Aden outfitted outdoorsy again for their interrupted Café Jarrod West meeting, Truman work attired in a red plaid shirt and khaki pants, and Valentina costumed in a kitschy pink velvet track suit.

Someone had also accessorized Truman and Valentina with flex-cuffed hands behind their backs.

"What is this?" Molka said.

Yeong pointed to an empty chair next to Truman. "Shut mouth! Sit down!"

Owen closed the office door and put his back to it. "You heard the man, doc. Have a seat."

"Why are they cuffed?" Molka said.

Owen took out his dip can, frowned, and put it back in his pocket. "The boss will be in shortly to explain everything. Have a seat."

Molka sat.

"I see they got you too, Molka," Truman said.

"Why did they get you?" Molka said.

"I'm not sure. First Sergeant Owen walked up to me, shoved the barrel of his machinegun in my face, and brought me here."

"Pipe down, flabby," Owen said. "Or I'll shove my barrel someplace else you'll like a lot less."

Molka turned to Aden. His chin lay on his chest and his lips pouted. "Are you ok?"

No response.

Molka addressed Valentina. "Is he ok?"

"No," Valentina said. "He is not ok. She told him he is in big trouble and—"

A door in the mahogany paneling behind the desk opened and the colonel—with holstered sidearm—entered. He moved to the desk's right side and faced everyone.

Besnik appeared from the door next, carrying his titanium attaché case. He opened the case, laid out three file folders on the leather desktop, moved to the desk's left side, and faced everyone.

After an uncomfortable pause, Darcy entered from the same door wearing a black off-the-shoulder sheath dress and black heels.

Yeong moved away from the desk and moved to guard the paneling door.

Darcy sat behind her desk. Her face alighted on Molka. "Hello, doll. Welcome to the conspirator's cabal."

"The conspirator's cabal?" Molka said. "Sounds like the name of a hot new club for our next sisters' night out."

Darcy smiled at Molka before glaring as she passed her hands over the folders. "What I have here are deep, comprehensive background checks exposing each of the traitors in this room. These were provided to me by an unimpeachable source high within the Canadian intelligence services. So, we're not going to have any debating or tearful denials." She rose and moved to the desk front. "Before I reveal what's contained in those folders, let me say it's immoral to destroy a school like this where a leader cares so infinitely as she cares, and tries to build a structure of caring; it's immoral, it's criminal," she slammed a fist into the desktop, "and you should get it, goddamn you! What have I done but dedicated my life to helping others? First as an educator, then with Doctor Moore, and now at this school. What have I sacrificed? I'm husbandless. I'm childless. I'm virtually without family. The only thing I have is this school. That's why I will never abide traitors to it! NEVER!"

Darcy composed herself and moved before Truman. "Custodian Truman, or should I say Inspector William, "Willie" Barkley of the Canadian National Police? You retired early for health reasons—arrhythmia—but you begged to come back for one more important assignment. And your red-coated cop friends asked you to treacherously imbed yourself here and spy on me."

Molka reevaluated Truman: *He's an undercover policeman? I never would've guessed.*

Darcy went on, "This is no real surprise though. We've taken it for granted the cops were spying on us. But what is a bit of a surprise is what we found hidden in your work closet. Colonel Krasnov, if you would, please."

The colonel reached behind the desk and lifted a MATADOR rocket launcher.

"Care to explain, Inspector Barkley?" Darcy said.

Truman/Inspector Barkley answered her with his pleasant smile.

"No?" Darcy said. "Well, perhaps you'll tell First Sergeant Owen in a more private setting at security headquarters."

"I can guaran-damn-tee you he will," Owen said.

"This will not be necessary," the colonel said. "It is obvious the police officer was gathering evidence to verify rumors of illegal weapons here."

"Well," Darcy said, "Dean Besnik is going to send him back to his cop friends with a little rocket of our own. A rocket that's going to explode in their faces with criminal complaints and civil lawsuits."

Truman/Inspector Barkley's face focused on Darcy, transforming from janitor-pleasant to cop-serious. "You have no authority to detain us."

"I have total authority here. This is my private property."

"Don't you mean your private dominion?"

"Best shut your mouth, flabby," Owen said. "Before it gets you in even more trouble."

Truman/Inspector Barkley twisted in his chair toward Owen. "You're the one who has real trouble coming, skinny man."

Darcy mock-sighed. "I guess you two boys will never be friends." She side-stepped and stood over Valentina. "Moving on to Valentina, or should I say Pink Pussy Cat? Because that's what your handlers in the Israel Security Service call you."

Molka reevaluated Valentina: *She's with the ISS? I should've guessed.*

Darcy went on. "They recruited you some years ago to gather pillow talk from various home country scientists and inventors—to make sure they didn't sell information or defect to the enemy. In exchange, you got help with the sloppy hot mess you call a career."

Aden lifted pained eyes on Valentina.

"That's right, smartacus," Darcy said. "Your girl was only watching you for her pimps." She viewed Valentina with scorn. "I got him away from you though. But then this poor dumb little old girl from Mississippi brought you all the way here to reclaim him, didn't I?"

Valentina's face filled with disgust. "You are a delusional and disturbed woman."

Darcy's eyes spewed hate on Valentina. "Death to traitors."

"Principal Darcy," the colonel said. "What are your plans?"

"First Sergeant Owen," Darcy said, "take the pink slutress and the fat cop to the detention cells. I brought them here first class, but I'm sending them back to Vancouver low class. The next bus from Alex Creek leaves in eight days. Put them on it."

"Yes, Principal Darcy," Owen said.

"First Sergeant," the colonel said. "Prepare bunks for the police officer and myself in the barracks room. The lady will sleep in my quarters."

"Yes, sir."

"No, sir," Darcy said. "They're trespassers who pose a clear and present danger to student safety. I want them locked up and held…what's the term, Dean Besnik?"

Besnik straightened his tie. "Incommunicado."

"Incommunicado," Darcy said. "That means no communication or contact with anyone except for security staff. Do you understand me, First Sergeant Owen?"

"Yes, Principal Darcy." Owen turned to Yeong. "Take the detainees to the detention cells."

Yeong removed Truman/Inspector Barkley and Valentina from the room at submachine gunpoint.

Valentina called back from the hallway. "You better take good care of Principe!"

"Guess I'm next," Molka said. "You won't need to get me a bus ticket though. I can call my own ride."

Darcy snickered. "I'll talk to you shortly, doll." She stood over Aden and shook her head. "How many more? How many more? Since your wonderful mother passed, almost every woman you've trusted has lied to you and hurt you, haven't they?"

Darcy paused for Aden's response. None. She went on. "But there is one woman who never lied to you and who never hurt you, isn't there?"

Aden focused on the floor and nodded.

"And who would that woman be?" Darcy said.

Aden spoke in a loud whisper. "You, Principal Darcy."

"I'm sorry? Speak up please."

Aden spoke in a louder whisper. "You, Principal Darcy."

"Yes. Your loyal, caring, loving Principal Darcy. And you'll never forget again, will you?"

"No. Principal Darcy."

"Good. Recess is over. Get back to work!"

Aden rose and daze-walked from the room.

Darcy watched him out the door. "Poor boy desperately latches on to woman after woman hoping they'll give him the love and acceptance his late mommy gave him. But they've always let him down." She smiled to herself, refocused, and addressed her desk flanking cohorts. "Thank you, Colonel Krasnov. You may leave. Dean Besnik, you may leave as well."

Besnik and the colonel departed. Darcy walked to the door, removed a key from her bra, locked the door, and dropped the key back inside her bra.

"Why are you locking us in?" Molka said.

"I don't want anyone walking in on what's coming next," Darcy said.

Molka leaned forward. "What are you talking about?"

Darcy addressed Owen. "Give us a moment. I'll call you when I'm ready."

"Yes, Principal Darcy." Owen crossed the office and stepped through the door in the mahogany paneling.

"Where's he going?" Molka said. "What's in there anyway? The apartment you never stay in?"

Darcy stood over Molka; her face saddened. "Now comes the hardest part. Sorry to keep you waiting, but I didn't want the others here for this. This is personal between you and me."

Molka leaned back in the chair again and folded her arms. "Alright. You caught me. I've been a bad girl. What's my punishment? Expulsion from your little school? Fine. But fair warning, if you try to put me in detention first, I won't go easy like those other two." She smiled sarcastic. "Principal Darcy."

Darcy laughed. "I do love your odd sense of humor."

"Now what?"

"Now we might as well get the unpleasantness over with, doll. Or should I say Security Officer Molka? No, I shouldn't call you that either. That's not really what you are." Darcy paused. "Is it? Maybe I should call you Doctor Molka. But, you're more than that too, aren't you?" She knelt and placed her hand on Molka's shoulder. "That night in Vancouver, you said you wanted to be like a sister to me. Did you mean it?"

"You were very drunk."

"I know what I was. Did you mean it?"

"I was trying to get you in the limo."

"It's a simple question," Darcy said. "Did you mean it?"

"I guess meant it when I said it."

"Do you still want to be like a sister to me now?"

"Everyone has a job to do," Molka said. "I've never held it against someone for doing theirs, even if it opposes mine."

"That doesn't answer my question. Do you still want to be like a sister to me now or not?"

"I'm not really sure what it means anymore to be sisters. But...."

"But?"

"But yes. For whatever reasons, I still want to be like a sister to you."

Darcy's face softened. "I feel the same way about you, doll. That's why I really hate to do this, but because of who you truly are, I don't have a choice."

"Choice for what?"

"I'm sorry."

"Sorry for what?" Molka said.

Darcy removed her hand from Molka's shoulder and stood. "Are you ready, First Sergeant Owen?

"Ready for what?" Molka said.

"Yeah, I'm ready," Owen said.

"Bring it," Darcy said.

Molka straightened. "Bring what?"

"Here it comes," Owen said.

Molka's focus shot to the hidden door.

Here comes what?

Darcy locked the door behind me.

Fifth-floor window.

No escape routes.

What's Owen bringing?

Death to traitors?

Molka leapt to her feet, jerked the chair over her head, and rushed toward the paneling door.

Owen emerged holding Valentina's white leather pet carrier with Principe's cute face peeking out.

Molka halted her charge with the chair still poised overhead to strike.

Owen startled, ducked, and stumbled to evade. "Damn, doc! What the hell? I thought you liked animals!"

Molka lowered the chair.

Darcy burst into laughter. "You love to keep him terrorized, don't you? That's called using a strong pimp hand." She laughed on and on and on until she caught her breath. "Oh me. Oh my. Ok, whew." She unlocked and opened the office door. "You better get out of here soldier boy, before she bites your other ear off and totally makes you her bitch."

Owen handed Darcy the pet carrier and moved to leave. "Both of ya'll are Kentucky crazy."

Darcy unlocked the door for Owen and relocked it behind him. She returned to Molka holding the pet carrier away from her body with two fingers. "If anything happened to this little barking brat while in my care, his owner's hundred million fans would ruin me. And you are a veterinarian and the most qualified person here. Still, I wouldn't impose this burden on anyone but family or someone I considered a sister. So can you please, just for me, take care of him until his owner leaves?"

Molka concealed an adrenaline filled exhale. "Of course."

Darcy set the purse on the floor and embraced Molka. "Thank you, doll. I love you like an older sister loves a younger sister."

CHAPTER 46

Go to an amusement park and ride the merry-go-round until you're completely disoriented and then go straight to the biggest roller coaster and ride it until you're emotionally spent and then go straight to the house of mirrors and try to make sense of things until you're totally confused, and then go straight back to the merry-go-around and repeat the process, This is how Molka would describe her task when Azzur debriefed her.

He might not appreciate her metaphor, but she appreciated his undeniable talents. His cleaning job on her background had not only withstood Darcy's deep comprehensive check, it had also reinforced Darcy's belief that Molka was just who Darcy thought she was: a troubled, lonely veterinarian and a newfound sister.

A critical error Molka could use against her.

And Valentina's ISS handler's critical error in not securing her legend could be useful too.

Three days left and successful task completion moved from probable to assured. Right?

Molka left the classroom-administration building, dropped Principe into Rosina's thrilled care at the clinic, and returned to her room.

She got into uniform and formulated how to cause yet another critical error to work in her favor.

Molka stood at ease before the colonel's desk, disappointed. The three MATADOR rocket launchers confiscated from Truman/Inspector Barkley sat stacked in the corner. Who knew when they would be returned to the armory where she could steal them again?

Oh well. One new humbling challenge at a time.

Owen entered. "You wanted to see me, colonel?"

"First Sergeant," the colonel said. "What is your procedure for the detainees?"

"I'll check on them every hour, open their cell doors for a member of the cafeteria staff who brings them their meals, and offer to take them out each day for a 30-minute exercise walk inside the Green Zone."

"And who will watch the detainees when you are sleeping?"

"I'll rotate a different team member to watch them from 2000 hours to 0600."

"The lieutenant who drives truck has suggested an alternative to your procedure."

Owen spun a chair around backwards and straddle-sat. "Has she, now?"

"She has volunteered to bunk in the detention area and watch the detainees around the clock for you."

"And why would she volunteer to do that for me?"

"She believes since one of the detainees is an attractive female, it would be more ethical for another female to guard her and to keep the rest of the team members away. I am inclined to agree with her assessment. What is your view?"

"The female detainee is a foreign agent," Owen said. "And the flabby detainee is an undercover cop trying to bust us on illegal weapons charges. We don't owe them any ethical treatment."

"The accusations made by Principal Darcy against the detainees have neither been proven nor disproven, and it is not our duty to speculate on their veracity." The colonel addressed Molka. "Lieutenant who drives truck, you will assume responsibility for guarding the detainees."

The security HQ detention area hid behind a heavy wooden door at the hallway's end. The wooden door opened onto a small bedroom-sized foyer containing side-by-side steel cell doors with bullet-resistant glass windows.

Truman/Inspector Barkley occupied cell number one on the left and Valentina cell number two on the right.

Molka jogged back to her room and gathered her alarm clock, some bottled waters, and a few protein bars. She returned to the detention area foyer to find Owen had begrudged her—by the colonel's orders—a cot, a small table, and a chair. The cot's mattress had sprung springs, the table wobbled, and the chair squeaked. But she could deal with the spite because her ploy had worked.

Talking her way into detention guard duty moved Molka from patrolling the perimeter wall to within meters of the Red Zone and Aden. She wanted to leave that night. But two things went against it.

First, she needed to obtain a new weapon to destroy Building A. Later, when everyone slept, she would have to sneak back into the armory, choose another rocket launcher type, and learn how it functioned.

The second reason for not going that night—Aden's mental state. The scene in Darcy's office had unnerved him and she had dropped her heavy mommy issues hammer on him for good measure. Giving him a day to process and compose would help him better handle the stress they would have to get through during extraction.

So they could leave early morning on Sunday the 1st—the last possible day.

Saturday the 31ˢᵗ could be used to contact and prepare Aden. And that day, Friday the 30ᵗʰ, could be her final prep day.

And start the prep by giving some gratitude and gathering some intel.

Molka unlocked and opened cell number one. Truman/Inspector Barkley lounged on the cot minus his pleasant smile.

"You're my hero," Molka said.

"Why is that, Security Officer Molka?"

"It's still just Molka, and you're my hero for not telling them where you got those rocket launchers."

Truman/Inspector Barkley raised a finger and whispered. "Are these cells audibly monitored?"

"I asked Hamu the same question," Molka said. "They're supposed to be, but he hasn't got around to it yet. You and the pink princess are the first two guests back here."

"Ok. Well, I appreciate the accolade, but I'm no hero. If that maniac First Sergeant Owen worked me over, I probably would have talked. Thank goodness the colonel stepped in, even though he was wrong about my intentions. I would never mishandle evidence like that."

"But you still could have mentioned me," Molka said. "So thanks again."

"You earned it." Truman/Inspector Barkley sat up. "Can you believe super-model, super-star, Valentina is working for the Israeli Secret…what's it called?"

"Israel Security Service. The ISS."

"What's their function, do you know?"

"Internal security," Molka said. "Similar to your agency or the NIB in the US."

"She's quite a get for them, isn't she?"

"Yes. Until she got got."

Truman/Inspector Barkley chuckled his pleasant chuckle. "You're funny, Molka."

"By the way, I'm sorry Darcy found out about you and put you in here. It's not right."

"Well, when I asked to come back to undercover service, I knew the risks. And I had to call in all my favors and sign a stack of waiver forms because of my health, but it was worth it. Retirement was killing me by loneliness. My wife divorced me years ago, and I don't have any kids. The CNP is my only family. I missed it horribly. And when I came back, it was nice to feel wanted again. Does that make sense?"

"Yes," Molka said. "My previous job was a little like that. You need anything?"

"An extra pillow would be nice. And maybe some magazines from my room to read?"

"Ok. I'll clear it with the First Sergeant when he gets back."

"And if you brought me something from the ice cream stand, I wouldn't complain either."

Molka smiled. "I'll see what I can do. And for what it's worth, I'm also sorry you didn't get to finish your investigation. I hope your people come back and finish the job."

Truman/Inspector Barkley smiled his pleasant smile. "*Maintiens le droit.*"

Molka unlocked and opened cell number two. Valentina sat on her cot with her back against the wall. Not a happy pop star.

Molka said, "I wanted you to know Principe is being well taken care of by Rosina. She'll bring him to you when you leave."

"Please thank her for me," Valentina said.

"Did the ISS really send you to bring Aden back?"

Valentina rolled eyes and looked away. "What do you know about the ISS?"

"Not much," Molka said. "I mean, I've heard of them."

Valentina focused lament on the floor. "It does not matter if they did or not. I have lost Aden again regardless. I was wrong;

you have taken him away from me. Or should I say, you have conveniently taken *me* away from him."

"I didn't. Darcy did."

"I will be gone, and he can fall in love with you next."

Molka shook her head. "We're just friends."

Valentina knifed to her feet and faced Molka. "You keep saying this, but we both know different. Now I will tell you what you are getting yourself into. When I first met Aden, all he talked about was the last woman he was with. A woman from Costa Rica named Isabel he said he was engaged to. It was Isabel, Isabel, Isabel. But within a week, he stopped talking about Isabel and began to talk about what our life together would be like after we were married, and he never mentioned Isabel again. Then I left to do a photo shoot in Martinique. When I came back a week later, I found we had a houseguest—in our bed. An American woman well known for her self-help programs."

"Darcy?" Molka said.

"It surprised me too, but their short affair was more of a temporary infatuation caused by his mommy issues. Then I found out her real reason for being there. One of Aden's rich friends put her in contact with him. She saw he needed help and convinced him she was the only one who could help him. And then it was Darcy, Darcy, Darcy non-stop. I left again enraged. When I returned a few days later, they were both gone. She had brought him to this horrible place. And now I arrive to find it is Molka, Molka, Molka with him."

"It is?"

Valentina braced herself against the stainless-steel cell sink and stared out the cell door. "Every day on my social media, thousands of strangers tell me they love me. All around the world, wherever I go, people shout their love to me. Some of the most beautiful, famous, and wealthiest men have promised me their love. I never believed any of it. Then I met a man once who did not even know or care who I was. And he told me he loved me, and I believed him. I believed him so deeply I told him I would give up my career just to be there for him always. And I would have." Her glistening eyes fell on Molka. "So, you are the latest love of Aden's life. My congratulations. But also, my condolences. Because you will not be the last."

Molka stepped back. "The way you said that—the way you just talked about him—the way you acted with Aden on stage, your whole act with Aden…. It's not an act, is it?"

Valentina curled onto her cot. "I was instructed an operative falling in love with their target is strictly forbidden by the rules. But what do rules know of the heart?"

 **CHAPTER 47**

From her chair and table outside the cell doors, Molka made a paperless final prep list. Two items in, an alternate weapon to destroy Building A smacked her dead center in the obvious.

How embarrassing!

But her solution soothed the pain of her negligence.

Was a tool to defeat the Red Zone's razor-wire-topped fence to get to Aden also parked in plain sight? Crude thinking suggested a ladder and wire cutters. However, the smoothest, least conspicuous way to breach a fortified fence is a casual walk through the gate. Obtaining another all-access security keycard would do the trick. Maybe slip into the barracks later while they slept and switch hers for one of theirs? Risky, but—

The outer wooden door mashed open, and Owen leaned in. "I just found out I've got a big problem."

Molka's face fell into mock sympathy. "Why is it the sickest ones are always the last to realize they have a problem? It's so sad."

"Very funny, doc. But my problem is Student Woodrow's dog got loose."

"Duffy? He's a cute dog."

"Well, it's not so cute he's running and barking and pissing and shitting all over the staff compound. He needs to be caught A-SAP."

"Nothing a big bad merc like you can't handle."

"Yeah, but I'm no dog catcher neither. Besides, the last time I saw that mutt, the little bastard tried to bite me."

Molka smiled. "Oooo. What a good boy he is."

"No, he ain't. That's why you're going to go catch him. Because if I do it, and he bites me, I'm going to shoot him."

Molka un-smiled. "No, you won't."

"Then go take care of it."

"What about the detainees?"

"You look after that bad dog." Owen threw a thumb over his shoulder at the cell doors. "I'll look after these."

Over 90 minutes into driving a cart around the staff compound—and stopping to search every possible hiding spot a tiny black and tan dog might squeeze into—an employee at the maintenance department flagged Molka down. He informed her that he had found a stray dog locked in their storage shed.

Molka carried Duffy to Student Woodrow's dorm room door and knocked to no answer. The door across the hall cracked open with a snooping eye.

Molka turned. "Do you know if Student Woodrow is here?"

The door opened on a hunched septuagenarian. "No. He's in organized activities, of course."

"Why aren't you?"

"I took today off. I'm not feeling well. You can give Duffy back to me. I'm Student Woodrow's friend, Student Blaine. I was watching Duffy for Student Woodrow today."

"Alright." Molka passed Duffy to Student Blaine. "But why did you let Duffy get loose?"

"I didn't. First Sergeant Owen came and took Duffy away from me a couple of hours ago."

Molka returned to security HQ to find Yeong and Gervaso, as usual, loitering in the squad room.

"Have you seen the First Sergeant?" Molka said.

Yeong ignored her with malice.

Gervaso nodded toward the surveillance room. "He's watching the show."

Molka entered the surveillance room. Hamu sat at the console viewing the monitors, Narcisse leaned against the wall also viewing the monitors, and Owen sat in the back corner holding a dip cup and viewing too.

Molka addressed Owen. "What was the point of the staged dog escape?"

"Just a training exercise," Owen said.

"Just a training exercise? I can't believe you said that." Molka noted all present focused on the same monitor. "What's wrong?"

Hamu answered. "The detainee is down 18 kilometers from the front gate."

"The detainee?" Molka spun around. The top left monitor displayed a drone camera overhead view of Truman/Inspector Barkley on his back next to the gravel road outside campus. Hamu zoomed in on Truman/Inspector Barkley's face. His eyes were closed, but he appeared to be breathing.

"What's he doing out there?" Molka said.

"He was walking fine," Hamu said. "Then he collapsed."

Molka lurched toward Owen. "You took him on a field trip? Are you insane? He has a serious heart condition!"

"Should I go pick him up in the gunship?" Narcisse said.

Owen spit into the cup. "No. That's what he wants. He's just faking."

Molka's face crowded Hamu's face. "Open the front gate or I'll ram it open!" She sprinted out the door.

Hamu rotated his chair to Owen. "Think she'll really ram it?"

"You bet."

"What should I do?

Owen spit into the cup again. "Best open the gate."

"I figured I would die before my time," Truman/Inspector Barkley said from the security SUV's backseat. "Same bad heart and almost the same age as my daddy. But I never expected it to happen in the back of a police car."

Molka drove with max effort. Gravel popped and flew from the tires and clanked in the wheel wells.

"Rest easy," Molka said. "I'll have you in the infirmary in 10 minutes. They're standing by. How do you feel?"

"Dizzy. Lightheaded. Bad. Not as bad as last time though."

"Just rest easy."

"Molka, I wasn't going to tell you, but it doesn't matter now, and I know you're on the right side of the bad things here. And I know you and the colonel were planning to do something about them. So, I don't want you to be here when they come."

"When who comes?"

"They're coming on the 31st.

"That's tomorrow. Who's coming?"

"Yes," Truman/Inspector Barkley said. "They're coming tomorrow. Thank goodness."

"Who's coming?"

"*Maintiens le droit.* My people. A major tactical operation. They have warrants for Principal Darcy, Dean Besnik, and Colonel Krasnov. All other Hazlehurst staff will be detained pending an investigation. A lot of miscreants took refuge here. They'll weed them out. But what they really want now is Aden Luck and what he's making in Building A."

"Do they know what he's making in Building A?"

"Yes," he said. "Jun told them. It's shocking. The operation was scheduled to happen in a few weeks. But when they found out about Building A, they moved it up."

"What type of force is coming?"

"Several ERT teams and support units. A massive operation. Maybe the biggest one in CNP history."

"How will they come?" Molka said.

"By helicopter assault, exactly 3:42 AM."

"Why exactly 3:42 AM?"

"Tactical reasons. That's the full moon."

"Makes sense"

"Leave tonight if you can, Molka. They'll block the road two hours before the assault. Don't let yourself get caught in Darcy's mess."

"Ok. I'll try hard to be gone before then."

"Molka?"

"Hold on a second, Truman." She spoke into her radio headset. "Hindu. This is Doc. Over…Arriving in eight minutes. Open the gate…Negative. Open the gate because I'm not stopping. Out."

Well, the CNP has forced the issue. I have to take Aden out tonight before they arrive!

"Molka? Please keep talking to me, Molka. I don't want to pass out. If I do, I…I don't think I'll wake up again."

"Alright," she said. "Communication. How were you communicating with your people?"

"You know why instead of drinking fountains the school has bottled water dispensers?"

"Because of the hard well water, right?" Molka said.

So much to do before we go! So much to worry about!

"Right," Truman/Inspector Barkley said. "And I'm in charge of sending back the empty dispenser bottles and receiving the refills on the bi-weekly supply plane. The water supplier is working with us, and we use special bottles with false bottoms to carry messages in and out."

"Ha. Now I understand where your 'word from the janitor's closet' came from."

Oh, no! Will I have time to get what I need from Darcy before we leave?

"You guessed it. Molka? Please keep talking to me, Molka."

"Um, ok, I'll go to your room and get the magazines you asked for and bring them to you in the infirmary. Any particular ones?"

"Hockey Preview. Training camps will open soon. I'm a huge Sens fan. The cup is ours this year."

"Got you," Molka said. "I'll also stop by the ice cream stand and bring you something if they let me."

"Yes. Ice cream would be nice. I've loved ice cream ever since I was just a little boy. Just a little boy. Just a little…."

"What flavor do you want?"

No response.

"What flavor ice cream do you want, Truman?"

No response.

Molka checked the rearview mirror. Truman/Inspector Barkley lay serene with a pleasant smile on his pleasant face.

"Truman?"

"Truman?"

"Inspector Barkley?"

 **CHAPTER 48**

Hamu straddled Molka's chest.

Gervaso pinned her left leg to the grass.

Yeong pinned her right leg to the grass.

Owen braced himself against the wall outside the security HQ front door.

"YOU KILLED HIM!" Molka yelled for the second time at Owen.

Owen yelled back. "He got a field trip for his smart-ass remarks to Principal Darcy!"

"YOU KILLED HIM!"

"I didn't kill that man! Fifty-five years of fried food and sittin' on his fat ass laid him low."

"Let me up!" Molka bucked and writhed against her restrainers. "You killed him! Now I'll kill you!"

Owen pulled bloody fingers away from his ear bandage. "Bleeding again! Shit! DO NOT LET HER UP!"

The colonel thundered out the security HQ door.

"*STOY!*

"STOP!"

"What is this foolishness?"

Owen pointed at Molka. "She asked me to step outside for a word and she jumped me. Kicked me right in my wounded ear. Ripped my uniform and tore all my gear off and pitched it in the bushes over there. Liked to stomp a hole in me until the boys heard my hollering and stopped her. She's crazy!"

"Release her," the colonel said.

The three released their grips. Molka jerked away and stood.

The colonel addressed her. "Lieutenant who drives truck, what have you to say?"

"Just a little soldier's quarrel, sir."

The colonel addressed Owen. "First sergeant, what have you to say?"

Owen exhaled hard. "Yes, sir. Just a little soldier's quarrel."

"Lieutenant who drives truck," the colonel said, "remain here. The rest of you are dismissed."

The team members moved to obey.

"Not you, Gervaso," Owen said. "Get a flashlight and try to find all my shit she scattered in the bushes. I need to go get my ear rebandaged."

Owen and Gervaso left the scuffle scene.

Molka came to attention.

The colonel inspected her with a covert smile. "Fear the goat from the front, the horse from the rear, and a woman from all sides."

"Sir?"

"I am assuming you got what you wanted from this...little soldier's quarrel?"

"Yes, sir," Molka said. "I got exactly what I wanted."

"Then resume your duties."

On the way back to the detention area, Molka reached down her pants front, into her panties, and removed Owen's all-access keycard from where she stuffed it after ripping it from his neck.

The callousness of empty cell number one's door left wide open, and the light left on re-enraged and saddened Molka.

Truman/Inspector Barkley deserved better. She turned out the light and closed the door with reverence.

Cell number two's occupant slept unaware.

Molka sat on her cot and briefed herself on what she must to do in the next few hours to complete her task and how she would attempt to do it.

When her briefing concluded, she only asked herself one question: Against the unforgiving odds she gave herself, could the killing luck possibly favor her again?

She didn't have the answer.

Molka checked her alarm clock: 10:11 PM.

Exhausted.

Get a little nap to be sharp for later. Critical to be sharp later.

She set the alarm for midnight, lay on her back, closed her eyes, and slumbered on a final thought: At least all the madness inside Hazlehurst Institute was about come to an end—one way or another—for everyone.

CHAPTER 49

The portly, bearded, middle-aged man in the expensive suit sitting at the bar in the posh Tel Aviv beachfront hotel asked the bartender again if he was sure.

"Yes, I'm sure," the bartender said. "She's not a hooker. The concierge only allows a few high-end girls to work the hotel, and she's definitely not one of them. If you ask me, she's more like a girl playing a woman."

"She keeps looking at me like a jungle cat looks at its prey," the man said. "I am mesmerized."

The predator mesmerizing him? Laili. She perched on the end barstool, sensualized into a sleeveless, backless, body-hugging, scandal-short gold dress and black high heels. Her hair and make-up were well-worthy of the ensemble. The legendary Lady Elka's best efforts had proved effective after all.

Laili stalked over to the stool beside the man. "I couldn't help noticing you noticing me."

The man smiled. "Yes, I noticed."

"Are you here at the hotel for business or pleasure?"

"To me, business is a pleasure."

Laili smiled, impressed. "A man of wit. You must be a foreigner."

"I am from Amman."

"I've heard Amman has the most beautiful women in the world."

"That is not quite true," the man said.

"Oh, why is that?"

"Because Amman does not have you."

Laili smiled seductively. "You are also a very charming man, mister…?"

"Please call me Walid."

"And you may call me Orah." Laili leaned into Walid's shoulder. "I have a confession to make. I'm very attracted to older men with wit and charm. Does this bother you?"

"Not in the least. And I have a confession to make as well. I am a married man with five children. Does this bother you?"

"Well, there are married men and there are happily married men. Which are you?"

"I am a married man. May I buy you a drink?"

"You mean here?" Laili said.

"Is there someplace else you would prefer?"

"Yes. The bar in your suite upstairs."

Walid smiled. "Shall we go now, Orah?"

"Are your bodyguards coming with us?" Laili pointed a sharp French-manicured nail at two big pretty boys occupying a side table.

"Are they that conspicuous?"

Laili smirked. "They're obviously noticeable. I mean—what I mean to say is—it's clear they are watching over you."

Walid sighed. "My wife's brothers. She insisted they accompany me on this trip for my safety. However, they are staying in the adjoining suite and will not disturb us."

Laili smiled turned predatory. "Perfect."

"Your turn to get naked now, Walid." Laili prowled from the master bedroom in his luxury suite wrapped in a small white towel, which barely concealed her breasts and crotch.

Walid set their drinks on the bar and removed his tie.

"Not in here." She gestured back to the bedroom. "Why don't you wait for me in the bedside jacuzzi? It looks so stimulating. I just need to use the little girl's room first."

Walid submitted with a submissive smile.

Laili closed the door after him and listened. After hearing Walid's entry splash into the jacuzzi, she tossed away her towel. Under it she still wore her dress—the bottom hiked up to give the illusion of nakedness. She pulled her dress back down, scanned the room for a few seconds, and padded to a coffee table with a crocodile skin briefcase atop it. She grabbed the case and padded back to the bar to retrieve her heels.

"What are you doing?"

Laili turned to a naked, dripping, furry Walid in the doorway and laughed. "How did you ever get five kids with that tiny thing?"

His face panicked on the briefcase in Laili's hand. "You are robbing me! You are a hooker!" He ran to the suite's connecting door and pounded. "Yamin! Ayham! ROBBERY! HELP!"

"Bad mistake, fat-ass." Laili hopped, skipped, and jumped a front kick into Walid's chin, flooring him unconscious. She landed, spun, dropped the briefcase, and flattened her back against the wall next to the connecting door.

The big pretty boys stumble-squeezed into the room, each holding a pistol.

Laili pounced.

Pretty boy one took a roundhouse to the rear cranium.

Pretty boy two caught a side kick on the temple.

Both sniffed the carpet.

She disarmed and covered them with their own weapons. "Just stay down there." She examined the pistols. "A Glock 17. Classic. And a CZ 75. I hear these are overrated."

"Please don't kill us," pretty boy one said.

"I might not." Laili grabbed the briefcase and her heels and moved toward the door. "But if anyone asks, this never happened, and I was never here."

"No problem," pretty boy one said.

"We've already forgotten you," pretty boy two said.

She halted. "What did you say?"

Pretty boy two said, "We've already forgotten you."

"You guys want to forget me?" Laili said.

"Yes," pretty boy one said. "Like he said, we've already forgotten you."

"Serious?"

The boys in unison: "Yes."

Laili stalked back and shot each in the buttocks with their own pistol. "But now you'll never forget me."

Laili punched through the hotel's rear emergency exit into a service lot. She carried her heels and one pretty boy pistol in her left hand and the crocodile skin briefcase and the other pretty boy pistol in her right.

A white van waited with its side door open.

Laili dove in. "Go fast! Go hard!"

The driver obeyed while trying to catch rearview mirror glimpses of Laili rolling out of her dress and into tight jeans, tank top, and tennis shoes.

The van jerked to a stop on a busy downtown corner.

Laili concealed the pistols in her waistband, sprung from the van with the briefcase, and ran-dodged the teeming sidewalk to Azzur sitting at an outdoor café table.

Laili dropped into the chair across from Azzur and slammed the briefcase tabletop. "Did I make it on time?"

Azzur laid some cash on the table, stood, and picked up the briefcase. Laili followed him to his curb-parked car and they both got in.

Azzur pulled into traffic. "Did you touch anything in his suite?"

"Only a towel and the case, like you told me." She pulled out the boy's pistols. "And these."

"You were to avoid contact with his security."

"Well, they started to contact me first, so…."

"Any other problems?" Azzur said.

"No. Like what?"

"What did he tell you?"

Laili laughed. "He said he was a married businessman from Amman. What a lame-ass fat-ass."

Azzur lit a cigarette.

"What's in his case?" Laili said. "Top secret plans for a big terrorist attack? Mega-cash to fund the attack?"

He turned into an alley, eased to an open dumpster, tossed the briefcase into it, and drove on.

Laili gawked back at the dumpster. "What the hell? What was in the case?"

"No idea."

"Then who was that guy?"

"Probably a married businessman from Amman."

"Well, isn't that just pleasantly wonderful. This was just training exercise." Laili helped herself to Azzur's cigarette pack and lighter in the cup holder. "Now what?"

"Now we go home and pack for our trip."

"Trip?" Laili smiled and wriggled. "Are we going on a vacation, daddy?"

"No. We are not going on a vacation."

"Where are we going then?"

"To work."

PROJECT MOLKA: TASK 3
SATURDAY, AUGUST 31ST
12:00 AM

CHAPTER 50

BEEP

 BEEP

 BEEP

 BEEP

 "You didn't invite me to your wedding."

 "It was small ceremony," Molka said. "We only had a few guests."

 BEEP

 BEEP

 BEEP

 BEEP

 "You have beautiful twins now I've never met."

 "I know," Molka said. "I am sorry. I wish you had."

 BEEP

 BEEP

 BEEP

 BEEP

 "You didn't even come to visit me on my birthday, Molka. Like you always did."

 "Well, I've been so busy with the kids and my work and my husband's work, and you're so far away from where we live."

BEEP

BEEP

BEEP

BEEP

"Did you forget about me, Molka?"

"Don't be silly."

BEEP

BEEP

BEEP

BEEP

"Why did you forget about me, Molka?"

"You were always so silly."

BEEP

BEEP

BEEP

BEEP

"You forgot about me, Molka."

"You forgot about me, Molka."

"You forgot about me, Molka."

"You forgot about me, Molka."

BEEP

BEEP

BEEP

BEEP

Molka woke to her alarm clock beeping, panicked from her cot, ripped open the door, rushed down the hall, tore out of the security HQ into the cool night, and cast anguish into the dark eastern sky.

No!

No!

No!

No!

I'm sorry!

I'm so sorry!

I haven't forgotten about you!

I'll never forget about you, my little Janetta!

CHAPTER 51

Molka left the security HQ, returned to her room, and logged onto Hazelnet. Both messages she had sent when she had gotten back from dropping off Truman/Inspector Barkley's body at the infirmary the previous afternoon had received the replies she wanted.

After a quick cold shower, she geared up again in black jeans, a black long-sleeve mock turtleneck, and her tac boots. She high-ponied her hair—with bangs swept across her forehead right to left to clear her aiming eye—and re-strapped her old pilot's watch on her left wrist.

She opened her black tactical duffle bag and removed and pulled on her leather tactical gloves. In the bag she packed her binoculars, several sets of flex cuffs taken from security supplies, more latex gloves from the clinic, Azzur's special Tampon box, and the commissary bought duct tape. The silenced .22 pistol got tucked behind her back and under her shirt.

At her little desk, she jotted in her notebook, tore out and folded the page, and tucked it into one front pocket. She slipped the all-access keycard she had stolen from Owen into the other.

Before slinging the duffle bag over her shoulder and leaving, she tore down the Darcy calendar and tossed it in the waste basket.

"Time's up."

The elegant—if not ominous—frontal view of Darcy's personal jet radiated under illumination in the airport's open hangar.

The lights in the adjoining hanger office blazed too. Molka walked to it and opened the door. Four men sat around a table: two aircraft maintenance men, Darcy's pilot, and Narcisse. Cigarette and cigar smog hung in the overhead fluorescents. Ashtrays, open beers, Canadian currency, and playing cards covered the table.

Molka approached to hands scrambling to hide contraband.

Narcisse offered Molka a wary smile. *"Belle!"*

"I want to talk to you," Molka said. "Tell your boyfriends to step outside and take a smoke break."

The bigger maintenance man slid his boot over the lit cigarette he had dropped on the floor. "Smoking at Hazlehurst is cause for immediate termination, Security Officer Molka."

"Yes, it is," she said. "And so is drinking alcohol and gambling. Principal Darcy would be most displeased to hear of all three happening in here every night."

"Are you going to report us?" the pilot said.

"Only if you don't step outside, fast."

They stepped outside, fast.

Narcisse's wary smile clinched into a nervous grimace. "What's in the tactical bag?"

"I need to take out some aggression," Molka said. "And I need you to help me."

Narcisse stood. "Do you want to beat me again?" He brightened. "Because I really am into S and M play."

"Maybe later. But does the offer to take a ride on your powerful gunship still stand?"

"Absolutely!"

Molka faked flirtatiousness. "Then tonight's your lucky night, handsome."

"Handsome?" Narcisse's nervous smile relaxed into a confident grin. "Her true affections are revealed. But what about your detainee?"

"She can get her own ride."

Narcisse laughed. "I love your attitude, *belle*."

"Do you have any high-explosive incendiary ammo for its cannon?"

"Yes. Why?"

"HEI is good for setting trees on fire."

"You wish to set trees on fire?"

"Yes," Molka said.

"Why?"

"Because they have way too many surrounding this place. I'm a desert girl. It annoys me. Let's go torch some."

Narcisse's face became appalled. *"Belle,* I must say you have shocked someone even as jaded as me. That is a very depraved, sick, and insanely twisted idea." Narcisse's face became delighted. "I love it!"

"Thought you would." Molka checked her watch. "I'll meet you back here no later than 2:30."

"I will count the seconds."

"And have your powerful gunship ready to go for me." Molka grinned. "When I come back here, I'll be in a desperate hurry to ride it."

 **CHAPTER 52**

Time: 1:56 AM.

Molka waited next to the safety railing on the west-side belfry opening in the campus bell tower.

Weather: clear and cooling.

The wind had increased a bit with some gusting—and crosswinds can be tricky things for a pilot—but maybe it would calm before the extraction helicopter got there.

Campus status: quiet.

No lights on in the student dorms. And only a lone light remained on in the staff housing units—the one she had forgotten to switch off when she had left her room.

Exposure risk: low.

Since no one had replaced her on night watch—Owen told Hamu to cover the perimeter wall with an extra drone until he reassigned the duty—there would be no eyes on inner campus activities.

Plan going to plan—so far.

Below, Darcy arrived at the classroom-administration building in her performance enhanced custom transporter—alone, as Molka's Hazelnet message had requested.

Light footsteps climbed the stairs. The hatch opened, and Darcy lilted in carrying a wicker picnic basket. She was dressed stylish-comfortable in a white funnel-neck sweater, gray jeggings, and adorable black ankle boots.

Darcy beamed. "Hey, doll! I was so excited when you asked for another sister-to-sister talk. I really needed a break with all the stress on me lately. And I love the idea of sneaking up in the tower; it's like our own little private hideaway." She set the basket on the floor and removed two bottles. "Ok, I brought a nice Pinot Grigio and some Don Julio 1942 if we want to take it up a notch." She reached back into the basket "For snacks, I brought some string cheese, cookie dough, and I'm not sure if you eat hot pork rinds, but trust me, they go great with any kind of alcohol…" She refocused on Molka. "Look at you. Looks like you're dressed for a casual funeral."

Molka smiled at Darcy. "I have a surprise for you."

Darcy hopped excited. "Goody! I love mysterious surprises. This is fun."

Molka reached into her duffle bag and removed the special Tampon box and the duct tape.

"Oh," Darcy said. "Is that why you're wearing dark jeans?"

Molka tore off two tape strips and stuck them on her shirt, opened the Tampon box, pulled out a tube with blue and white writing on the wrapper, tore it open, and removed the signaler. She moved to the west-side opening, placed the signaler atop the safety rail—with the open end aimed at the foothill containing the contractor's sensor—used the tape strips from her shirt to secure the signaler in place on the rail and rechecked her watch: 1:59 AM.

Darcy stared perplexed. "What in the world are you doing?"

"It's part of the surprise." Molka counted her watch to 2:00 AM and pulled the signaler string.

The green beam fired out too bright at the source to view.

Darcy shaded her eyes with both hands. "What in the…what is that thing? Laser pointer?"

Molka retrieved her binoculars, took a knee behind the signaler, and sighted the beam's ending point near dead center of the foothill 4.6 kilometers away. And above and to the right, a faint amber light appeared—the sensor's acknowledgment signal.

The extraction helicopter would be on the way.

"Who are you spying on?" Darcy said. "Aden?" She giggled. "Messing with him and his girl with that laser pointer? Is that my surprise?"

Molka stood, pulled the signaler string to shut off the beam, removed it from the railing, dropped it and the binoculars back in her bag, and took two steps toward Darcy. "I have something I want you to know, before what's about to happen, happens."

Darcy hopped excited again. "My surprise? What's about to happen?"

"Before what's about to happen happens, I want you to know I relate to you in some ways; strong women are often misunderstood. And I feel sorry for you in other ways; you had a traumatic childhood you'll never fully get over. And, on some level, I admire you; the world smacked you in the face and you smacked the world right back."

Darcy's face softened sentimental. "Aww, that is so sweet of you to say. I wasn't sure if you truly even liked me. You're going to make me cry."

"I'm leaving with Aden," Molka said. "Tonight."

"Poor doll." Darcy frowned, sympathetic. "I figured that's what you wanted to talk to me about. After I got the pink whore out of your way, you thought you could get your man back, didn't you? Run off with him and make him fall in love with you. Because you really are in love with him. But like I said, he's not the one for you. He's—"

"I didn't bring you here to talk about Aden." Molka walked to the hatch, closed it, pulled her pistol, and faced Darcy.

Darcy caught her breath at the pistol and then her face disgusted on Molka. "Which one are you, traitor or cop?"

"I guess as far as you're concerned, I'm both."

Darcy's arms lowered to her sides with fists clenched, and she smiled. "Aden is here of his own free will. And I promise he'll tell you that himself. You have no legal standing to make him leave with you, cop. Even this poor dumb little old girl from Mississippi knows that much."

"Tell me the identity and location of the one you sold the drone swarm to."

Darcy feigned bewilderment. "What's a drone swarm?"

"It's too late for games," Molka said. "We know everything. Tell me the identity and location of the one you sold the drone swarm to."

Darcy smirked. "When are your cop friends coming for me?"

"They're on the way as we speak."

"Then all is lost." Darcy sat on the floor.

Molka rechecked her watch. "Tell me the identity and location of the one you sold the drone swarm to."

"Such unappreciation," Darcy said. "A few malcontent students cry to their families they're being mistreated, and their greedy families go to the cops and tell them their money suppliers are being mistreated. Mistreated? They've never been treated so well as by their caring Principal Darcy. But it gave the cops the excuse they were looking for to investigate everything about me."

"Tell me the identity and location of the one you sold the drone swarm to."

"You cops are just doing your jobs," Darcy said. "I suppose. The students are the real traitors. Even the ones who didn't complain are traitors because they didn't stop the malcontents. They didn't get their minds right."

"Tell me the identity and location of the one you sold the drone swarm to."

"They all begged me to let them come here," Darcy said. "And I accepted them with open, loving arms. And look how they've thanked me. It's immoral to destroy a school like this where a leader cares so infinitely like—"

Molka stepped forward and put the barrel to Darcy's forehead. "I don't have time for that speech again. Tell me the identity and location of the person you sold the drone swarm to."

Darcy's eyes defied Molka's. "I can't tell you."

"Then I'll kill you right here, right now."

Darcy smiled with contempt. "You can't con a conner. I know you won't just shoot me, cop."

"You know nothing about me and what I'm capable of. Tell me the identity and location of the person you sold the drone swarm to. NOW!"

"Only thing I'm going to tell you is to take a flying leap off this tower, cop."

Molka tucked the pistol behind her back, grabbed Darcy by the hair, yanked her light weight to her feet, grabbed her petite throat, and pushed her back-first into the safety railing.

Darcy glanced behind her, panicked, and grabbed Molka's wrists.

Molka pushed Darcy by the neck and bent her over the railing. "A few weeks ago, I threw a man off this tower who didn't have anything I needed. You have the only thing I need. So, believe me. I will kill you too."

Darcy's eyes widen in terror. "No, you won't kill me."

"I will kill you."

"I know you won't kill me."

"Believe me, I will. I will kill you."

Serenity chased terror from Darcy's face. "Yes. Yes, I believe you. You will kill me. You won't let me end up back in Mississippi dancing at The Eager Beaver, will you? You won't let me suffer anymore humiliations. Yes, kill me. Don't let me suffer anymore. Thank you, doll. You're a true sister to me."

Darcy let go of Molka's wrists.

Her body went limp.

Molka placed her mouth to Darcy's ear and whispered. "The one you sold the drone swarm to is responsible for killing my little sister. Please tell me."

Darcy closed her eyes. "I love you like an older sister loves her younger sister."

Molka bent Darcy farther over the rail. "Who killed my little sister!"

"I love you like an older sister loves her younger sister."

Molka bent Darcy even farther over the rail. "I loved my little sister! Tell me who killed her!"

"I love you like an older sister loves her younger sister."

Molka released Darcy's neck, lifted her, and held her in dropping position over the railing. "WHO KILLED MY LITTLE JANETTA?"

Darcy's eyes remained closed. "I love you like an older sister loves her younger sister."

Rapid clunking sounded behind Molka.

Heavy boots charging up the tower steps.

Prepare to defend!

Molka brought Darcy back inside the railing and dropped her.

Darcy's repetitive babbling continued.

Molka silenced her with a chin shot and propped her into a sitting position against the pillar.

The hatch opened.

The colonel entered.

His sidearm holstered.

"Lieutenant who drives truck, did you activate a signal laser from this tower?"

"Signal? Laser?" Molka faked a laugh. "No, no, we were having a little private girl talk. We brought a laser pointer because it's so dark in here and we were playing around with it."

The colonel viewed Darcy's unconsciousness.

"We were also drinking," Molka said. "She passed out."

The colonel moved to the railing and looked down. "From below, I observed you two quarreling and you seemingly about to drop her to her death." He turned back to Molka. "Do you wish to continue insulting me with this absurd explanation?"

"No, sir. Colonel, the Canadian National Police will conduct a major operation here at 0342 hours. They're coming for Darcy, Besnik, and you."

"This I have always expected."

"And I don't have time to explain, but before they arrive, I'm taking Aden out of here and destroying Building A, and if anyone tries to stop me," Molka pulled her pistol again, "I'll kill them. So tell me now, do I have to start with you?"

The colonel's booming laugh resonated within the tower. "Azzur warned me of your unpredictable volatility."

Molka lowered her pistol and winced. "You removed the previous veterinarian so I could come here. You assigned me to the Red Zone when I came on your team. You covered for the MATADORS I gave Truman to hold. You approved me as detention guard when Darcy had me moved out of the Red Zone. How many more hints did I need that you're Azzur's asset here?"

"Azzur also told me of your exceptional perseverance and cleverness. He did not exaggerate."

"Thank you, sir," Molka said. "I won't even ask how you know Azzur or how you've been communicating with him."

"Good. This will save me the trouble of not telling you."

Molka put her pistol behind her back and removed three flex-cuff sets from her bag.

"It will not be necessary to detain her," the colonel said. "My SUV is downstairs; I will take her to the dean's residence where we will await our fates together."

"I'm not detaining her. I'm restraining her. I'm about to give her an enhanced interrogation." Molka dug out the latex gloves and started to pull them over her tactical gloves. "She has information I need."

"Fear has failed, so now you will resort to force."

"You may not want to stay for this, sir."

"Is the information you seek from Principal Darcy crucial to your mission?"

"Not exactly, sir."

"What then?"

"Information of a personal nature."

"Lieutenant who drives truck, you are an outstanding soldier. And as such, you are aware you cannot allow a personal matter to compromise your mission."

"Yes, sir. But this is…this is a personal matter of extreme importance to me."

"Do not give me the details of your plan because I will soon be questioned by the authorities and will not lie to them, but is it safe to assume it is very time constrained?"

"Yes, sir."

"And can I also assume the time you allotted to obtain this personal information has now passed?"

Molka consulted her watch: 2:10AM. "Yes, sir."

"Then you must go now."

"I can't, sir."

"Take Principal Darcy's cart to expedite your movements. I will order security confined to barracks. But I can assist you no further. Go now."

Molka's jaw clinched. "No, sir." She pointed at Darcy. "She's probably going to prison. I'll never get this chance again."

"And the countless potential victims of her appalling weapon will never get this chance again either."

"But the situation has changed, sir. If I don't destroy Building A and leave with Aden before the Canadian authorities get here, they'll secure the slaughterbots and keep Aden for themselves. And they'll never use them. And they'll never allow Aden to fall into the wrong hands again."

"Such determinations by you do not fall within the parameters of your mission and are certainly not your privilege."

"I know, sir. But—"

"Will you honor your mission?" the colonel said.

"Sir, I just can't leave without—"

"Will you honor your mission?"

Molka spun, rage-gripped the railing, and swore softly into the darkness. Azzur was right. Her inner rogue had tried to talk her into committing a selfish personal act. *Damn him! Why is that bastard always right?*

"Will you honor your mission?" the colonel said.

Molka thrust off the railing, spun back, and inhaled, defiant.

"Lieutenant who drives truck, will you honor your mission?"

Molka exhaled, resigned. "Yes, sir."

CHAPTER 53

"**I** come in peace," a double peace sign gesturing Molka said from the surveillance room doorway.

Hamu flinched and swiveled his chair around. "The colonel ordered a barracks confinement drill. That means everyone must remain in barracks until he orders otherwise."

"I know what it means."

"Your barracks is back in detention. Why are you bothering me in mine?"

Molka left her tactical bag in the hall, entered, and peered over Hamu's shoulder at the monitor screens. "Still using your drones to peep on those pretty young girls from the laundry staff?"

"Who told you?"

"A lifetime of being peeped on by degenerates like you."

Hamu seethed on his monitors. "I'm still going to kill you someday."

"Glad you said that. Makes this easy for me."

"Makes what easy?"

Molka's roundhouse kick flung him unconscious from chair to floor.

She snatched her bag, jogged back to the detention area, flipped on the florescent lighting for cell number two, and opened the door.

Valentina rolled over in her bunk, blinking. "Breakfast already?" She sniffed her track suit's sleeve. "Yek. Can you bring me a change of clothes today?"

"I don't have time to ease you into this," Molka said. "The Counsel sent me to take Aden out of here."

Valentina laughed. "The Counsel sent you." Her laugh blunted on Molka's unamused face. "The Counsel sent you?"

"Yes."

"I thought the Counsel did not have people for these types of operations anymore."

"They don't," Molka said. "I'm going to release you, but first I need you to tell me what your plan for getting Aden out was."

"Why?"

"To make sure it won't interfere with mine."

"I was to convince Aden to leave with me, and first chance we got, set fire to Building A to destroy all the drones and steal and fly out on Darcy's jet. He is a pilot, you know?"

Molka raised sarcastic eyebrows. "That's the best the ISS— with all their legendary brain power—came up with?"

"Time limited the options. Darcy only approved my visit two weeks ago."

"Ok. But the jet's been here since you arrived. What were you waiting on?"

"Aden was not ready," Valentina said. "He said it was his loyalty to Darcy. But I think it was really you he was not ready to leave."

"And if you brought him back, would you be allowed to stay with him again?"

Valentina frowned. "Yes, we would be together again like nothing ever happened. What is your plan?"

"A contractor team will extract us by helicopter."

"When?"

"Less than an hour," Molka said. "And there's something else. In less than two hours, the Canadian National Police will conduct a tactical operation here. They have warrants for Darcy,

Besnik, and Colonel Krasnov. Everyone else will be detained for questioning. But what they really want is Aden and what's in Building A."

"Who doesn't."

"I have something to ask," Molka said. "We don't play for the same team, but both our teams play in the same league. Right?"

"I do not understand."

"Ok. We don't play in the same band, but both our bands play on the same label. Agreed?"

"Yes, I would agree."

"I'm running a little behind. I could use your help."

"Remember, I am not a real spy girl. I am just a clueless diva high on my own fame. What could I possibly do to help?"

Molka pulled out Owen's keycard and handed it to Valentina. "I know Aden's upset and disappointed with you—"

Valentina. "You think?"

"But go to him right now and tell him I said we're leaving for home tonight. Then get him out of the Security Zone immediately. Don't bring anything with you, including any drones. I'm going to destroy Building A in the next 30 minutes."

"How?"

"Violently," Molka said. "Open the loft's curtains and turn on every light as you leave. That will be my signal you're out." Molka took the folded notebook paper from her pocket and gave it to Valentina. "That's Rosina's housing unit number. Take Aden there. Rosina is expecting you. She has Principe with her. Wait there until 2:50 AM and bring Aden to the central courtyard. That's the extraction point. It's only a 5-minute walk, but make sure you have him there no later than 3:00 AM. Understand?"

Valentina nodded. "Yes. What time is it now?"

Molka consulted her watch: "2:24. Repeat my instructions back to me."

"Get Aden out of Building A right now. Don't bring anything including drones. Open the curtains and turn on the lights before we leave. Take Aden to Rosina's room. Wait there until 2:50 AM and then get Aden to the central courtyard. Make sure he is there no later than 3:00 AM."

"Wow," Molka said. "That was good."

"And will I be leaving with you and Aden?"

"The contractor team is only expecting two passengers. They don't make exceptions."

Valentina exhaled, thoughtful. "I guess I could steal a vehicle and head for Vancouver."

"They're blocking the road out of here. They might shoot you if you try to run it. Let's go."

Valentina followed Molka into the foyer area. "When Darcy or Besnik or Krasnov tells the police I work for the ISS, I'll be detained again. Legitimately this time."

Molka opened the outer door and faced her. "I know. I'm sorry."

Valentina fluffed out her hair. "Well, there goes my career. Both of them."

"These things are usually kept quiet. It's embarrassing to both sides. Maybe your people can work out an exchange in a few months or a year. Until then, I've heard Canadian jails aren't that bad."

"Thanks," Valentina said. "Very comforting." Her eyes jumped over Molka's shoulder, and she whispered. "There is a big guy coming down the hall with a gun."

Hamu stopped and aimed. "I told you I would kill you someday! Today is that day!"

Molka whirled and crouched simultaneously; her pistol was in her hand when she faced Hamu. Two rapid, silenced chest shots ended his threats forever.

Valentina's astonished gaze turned to Molka. "You are a hard woman."

"I was almost too soft. I should have taken time to cuff, if not, kill him." Molka motioned toward the utility closet across the hall. "Help me drag him in there."

They dragged and stuffed Hamu's bulk into the tiny space, squeezed the door shut, and ran to the security HQ front door.

"Wait. Before you go." Valentina stopped Molka by the arm. "If I do not get a chance to tell you later, take care of Aden when you get him back home. He really is just a lost, scared little boy."

"I'll see you and Aden in the central courtyard soon."

"What will you be doing until then?" Valentina said.

"I have a date."

CHAPTER 54

Darcy surrendered herself to the bed in the dean's residence. A wet washcloth covered her eyes, and an ice pack rested on her delicate chin.

A tranquil-faced colonel sat in a chair to her right.

A turmoil-faced Besnik sat in a chair to her left.

Greenie Greg waited outside the door.

Besnik buried his toad face in his toad hands. "I have dedicated over 30 years to the law and to building a stellar reputation. This was not supposed to be my destiny."

The colonel unleashed his booming laugh. "Destiny; a tyrant's authority for crime and a fool's excuse for failure."

Besnik lowered his hands and raised his head. "At least I will not be subjected to your banal Russian proverbs much longer."

"That is not Russian," the colonel said. "In Russia, we say 'after losing one's head, one does not grieve over the hair.'"

Besnik glared. "Screw Russia."

The colonel boomed another laugh.

Darcy removed the cloth from her face and set the ice pack aside. "Colonel Krasnov is—" She cringed and touched her jaw. "Oww. Colonel Krasnov is right. We should face the inevitable with professionalism rather than emotion." She rolled on her side toward the colonel. "How did you say Doctor Molka would get Aden away from here?"

"I did not say, and I do not know, nor do I wish to know."

"Sounds like you approve of their vile, back-stabbing traitorous action."

"I do not approve nor disapprove."

"And that's a non-approval approval. Just like one of Dean Besnik's dirty little legal tricks. But you didn't bring me here because you're concerned about my mental and physical wellbeing." Darcy pointed to the colonel's sidearm. "You wanted to make sure I don't run off. Because you're in on it too. Right?"

The colonel smiled, relaxed. "I cannot agree nor disagree."

"And what time did you say Doctor Molka's cop friends would arrive?"

"I did not say. However, I will tell you, our freedom will end shortly after 3:42 AM."

Darcy rolled off the bed to her feet. "Friend Greg, please come in here."

Greenie Greg entered. "Yes, Darcy?"

"I believe there are two bottles of the blue-labeled vodka Colonel Krasnov enjoys on the bar downstairs. Please bring them to me along with three shot glasses."

"Yes, Darcy." He ran to obey.

"We'll drink a toast to our demise," Darcy said.

The colonel offered an amiable smile. "An excellent suggestion."

Greenie Greg returned with the goods.

The colonel's face lit up. He and Besnik stood.

"I'll take those, Friend Greg," Darcy said. "And please wait outside."

Greenie Greg passed Darcy the two full vodka bottles and three shot glasses and excused himself.

Darcy handed the colonel one bottle and the shot glasses and retained the other bottle in her right hand. "Colonel Krasnov if you would please do the honors. You may use the dresser as a bar."

The colonel put his back to the wall beside the dresser, placed the shot glasses on the dresser top, poured, and distributed the round.

Darcy raised her glass. "To tragedy!"

The colonel and Besnik in unison: "To tragedy!"

All three downed.

"Whew!" Darcy examined the vodka bottle she still held. "This stuff's no joke. I like it though. Let's do another. I have a special toast I would like to make."

The colonel put his back to the wall beside the dresser again and poured and distributed another round.

Darcy raised her glass and faced the colonel. "I know I haven't been easy to work for. And I never gave you the appreciation for all the fine work you did for me. So in the spirit of better late than never, I thank and salute Colonel Nikolai Vasilyevich Krasnov—an honorable soldier."

The colonel's adamant blue eyes teared over.

All three downed.

Darcy hopped in place. "Woo-hoo! Now it's a party! You're turn, colonel. Do you know any funny, dirty toasts?"

The colonel smiled playfully. "I may be able to recall a few dozen." He turned his back to the party-goers to repour.

Darcy eased behind him, raised the bottle in her hand over the colonel's head, and swung down.

CUNK!

The colonel landed loud and lay silent.

Greenie Greg burst back into the room. "Are you alright, Darcy?"

Darcy bent and examined a burgeoning hematoma on the back of the colonel's hatless head. "In movies, the bottle breaks on the skull. In real life, the skull breaks on the bottle."

Besnik bent to inspect the wound too. "You might have killed him."

"If I didn't, I should have."

"It was your complimentary toast to him," Besnik said. "He was very moved. He dropped his guard. You always uncover the exploitable weakness, Darcy."

"Death to traitors." Darcy rushed into the walk-in closet and started stripping. "Come in here, both of you."

Besnik and Greenie Greg stepped into the closet.

"Friend Greg," Darcy said, "I want you to sound a campus fire drill."

"Yes, Darcy."

"Then get First Sergeant Owen and tell him I have relieved the colonel of his duties and chosen him to be the colonel's replacement."

"Yes, Darcy."

Darcy slithered into a tight black cocktail dress. "Tell him the reason for the colonel's dismissal was he showed up here drunk and belligerent and had to be subdued by the Friends, and he remains sedated in the care of the school physician."

"Yes, Darcy."

Darcy exited the closet carrying black heels. Besnik and greenie Greg trailed her out.

Darcy sat in a chair and slipped on the heels. "Then tell First Sergeant Owen that Aden and Doctor Molka are attempting to leave the school tonight. He is to lock it down to prevent this. And then he is to bring Aden, Doctor Molka, and Valentina to me at the stadium. And tell him to stay off the radios. Doctor Molka may be listening in, so you will act as his messenger boy. Do you understand?"

"Yes, Darcy."

"Go."

He ran to obey.

Darcy rose, moved to the vanity mirror, and brushed her hair.

"The fire drill is an excellent idea," Besnik said. "When the persecutors arrive, they will not find a disorderly rabble, but an orderly assembly. We will show them the true dignity of Hazlehurst Institute."

Darcy laid on a string of pearls. They popped lustrous on her black dress. "How do I look?"

Besnik's face unmasked longing. "Exquisite. Gorgeous. Spectacular. You have never looked more beautiful in my eyes, Darcy."

Darcy applied two Clive Christian No. 1 sprays and turned to Besnik. "I'm not going back broke to Mississippi after a Canadian prison term. I have another final destination in mind. But before I go, I'm going to drop a world-class tragedy on the persecutor's asses. They'll spend the next 50 years pointing their hypocritical blame fingers at each other."

"What will you do, Darcy?"

"When the students are all gathered in the stadium, I'm deploying their Personal Security Drones as a swarm."

"Deploying them? But they..." Besnik returned to his bedside chair and buried his toad face in his toad hands again. "Darcy, when you asked me to instruct Aden to weaponize the PSDs, I understood it was a loyalty test for him. And also, for me, because ours were included. But I never thought we would actually...You really wish to kill the students?"

Darcy began refreshing her makeup. "They were already dead when they came to me. Every day they've lived since has been a bonus. A gift I gave them. And without me, they'll all give up and die miserable anyway. Why make them suffer that in their remaining years? This will be my final act of merciful loving kindness to them."

Besnik raised his face. "Even so, it would be a horrible legacy."

"Well, if you have to go down, you may as well go down like a boss, right? And after I deploy the student's PSDs, and I see what's done is done, I'm going to deploy ours. Are you with me?"

Besnik started at her mortified. "Ours too?"

"Yes, ours too. The true Doomsday Scenario is upon us."

"I know we have talked about the Doomsday Scenario for years, and what we would do if things really went sideways, but I just never believed it would really happen."

Darcy reapplied her lipstick. "Face it, you're much too delicate for prison, Bezie. After one day, you'd be made some 385-pound. drug dealer's bitch boy on your knees trimming his toenails and doing much worse, wouldn't you?"

"Probably."

"Then are you with me?"

"Darcy, I...I..."

"Are you with me?"

"Darcy, what you ask me to—"

Darcy rushed to Besnik and grabbed his face. "We've lived more in these last four years than most people could live in 400 lifetimes. And we lived them on our own terms, haven't we?"

"Yes, Darcy."

"Now let's take it all the way and die on our own terms too. Together." She kissed him hard on the mouth and pushed him away. "Last time I'll ask—are you with me?"

Besnik's face enraptured. "Oh yes, Darcy. Yes, I am with you. I am with you until the end."

"Get me pad and pen."

Besnik produced both items from another room and handed them over. Darcy wrote on the notepad, tore off the page, and gave it to Besnik.

"What is this?"

"Our final statements. Take out your phone and video yourself reading it."

"Yes, Darcy."

Besnik removed his phone from his jacket breast pocket, held it for a selfie-video, and read:

"To the persecutors—this is my final statement. We came here to live and work in peace but lying traitors from within and without have betrayed us in the most vile and unfair manner. We will not allow you to take our freedom because the authority by which you come to persecute us is illegitimate. Therefore, we chose to commit an act of revolutionary suicide protesting the conditions of an inhumane world. I bear full responsibility for what occurred here on this night. Death to traitors." He stopped the video and admired Darcy. "A beautiful indictment."

"Put your phone back in your pocket," Darcy said. "So, the persecutors can find it when they find you."

"Yes, Darcy."

"My turn."

Darcy removed her phone from a purse and took a selfie-video of her reading the statement.

Besnik did not notice she failed to push the record button.

Darcy finished and tossed her phone back in the purse. "Let's get to the stadium." She bent and pulled the Black Night Case from under the bed. "Now listen carefully to what I'm about to tell you…"

Darcy left the room with Besnik at her heels.

The colonel opened his eyes.

 **CHAPTER 55**

"What are you doing with Principal Darcy's personal transporter?" Narcisse said, standing beside the gunship on its landing pad.

"Hurrying things along." Molka hopped from the driver seat. "Have you been too?"

"Yes. We can takeoff whenever you are ready."

Molka peeked in the cockpit. All systems were powered up including the pilot's helmet-mounted display.

Narcisse tapped the feed chute on the 20-millimeter cannon. "And I loaded 500 rounds of HEI for your tree burning fetish."

"Perfect," Molka said.

Narcisse's eyes fondled her. "*Belle*, you look so beautiful out of uniform. Maybe I will see you even more out of uniform before this night is over?"

Molka feigned playfulness. "Anything is possible tonight. And since you mentioned it, why don't we run into the hangar office for a little pre-flight fun?"

His lascivious face didn't argue.

Molka fast-jogged toward the hangar. Narcisse kept pace alongside. Halfway there, the campus loudspeakers spoke:

Attention, students. This is a fire drill.

Report to your assigned seat in the stadium immediately.
Attention, students. This is a fire drill.
Report to your assigned seat in the stadium immediately.
The prerecorded message looped on.

Narcisse shook his head. "Dragging these old people out of their warm beds for a fire drill at this hour? I tell you, Principal Darcy gets more and more crazy by the day."

Molka followed Narcisse into the hangar office.

Narcisse eyed Molka's duffle bag. "You still have not told me what is in your bag."

"You're about to find out. But first, you won't be needing your weapon. Take it off. Quickly."

He removed his shoulder holster, tossed it on the card table, and smiled. "Should I keep taking things off?"

"Not yet." Molka pointed to a chair. "Sit down. Move fast."

"Yes! I love when you order me." He sat fast.

Molka removed flex cuff sets from her bag.

Narcisse's face perked with arousal. "How did you know I crave to be restrained by a beautiful woman?"

Molka cuffed his hands behind his back and each ankle to a chair leg.

"Try to stand," she said.

He tried. He couldn't.

"Try harder."

He tried harder. He still couldn't.

"I am totally at your mercy," Narcisse said. "What will you do to me now?"

Molka re-zipped and re-slung her bag. "You really like pain?"

Narcisse bowed his head. "Please do your worst, *Mistress Belle*."

"Ok. Ever had your pride whipped?"

"What?"

Molka ran out, slammed the door behind her, and sprinted toward the gunship. Ten meters from reaching it, something in her periphery turned her head.

Did someone just run into the hangar? No. Seeing things in the dark.

Molka opened the gunship's pilot door, tossed her bag into the backseat, slid into the pilot's seat, and strapped in. She took a moment to familiarize herself with the cyclic, collective, and pedals. And even though Narcisse had implied he had already done an engine prestart check, old training habits took over.

Rotor break: RELEASED.

Fuel shut-off lever: FORWARD.

Twist grip: IDLE.

Starting selector…

Movement in her periphery again.

Someone exiting the hangar office.

Narcisse!

Charging toward her!

Pistol aimed at her!

Molka unbuckled, pulled her pistol, opened the co-pilot's door, dove onto the apron, and rolled.

Narcisse charged on. His face transformed from masochist to sadist. "LIAR! TRAITOR! GET AWAY FROM MY GUNSHIP!"

He fired.

His shot tore into the concrete next to Molka's head.

Warning shot? No time to find out.

Molka's return shot tore into Narcisse's head.

She ran to his dead body. *Fool! You're a fellow pilot, I was trying to let you live. How did you get free?* Her eyes flicked to Greenie Greg standing outside the open hanger office door. "That's how." She aimed a combat stance on him. "Hands on your head."

He complied.

"Get over here! Run!"

Greenie Greg ran to her with hands on head.

"Face down!" Molka said.

He complied.

Molka frisked him for a weapon. None.

"Are you going to kill me too?" Greenie Greg said.

Molka tucked the pistol behind her back. "No."

"Why did you kill Security Officer Narcisse?"

"Did you cut him loose?"

"Yes."

"Then you killed him. Stand up."

He complied.

Molka's blur-quick boot-to-the face front kick laid him right back down.

Molka returned to the gunship, re-strapped in, pulled on the helmet, and flipped the starter switches.

The turbines spun up.

The blades started rotating.

The cabin rocked with their building power.

The engine's high whine transitioned into a thumping roar.

The old thrill electrified Molka.

It had been a long time.

She had missed it even more than she knew.

But no time to savor memories.

She checked her watch: 2:31 AM

She lifted off and flew toward Building A.

CHAPTER 56

Three hundred and seventy-nine sexagenarian, septuagenarian, and octogenarian students—clad in sweaters and jackets over pajamas—sleepwalked into Hazlehurst stadium. A dozen greenies helped them to their assigned fire drill seats in the grandstand.

A microphoned podium waited on the lighted field below. Darcy, flanked by dual greenies, stood behind the podium with her back to the students and admired her illuminated statue across the river. Her left hand held the Black Night Case.

Besnik shivered at her side.

"How long does it usually take them to get here and get seated?" Darcy said.

"About 25 minutes," Besnik said.

"Sweet Savannah. Good thing we never had a real fire. What time is it now?"

Besnik used his right hand to steady his left wrist to view his luxurious gold watch. "Two thirty-one, Darcy."

Darcy smiled serene and placed a hand on Besnik's shoulder. "Be brave, Bezie. It's nearly over."

"Yes, Darcy."

Owen herded Aden and Valentina at submachine gun point across the running track and to the podium. "Caught these two leaving the Security Zone in a helluva hurry. Miss Valentina won't tell me who sprung her, but it had to be the doc."

Aden motioned at the students struggling into their seats. "Principal Darcy, is that really necessary? And is this really necessary?" He pointed at Owen's weapon pointing at him. "Why be vindictive now?"

Darcy scolded Aden over her shoulder. "Vindictive? You never appreciated anything I did for you."

"Principal Darcy—Darcy—it's over."

"Not yet, smartacus. But all thanks to you, it soon will be." Darcy turned back to her statue.

Aden viewed the Black Night Case in Darcy's hand, looked again to the students still congregating in the grandstand, and focused back on Darcy adoring her statue. "Darcy…what are you thinking about? I hope you're not thinking about doing something reckless and horrible here. It's not right to hurt innocent people for your mistakes. Darcy?"

Darcy kept her back turned. "First Sergeant Owen?"

Owen stepped around Aden and Valentina. "Yes, Principal Darcy?"

"Where is Doctor Molka?"

"Not sure. The front gate is locked down and no vehicles are missing. So, she ain't likely left campus. Hamu isn't in surveillance though, so we don't have eyes on her yet."

"And where is Security Officer Hamu?" Besnik said.

"I don't know that either. Sometimes when the colonel is away, he likes to go play. Probably chasing some young tail over in the staff compound. I'll kick his ass from here to the Yukon later. But I have Gervaso and Yeong searching for her. And I sent Greenie Greg to tell Narcisse to get the gunship up to help look. You can hear him up now. We'll find her in a—"

THUNG!
THUNG!
THUNG!
THUNG!
THUNG!
THUNG!

The successive explosions rocked the Security Zone.

All heads swung toward them.

"What the hell?" Owen said.

Light-gray smoke plumed over the Red Zone area.

Owen pointed. "I think Building A exploded!"

All watched the gunship fly through the smoke, bank around, hover, and spew a hot red-orange stream of 20-millimeter cannon rounds downward.

"Holy shit!" Owen said.

A disconcerted murmur emanated from the students.

Another 20-millimeter cannon burst and...

HUGE EXPLOSION.

"Narcisse has lost his damn mind!" Owen said.

Darcy smiled sly. "Hell must know I'm on the way." She turned and addressed a female greenie on her left. "Friend Jennifer, please bring me my Range Rover."

"Yes, Darcy." She ran to obey.

Darcy laughed past Owen's shoulder. "First Sergeant Owen, you've lost your sheep."

Owen twirled and watched Valentina—pulling Aden by the hand—running toward the stadium exit. "Damn it! I'll go fetch them back."

"Let them go," Darcy said. "They can't run from their punishments. Get the front gate open for me."

"Open the front gate?" Owen said.

"Yes. It's time."

"Time for what?" Owen said. "And are you going to tell me the real reason you have the colonel sedated? Because I'm not believing the drunk and belligerent story. The colonel gets drunk to keep from being belligerent."

"Please open the front gate," Besnik said. "Principal Darcy wishes to leave the campus."

Owen shot Besnik a puzzled look. "What's going on here?"

"Just open the gate and do your job as we agreed. Your reward awaits."

"Ok, Deanie. I got you." Owen ran to obey.

Darcy stepped to the podium, raised her hands to still the students, and spoke into the microphone. "Students. Please compose yourselves."

They composed.

"The noise you hear and smoke you see is part of this fire drill exercise. Our brave campus fire department needs to practice too."

A relieved murmur emanated from the students.

"So everyone maintain calm while the drill continues."

A compliant murmur emanated from the students.

"Would you like to sing our school song while we wait?"

The student body cheered approval, arose, and sang:

I love me, this I know,
For Principal Darcy tells me so;
To myself I belong;
I was weak, but now I'm strong.
Yes, I love me!
Yes, I love me!
Yes, I love me!
For Principal Darcy tells me so!

Darcy soaked in the admiration until the last note's echo faded and presented a smile to charm the ages. "That was lovely, students. Now I must leave you for a moment and inspect the drill. I would like all of you to remain seated until I return. No matter what you may see or hear, please remain seated and remain calm. I promise you, this will all be over very soon."

Darcy's Range Rover arrived on the field beside the podium. Darcy approached the driver's door. "Thank you, Friend Jennifer. I will drive myself."

Friend Jennifer and Darcy exchanged places.

Darcy waved Besnik to the driver's window and passed him the Black Night Case. "Are you ready to follow my final instructions?"

Besnik averted his eyes. "Yes, Darcy."

"Look me in the eyes and tell me."

Besnik surrendered to Darcy's eyes and straightened his tie. "Yes, Darcy. I am ready to follow your final instructions."

She pinched Besnik's toad cheek. "Exactly what I expected from you, Bezie."

As Darcy drove from the stadium, the students serenaded her again:

I love me, this I know,

For Principal Darcy tells me so;
To myself I belong;
I was weak, but now I'm strong.
Yes, I love me!
Yes, I love me!
Yes, I love me!
For Principal Darcy tells me so!

# CHAPTER 57

Good work, Valentina!

All the curtains stood open, and all the lights blazed in Aden's loft.

Target clear of friendlies.

Free to engage.

Molka hovered the gunship over Building A at a safe firing distance, targeted the roof through the helmet-mounted display, and triggered a six-round 40-millimeter grenade salvo:

THUNG!

THUNG!

THUNG!

THUNG!

THUNG!

THUNG!

The roof disappeared under the explosions and a light gray cloud. She orbited around to clear the drifting smoke and admired a massive hole extending through all three floors.

She hovered again, targeted the opening, and fired the 20-millimeter cannon.

The gunship shook as the cannon buzzed out a hot red-orange high-explosive incendiary projectile stream at 6,000 rounds per minute.

Flames leapt from the hole.

She sent in another cannon burst and…

HUGE EXPLOSION.

Building A collapsed.

Its terrible contents engulfed.

Target destroyed.

Time to leave.

Molka headed for the central courtyard.

CHAPTER 58

The colonel agonized onto his back, rose tormented to his knees, and moaned to his feet. He swayed across the bedroom into the master bath, turned his back to the mirror, squinted over his shoulder, parted red sticky, blood-matted hair, and examined a nasty wound but an intact skull.

"When you make the decision to strike a deathblow, leave no one behind to disagree."

He swayed less returning to the bedroom, seized the vodka bottle from the dresser, fortified with a long swig, and with struggling determination, left the room.

CHAPTER 59

"**P**rincipal Darcy wishes to leave the campus!" Owen mock announced inside the dead silent security HQ. "Great idea. Let's all leave this goddamn madhouse."

As ordered, he opened the front gate from the surveillance room master control panel, jogged to the squad room, and checked the vehicle key cabinet. Still no keys missing.

He grabbed the keys to an SUV and jogged up to the barracks room. He unslung his submachine gun and unfastened his duty belt, tossed both on his bunk, and stripped his uniform. He opened his locker and popped the tags from a new fishing logo tee shirt, new blue jeans, a new truck logo cap, and unboxed new cowboy boots.

Reoutfitted, Owen re-slung his submachine gun, packed a quick dip, and resumed his jog back downstairs, out the rear door, and over to the armory. To gain access, he used a new keycard he had obtained. Gervaso reported he couldn't find his last one that Molka supposedly threw into the bushes when she jumped him.

He jogged to the pistol section and grabbed a small semi-automatic Walther PPK. He loaded it and concealed it in his right boot.

Next, he hustled over an aisle and grabbed a long olive-green metal case containing a Stinger portable shoulder-fired missile. He carried the case outside to his chosen SUV, opened the tailgate, and rested the case on it.

Gervaso and Yeong exited the security HQ rear door and ran toward Owen.

"What are you two jackasses doing back here?" Owen said.

"We came to report," Gervaso said. "You told us to stay off the net. We couldn't find Molka anywhere on campus." He viewed Building A's smoking carcass. "What the hell happened?"

"Crazy ass Narcisse has finally gone full-on-crazy," Owen said. "You seen Hamu?"

"Negative."

"What about Aden? You seen him in the last few minutes?"

"Negative."

Owen spit dip. "Something majorly fucked is going on around here." He looked to Yeong. "Turn the floodlights on."

Yeong ran to obey.

Gervaso said, "Do you want us to start searching the staff compound for Molka?"

"Forget her. Deploy your twin 23s and take down Narcisse before the fool kills us all."

"Roger that. I just saw him over the central courtyard."

Owen popped the latches and opened the case. "Refresh me, weapons expert. Once you insert the battery unit into the launcher, the missile is ready to rock, right?"

"Right. What do you need the Stinger for?"

Owen reclosed the case, pushed it in the cargo area, and slammed the tailgate shut. "If you miss Narcisse, I don't want him getting me."

Owen jumped into the SUV and burned tires.

On the zigzag road exiting the Security Zone, his headlights hit Greenie Greg waving from Darcy's transporter.

Owen skidded to a stop next to him. "Where the hell have you been? Never mind. I don't need you anymore. Tell Besnik I quit and I'm leaving. But first I'm taking care of the job. I'll meet him at his office in Vancouver tomorrow to collect." He squinted at an ugly swollen knot over Greenie Greg's left eye. "Damn, son. Who hit you?"

"Doctor Molka. She shot and killed Narcisse, kicked me in the face, and flew off in the gunship."

"The hell you say."

"It's true!"

Owen leapt out, snatched Greenie Greg's left arm, and twisted it behind him into a merciless armlock.

Greenie Greg screamed.

"Hurts, don't it?" Owen said. "That unbearable pain burning in your elbow is your bursa sac about to rupture. And the only way you can stop it is to tell me what the fuck's really going on here!"

CHAPTER 60

Molka landed in the central courtyard on the opposite end from the ice cream stand to give the contractor helicopter maximum room. She cut the power, unbuckled, removed the helmet, and jumped out.

Aden and Valentina emerged astonished from crouched concealment behind a bench.

Molka ran to them.

"And you're a pilot too?" Aden said.

Molka smiled. "Surprised?"

"With you, not anymore. But Molka—"

Molka checked her watch. "You're early. About 18 minutes to extraction. Thanks, Valentina. You're not quite the clueless diva high on fame you claim to be."

Valentina managed a faint smile. "Please do not tell my fans."

"Molka," Aden said.

Molka admired the flaring flames rising above the Red Zone. "Look at that baby burn! I have to admit, that was a lot of fun."

"Molka," Aden said again.

Molka rattled on. "Things are working out better than I thought. The colonel is with us. He stood security down. Wonder if he turned the floodlights on to help the extraction chopper? But I'll explain everything later when we get home. Home. I can't wait until we get home…"

Valentina laid her head on Aden's shoulder and fought tears behind closed eyes.

"Molka!" Aden said. "Listen to me! Darcy had a breakdown!"

"I know," Molka said. "It's sad. Hopefully, she'll get help in prison."

"She's in the stadium with all the students. We just saw her. I don't think she's going to let them arrest her."

"She's not with the colonel?"

"The colonel wasn't there," Aden said. "I think Darcy wants to kill herself. But first she's going to deploy everyone's Personal Security Drone."

"Didn't I just destroy them?"

"No. She had me move them to a secured container inside her statue's pedestal. That's probably why she called the fire drill, to concentrate the students in the stadium right across from the statue—to make it fast and easy for their PSDs to find them as a swarm."

"Find them for what?" Molka said.

Aden sat on the bench and dropped his chin to chest.

Molka knelt before him. "Aden, if Darcy has a death wish, why would she bother deploying all our PSDs to find us?"

"I've made a horrible mistake."

"Why is she deploying the PSDs?"

Aden whispered like a scared little boy. "It was a loyalty test. It was just supposed to be a loyalty test." He dropped his chin and again. "What have I done?"

"Loyalty test?" Molka said. "What did you do?"

"I've helped her kill us all."

"Kill us? Did you…are those drones…did you weaponize the PSDs too?"

Aden whimpered. "It was only supposed to be a loyalty test. The Doomsday Scenario Dean Besnik told me about wasn't a real thing. It was just a loyalty test. But they lied to me. She lied to me. They always lie to me."

Molka clutched Aden's shirt front and yanked his face to hers. "ARE THE PSDs WEAPONIZED?"

"I'm sorry." Aden's eyes pled to Molka. "Please don't hate me."

Valentina held up hands. "Wait, wait, wait. No, no, no, dying; was definitely not in my agreement."

Molka addressed Valentina. "How long ago did you see Darcy in the stadium?"

"Maybe 10 minutes ago," Valentina said. "But she ordered a greenie to bring her Range Rover for some reason."

"To drive to the statue." Molka pulled Aden to his feet. "How are the PSDs released?"

"By entering a code into a keypad inside the pedestal."

Molka checked her watch. "Extraction in about sixteen minutes. It's a 20-minute drive from the campus to the statue. But less than a minute's flight from here. I might have time to use the gunship to destroy the PSD swarm in the pedestal before she deploys it."

Valentina clutched Molka's arm. "NO! You still have time to fly us out!"

Molka addressed Aden. "Is it possible to outrun the PSDs?"

"Yes," Aden said. "They're only programmed to search for their targets within a five-kilometer radius of the campus."

"We could clear that quickly," Molka said. "But there's only fuel left for about 500 kilometers—150 short of Vancouver."

"It does not matter!" Valentina said. "We can walk the rest of the way if we have to! Get us away from here!"

Molka confronted Aden and Valentina's panicked faces. "Alright."

All jogged toward the gunship.

Scenes from Azzur's slaughterbot horror movie replayed in Molka's head. Would it play out in real life as terrifying and gruesome on the innocent elderly students waiting in the stadium grandstand?

Shame sickened her.

Molka stopped and turned. "I've got to try."

Valentina clutched Molka's arm again. "Oh no, you do not!"

Molka jerked away. "Yes, I do!"

"No, you do not!"

Aden placed calm hands on Valentina's shoulders. "Yes. She does."

Molka checked her watch again. "Extraction in about 14 minutes. I'll be right back. But if I'm not—"

"If you're not, it won't matter," Aden said. "We'll all be dead."

 **CHAPTER 61**

The nimble little gunship featured a much faster rate of climb than the big rugged old Black Hawks Molka had flown with the Unit.

Thank goodness.

Within 30 seconds, she cleared the trees surrounding the central courtyard, cleared the campus building rooftops, and sped forward across the river toward Darcy's lighted likeness.

She reached the statue and hovered low at the thick stone pedestal's rear. It presented as a stout bunker-like structure with a keypad-locked heavy steel door. But the 40-millimeter high-explosive grenade rounds would break it.

They had to.

Molka climbed and moved off to a safe firing distance. When she turned back, hovered, and locked on the target, Darcy's Range Rover skidded to a dusty stop behind the pedestal. Darcy sprung from the driver's side, tapped on the pedestal's entry keypad, opened the door, and entered.

Wow. She's really going to do it. Kill us all.

The colonel's SUV skidded to a stop next to the Range Rover.

What's he doing?

The colonel charged inside the pedestal.

He had said he would hold Darcy for the police.

Did he join her insane mass murder-suicide pact?

But they had driven separate vehicles.

Was he chasing her?

Was he trying to stop her?

Can't chance it.

Prepare to fire!

Molka's thumb went to the trigger.

Killing strangers in combat was hard enough.

But I know them.

And I like one and respect the other.

Why did this fall to me?

How long does it take to punch in the swarm deployment code?

Sorry, colonel.

Sorry, Darcy.

Molka fired a long grenade round salvo.

Orange flashes and light-gray smoke encased the pedestal.

Atop it, the 80-foot-high granite Darcy statute shuddered, broke loose, and pitched headfirst toward the river below. Her outstretched arms made her descent look like a graceful swan dive.

She vanished with a geyser-like splash.

Molka pushed forward and damage assessed the pedestal remains—burning mutilation no drone could survive.

Ten meters to the wreckage's right, a larger blackened figure dragged a smaller blackened figure away from the flames.

Smoke rose from the larger blackened figure's back.

Molka didn't want to see anymore.

She checked her watch—about 10 minutes until extraction.

Molka went full throttle back toward the central courtyard. She re-crossed the river. On her right, the student body still filled the stadium stands despite the destructive drama occurring across from them.

Principal Darcy's cult of personality gripping on to the end.

WATCH OUT!

Glowing green tracer rounds crossed the gunship's nose. Molka banked hard left and identified the weapons carrier truck positioned outside the auditorium. Gervaso fired the bed mounted twin 23-millimeter cannons at her, and Yeong stood beside the truck hoisting ammo boxes.

Molka went into S-turns with large bank angles. More tracer rounds streaked underneath her. Gervaso could never hit her if she continued those evasive maneuvers. But his weapon might come as a lethal surprise to the contractor chopper.

It had to be taken out.

Molka came back around, went into a shallow dive, and aimed between the 23 millimeter's barrels.

Yeong recognized Molka's attack run, dropped an ammo can, and ran.

Molka triggered a four-round grenade salvo at the same moment Gervaso cut loose on her again.

She pulled up and banked hard right.

BOOMPH!

The huge thud came from the engine compartment.

Warning lights flashed.

Warning tones beeped.

Oil smoke entered the cabin.

You got to be kidding!

A 23 millimeter takes me down again!

Power faded.

Molka angled for the central courtyard.

Think I can make it.

It's going to be a hard landing though.

She passed over the weapons carrier. It burned with a charred Gervaso still seated at the cannon's controls.

Power faded further.

She scraped the treetops surrounding the courtyard.

Almost down!

Come on, girl!

As soon as she was over the ice cream stand, the engine seized, and the gunship dropped.

The nose crumpled.

The windshield shattered.

The last things Molka saw before blacking out.

CHAPTER 62

The first thing Molka saw when she came to—seconds later—was Yeong. Half his face was enraged face; the other half was burned off, like he had laid his head on a BBQ grill and fallen asleep.

Most of his uniform was also burned off.

He was also missing his right hand.

He had tried to outrun Molka's last grenade salvo.

He hadn't quite made it.

He opened the pilot's door with his left hand, ripped Molka's helmet from her head, and yelled, "You kill me! Now I kill you too!"

Molka moved for her pistol, but Yeong carried no weapon and waned into shock, mumbling something in Korean.

Molka unbuckled, grabbed her tactical bag from the backseat, and tried the co-pilot's door. Jammed. She spun in her seat and double kicked Yeong—not to hurt him, to move him. The engine still smoked, and fuel waited to explode.

Molka pushed past Yeong. He took her place in the pilot's seat and kept mumbling. She didn't argue. A man should be allowed to die where he wants.

The gunship's landing skids had punched through the ice cream stand's roof, and the fuselage balanced on the rafters.

Molka jumped to the ground, spotted Aden and Valentina across the courtyard, and ran to join them. "Not one of my better landings, but—"

BAWHAMWAH!

The gunship detonated into orange-red-black carnage.

Molka flinched, turned back, and winced. "Sorry, girl."

Aden hugged Molka. "Molka, baby."

Molka hugged him back. "Darling."

"Did you—"

"I got there right before Darcy. The pedestal is completely destroyed. No drones made it out."

"What about Darcy?" Aden said.

"She made it out, but she didn't get far."

"Is she dead?"

"Dead or dying," Molka said. "Couldn't be helped."

"You're saying she can't hurt anyone?"

"Yes, she can't hurt you anymore."

"Then it's over," Aden said. "And we're really going home?"

Molka checked her watch. "About six minutes until extraction." She looked up to see Valentina with freshly tear-swollen eyes.

"Molka, baby?" Aden said.

"What, darling?"

"We're really going home?"

"Yes." Molka laid her hand on Aden's shoulder. "You're really going home."

Aden captivated Molka with his heart melting dimples. "So, when we get married, we'll live in Tel Aviv."

"Haifa."

"We'll live in Tel Aviv but have a vacation home in Haifa."

"Beachfront?" Molka said.

"Naturally."

Molka nodded. "I could work with that."

"And we'll have a Persian cat named Avro."

"A Boston Terrier named Shakespeare."

"And our first born will be a beautiful son named Zeke."

331

"No," Molka said. "A strong daughter named Dava."

"How about this: Our first born will be strong beautiful fraternal twins, Zeke and Dava."

"Adorable."

"And every Sunday morning we'll sleep late, then head over to—"

"Café Jarrod for smoothies."

Aden jumped boyish jumps. "Yes! You see, our marriage will be perfect!"

"Yes. It would have been perfect."

"And they all lived happily ever after." Besnik stepped from tree concealment 10 meters away. "Well, not all."

Molka smirked. "There's a lawyer who needs a lawyer."

Besnik started to answer, but the gunship's few remaining rounds cooked off with ferocity in the helicopter inferno and silenced his retort. Instead, he moved under a lamplight and laid the Black Night Case on the grass at his feet.

"Oh no," Aden said. "She didn't."

"I am afraid she did," Besnik said. He opened the case, removed three drones, and placed them on the grass beside it.

"More drones?" Molka said. "Where did those come from?"

"Oh no," Aden said. "She gave him access to the Black Night Case."

"What's a Black Night Case?" Molka said.

Besnik pulled a control pad from his jacket pocket. "In the event of her death, Principal Darcy's final order was that I deploy the Personal Security Drones of quote, 'the two bitches most responsible for her downfall' unquote. And then deploy my own. However, I made a slight amendment to her wishes." He stomped one of the drones into scraps. "As I have a private jet to borrow and a stellar new reputation to build in West Africa."

"You don't have to do this," Aden said. "Just put the control pad down and go."

"No." Besnik's toad face cringed in shame. "I must do this. Because I am weak. I failed her when she asked for my ultimate loyalty. I owe her this final act of devotion for everything she gave me. And everything I took from her."

"Have you gone insane too?" Aden said.

"Not to worry, Aden. You are safe as well. Principal Darcy said your punishment is witnessing and living with the consequences of your creation."

Aden turned to Molka. "SHOOT HIM!"

Molka reached behind her back for her pistol.

Gone!

It must have fallen out in the gunship crash!

Aden broke toward Besnik.

Besnik tapped the control pad. The quad-propellers on the remaining two drones activated, and they buzzed away in different directions.

Aden stopped and ran back to Molka and Valentina.

"Where did they go?" Molka said.

Aden's face desponded. "Their target acquisition software is booting. They'll be back in about 10 seconds."

Valentina held up hands. "Wait, wait, wait. No, no, no. Dying was definitely not in my agreement."

One of the drones swooped back, did three fast circles around the Aden, Molka, Valentina trio, hovered, and moved to Besnik.

Besnik's voice choked with terror. "What?"

The drone circled his head three times. "No!"

He pointed toward Molka and Valentina. "It's her!"

The drone hovered before his toad face. "Not me!"

He closed his toad eyes. "Of course, me."

He smiled his toad smile. "You always uncover the exploitable weakness, Darcy."

The drone veered into Besnik's forehead.

FLASH-BANG!

Besnik hit the grass dead.

Molka and Valentina tensed.

Aden slumped. "I'm so sorry, Dean Besnik."

The second drone returned, did three fast circles around the trio, and slowed to a hover in the middle.

Six eyes transfixed on it.

Valentina squatted, hugged her knees, and chanted mantra-like:

"Dying was definitely not in my agreement!"

"Dying was definitely not in my agreement!"

"Dying was definitely not in my agreement!"

But the drone didn't circle her.

It moved to Molka.

Aden yelled: "NO!"

The drone circled Molka's head three times.

Aden moved toward Molka. "NO! NO! NO!"

Molka yelled: "Stay back!"

The drone hovered before Molka's face.

"I'm so sorry, Molka baby."

Molka smiled. "It's ok, darling."

The drone veered toward Molka's forehead.

The motors stopped.

It dropped to the ground.

Aden rushed to and snatched the drone. "Harmless. The weapon feature's been deactivated." He ran to Besnik's body and recovered and examined the remnants of his death drone. "And this one was originally assigned to Valentina. Obviously, Darcy didn't inform poor Dean Besnik about the changes she made."

"Quick question," Molka said. "Please tell me there are no more drones lurking around?"

Aden ran to and hugged Molka. "They're all gone now, Molka baby."

The contractor helicopter came in low and somewhat muted over the classroom-administration building.

Molka checked her watch—3:06 AM. Dead center of the extraction window.

Valentina peeked from her cowered position. "Are we safe?"

"Yes." Molka grabbed Valentina's wrist, pulled her to her feet, and raised her voice over the increasing rotor noise. "You're leaving with Aden. Give him back to the ISS. I'm staying."

"What?" Aden yelled. "No! Why?"

The helicopter hovered over the courtyard and started a careful descent.

Molka embraced Aden and placed her lips to his ear. "I can't be with you."

Aden put his lips to Molka's ear. "Then you lied to me like all the others."

"No. I've been lying to myself. And I just now faced it."

Aden clung hard to Molka. "What about our dream life?"

"It was a beautiful dream, darling. But only a dream. To make someone truly happy, you have to be happy with yourself and who you are. I'm not that person anymore. And I don't know if I ever will be again."

"Molka baby, I don't understand. I thought we were—"

Molka looked over his shoulder at Valentina. "She's a good woman. She loves you. You have important work to do. It's going to be very hard on you. She can be there when you need someone. I can't promise you that."

The white and red Bell 407 helicopter landed. It was fitted with an underside auxiliary fuel tank and had *Alex Creek Logging Company* displayed in black letters on the tail boom.

"You have to go," Molka said.

Aden embraced Molka harder. "Molka, I—"

"I know." Molka kissed Aden and pushed him away. "So do I."

The helicopter's side door opened. A man—disguised in logger attire—crouch-jumped out, ran to them, and scanned from Molka to Valentina and back to Molka. "Departure in 60 seconds!" He took Aden's arm and pull-jogged him to the helicopter.

Molka turned away and yelled at a mystified Valentina. "GO!"

Valentina came close to Molka and yelled back. "What about Principe?"

"Rosina will get him back to you."

"What about you?"

"I've heard Canadian jails aren't that bad."

"The Counsel will probably crucify you for turning him over to my people."

"Only if I'm lucky," Molka said.

"Why are you really doing this?"

"Because the affairs of the heart must always bow to the affairs of the state."

"That is an order," Valentina said. "Not a reason."

Molka put her mouth close to Valentina's ear. "You're right about Aden; he's really just a lost scared little boy. Take good care of him. NOW GO!"

Valentina hugged Molka around the neck, ran to the helicopter, and climbed in.

The side door shut.

The helicopter throttled up and started an ultra-slow ascent— the pilot exercising extreme caution as he maneuvered the large rotor diameter within the dark narrow courtyard confines.

Molka crouched to avoid being blown back in the propwash.

Leaves and debris swirled around her.

Something flew into her eyes.

She rubbed them.

They were already wet.

She lowered her head.

 **CHAPTER 63**

Molka raised her head to watch Aden fly from her life.

Her eyes never made it.

They halted on movement across the courtyard.

Security SUV stopped on the grass.

Driver exited.

Driver?

Owen.

Owen opened the tailgate.

Owen removed a long olive-green aluminum case.

Case contents?

Stinger shoulder-fired missile.

Purpose?

Preparing to fire.

Target?

Aden's helicopter!

Molka, about 100 meters away, sprinted toward Owen's back.

Owen dropped the case on the grass.

Molka 90 meters away.

Owen knelt and opened the case.

Molka 80 meters away.

Owen removed the launcher.

Molka 70 meters away.

Owen removed the launcher's battery unit.

Molka 60 meters away.

Owen inserted the battery unit into the launcher.

Molka 50 meters away.

Owen stood and rested the launcher on his shoulder.

Molka 40 meters away.

The helicopter cleared the courtyard treetops.

Molka 30 meters away.

Owen sighted and aimed.

Molka 20 meters away.

The helicopter moved off.

Molka 10 meters away.

Owen placed his finger on the trigger switch.

Molka slammed a crushing flying side kick between Owen's shoulder blades.

Owen's body flew forward, he fumbled the launcher, and face-planted hard into the grass.

Molka unslung his submachine gun from his shoulder to hers, snatched the launcher, removed the battery unit, and heaved both components as far as she could in opposite directions.

Owen recovered his wits and crab-walked to his feet. "Doc?" His head jerked toward Aden's helicopter fading into the distance. "Damn you! You just cost me my retirement!"

Molka aimed the submachine gun at Owen. "Put your hands on your head."

Owen complied. "Easy, doc. As you can see, I'm out of uniform." He removed and flipped away his hat, lifted his shirt, and twirled 360 degrees. "And I'm unarmed now. I don't work here anymore."

"Put your hands on your head. Turn away from me."

Owen complied.

"Get on your knees, interlace your fingers, and cross your ankles."

Owen complied and said, "Someone begged me to believe you killed Narcisse and took his gunship. But I still had to go see for myself. And sure enough, I found him with a .22 caliber headache and found out we have a new pilot. Guess you did a bit more than driving trucks in the IDF."

Molka crinkled her nose. "Just a bit."

"But I saw the gunship crash. So I thought that was you I smell chargrilling in the wreckage over there."

"That's one of your friends."

"Which one?"

"Yeong," Molka said. "Gervaso is still simmering in place on his 23s."

"You also make Hamu disappear?"

"He was hiding face down in a closet last time I saw him."

"You've been hell on your fellow security officers tonight. The colonel might have something to say about it though."

"Not likely," Molka said. "The colonel got caught in some friendly fire by me. Same for Darcy."

"Well, aren't you the little killing machine?" Owen nodded at Besnik's body across the way in the grass. "And who was that?"

"Dean Besnik."

"You end his night badly too?"

"No," Molka said. "Darcy set that up for him. My turn to ask questions. Was the Stinger originally for me?"

"Yeah, until I spotted the second chopper coming in and figured it to be Aden's ride out of here. Why did you take down Building A?"

Molka circled around in front of Owen keeping him covered. "I'm not done questioning you. What did you mean when you said I cost you your retirement?"

"I think I have the right to remain silent, cop."

"Fine. You can do it in one of your own detention cells. Stand up."

Owen cocked his head to the side. "Hold on a sec. I'll tell you. It don't matter now anyway. I had a fuck-you-money job to make sure your boyfriend never left here alive."

"Darcy's orders?"

"No. It was the buyer of his little killer drones. They wanted to make sure they were getting never-to-be-reproduced one-of-a-kinds."

Adrenaline blindsided Molka. "WHO…" She tempered her tone. "Who was the buyer?"

"No idea. I got the job through a middle-man."

"You mean Darcy?"

"Nope. She never said a word about it to me."

Molka tensed and stepped closer to Owen. "Who's the middleman?"

"If I tell you, will you cut me a break?"

"If you don't tell me," Molka tapped the submachine gun, "I'll cut you in half."

Owen grinned. "I don't doubt it. Relax though. The deal's dead."

Molka took another tense step toward Owen. "Who's the middleman?"

"Old boy Deanie, over there."

"Besnik?"

"Yeah. He told me eliminating Aden after he finished the drone swarms was the real reason he hired me."

"Besnik?"

"I know, right? I didn't think he had that in him either."

"Besnik?"

"Hey, I got no reason to lie now."

"Besnik." Molka reached behind her head and tugged on the base of her ponytail. "If I'd known, all I would've had to do is give him one dirty look."

"Give him a dirty look for what?"

Molka checked herself. "Nothing. Detention for you. Stand up."

"You got some strange ways, doc."

"Stand up."

"I don't think I want to be detained for your cop buddies."

"I don't blame you," Molka said. "When they find out about your involvement in Truman…Inspector Barkley's death, I'm sure they'll convert your short-term detention stay into a nice long-term cell."

Owen grimaced. "Damn. I forgot about that. But I also may be wanted in connection with a few assassinations during a coup attempt a few years back."

"And let me guess, you ended up on the attempt side of the coup?"

"Right. Which means I got none of the money and all of the blame."

"Forget the nice long-term cell; they probably have a nasty permanent cage in mind for you."

"Well, I'm not ready for a nasty permanent cage either."

"I've heard that one before," Molka said. "Stand up."

"You know, in ancient times, a soldier in my situation would be allowed to fall on his sword."

"Got one handy? I'll be happy to give you a nice shove."

"The only sword I have is the one between my legs." Owen grinned. "And it's always up for some hot dueling action."

"Perfect. You can have all the sword fights you want with your new prison pals in the showers."

"Funny. But how about we finish the fight we started in the gym? Except this time the colonel won't be here to save your ass."

"I thought he saved yours." Molka smiled. "Or at least the rest of your ear."

Owen smirked. "Anyways, you make me tap out, I'll go take my punishment. I make you tap out, you let me get out of here."

"You can't get out of here. They've probably already blocked the road."

"I'm not leaving by the road. I'm heading into the mountains. I was raised in the mountains. I can stay in them for weeks, months, years if I have to. They'd never find me, let alone catch me." Owen grinned again. "So you havin' any of it?"

"I think I'll stick with the cage option for you. Stand up."

"Maybe this will change your mind: Principal Darcy didn't order the field trip for your flabby cop friend. That was all my doing."

"Because you hate cops as much as her?" Molka said. "Or did you have a darker reason?"

"Don't flip the race card on me. Half the men in my company were black, brown, and yellow guys. They called me a lot of things, but racist was never one."

"Why then?"

"Just something to do on another boring afternoon," Owen said. "His death was totally senseless and unnecessary. So I guess you were right. In a way, I did kill him. Now you havin' any of it?"

"And I could trust you to keep your word because of what?"

"Soldier's honor. Between us. Something your cop buddies probably wouldn't understand."

Molka didn't mention her cop buddies were no buddies, and she would probably soon join him in a detention cell. But if Truman/Inspector Barkley hadn't warned her about the police operation, Aden would be in detention too and her task a failure. Maybe a posthumous payback beatdown of Owen was as much gratitude as she could give that good man.

"Alright," Molka said. "Soldier's honor." She dropped her bag, removed the magazine from the submachine gun, flung it far into the darkness, unslung the weapon, and tossed it well aside in the grass.

Owen nodded. "That's a way." He lowered his hands and stood.

Molka assumed a Krav Maga stance.

Owen assumed a boxing stance. "For the record, I ain't afraid of Krav Maga. I think it's over-hyped bullshit. I mean, what kind of martial arts don't even have a sporting division. Get ready for your worst ever ass whippin'. And no hard feelings, right, doc?"

Molka shook her head. "Nothing is decided until it's decided."

Owen came at Molka, slipped her right cross, walked through her left hook, and tagged her with a blur-fast left jab, right cross, left hook combination.

Molka kneed grass and viewed stars in the stars.
Ouch.

She had taken some nasty bare fist shots before. But Owen's landed different—harder than bone hard. More like tempered steel.

Instincts got Molka back on her feet and back into her fighting stance.

Owen grinned and invited her to come get some.

Molka accommodated.

Owen ducked Molka's wild uppercut and tagged her with an overhand right, left uppercut combination.

Molka took another knee.

Nose bleeding.

Eye throbbing.

Remember your training.

Never box with a boxer.

And the aggressor always sets the rules.

Owen ordered, "Stand-up. We ain't done."

Molka launched at Owen.

Owen took a surprised step back. His new cowboy boots slipped on dewy grass. He recovered but unbalanced.

Molka launched again, caught Owen in a neck clinch, pulled his head down, and fired five quick knee strikes to his ribs and groin.

Owen dropped his hands to block.

Molka exploited with consecutive roundhouse kicks.

Kick two connected solid.

Owen fell.

Molka pounced on his back and chomped teeth into his bandaged ear.

Owen screamed and squirmed and squirmed and screamed.

Molka released her bite, dropped a stunner elbow into the back of Owen's head, straddled him, and pulled his left arm behind his back into a merciless armlock.

Owen screamed.

"Hurts, don't it?" Molka said.

Owen screamed again and flailed his free arm back at Molka.

Molka leaned forward and pressed her face cheek to cheek with Owen's. "That unbearable pain burning in your elbow is your bursa sac about to rupture. I've heard it's one of the worst looking injuries you'll ever see."

Owen screamed again and pounded the grass with his right hand:

"I tap out!"

"I tap out!

"I tap out!"

Molka released him, arose triumphant, and used her shirt to wipe the blood from her nose. "It's the nasty permanent cage for you after all. And no hard feelings, right? First Sergeant."

Owen rolled onto his side, pulled the Walther pistol from his right boot, and aimed at Molka. "The hell there ain't."

Molka sighed, disgusted. "Soldier's honor."

Owen stood. "When you live by the feud like I do, honor don't enter into it. Now. YOU get on your knees, put your hands on your head, interlace your fingers, and cross your ankles."

Molka complied.

Owen circled behind her and pointed the pistol at her head. "Well, doc, time for me to run. But I can't leave and leave you alive, and it's your own fault."

"How so?"

"You're too good."

"Don't worry," Molka said. "I won't come feuding after you. Believe me, I have much more important things to do than you."

"Even so, you're still the type of loose end who could pop up and garotte me anytime I wasn't looking. So why risk it? That's another compliment, by the way."

"Thanks."

"Any last smart-ass comments?"

"No," Molka said. "Just a last request, soldier to soldier."

"What?"

"Allow me to die on my feet, not on my knees. I've earned it."

"Sure," Owen said. "Whatever turns you on."

Molka stood and dropped her arms to her sides.

Owen moved to within arm's reach and placed the barrel to the back of her head.

"Are you really going to shoot me?" Molka said.

"You bet."

"Then do it like a man, close and personal." Molka stepped back and pressed her rear end into Owen's crotch. The intimate position required he adjust the barrel around to her right temple.

"Mmm…" Owen said. "Yeah, close and personal. That's the way I like it."

"Me too."

In an almost un-seeable flash, Molka's right hand came up, grabbed the barrel, and turned it away from her head. Simultaneously, her left hand came up and grabbed the back of the pistol. She punched both arms forward—ripping the pistol from Owen's hand—spun around and pointed the barrel into his chest.

Owen's eyes widened and he grinned. "What a move! Damn. I take back what I said about Krav Maga. It isn't over-hyped bullshit. It is the shit."

"So says Yossi. But I believe we were on our way to detain you for my cop buddies."

"You ain't a cop."

"I'm not?" Molka said.

"Nope."

"What changed your mind?"

"The cops are coming to seize Building A and grab Aden. But you destroyed Building A and helped get Aden out of here. You pulled an impressive op for someone."

"I did?"

Owen laughed. "Well, whoever you work for, I'll say this: You're a damn good soldier for them. And there was a time...a long time ago, there was a time, when I would've been proud to have you serve in my company, Doctor Molka."

"And at that time, I'm sure I would have been proud to serve in your company...Top Sergeant."

Owen nodded respect.

"Ready to go?" Molka said.

"Yeah. I'm ready."

Owen shot his hands forward and grabbed Molka's gun hand.

POP!

Molka could always tell herself she wasn't sure if Owen's sudden grip had made her pull the trigger or if Owen had pulled the trigger himself or if the beatdown hadn't been enough gratitude for Truman/Inspector Barkley.

Owen stumbled and viewed his chest wound. "Killed with my own weapon. That's a helluva note." He staggered back, braced against a tree, and slid into a sitting position. "Where's my dip?" He struggled the can from his pocket, dropped it, and stared into the clear star-filled sky. "You know, it's funny. Of all things, right now I'm thinking about…I'm thinking about…my little dog…my sweet little dog, Sarge."

Owen's eyes remained open but saw no more.

Molka found Owen's hat in the grass a few paces away and returned to his body. She picked up his dip can, placed it in his hand, and placed his hat on his head with the brim covering his eyes.

She walked away, recovered her bag, slung it over her shoulder, and headed for the bell tower.

CHAPTER 64

Leaning against a pillar in the belfry, Molka observed the entire thing.

At exactly 3:42 AM—full moon's peak—three dark-green Griffon helicopters came in low and fast. One each hovered above the Red Zone, the security HQ, and the dean's residence. The helicopter over the Red Zone—finding their target a smoking ruin—moved to their secondary target: the student dorms.

Black clad tactical teams repelled from each helicopter to achieve their objectives.

Of course, their efforts went unfulfilled. The security HQ sat unstaffed, the dean's residence stood vacant, and all the students waited in the stadium.

Exactly five minutes later, eight more Griffon helicopters landed in echelon on the airport apron. Each one disgorged eight uniformed and armed officers who formed into individual units. The units moved fast to secure the airport—including Darcy's jet—the front gate, the outer perimeter, and the classroom-administration building. Other units cleared the rest of the campus building by building.

Exactly 15 minutes after that, two big twin-rotor Chinook helicopters landed alongside the others. One contained medical personnel. The other offloaded about 25 officers wearing blue police Jackets and carrying laptop cases.

And exactly 10 minutes after that, two newer model 737 passenger jets landed followed by two older Dash 8 turboprop commuter aircraft. Molka reasoned that the comfy 737s would fly the students out, while the staff would leave on the less glamourous Dash 8s.

A well-planned and efficient operation. Impressive.

At about the 30-minute mark, a polite Canadian accented voice came over the school PA system:

"Students of Hazlehurst Institute, this is the Canadian National Police. Do not be alarmed. We are here to help you. By order of the Canadian Government, this school is being closed immediately. Pack one bag of personal belongings and bring it along with your student ID and any pets to the central courtyard. If you need any assistance, ask the nearest officer. Again, do not be alarmed. We are here to help you."

A less compassionate announcement followed:

"Faculty and staff members of Hazlehurst Institute, this is the Canadian National Police. Bring your staff ID and report to the school cafeteria. Non-compliance will result in arrest."

Their mop up also progressed well organized. They discovered and removed Owen and Besnik's bodies and commandeered the campus fire truck to extinguish the still burning helicopter/ice cream stand. Yeong's stench lingered after the suppression foam though.

Officers also videoed Building A's ruins and others crossed the river in a helicopter to investigate the smoldering Darcy statue pedestal.

Before the announcements, the students—bless their little brainwashed hearts—remained seated in the stadium waiting for Darcy's return. After the announcements, they filed out and headed to their rooms. And soon after, the staff compound gate opened, and confused, stunned staff members flowed toward the cafeteria.

Molka watched for another half hour, left the tower, got her staff ID from her room, and joined the growing courtyard crowd.

The student body—most still in jackets and sweaters over pajamas and dragging their one bag and pet if they had one—

congregated as a scared flock. Officers herded them into three separate lines. Other officers checked their student IDs against lists on tablets, split them into groups of 25, loaded them onto the institute's transporter trams, and shuttled them to the airport.

As Molka passed one line, Student Woodrow—holding Duffy on a leash—broke ranks and grabbed her arm. Duffy tail wagged, and Molka bent to pet him.

Student Woodrow cast panicked, wet eyes onto Molka. "Doctor Molka, what happened to Principal Darcy?"

"I'm not sure," Molka said.

"They're closing the school."

"I know."

"What do I do now?" Student Woodrow said.

"Go home."

"Go home and do what?"

"Grow up."

Rosina, carrying Principe in his carrier purse, jogged to Molka. "You said there would be some excitement tonight, and girl, you weren't lying! But Valentina and the genius guy never showed up."

Molka petted Principe's peeking nose. "They're gone. On their way to a happy home."

"What about Principe?"

"Take good care of him. You're about to get your fame moment: loyal fan returns superstar Valentina's lost dog."

Rosina's face broke into an enchanted smile. "Wow, really? Me, famous?"

"Better get to the cafeteria and follow their directions."

"I will. But she asked me to find you first. She wants to talk to you in the infirmary."

"Who wants to talk to me?" Molka said.

"*She* does."

Molka reached the infirmary door as two shotgun-carrying officers exited, followed by two paramedics rolling a wounded man on an ambulance stretcher. Their closed-eyed patient—the colonel—wore a hospital gown, a head bandage, and handcuffs.

Molka walked alongside. "How is he?"

A paramedic answered. "Full of fragments, badly burned, and a wicked skull fracture, but he's going to make it. Rasputin's got nothing on this tough Russian bastard."

The colonel opened his eyes to Molka. "Your task?"

"Completed."

"Congratulations."

"Thank you, sir. Sir, your wounds. The pedestal's destruction. I'm—"

"I know. This could not be helped."

"It's amazing you survived though," Molka said.

"I spotted you positioning to fire. I managed to grab Principal Darcy just before your first round struck. We made it out, but not far enough away."

"Again, I'm sorry."

"My team?"

Molka shook her head.

The colonel shrugged. "When wood is chopped, woodchips will fly."

"If I may say so, sir, they weren't worthy of you."

"But you are worthy. Most worthy. Lieutenant."

"Don't you mean, lieutenant who drives truck?"

He smiled. "Perhaps we shall have the good misfortune of serving together again one day."

"Thank you, sir. I really appre—" Molka stopped. "Wait. Was that a compliment or a Russian curse?"

Colonel Krasnov's booming laugh echoed across the campus as they pushed him toward the airport and his day of reckoning. Those who passed judgement on him were no doubt confident and relieved they had finally and permanently trapped the Red Wolf.

Ha. Believe it when you see it.

350

The Friend of Darcy nurse who cleared Molka with the officer guarding the ICU said Darcy was resting in a critical but stable condition. And they would soon transport her to a Vancouver hospital, and that she faced a couple years' worth of surgeries.

Before they left Molka alone with their patient-defendant, the officer quipped she also faced a couple years' worth of trials.

Darcy lay attached to a multi-bag IV stand and several monitors. Bandages and sheets covered her whole body, except for a circular opening around her face which, which incredibly, only had one small bruise on it.

Darcy smiled at Molka. "Hi, doll."

"Hello, Darcy."

"If I didn't know better, I would say you look overjoyed to see me alive."

Molka carried her overjoyed smile to Darcy's bedside. "You have no idea."

"Raise me up, will you, please? My hands aren't working too well right now. Neither are my arms or legs for that matter."

Molka used the bed controller to raise Darcy into a sitting position.

Darcy grimaced as she shifted herself a little more upright. "They tell me the only part of my body either not bruised, broken, or burned is my face. How does it look?"

"Beautiful as ever."

Darcy smiled and teared up. "They're taking my students away from me."

"I know."

"The persecutors will get them to say the vilest things about their time here. And about me. Mostly lies, but they'll repeat whatever their new caretakers wish to hear. They're all so fragile. They'll never survive their *rescue*. They'll all return to the old miseries that were killing them. And they'll all die miserable. And it's so sad, because all they ever wanted was the love and acceptance they didn't get as children. And now that's impossible for them."

"At least they'll be back with their loving families."

Darcy smirked. "Money-loving families. If their families really loved them, they never would have come to me." Her face blazed defiant. "I know what you're thinking right this moment, doll."

"You do?" Molka said.

"I do indeed. Want to know a secret?"

"I was about to insist you tell me one."

"If they would ever let me, I would be their Principal Darcy again. For free."

Molka considered wiping the tear flow from Darcy's cheeks. Instead, watched it soak into her bandages and said, "Why did you want to see me?"

Darcy blinked and composed herself. "I wanted to hear it from your own mouth."

"Hear what?"

"Before the cops dragged him away, Friend Greg said you did this to me. Is that true?"

"Yes," Molka said. "It wasn't personal though. I would've done this to anyone trying to do what you tried to do."

"I could have let Besnik drone you, and considering the way you betrayed me, I should have. And I almost did. But I just couldn't do it."

"Why not?"

"Because I truly hoped we would become as close as sisters." Darcy's eyes teared anew. "And I still do. You're the closest one to a sister I'll ever have."

Molka started to lay her hand on Darcy's sheet-covered arm—the thought of inflicting further pain stopped her. "Darcy, if you really want to be as close as sisters, I want you to tell me, tell me now, the identity and location of the one who was going to buy the drone swarm."

"A little while ago, two polite Canadian cop friends of yours visited me and asked the same question."

"What did you tell them?" Molka said.

"The same thing I'm going to tell you: I can't tell you."

A chair with an extra pillow on it sat beside the bed. Molka picked up the pillow, moved the chair to the door, wedged the chair back under the door handle, returned to Darcy's bedside, and lowered her voice to a dead serious tone. "Darcy. You will tell me now the identity and location of the one who was going to buy the drone swarm. If you don't tell me now, I will without hesitation or mercy or fear of the consequences—"

"You'll what?" Darcy said. "Snuff me out?"

Molka double clutched the pillow. "Yes."

"You won't do it. Just like you wouldn't do it in the tower. And you won't torture me either. You've crippled me. And you'll have to live with that. Add it to the guilt I know you suffer with over your little sister's death. Guilt is your real enemy. It's your exploitable weakness."

Molka closed her eyes and crushed the pillow into a ball.

"Did this person really kill your little sister?" Darcy said. "Or is that story a cop trick to make me talk?"

"It's not a trick. It's the truth."

Darcy searched Molka's tormented face. "Ok, doll. I believe you. But I still can't tell you. Because Besnik arranged the deal. I have no idea who the person was."

Molka opened her eyes and sighed.

"You don't believe me?" Darcy said.

"I don't believe Besnik, or anyone close to you, did anything without your total knowledge and consent. You're the Grande Dame genius of probably one of the most lucrative, gutsy, and—dare I say—brilliant scams ever. I told you before, I respect talent. Please don't disrespect me by denying it."

"You're giving me too much credit," Darcy said. "Besnik was the real mastermind of my success. He was the CEO and President of Hazlehurst-Moore Incorporated. I'm listed as an Executive Vice President—whatever that means—but I had absolutely nothing to do with the day-to-day operations. I never have. Besnik made all the business decisions. That's why the charges they're bringing against me for accounting fraud, wire fraud, bribery, and human trafficking, won't turn up a single document with my signature or a single witness implicating me. He was also embezzling funds from behind my back for years." Darcy smiled. "All I ever wanted to do was help people. And my only crime is being too naïve and trusting."

Molka crinkled her nose. "And I suppose the insane idea to build the slaughterbot drones was all Besnik too?"

"Absolutely. Granted, Besnik told me Aden's research may have future military applications. But I was only concerned with Aden getting well and I knew his work was an important part of that. So, I built him a research facility and encouraged him. However, I didn't pay attention to the specifics of what he did there."

"Aden may tell a much different story of your involvement."

"Well, I doubt Valentina's people will allow him to speak publicly about his time here anytime soon." Darcy grinned. "Or ever."

Molka crinkled her nose again. "But of course, Besnik paid very close attention to Aden's work. And it was he who thought of the plan to sell the drone swarms to very bad people for very huge sums?"

"Yes, sadly."

"I wonder why he would think to do that?"

"He was desperately in love with me for years. All the Friends will swear to that under oath. I rejected his advances. I guess he thought this ill-conceived money-making scheme would win me over in some bizarre way. But obviously, it was the product of a very disturbed mind."

Molka's nose crinkled yet again. "Obviously."

"Besnik also ordered Aden to weaponize the Personal Security Drones. And when he went crazy last night and wanted to deploy them on the students and staff and himself, I found out and tried to destroy them first. But you showed up and almost killed me for my efforts."

Molka folded her arms across the pillow. "You're precious, Darcy."

"The two polite Canadian cop friends of yours also showed me a video confession Besnik recorded on his phone. They said it—and my story—sounded dubious. I said dubious is a matter of opinion. Then they said Colonel Krasnov had a much different account of things here."

Molka flashed an optimistic smile. "I'm sure the colonel contradicted you radically."

"He did. However, I pointed out it was my word against the colonel's, and he faces much more serious charges and might say anything to lessen his legal peril. Well, that gave them some second and third thoughts. And then they said my story still sounded dubious and they would just have to trust an honest jury to decide what to believe."

"Yes," Molka said. "And an honest jury can be a very inconvenient thing to a less-than-honest story."

"True. But after I tell the jury all about my tragic early life—and have them crying out of the palm of my hand—and then explain my version of events here—in my own charming way—and with poor Bezie not around to deny it, and after they watch his damning video confession, well..." Darcy's smile was crafty. "I'm as good as acquitted. The media will call it the, 'I'm just a poor dumb little old girl from Mississippi' defense. I'm already planning a book, a movie, and a streaming series with that title."

Molka smiled and shook her head. "All figured out. You're wrong about one thing though. I haven't given you too much credit. I never gave you enough."

"Does that mean you believe I don't know who killed your little sister?"

Molka paced the room and punched the pillow. "You put a buffer between yourself and anything incriminating. Buffer Besnik. And when they came for you, the buffer got buffed out. You're a master of manipulation. Look what happened last night. In just a few hours' time you moved from unleashing a horrible weapon on the world, to mass murder-suicide infamy, to formulating a winnable legal defense strategy. And even your paranoid instincts proved valid. Turns out you had a foreign intelligence operative, undercover police surveillance, and a disloyal security chief infesting your little empire and you're still going to get away with everything." She stopped pacing and punching and marveled at Darcy. "You're probably the sanest most insane person I'll ever meet."

"Does that mean you believe I don't know who killed your little sister?"

Molka transformed from marveling to morose. "Yes. I believe you."

Darcy smiled, elated. "Thanks, doll. Then we can still be as close as sisters."

Molka removed the chair from the door and tossed the pillow back on it. "Are you in a lot of pain?"

"Not so much anymore. All the concern over Fentanyl is legitimate. It's dangerously great stuff. How are you managing your pain?"

"My pain? Oh, you mean—" Molka viewed the dried blood on her shirt from the Owen fight. "That was just a little bloody nose. I've had much worse. I'm not in any pain."

"I wasn't talking about that type of pain. Aden left with her, didn't he?"

"Yes. So what?"

"You can't con a conner," Darcy said. "Your pain is on the inside."

Molka forced out a laugh. "No. I'm perfectly fine. He didn't really mean anything to me. Just another task to complete, forget about, and move on."

Molka left the infirmary and headed to the cafeteria for her interrogation. Cutting across the central courtyard, she investigated the empty, dawning sky until she located the exact spot she had last viewed Aden's helicopter.

No. I'm perfectly fine. He didn't really mean anything to me. Just another task to complete, forget about, and move on.

PROJECT MOLKA: TASK 3
TASK COMPLETED

CHAPTER 65

Molka sat in the same cafeteria seat at the same cafeteria table as she had the first time she had lunched with Aden.

But the various gourmet meal aromas from that occasion had been replaced by the various body odors of the entire groggy, bewildered, and agitated Hazlehurst staff occupying seats around her.

Their protestations and speculations came muted but constant:

"Cripes. How long is this going to take?"

"I heard Principal Darcy got badly injured stopping a terrorist attack."

"I heard Building A exploded and Dean Besnik committed suicide."

"I heard they locked Greenie Greg and the rest of the Friends in the gymnasium."

"I heard someone on the security team went crazy and they were all killed in a huge firefight."

"But wasn't she on the security team?"

"Cripes. How long is this going to take?"

They waited to be called to a table at the cafeteria front where light blue uniformed officers sat with laptops and conducted interrogations.

Rosina and Principe got called and cleared fast. The nice older ladies from food service received a longer inquisition though. The utility workers and maintenance crew followed. No hurry to get to Molka. Maybe they didn't know her role in the mayhem yet? Or maybe they wanted to save the worst for last.

Molka rested her arms on the table and rested her head on her arms. Her adrenalin tide ebbed, leaving an empty beach of exhaustion.

Aden's in Vancouver by now.
Maybe even on the way home.
Good for him.
Good for them.

She closed her eyes.

An hour or so later, a voice awoke her. "Pardon me, miss. Are you Molka?"

Molka raised her head. A black tactical-uniformed policeman, carrying an AR-15, stood over her.

"Yes. I'm Molka."

"May I see your ID please, miss?"

Molka handed him her staff ID card.

He verified her identity and handed it back to her. "Thank you, miss."

"Your colleague, Truman—I mean, Inspector Barkley—is in the morgue in the infirmary."

"We know, miss."

"He was a good man."

"We know that too, miss."

"I killed the man who killed him," Molka said. "Actually, I'm not sure about that. But if I did, it was self-defense. I also killed the other four members of the security team; each one of those was self-defense too. And I hit Principal Darcy and Colonel Krasnov with friendly fire. That couldn't be helped though. Oh, and about a month ago, a mercenary tried to throw me out of the bell tower, but I was able to fight him off, and he fell to his…I sound like a terrible person, don't I? Am I supposed to tell you all this? Because you don't look like the other interrogators here."

"I wouldn't know anything about all that, miss."

"Are Canadian jails as nice as I've heard?"

"I'm to escort you to your ride."

"I don't have a ride," Molka said.

"Apparently you do now. Please bring your bag and follow me, miss."

Molka followed him from the cafeteria and into a security cart. They drove in silence through the deserted campus on a bright, cool British Columbia late summer morning.

What did he mean escort her to her ride? Was she getting a free pass from interrogation?

They entered the airport. Officers clustered around their helicopters talking and laughing, a familiar post-mission unwind scene when it's all over but the debrief and the folklore.

Both 737s had departed—presumably with the students— and ahead on the runway, both Dash 8 aircraft waited with doors open—presumably to board the staff and her.

Molka's escort didn't stop though. He proceeded on to the apron's outer edge, where a beautiful metallic gold and black Bell 429 helicopter waited.

The officer stopped the cart beside the helicopter. "Here you are, miss."

"This is my ride?"

"Yes, miss."

Molka exited.

The helicopter's side door opened, and a tall serious gray-haired man—distinguished in a dark-blue police uniform displaying gold commander insignia—ducked his head and stepped out. He paused and acknowledged Molka with a silent mixture of respect and disappointment, boarded the cart with her escort, and rode off.

Molka stuck her head inside the helicopter.

In the rear-facing passenger seat behind the pilot—wearing his usual brown leather jacket—sat Azzur.

Molka climbed in and sat in the seat facing him. "I know why you're here. But first tell me, is—"

"That's her?" Laili—outfitted in a tight yellow and black flight suit and cool aviator sunglasses—sneered from the pilot's seat at Molka. "She doesn't look like the bad-ass you said she was. She looks standardly average."

Molka shot Laili with a look of annoyance and went back to Azzur. "Can we talk in front of her?"

Azzur took out and lit a cigarette. "Yes."

"Is Aden safe and on the way home?"

"Yes."

Molka relaxed back into the seat. "You shouldn't smoke in here, by the way. Alright. You want to know what happened. So... Well, first—"

Azzur interrupted. "On the flight from here to Vancouver—a flight Miss Valentina should not have been on—she convinced one of the contractors to allow her to use his phone, purportedly, to message her worried mother. But she did not message her worried mother. She messaged four colleagues instead. These four operatives arrived at the private airport before we did and concealed themselves. And when the contractor helicopter landed, and the door opened, and I awaited you to deliver Mr. Aden Kayne Luck to me, imagine my surprise when instead of you, Miss Valentina accompanied him. And imagine my further surprise and anger when the four colleagues showed themselves and held us at gunpoint."

Laili turned to Molka again. "Daddy was furiously enraged."

"Daddy?" Molka said.

Azzur flicked ash out the door. "And imagine my extreme disappointment when Miss Valentina and her armed colleagues boarded a waiting jet with Mr. Luck and departed. Now you may tell me what happened."

"Insanity." Molka made a twirling motion with her a finger. "A merry-go-round, roller coaster, house of mirrors. I had everything lined up when out of nowhere, *the* Valentina showed up. And I'm hit with the fact she's not only Aden's fiancée, she was also, as you found out, sent by the ISS to bring Aden back. Obviously, that complicated things for me tremendously. Long story, short, the only way I could get Aden to leave is if he left with her instead of me. So, I had to allow it to get our engineer back—which was my task—and everything worked out anyway."

"Yes," Azzur said. "Everything worked out magnificently. I am told the Prime minister wept in elation upon hearing about

Mr. Luck's sudden recovery. All courtesy and credit to a brilliantly conceived and flawlessly executed operation by the heroic and resourceful ISS."

Molka raised a hand. "Ok. I admit I handed them a big prize. Huge. Things got messy though. I had to make adjustments. Tough decisions. It wasn't pretty, but in the end, we still got our engineer back. Right?"

"Even so, you did not technically complete your task."

"What do you mean technically? Are you trying to deny me credit for the task on a technicality?"

Azzur leaned toward Molka. "I instructed you to personally hand over Mr. Luck to Counsel representatives for processing."

Molka leaned toward Azzur. "Well, I'm sorry the Counsel representatives didn't get the Prime minister's weeping praise, and when you say Counsel representatives, you mean you."

"In any case, you failed to do so. I am not satisfied with your performance."

"Well, I'm not satisfied with yours either. You promised me Darcy—Mrs. Hazlehurst-Moore—had information on the one I need. But she didn't know anything."

"I did not promise. I told you our latest and best assessment said she had such information. What information did she have?"

"None. I just told you that."

Azzur blew smoke. "Unfortunate."

"Yes. Very unfortunate. Mainly for me. And let me guess, out of appreciation or compassion, you won't be giving me the information I need either, and our previous agreement continues."

"That is correct."

"Oh well." Molka slammed back into her seat. "Three tasks down. Seven more to go."

"Again, I am not satisfied with your performance."

"Noted. Wait, do I still get credit for the task?"

"Failing to follow my instructions is inexcusable."

Molka's voice escalated. "Do I still get credit for the task?"

"Because every instruction I give you is done for a very specific and vital—"

"DO I STILL GET CREDIT FOR THE TASK OR NOT?"

Laili removed her sunglasses. "Does she always whine like this?"

Molka glared at Laili. "Who is she?"

Azzur flipped his cigarette butt out the door. "At the highest levels, it is believed you working with Valentina was a positive step toward better inter-agency cooperation with the ISS. And as you said, ultimately, we got our engineer back. Therefore, yes. You will get credit for successfully completing your third task."

"Good," Molka said. "Why didn't you say so in the first place?"

"It is also believed the bonding experience of escape you helped arrange between Mr. Luck and Miss Valentina will discourage him from wanting to run off again by rekindling their romance."

Laili laughed. "And she was rekindling all over him. Can't blame her though. He's pretty hot for an older guy."

Molka folded her arms across her chest. "I'm so happy I could help get those two back together."

Azzur went on. "Therefore, I was instructed by the director to pass along personal congratulations."

"Congratulations?" Laili lashed Molka with a disrespectful stare. "For what? You just said she disobeyed your instructions and failed to turn the target over to our people. And it's her fault we got guns in our faces and had to waste time coming here to get her. We're not on vacation, by the way, we're working. I mean, it's a fucking miracle things worked out despite all her fuck-ups. Fuck congratulations. She just had the luck."

Molka pointed at Laili. "Who is this rude nasty mouthed little brat I'm about to slap?"

Laili released her seat belts, stomped into the cabin, and bowed up on Molka. "Oh, please, please, try to slap me. Because I would LOVE IT, bitch!"

Molka bowed up on Laili. "You picked a VERY BAD DAY to annoy me, brat!"

Laili tossed her sunglasses into the pilot's seat. "Say that to me again. Outside."

"Alright." Molka jumped out the door.

Laili jumped onto Molka's back and raked both Molka's cheeks with her sharp nails.

Molka dipped her shoulder and judo-slammed Laili onto the concrete.

Laili's quick roll to her feet surprised Molka.

Laili's instantaneous jump kick to Molka's chin surprised her more.

Molka reeled, ducked Laili's hook kick, and chopped Laili down with a side kick to her long leg's right knee.

Laili raged to her feet and charged Molka.

Molka blunted Laili's recklessness with an elbow strike to the mouth.

Laili snubbed, the pain and her first blink-fast roundhouse kick missed Molka's head, but her second didn't miss Molka's ribs.

Molka gasped and let her instincts unleash back-to-back defensive front kicks.

Laili wobbled.

Both women stepped back and paused to pant.

Molka tasted blood and tongued a split lip.

Laili licked blood and spit blood and rubbed her right knee.

"Playtime's over," Molka said. "Time to get serious."

"Bring it," Laili said.

Both assumed Krav Maga fighting stances.

Azzur leapt from the helicopter and got between them. "Project Molka, meet Project Laili. Project Laili, meet Project Molka. I am assigning you each a new task."

Laili glared at Molka.

Molka glared at Laili.

Azzur continued. "Do you both understand me?"

"Yes," Laili said.

"Yes," Molka said.

Laili seethed at Molka. "I'm still going to kill you, bitch!"

Molka seethed at Laili. "You'll die trying, brat!"

Azzur fired a side kick into Molka's chest, spun, and speared a front kick into Laili's abdomen.

Both women hit the cement, wince hard.

Azzur stood over them:

"You may finish your fight on your own time."

"Right now, you are on my time, so shut up and listen."

"Your new tasks have the highest priority."

"They are crucial to the nation's survival."

"You must complete them successfully."

"And like it or not, hate it or not, hate each other or not, to complete your new, high-priority, crucial tasks, you will work together as partners."

"Effective immediately."

What Happened Next? Keep Reading!
PROJECT MOLKA Book 3!

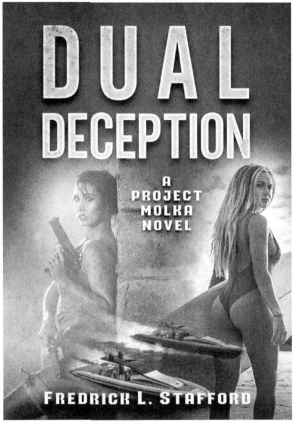

Available on Amazon!
https://www.amazon.com/dp/B0846SZ88T

Scan Me

Printed in Great Britain
by Amazon

21134705R00215